REBELLION

DIVIDED ELEMENTS - BOOK II

REBELLION

DIVIDED ELEMENTS - BOOK II

MIKHAEYLA KOPIEVSKY

KYRIJA

1 3 5 7 9 10 8 6 4 2

KYRIJA
North Arm Cove, NSW, Australia
www.kyrija.com.au

A CIP catalogue record for this book is available from the National Library of Australia

ebook ISBN 978-0-9954218-1-3
paperback ISBN13 978-0-9954218-4-4
paperback ISBN10 0-9954218-4-6

Cover Illustration by Ethan Scott

For Elijah

࿐ ⌒ ♯ ✕ ▪ ✕ ↘ ♥ ᨄ ‿ ↘ ⌒ ↗ ✳ ♥ ‿ ‴ ⌣ ∴ ↗ ‴ ↘ ▪ ↗ ⋯ ▪ ≈ ↘ ⌒
✳

ONE

The sky over the Edges shimmers then falters. Hovering between night and day, the dawn has come and trapped it between two very different realities – blurring it at the fringes until it becomes impossible to tell whether it's in one state or the other.

Maybe both, maybe neither. Maybe something altogether different.

Anaiya holds the ambiguity in her mind, letting it pull at the strange and hidden emotions lurking just below the surface. Like the sky, she is caught in her own dichotomy – not just a Fire Elemental anymore, not really an Air Elemental.

The idea skitters across the surface of her thoughts, never taking hold. Dwelling on her Heterodox existence no longer sends cramps to her belly or cold sweats to her temples; she no longer spends her nights waiting for Peacekeepers to come and detain her or for Technicians to escort her to the Execution Pillar.

Three months after Rehhd's Execution and her own failed realignment, she has finally learned that you can only be found guilty if you get caught. And Anaiya has become good at hiding.

A tug at her wrist draws her gaze down, a rope leash stretching taut and cutting into her skin. Delacroix, his fur matted but lice-free, sniffs too close to the edge of the air recycler's flat roof, his curiosity ignorant of the dire consequences.

She pulls the pup away from the danger and returns her

attention to the vista that stretches towards the city. The unrelenting lights of the nearby precincts are winking off. Minutes ago, they overwhelmed the delicate twinkling of the night's stars; now, not so much. There is a limbo – a moment where one fades and the other gains dominance. Anaiya's fractured identity is drawn to both, switching from the shimmering of one to the flickering of another.

Her fingers move of their own accord against the glass screen resting in her lap. At each touch, the device sends bright, harsh notes to echo against the dense concrete of nearby air recyclers. The first notes are always the most tentative, the most raw. But then, as it always does, the music calms the inner demons before they can shout their protest and, slowly, the symphony eases into a more cohesive structure.

The heavy notes stumble into wavering melodies, filling the sky until they are no longer different from the lights that inspired them, but just another manifestation.

The music is nothing like the fast, dense, chaotic symphonies she had listened to as a Peacekeeper. But she is no longer a Peacekeeper, and nothing is as it was a year ago.

In the isolation of the Edges, protected by the final hours of curfew, her creation should be safe from detection; but there is always the risk that someone – a patrolling Peacekeeper or an Unorthodox truant – will discover her. The former would generate unwanted scrutiny that could lead her all the way to the Executioner's needle. The latter to a confrontation with the guilt and confusion she banishes with her music.

And, yet, she plays on. Peacekeeper patrols are predictable and there is only one group of truants that would break curfew to venture to the Edges. Only one truant that she both dreads and desires.

Sensing her disquiet or spurred by the music, Delacroix shuffles closer to press his lean body in against her own. The pup squirms in tighter, sinewy limbs seeking a warmth and comfort denied by the recycler.

Anaiya's chest tightens with affection. And anxiety. Like the music, her attachment to the pup betrays her Heterodoxy and risks her discovery.

His emaciated frame should have wasted away in the Edges or been torn to pieces by the few predatory animals that survived there. As barely tolerated nuisances, animals were an unwelcome reminder that even Otpor, in all its ordered and synthetic glory, would never truly escape its past.

Showing them anything but disdain was Unorthodox; the kind of forbidden action that was just enough to raise a few eyebrows and set a few tongues tutting. Protecting one was Heterodox; it demonstrated the kind of wrong thought that could only be borne of a compromised mind. That could only be cured with death.

Her music shivers, the cold of dawn finally putting tremors to her fingers. Time has escaped her; caught in the hypnosis of errant thoughts, Anaiya has missed the end of curfew.

Putting down the glass screen, she looks to Delacroix. The pup snoozes at her side, oblivious to the messy contradictions in her head and the complexity of their strange relationship. She runs her fingers through his fur, picking at burrs and unravelling knots.

"Time to go, peu d'ombre."

Her little shadow scampers up over her legs – paws scratching along the glass that is already textured by similar journeys – and settles down into the front of her hooded jacket. She zips it up, taking care not to catch his fur in the unforgiving teeth of the zipper.

Reluctantly, she secures the glass screen in one of the crevasses ravaging the concrete surface. It will be another week before she can return – the screen will be safe until then, but she will miss the opportunity to compose her music.

Cradling Delacroix against her chest, she ruffles his head and starts the climb down the recycler. The pup's scratchy tongue laps at her cheek, leaving a sticky trail along the skin. She laughs and hums in his ear remnants of the tune that had rushed from her fingers moments ago.

As her feet crunch on the gravel, he scrambles from his confines and races off, pulling up short only when his leash reaches its limits. Anaiya tugs on the cord, but the pup resists, pulling against her and barking a series of short yelps.

"Delacroix!"

No doubt a rat, or dead pigeon, has attracted his attention. If dogs were Elementals, this one would be Air – easily distracted and impulsive to a fault.

"Ease on, petite fourrure." The unexpected voice carries loudly to Anaiya. Her heart catches at the familiarity of it and seizes as Kaide walks into view. He is not the rebellious Air Elemental she had thought would find her. He is not Seth.

Relief and disappointment loosen her chest.

He looks as surprised to see her but hides it quickly – bending down and scratching behind the pup's ear, turning the yelps into a gentle growl of satisfaction.

Finally, he looks up at her. "That was you?"

It has been months since she has seen him, months since the Execution. Dark circles accentuate dark eyes and the lean angles of his face make him seem even more serious.

Perhaps Rehhd's spectre keeps us both from sleep.

It would not surprise her. A silent bargain had been struck the night they saved Seth from the Pillar and handed over Rehhd in his place. The betrayal and guilt of that night were large enough to ensnare them both.

He straightens, hands resting casually by his side, gaze sharp. "The music – that was yours?"

Anaiya tugs on Delacroix's leash, grateful to see the dog trot faithfully back to her. "What are you doing here, Kaide?"

"What are *you* doing here, Anaiya?"

And just like that, the old battle lines are drawn. Both rising to the challenge, neither willing to back down.

It had made them uneasy allies during her deployment. It makes them cautious enemies now.

With the morning light still thwarted by the Border Wall, they stare at each other in the shadows. It reminds her of a lifetime ago; of their silent battle in an izakaya basement while a Fire Trainee sat bound and gagged on the floor and a livid Rehhd spat a stream of vitriol. Back when Rehhd was alive. Before everything unravelled.

Before her life fell apart.

"Your Peacekeepers are getting feisty," he says, finally breaking the silence.

"Not my Peacekeepers anymore." The admission has lost the sting it carried just a few months ago.

His gaze tracks over the nondescript kevlar jeans and loose cottonex shirt so far removed from the dark, form-fitting Peacekeeper uniform. "This deception is at least more believable."

Deception?

Kaide frowns, his eyes narrowing as if he sees her confusion or senses a puzzle to be solved. He has always been more methodical than the other Air Elementals she has encountered – more intrigued by the mechanics of things.

He looks to Delacroix and then back to Anaiya.

"Their experiment didn't work, did it?" He says the words slowly, drawing them out as the realisation dawns on him. "They couldn't realign you back."

Anaiya's heart is beating too fast, too loud. She needs to dissemble. "The only experiment I see failing is Seth's."

It is still hard to say his name aloud, but it has the desired effect. The surprise in Kaide's eyes turns to anger and suspicion.

"His Resistance, his vision," she continues, "not the righteous, pure thing of beauty anymore, is it? What, with all the broken bones and blood and scar tissue."

Rehhd's Execution had changed everything – gone was a Resistance content to splash forbidden murals on crumbling Otpor walls. A new rebellion was borne, one thirsty for vengeance and armed with improvised explosives. Less than six weeks after the Execution, bloody retribution sang through Otpor streets.

"It is difficult," Kaide says, bringing Anaiya back to the present, his face hard and his voice accusing, "to maintain support for a peaceful resistance when your enemy murders an innocent protester."

Thoughts of Rehhd threaten to unleash a familiar rush of emotions, but she shakes them away, unwilling to indulge the nightmare that plagues her every other waking moment.

Besides, culpability for Rehhd's Execution is not her burden alone.

"Would you have preferred us to have Executed the guilty?" She speaks softly and yet the words strike with all of the weight of the past. Kaide flinches and looks away.

"You may still, yet," Kaide finally says, looking back to Anaiya. "We may still, yet."

Anaiya shivers; from the dawn breeze, from Kaide's cold assessment, from the threat or premonition in his words.

She has no response. Has no willingness to stand here in the shadows, held captive by the past. This uneasy rush of emotions, this feeling of control slipping from her grasp – she thought she had left it all behind. She still wants to leave it all behind.

Tugging on Delacroix's leash, she turns and strides away from Kaide, heading back towards the city. Kaide doesn't call out to her and doesn't follow. It is a relief, but a short-lived one; she shouldn't have allowed him to bait her, she shouldn't have engaged.

Engaging means detection, and staying hidden is her only real defence against everything that can bring her undone.

TWO

A week later, Anaiya's thoughts are still plagued by her confrontation with Kaide.

"Would you have preferred us to have Executed the guilty?"

The question burrows itself deep in her mind, spinning and twisting, forming an incessant backing track to her usual thoughts of Rehhd and Seth and Executions and Heterodoxy.

They were all culpable to some extent – all had some hand in Rehhd's Execution. Although some hands were stickier with her blood than others ...

She wipes her palms on her jeans. Guilt arrives as it always does – swift and sharp, digging with nails and scraping with razors. It fills her belly with sand and makes her want to claw out her insides.

Most days she can bear it, or at least keep it at bay. But this afternoon, in the small space of her apartment, it seems to grow; sucking out the available oxygen and magnifying the oppressive heat. She suffers it until it feels like her lungs will collapse under its weight.

But escaping the confines of her room for the city beyond merely trades one kind of torture for another. The heat of the day still leaks from the precinct's ubiquitous concrete and metal, stealing her energy and slowing her feet. The only blessing is the quiet streets and the knowledge that evening is on its way.

With her Infrastructure Protection shift not due to start until well after curfew, she pushes against the resistance and lethargy in her muscles and breaks into a slow jog. Part of her wants to take the movement to the next level, to push the jog into a free-run. But only Peacekeepers free-run, and she is not a Peacekeeper.

Hours stretch on and on, until finally the sky darkens and the city lights emerge. It should bring her joy, but all she feels is tired and sticky and dirty. And guilty.

Sighing, she leans against a nearby wall. The streetscape ahead is shadowed, victim to mandatory blackouts so the Cooperative can boost power to precincts where Heterodox activities are more prominent. Just another neighbourhood left without light from dusk till dawn.

She peers into the darkness, her limited vision able to make out the distinctive shapes of nearby buildings and markers. She knows this place; Lei Zhardan du Ruiso.

Air Elementals, drawn to the irrational and unknown, have come to the Ruiso Gardens for generations. On the Seventh day, they arrive en masse, crowding around the small stone water basin to perform the ablution ceremony. To wash away their sins.

If only sins were so easily erased.

Wiping the sweat and grime from her bare arms, Anaiya tentatively steps out, seeking the set of stairs that descend to the gardens.

Gardens. An ancient name for an extinct reality. If you were to believe the synth-addled ramblings of older Elementals, Otpor was once dotted with oases of chaotic, natural life – trees, plants, fleurs. Names that survived the extinction of their origins.

It is difficult to imagine that clusters of delicate, colourful beauties once sprung from a fertile ground, uninvited and spontaneously. Imagining natural colour under a brown Otpor sky is like imagining massive metal synthflies that could carry Elementals across the Wasteland – a romantic fantasy about an impossible past.

Her feet crunch on the loose stones of the courtyard below. Despite the deep shadows, something shimmers on the wall ahead – catching and reflecting the dull echoes of a far-away light. She hesitates, her fingers hovering over her wristplate; wanting to switch on the diode and not wanting to fall back into the drama that always comes from shining a light on things in the darkness.

Damn it.

The light explodes around her.

Details obscured in the dark flash bright and overexposed; the concrete terraces and mosaic walls, the deep water basin and antique sculptures. It is as beautiful and enigmatic in the light as it is in the dark. Marred only by age and, in the case of the wall ahead, familiar red paint.

But this time, she is not confronted with the singular call for resistance that has plagued the murals of her recent past, but something more complex. The script is not angular or stencilled – instead it flows free-form like a rivulet.

Divide and conquer, weaken and dominate, love and enslave; this is the holy trinity.

The natural cadence of the verse reminds her of Otpor's state motto. But the familiarity runs deeper than that. The words tickle at the edges of her subconscious – a new reflection, an old echo. She struggles to place them; words that shouldn't be familiar, yet are.

Caught in a moment of deja vu, Seth's form shimmers in her memory. And in that brief second, she doesn't see him as Seth anymore; doesn't see him as the leader of the Resistance, the charismatic Air Elemental that had distracted her from her mission to uncover the heart of rebellion, the one who had pulled her further out of alignment and away from her Fire Element.

In that moment, he merges with the other Resistor she had loved.

She sees him as Kane 148.

"That's enough for tonight, Anaiya."

Kane's voice bounces off the dense bricks of the necropolis and draws her up short. She lands her dash vault and swivels around to locate him, finding him standing at the junction of the eastern and northern walls.

Watching him, Anaiya is hit with a familiar wave of vague unease. It has been following her for weeks now and, while she can't place its exact origins, she knows it has something to do with Kane's new demeanour.

That he no longer calls her Trainee, but Anaiya, is part of it. But it's more than just that – it's the long stares, the drawn-out pauses, the shift from action to contemplation.

Like now – he just stands there, running his fingertips over ancient and worn bricks. As if he has forgotten she is there. Has forgotten who he is and what he is supposed to be doing. As if the world has shrunk to the centimetres between him and the necropolis.

She shifts on the balls of her feet, wanting to do anything but stand still, to be anywhere but here watching her mentor … change.

Change. It is a strange word – a word that is slightly Unorthodox. Slightly Heterodox.

The world, her world, should not change. Why change something that was already right? That had already corrected the flaws of the past? And Elementals; they should never change. Grow, develop, excel; yes. But change? Never.

She glances back to Kane and quickly looks away.

He wasn't always like this.

When Anaiya had first been assigned to the Peacekeeper Corps, her joy at the selection had been immediately superseded by the announcement that Kane 148 was to be her mentor. Already the stuff of Peacekeeping legend, he exuded a calm confidence, a righteousness, a superiority that was less ego and more inevitability.

The same Kane 148 that first executed the kaiju aerial. The same Kane 148 that kong vaulted the River Syn in pursuit of a synth-addled Earth serial killer.

The Fire Elemental before her now is not that same Kane 148.

She takes a hesitant step forward.

"This necropolis has remained for centuries." His voice is softer now. "For centuries. Before the Emancipation. Before the Singularity."

Anaiya cringes at the Unorthodoxy. It is not right to dwell in the past.

"Yes, if you dig beneath the surface you will find the ashes of Air Elementals. But, if you dig a little deeper, you will find the dust of ancient peoples."

She shivers, the words raising bumps along the flesh of her arms. No, this is not the same Kane 148. Why is he saying these words, these terrible words? Why is he saying them aloud?

If she were an Air Elemental, she would imagine them catching with silver-plated barbs on the slight, warm breeze. Imagine them being sucked into the bellies of air recyclers before being pushed out for consumption by the citizens of Otpor.

But, as a Fire Elemental, she cannot see anything but a fractured hero. Can't hear anything but his words, his terrible, Unorthodox words.

"Air Elementals rightly concern themselves with the holy." His voice is still soft, but it has taken on a darker edge. A strange kind of fervour clouds his eyes and Anaiya has to look away again. Part of her wants to free-run all the way back to the Trainee Barracks. But the part of her that knows only obedience, that was properly conditioned as a Premie to respect her superiors, roots her feet to the ground.

Unable to look at her mentor, Anaiya looks back along the eastern wall. She sees the footholds and swing props and opportunities for demitours.

"And the Cooperative teaches us their own holy trinity. Liberty. Egality. Fraternity."

The words of the state motto sound broken and corrupted on his tongue.

"But it is not the true trinity."

Anaiya looks back at him, despite herself. His hand still brushes against the jagged surface of stone and mortar, but now he looks at her. His eyes clouded with sadness.

"No, Anaiya. That is not the true trinity. Divide and conquer, weaken and dominate, love and enslave; this is the holy trinity."

THREE

Anaiya wrinkles her nose as the stench of rotting rat flesh wafts through the mezzanine level of the administration building she is Protecting. Even with the windows open, the sour, bittersweet smell of decay assaults her.

She sits cross-legged on the floor, staring at the blank wall opposite her. The worn acrylpoly carpet beneath her offers no comfort, but maybe that's as it should be.

For hours she had fixated on impossible questions; How did Kane 148's words end up on a city wall two generations after his Execution? What do they mean in this new context? Why have they been resurrected?

By the time the Station Manager arrives to signal the end of the night shift, Anaiya's insides are coiled tight.

The Manager unloads in that pinched voice of hers about the mess on the ground floor, but Anaiya ignores it. For some stupid reason, the greying Earth Elemental thinks she is also a Cleaner. Swiping her wristplate over the terminal at the warehouse entrance, Anaiya pushes through the service door without a backwards glance.

No doubt the old rodent will report her for unprofessional conduct, but the thought barely makes a dent; she is too wrapped up in darker thoughts and the threat of demotion had lost its power when they first stripped her of her Peacekeeper badge.

Her feet beat out a steady rhythm towards the Ravignan Strip; the route to the Air entertainment sector is one she treaded many times before. Returning feels as foolish and inevitable as the return of a perpetrator to the scene of their crime, or the flight of a synthfly drawn to a fluorescent globe – ignorant of the consequences or unable to resist them.

Not that she ever actually returns. Some days she ventures closer than others; the days when her Air identity is ascendant and the memories of late nights at izakaya pull at her. Mostly, she just skirts around the edges, indulging the persistent and spiky emotions that demand she do something other than just stay hidden.

This morning she starts to turn away from the Strip's direction earlier than she would normally. She is too amped up, too much inside her own head – too unpredictable. The run-in with Kaide in the Edges and the discovery of Kane 148's forbidden words in Lei Zhardan have spooked her and she is unwilling to take unnecessary risks. The barbed wire in her brain will need to be dulled with something else.

And then she hears it. With curfew lifted not twenty minutes ago, it is too soon for the alcohol-addicted to be making their way to barely opened izakaya, and yet music and laughter echo off the buildings that line the narrow street.

Laughter. It is a sound that is rare and precious, and wholly unnatural in this new era of conflict.

She approaches the entertainment sector cautiously, pressing herself to the brickwork of nearby buildings and lurking in their shadows. The deep recessed door of a closed izakaya provides the perfect balance between a good vantage point and useful hiding spot.

Just a quick look. Just enough to sate the monster within.

Air Elementals have turned the narrow street into an explosion of colour and music. They weave between and around tattered polyester lounges and upended delivery crates, talking and gossiping and flirting.

So perplexed is she by this sudden demonstration of joy, in a city that has seen nothing but bleak violence for months, that it is minutes before Anaiya sees the real revelation.

The once-plain wall that separates the izakaya from its neighbour is awash in forbidden paint. Stylised ribbons of auburn hair tumble down the brickwork and Rehhd's impossible orange eyes gaze down on the crowd celebrating below. Anaiya's chest feels like it has been doused in liquid nitrogen. Her breath catches and when she finally sucks it in, it burns down her throat.

A song emerges from the mess of noise, its dense beats and lilting melody taking her back to a time before she was broken … or only half broken. Anaiya distractedly pulls up her wristplate, the date confirming what she already knows. This is Rehhd's semester celebration.

I can't be here. I have to leave. I have to …

Leaving the safety of her hiding spot, Anaiya steps out into the street. Her heart slams against the walls of her ribcage and panic fractures her thoughts.

I just need to leave … I …

She throws a quick glance over her shoulder. It is a foolish move, she knows as soon as she does it; but her Fire training demands that she turn and take stock of the threat her body is reacting to.

Her eyes are immediately drawn to the immense mural of Rehhd, so like the Heterodox murals that pushed her and the rest of the city into a dysfunctional spiral. A flash of mourning black below the portrait captures her eyes – anachronistic for the Air Element and completely at odds amongst all the colour and music and festivity around it. Yve, Rehhd's widowed partner, stands talking with another Air.

But it is not Yve that Anaiya locks gazes with. It is Seth.

For a moment they just stare at each other. Seconds, minutes. It feels like forever.

And then all the other details come rushing into focus. He is not alone. His usual shadow is right there beside him.

Kaide's eyes flick from Seth to Anaiya. He is clearly not happy with this development.

Heads begin to turn at the sudden change in mood and focus.

"You fucking Fire fascist piece of toxic …" Yve shrieks, her face contorted, her arms working to get past the group of Elementals in her way. Long folds of black fabric tangle beneath her, tripping her up, slowing her down.

Seth remains where he is, arms crossed, watching passively as the scene unfolds. Kaide shakes his head and strides forward, reaching Yve and wrapping her up in his powerful arms before she can unleash her rage at Anaiya.

"Let me go!" she screams, thrashing against her temporary restraint.

Anaiya clumsily future-searches, seeking the best course of action. While her realignment did not rob her of the ability, the visions are not as clear as they used to be. More variables seem to come into play, alternate endings fighting for attention and dominance.

As her thoughts speed up, the scene in front of her appears to slow. Yve's movements become long and exaggerated; Kaide's eyes, unflinching and intense.

More and more rapidly, her mind sorts through the available data, struggling against her biased observations and chaotic emotions. She sees herself walking away, sees Kaide letting go, sees Seth intervening. But the search is distracted.

There is something tickling at the periphery. Her head twists to the right, her eyes catching the first glimpse of a Peacekeeper rounding the corner not thirty metres from where she is standing.

Time escapes the sticky residue holding it in slow motion and Anaiya is thrust back into the loud chaos of the moment. Panicked, she steps back into the hidden recess of the doorway. Yve's screams pitch higher, oblivious to the kevlar-clad Trainee that repels off izakaya walls.

Anaiya tries to future-search again, but her mind resists. Caught up in the unfolding drama, she is unable to separate the present from the rush of memories that come unbidden – of herself as a Trainee, free-running beside Kane 148 as he showed her the forms; of the smell of genievre as a Peacekeeper Trainee slammed a drunken Earth Elemental to a subworm station floor on the day of her deployment; of a Peacekeeper Trainee restrained in an izakaya basement before it all went black and the world turned upside down.

And behind all of it is the real and urgent fear that she risks coming out of hiding. The hiding that has kept her safe. Kept her alive.

A loud, sharp shout cuts through the noise. The Air Elementals seem to pay it no mind, but it runs like fire down her spine. It is a call for reinforcements. A call to tribe.

The other Peacekeepers round the corner; a swarm of synthflies with a hunger for raw meat.

Finally, Yve turns around, let loose by Kaide's distraction. She squirms out of his grasp as the Peacekeepers set upon the Elementals closest to the mural, restraining without cause or concern.

It is the way of this new world order – *There is no such thing as an innocent bystander anymore.*

Yve is running towards a Senior Peacekeeper already preoccupied with two other Air Elementals. Anaiya doesn't need to future-search to know what will happen next. She steps out from the doorway, pushing aside the sudden anxiety at being exposed, and runs after Yve.

With the other Elementals restrained, the Senior Peacekeeper turns her full attention to the new threat. She relaxes her stance and throws a well-timed punch at Yve. Still stumbling, the Air manages to catch only a glancing blow to her shoulder. The impact knocks her further off-balance and she tumbles to the cobblestones.

Anaiya accelerates. Brushing past Kaide, she fends off his attempt to grab her.

"Distract her," she whispers fiercely, not turning around to see if he has heard or will comply.

Yve is pushing herself up, but the Peacekeeper, sensing a new target, turns and sets her sights on Anaiya. Her eyes widen at the sight of Anaiya's uniform and then shift to the right, narrowing at another threat.

Anaiya keeps her eyes on Yve. Vaulting over the bodies of restrained Elementals, she launches into Yve and locks her arms around her. The tall Elemental thrashes in her grip, but Anaiya holds tight, kicking Yve's legs out from under her and barrelling her towards the entrance to Veritas.

Wrenching away Yve's arm before it can strike her, Anaiya jams it against the access panel, wincing at the unnatural angle and Yve's cry of pain.

Not now. Just get her inside.

With Yve temporarily disabled, Anaiya wrenches the door open, sending the two of them tumbling inside. She falls awkwardly, twisting to cushion Yve's fall and grunting as the Air collapses on her. The door shuts behind them, sealing them away from the light and the noise and the chaos.

Anaiya gently pushes Yve off her, unnerved at the Elemental's sudden silence. And then she hears it. Worse than the shrieking, worse than the cursing and the shouting and the sound of Elementals dropping to the road.

Sobbing. Deep, wrenching sobs that gasp and splutter and rend.

"Yve ...?" Anaiya whispers, tentatively reaching out to comfort her.

The Elemental rounds on her, throwing herself on Anaiya and pounding her with fists. Anaiya lays still, letting the blows rain down on her, unable to take her eyes off the wretched face above, contorted in grief and anger and pain.

Tears fall from Yve's cheeks to Anaiya's and still Anaiya remains motionless. This is her punishment.

The blows come heavier, and then with nails, scratching at skin. Yve's hysteria worsens, the sobs wracking her chest, her eyes wild and unfocussed.

Anaiya's chest fills to bursting. With a loud wail she finally reaches up and pinches her fingers into the soft spot on the side of Yve's neck where her Peacekeeper restraint needle would have once pierced. Clenching her eyes shut, she squeezes her grip tightly, feeling the last bit of resistance give way.

Yve falls quiet as her body goes limp. It should be over, but the sobbing continues. Softer this time, but no less harrowing. She can't stop them. They rush from Anaiya's chest and suck the air from her lungs. Tears course down her face and with what little energy she has left, she gently rolls Yve's leaden body off her and sits up.

The sobs die in her throat.

Seth and Kaide stand at the door to the wet room. Kaide stares at her, a frown beginning to crease his face. Seth's stricken eyes flash from her to Yve and back again.

"What have you done?"

FOUR

Kaide is the first to break from the spell, rushing over to kneel beside Yve's still body. He lifts up her arm, cradling it against his chest while he brings up her vitals on the wristplate. Looking over to Anaiya, he frowns again. She runs her hand self-consciously over her face to wipe away the tears and erase the bloody scratches.

"What did you do?" Seth's voice cuts again into the silence. His voice and face are so hard it is impossible to remember a time when they looked on her with anything but malice and hatred.

"Nothing," Anaiya splutters. "She's fine. I just restrained her."

The word is a charge and Seth explodes. "You *restrained* her. For *what*? She was doing nothing *Unorthodox*." He spits the last word, his feet pacing back and forth, hands running tense fingers through his hair. "She was celebrating the semester of her lover's death. The lover *you* Executed."

"Seth." Kaide's voice is low and harsh. He shakes his head and returns his attention to Yve.

"No," Seth yells back. "She is no better than the lache armes out there."

There is an ugliness to his voice as he throws out the popular insult used by Air dissenters against Peacekeepers. *Lache arme.* Loose weapon.

"She killed Rehhd and now she assaults Yve," he continues. "She is the lowest of them. She is feu mort. She is *dead fire.*"

Anaiya's heart hardens, her liquid emotions setting like amber and stripping her of the vulnerability that suffocated her just minutes ago.

"You think you are *better* than me?" she shouts back, her own emotion bubbling over. "You think your culpability is somehow *less* than mine? Your Heterodoxy killed Rehhd and now it kills others. You started a movement you can't control. You infect them like you infected Rehhd, manipulating them with your grand visions of resistance only to stand back while they run rabid in the streets. While they set fire to buildings and throw bombs from shadows."

The dynamic in the room has shifted. Kaide stands, keeping Anaiya at arm's length but not intervening. Seth glares at her, opening his mouth to respond, but she ignores him. She is not finished and this is a rage that for months has begged for release. A rage that burns hot to mask her guilt and confusion and fear.

"You hide away in your delusion that Rehhd was some innocent victim. The *martyr* for your righteous cause. But Rehhd's Execution was guaranteed the moment she took that Trainee. What did you think she was going to do, Seth? Just release him?" A harsh, caustic laugh rips from her lips. "Rehhd had years of cuts, bruises and scars to pass on. She would never have stopped. Not until the whole city burned. And now you are doing her work for her."

It is too much; her voice breaks and a deep tiredness floods through her body. "You lead your little army through Otpor, promising them a better future, but leaving nothing but destruction and disunity."

She steps towards Seth, halted as Kaide's arm comes up as a protective barrier. She glances briefly at him, momentarily surprised at the melancholy behind his eyes, but then turns her full attention back to Seth. The agitation radiates from him in waves, but he doesn't voice it. Just stands there, staring at her with hatred burning in his eyes.

"You may have been a visionary once, Seth. But now you are just a Demolition grunt. What hope will be left once you've destroyed everything? How many more are you willing to sacrifice in pursuit of this grand vision? This beautiful Resistance?"

She is spent. Pushing away Kaide's arm, she heads for the

izakaya exit. As her hand reaches for the door, she throws a final glance back. The pair of them stand together, regarding her silently. Once upon a time, a small part of her had wanted to be just like them. Now, she wants nothing to do with them.

Seth's voice echoes in her memory, taking her back to that night at the Trocadero when the lights from the Execution courtyard had continued to shine, long after Rehhd had taken her last breath. Anaiya had tried to protect him even then. Tried to shield him from detection as he defiantly broadcast his Heterodoxy. She had burned hot with the desperation of it.

And then he had turned cold eyes to her and with a colder voice uttered a string of words that have never left her. *You are dead to me, Anaiya.*

She looks at him now, his eyes still devoid of any tenderness or hope or life. And something inside her shifts. *You are dead to me, too.*

FIVE

Outside, the contingent of Peacekeepers has grown from a handful to a dozen. And yet, they do not dominate the crowd. Air Elementals, drawn by the noise and the heat of a new Otpor day, run from nearby streets to join the fray, rushing at Peacekeepers with shouted insults and makeshift weapons.

A number of Peacekeepers already sport long gashes and wounded heads, but the injuries pale in comparison to the bodies of restrained Air Elementals that litter the ground. Trainee Peacekeepers pile them up like boxes of soylent in Earth Elemental stores, clearing the way for more efficient manoeuvres.

The Fire part of Anaiya's brain recognises the functionality of the action, but the Air part shudders in abhorrence. There is something unnatural and macabre in the walls of incapacitated and broken bodies.

One Trainee moves amongst the bodies, bending down to tag Unorthodoxy codes into wristplates. Anaiya watches his face for signs of revulsion, but he merely goes about his task, never really stopping, never hinting at anything beyond a mild boredom or irritation.

That used to be me.

She can imagine it so clearly. Dutifully obedient to her superiors, but itching to be part of the action, to unleash her Fire.

Movement to her left brings her back to the moment. An Air

Elemental, three generations older than Anaiya and too old to be caught up in the violence, advances on the preoccupied Trainee. He is slow and haphazard like most Airs, but his eyes are sharp and unmoving. This is an Elemental seeking vengeance.

This is not my fight. I can't get involved. I need to stay hidden.

He is closer now. A broken bottle, its jagged edges like liquid in the morning light, is gripped tightly in his hand. In a few seconds his advance will turn to bloodshed.

Groaning, Anaiya rushes at the Air Elemental, tackling him from behind. The unexpected force knocks the weapon from his hand and she faintly registers the sound of it shattering against the cobblestones as she twists yet again to cushion her victim's fall.

The Trainee swivels in surprise and without hesitation reaches for a syringe to complete the restraint.

"I thought Infrastructure Protectors were supposed to be slow," he says as he injects the needle into the neck of the squirming Air. The older male stills and Anaiya winces as the Trainee lifts him and adds him to the nearest pile of bodies.

"I thought Peacekeepers were supposed to be alert," she replies.

The insult causes his face to tighten, but Anaiya doesn't waste time on it; her attention is called to the two Air Trainees advancing towards them. The tall male is the first to start running, his stride lengthening as his scowl deepens.

Their collision is just seconds away. In her mind's eye, she sees herself pull at his forearm, crush fingers into the stomach nine pressure point. *Not too heavy. Just enough to drop him …*

He grunts as the impact forces air from his lungs. Anaiya wraps her arms around him. Fingers reach for that tender spot in his neck and then, inexplicably, flinch away. Caught off guard by her own hesitation, she shifts her hands to his hips, spinning him around. Swivelling herself, she kicks out, sending him sprawling.

It will hurt and it will leave scars, but it will not damage him.

The female wails as she begins her own sprint towards Anaiya. Her light feet identify her as Dancer, her poise and agility out of sorts with the high-pitched wailing that spews from her lips.

Anaiya crouches, ready for the confrontation. Wanting it.

Nails slice at the skin protecting her clavicle. Fitting that it should be the part that separates her head from her heart.

She lets them dig in, savouring the white, hot shreds of pain. *Three. Two. One.*

Her hand flicks out and grabs the wrist. Turns. Twists. There is that moment, when the give of muscle and tendon reaches a place of limited options, where there is nothing else but escape or bone to break.

A cold sweat breaks out over Anaiya's skin. Her grasp falters and she lets it – watches, almost distantly, as the female falls to the ground, sobbing and grabbing uselessly at the wrist that is still intact, but compromised.

Anaiya stands, satisfied the threat is contained and unable to look any longer at the bodies damaged by her hand. Around her, the situation is winding down. More Peacekeepers are arriving and order is slowly being imposed on the unruly Strip.

Lumen, a former Peacekeeping colleague, stands amongst the new arrivals. She looks from the Trainee to the pile of Restrained bodies to Anaiya. She frowns at seeing Anaiya, but quickly launches into action, throwing herself at a large cluster of Air Elemental who have cornered a younger Peacekeeper.

Anaiya turns away; she has seen enough violence for one day. Her gaze passes quickly over the crowd, looking for a clear exit. She finds it to the west, but not before her attention is drawn back to the izakaya. Kaide stands in the doorway, partially shadowed, hidden like Anaiya was earlier in the morning. For a moment, she thinks he will step back into the fray and her chest tightens. But he stays where he is.

Watching but not engaging.

For the briefest of moments, she wonders what he sees in the mess before him. What he thinks of it, what he is planning. Because he will be planning something.

It is a minor distraction. With nothing else holding her to this place of chaos, she turns her back on it all, abandoning it to its fate.

SIX

Anaiya wakes to a vibration at her wrist and Delacroix's sticky tongue to her cheek. Afternoon light streams through the threadbare curtains of her bedroom, ratcheting up the temperature.

Moving the mangy pup off the bed, she sits up and plugs her lifeline into her ear.

"Anaiya, it's Niamh."

And the nightmare continues.

The last time she had spoken with her former patrol partner had been months ago. Niamh, finally satisfied that Anaiya's 'mind descent' had stalled and stabilised, no longer needed to check in on her every week. No longer needed to protect his once-investment, now-liability.

He had looked at her in the same way that all Elementals looked at hypoxia-demoted colleagues – with an air of fear and repulsion. It didn't matter; Anaiya had used it to her advantage, playing up her pathetic state to reassure Niamh that her Heterodox mind had recovered and reset in its new, demoted role.

"Are you there?" He sounds mildly frustrated.

"Yes, I'm here."

"How are you feeling?"

The question takes her aback. Niamh is capable of many things, but concern and sympathy are not among them.

"How am I feeling?"

It is always difficult talking to her old patrol partner. She invariably second-guesses herself – stumbling over her words and cringing at how weak she sounds. Every interaction with Niamh seems to leave her feeling smaller, inadequate. Redundant.

"Yes, Ani. How are you feeling?" He speaks the words slowly, over-enunciating the syllables. As if she were a pre-form. As if her agreed pretence of hypoxia is real.

"Fine … Why?"

"Be at Eastern Area Command in fifteen."

"I'm not a Peacekeeper anymore, Niamh."

"Twenty-five."

The line clicks dead as he disconnects.

"I meant, you can't order me around anymore," she mutters.

Sitting up, she pulls on the boots lying half-chewed under her bed. Even with the extra ten minutes, she will need to hustle. Delacroix sniffs at the laces.

"Sorry, pup, this one's a solo mission."

"You've lost tone, Ani."

Niamh sits behind a desk, barely glancing up when she walks into the office. "Infrastructure Protection doesn't become you."

He says it matter-of-factly; a simple observation. She ignores the small sting it brings. Easier to expect an Earth Elemental to solve synth toxin build-up, than a Fire Element to show tact.

"You're the one who demoted me," she says, taking the seat opposite him without waiting to be asked.

He raises an eyebrow, but lets her comment pass.

"Why am I here?" Frustration creeps into her voice and she imagines reaching over the table and pulling his head back until his gaze meets her own. Patience is a virtue that neither Fire nor Air possess.

"Lumen debriefed me on the Ravignan Strip incident."

Thoughts of Yve and Seth and piles of restrained bodies threaten at the edges of her memory.

"It seems you were quite effective in assisting the Peacekeeping effort."

Finally, he looks up at her. She expects to see some level of emotion behind his eyes, something to indicate that he is interested or impressed, but he gives nothing away. Merely a Peacekeeper assessing a situation.

"It was just a couple of Air Elementals," she says.

He watches her closely and the feeling of being a target under surveillance starts to itch along her nerves. The urge to squirm under his scrutiny grows with each second that passes in silence. Digging her fingernails into her palms, she waits it out. Competition with Niamh has always been her default position.

"The idiots painted a seven-metre high mural of Rehhd 020," he says eventually, his face relaxing into open scorn. "It was like they were inviting us to drop them. What was your take on it?"

She shrugs non-comitally; there is no right answer to this question. Either she rejects his assessment and comes under more scrutiny or she accepts it and sends more violence to the Elementals she still feels indebted to.

"It was messy. Too many Trainees who weren't ready to deal with the situation." It's low-level intel; nothing that Niamh would not already know.

"There's just not enough of us," he says, drumming his fingers on the desk. "Population requirement analysis doesn't factor in major cases of Heterodoxy – not that it should, obviously. Why factor in something that shouldn't happen? But Peacekeeper numbers haven't exceeded two per cent in more than ten generations. *Ten.* I saw the Water projections report just the other week; more Repair Mechanics and Retail Workers will graduate out of the Nursery over the next three generations than all Fire competencies combined."

She stares at the insignia on his shirt; the red thread in sharp contrast to the black kevlar, a single flame inside three concentric rings. Area Commander – one step away from Deputy Peacekeeper. Not that Niamh's ambitions would halt there ... Still, he is already high enough the hierarchy to be getting population briefings.

I wonder what else he knows.

"... which is why I need you back on deck."

Back on deck?

Niamh looks at her expectantly. She frantically searches her subconscious to pick up the thread of conversation buried behind her distraction. Something about numbers being tight. And Peacekeeper injuries. Trainees taking too long to refine their conditioning.

"You're promoting me?"

"Not exactly. Your mental distractions and lack of physical conditioning aren't exactly inspiring confidence. If we weren't so desperate for numbers, I wouldn't even consider it. Yet, here we are."

Again, there is no malice, just a complete lack of tact. The fantasy of slamming his head into the desk screen is satisfying for only a second; for as long as it takes her to realise she can't act on it.

Niamh glances back down, frowning as he taps and swipes through the various tabs, Anaiya forgotten.

"What exactly are you proposing, Niamh?"

His frown deepens at the interruption; as if he is the one being inconvenienced, as if it were Anaiya who pulled him out of his life and not the other way around.

"You'll be paired with a Shadow," he says, glancing up. "Someone I can trust. Who knows? Your exposure to the Resistance may prove valuable. You seem to have a knack for finding Rehhd associates we haven't previously tagged ... I'll sort out the data transfer, you begin tonight. A7 is your new shift station. Your Shadow will be waiting for you at 1700 hours."

The room feels smaller, her rage replaced by an insidious tightness that builds in her chest. Niamh doesn't see any of it, his head already bent again, his focus consumed by whatever flashes on his screen.

The conversation is over. Not that it was a real conversation. *Just him ordering me around again.*

Her traitorous, Heterodox mind wants to rebel, to say no. She doesn't want this – doesn't want to be back on Niamh's radar and under his command.

But she is not Seth; she will not suffer for a rebellion of which nothing good can come.

Niamh has too much leverage over her, knows too much,

holds too much power. Saying no will only lead to more suspicion, reinstated surveillance. Maybe a Heterodoxy charge. Maybe an 'accidental' injury.

Is he really capable of that? It's hard for her to discern the line between her warped perception and reality.

So, here she is again. Confined in a room and left without options, her future already decided, her opinion irrelevant.

The rebellion in her mind is shouting at her, urging her to halt a return to this madness, but she stops it from gaining control. Not just because saying no would be stupid, but because the idea of being a Peacekeeper again excites her.

There had been an uneasy kind of rush when she had intervened at the Strip, a guilty thrill when she had felt the stirrings of a Fire identity that had been silent for too long.

There had been a feeling of compatibility and rediscovery, of pieces fitting together. She wasn't just sitting around in dusty industrial sectors, staring at walls, waiting for disturbances that never came.

"Ani?"

"Huh?"

Niamh is staring at her, his frown still there. "You're dismissed."

SEVEN

The tight black kevlar of her Peacekeeper uniform feels heavy against her skin. Anaiya pulls in vain at the fabric, urging it to deny its material limitations and stretch.

She runs her hands down the sleeves, taking in the absence of scuffs and scratches. It is not her old uniform, with its characteristic dents and dings – that would have been incinerated like the rest of her belongings left behind in Precinct 5.

Her heart twinges, a tiny ripple of emotion, but she halts it before it can entrain. She had never thought of her apartment in Precinct 5 as a home while she had lived there. Only now it is stripped away does she retrofit her Air emotions to it.

Air emotions. They pull everything into high definition. Nice when a lover's kiss is grazing your neck. Not so nice when they resurrect memories that should stay buried.

Delacroix sits on her bed with his head cocked to the side, occasionally growling at the strange figure that stands in front of him. He senses the pretence as much as she does.

She had hoped that pulling on the uniform would have given her an answer – would have stilled her uneasiness and halted the contradictions of her mind. Ended all this uncertainty. Erased the Heterodoxy.

Staring at herself in the tarnished mirror, her reflection offers no solace. The image before her is a stranger.

Get it together, Anaiya. You're just nervous.

Before her realignment, the flutter in her belly was just the flood of adrenalin pushing along her veins. Life was so much more complicated, now.

The free-run back to Headquarters does nothing to smooth out the ripples. Her kash vaults are clumsy, her footholds unsteady. And building with every metre gained is the irrational fear that Elementals are watching her, judging her. Finding her wanting.

By the time she reaches the Peacekeeper building, every molecule in her body is magnetised and pulling her back to the Northern Area. Gripping her hands into tight fists, she compresses the ball of anxiety in her belly and steps through the entry.

Inside, the foyer is a hive of activity, but the elevator space is empty. Peacekeepers don't do well standing still in confined spaces – it's a wonder they ever bothered to install one. Their aversion is her reprieve.

Ducking her head to avoid scrutiny, she rushes to the narrow corridor and waits until the small bell on the wall rings once, announcing the arrival of the metal cage. The descent to the basement is short but takes a lifetime. There is an unbearable urge to move, to shift, to fidget. Instead, she stares at the lights on the elevator dashboard, watching as the numbers count down, subconsciously creating a melody to ease her mind.

When the jaws of the cage open, bright lights announce the rows of shift stations. A long corridor runs down the centre of the room, ten pods of partitioned offices arrayed either side. Each step past the sterile cubicles pushes her to rebel, to retreat. There is no escaping scrutiny here.

Peacekeepers in dark kevlar turn and cast their unimpressed eyes over her. Clenching her jaw, she forces herself to continue her march past them, her belly swarming with synthflies as she seeks out her shift station.

Unlike the other stations, A7 is sparsely populated. The tightness in her chest relaxes a little. And then the senior Peacekeeper halts her discussion with the Administrator and looks over her shoulder; her attention drawn to the anomaly that is Anaiya. She is prepared for what she sees; only the faint shadow of a grimace betrays any emotion.

But Anaiya is reeling. The senior Peacekeeper is not just another unfamiliar face in a sea of disapproving stares.

It is hard to look at Jenna and not be assaulted by the same anger and jealousy she had felt towards her during her realignment and deployment. Even now, confronted with Jenna's promotion to a higher rank, Anaiya feels as though the Peacekeeper has stolen the future that was meant for her.

It was Jenna who had kept her Fire identity while Anaiya's was stripped away. It was Jenna who had taken Anaiya's place by Niamh's side as consummate Peacekeeper. Who had never faltered in her perfect conditioning, while Anaiya's identity fractured beyond repair.

And it is now Jenna, who just by being here, throws all of that back at her, reminding her that she is damaged and inferior.

"OK, Premie," the senior Peacekeeper says, striding past Anaiya without any recognition of the chaos within her. "Let's patrol."

The insult burns, but Anaiya doesn't react. This is Jenna's world and, as far as the Peacekeeper is concerned, Anaiya is just another damaged Elemental; hypoxia rendering her capable but unproven.

Except that Anaiya is not hypoxic; a secret Jenna knows too well. Damaged, yes; but not through injury and not by accident.

"Keep up, Premie," Jenna calls over her shoulder, not looking back. "We don't have all night. Let's run."

There is no pity, no irony. A simple direction. An assumption that the very familiar words will trigger a very natural response.

Jenna ignores the elevator – just another piece of redundant infrastructure to a Peacekeeper – entering the stairwell at pace and taking the steps three at a time. Anaiya keeps up, but feels her legs and lungs push to meet the unexpected demand.

Questions about where they are going and what they will be doing fill her thoughts but avoid her tongue. As a 'Trainee' it is not her place to know. Just to follow.

They exit the building without slowing, launching into the free-run despite the clusters of Elementals that crowd the street.

Flashes of jealousy mix with appreciation at the sight of Jenna's execution. Every launch is flawless, every vault a perfect sinuous curve of movement.

The ease of her confidence, the natural assuredness, is a sharp rebuke and a heavy reminder. Anaiya was once this consummate Peacekeeper – was easy and uncomplicated. The manifestation of Orthodoxy. Perfectly optimised.

But now she is corrupted and unnatural. Heterodox.

She falters, recovering quickly, but not quick enough. Jenna throws a quick glance in response to the stumble, narrowing her eyes at Anaiya's unsteady gait, but never slowing.

Flushing with the shame of it, Anaiya pushes harder to catch up, forcing her muscles to remember the forms, begging her arms to reach higher, her feet to kick-off more forcefully.

Her hand scrabbles against a crumbling brick wall, losing purchase and threatening to give her over to gravity's mercy. She curses and tucks her body into a tight roll. Landing awkwardly on her shoulder, she turns the mistake into a manoeuvre of sorts, somersaulting on an ugly axis across the cracked bitumen.

The impact knocks the air from her lungs and sends a weight to her core. For a moment, she just lies there, waiting for her body to recover.

"Get up, Premie. We've got work to do." Jenna stands over her, her athletic frame blocking the brown rays of Otpor's sun.

Anaiya reluctantly meets her gaze. Somewhere behind that carefully controlled facade is the repulsion and apprehension that all Elementals feel when looking at the hypoxia-affected, at the damaged Elementals, the 'less-than' optimal. But she hides it well, showing only hints of irritation and impatience – the perfect conditioning of a functional Fire Elemental.

Taking a deep breath, she pushes herself up, fighting the urge to wince as pain trembles from her shoulder to wrist. She cradles the arm against her side and looks around. So caught up in the free-run, she has failed to notice their arrival in the Northern Area's upper precincts.

"What are we doing here?" she asks, gritting her teeth against the pain and momentarily forgetting that Trainees don't have the luxury of asking questions.

"We're on heat-map duty," Jenna replies, frustration now more evident in her tone. She speaks as though Anaiya should already know this. As though she should understand what 'heat-map duty' is.

Seconds pass before Jenna realises the cause for Anaiya's uncomfortable silence. "He didn't tell you?"

Anaiya shakes her head.

"What did he tell you?"

"That numbers were tight and he needed an experienced Peacekeeper on active duty."

Jenna clenches her fists at her side, the only indication of any depth of emotion.

"I hope he knows what he is doing," she mutters, appraising Anaiya with more scrutiny than before. "OK, so intel has identified hot-spots of Unorthodox and Heterodox activity. Heat-map teams patrol the areas with the most significant activity. Normal Peacekeeping protocols don't apply – no code call-outs, no warnings, no opportunities for defence. If anything looks out of order, don't bother future-searching. It's restrain first, ask questions later."

Anaiya's belly falls cold and hard. She recalls the incident at Ravignan Strip, visions of unconscious bodies piled as bricks in a wall. She had been absent for most of it and her brain struggles to remember the details. Had Peacekeepers followed protocol? Just how far had the corps shifted in the last six months?

Jenna sighs, likely mistaking her continued silence as the mark of a slowed mind. "Just follow me, OK? And don't do anything stupid."

The northern reaches of Precinct 19 are unrecognisable. Electronic stores and convenience shops sit abandoned, their broken windows patched with boards of cheap micro-lattice. Anaiya's feet crunch on the deposits of shattered glass.

She and Jenna had slowed their approach a few blocks back, the signs of disrepair starting to show in the sand-covered streets and empty storefronts. It had hinted at what was to come, yet Anaiya is still unprepared for the scope of desolation.

Thick coats of unnatural white polymer cover every wall, announcing the Heterodox graffiti they hide simply by their presence. The harsh colour serves as an unforgiving backdrop to the damaged infrastructure and litter-filled streets.

Anaiya's boots track prints in heavy drifts of Wasteland sand, avoiding the debris and destruction. Her stride becomes slow, an uneasiness settling on her shoulders.

The Heterodoxy and violence had always been shocking, a jolt of electricity that was easy to rage against. But this – the emergence of places bereft of Water technology, Earth maintenance, Air creativity or Fire enforcement – is less shocking and more insidious.

Beneath the sand and debris and broken glass is the hint of something bigger; something that will outlive the chaos. A purer form of anarchy. Heterodoxy in its ultimate manifestation.

A singsong chant swells into the quiet and pulls her from her thoughts. Jenna stops and pivots, crouching low and balancing on her back foot. Seeing her seamless shift into combat mode throws Anaiya and she stumbles into a poor approximation. Jenna gives no indication she has noticed the blunder, her eyes carefully trained on the laneway two blocks ahead.

The broad-shouldered Earth Elemental emerges as if on cue, still singing the simple nursery rhyme his Element learns in the Nursery.

"Under the sun, I'll work and play. I'll do the same as yesterday. I'm simple and tough, and easy to please. Time for you to catch this disease."

Beat. Beat.

The gears in Anaiya's mind grind against the intrusion.

No. That's not right.

The words are wrong. *You've never seen hands as strong as these.*

Jenna is already in full flight, hurtling towards the male. He stands there and watches calmly as she barrels towards him, starting his rhyme over again.

In spite of Jenna's early direction, Anaiya future-searches. As she expects, it is clumsy and awkward, compromised by her unease and the insistent shouting of her mind that something is very, very wrong.

Her Fire identity provides the structure – taking into consideration the perpetrator's profile and stance, and the surrounding environment. That alone would present her a simple assessment and she would be running alongside Jenna to follow up what should be an easy restraint.

Except her Air identity draws alternative conclusions. It picks up on the inconsistencies; the alternative lyrics, the atypical response to Jenna's impending restraint, the shadows stretching along the white-washed walls, the criss-crossing of footprints in the sand drifts.

He is not alone. This is not a simple restraint or chance encounter.

This is a trap.

Anaiya opens her mouth to sound a warning, but the words evaporate before they make it to her lips. Earth and Air Elementals stream from the arcade; unlikely allies who share only their preference for the intuitive over methodical.

Finally, her body catches up with her mind, bracing for the explosion of energy she'll need to catch up to Jenna.

A firm grip encircles her forearm. She swivels on instinct, her free arm raised to deliver the short punch her muscle memory begs to unleash.

Kaide's face swells in her vision. "Back down. This is just a distraction."

Heart still racing with unspent adrenalin, she pulls away and looks over to where Jenna is easily restraining the slower, less-coordinated Earth Elementals.

"Take this." His hand brushes down her arm, pressing something fragile into her palm. "You can make things right again, Anaiya."

Her earlier panic is subsiding, her mind slowing to take in more details. Kaide's eyes flit erratically between hardness and pleading. There is a desperation there. And a challenge.

Noises behind her draw Anaiya's gaze back to Jenna. The rush of Elementals has dissipated and only a few lie motionless on the dirty street. The Peacekeeper is in full control, restraining the last of the aggressors with a simple feint-attack manoeuvre.

Anaiya turns back to Kaide, but the space behind her is empty. No sign of the enigmatic Air Elemental; no indication that he was ever really there, except for the crumbly sheet of material in her hand. It sticks to her palm, adhering to her skin as it sucks up the beads of sweat.

She doesn't have time for this. Crumpling the sheet into a smaller shape, she stuffs it into her pocket and launches into a sprint towards Jenna. The Peacekeeper barely glances at her as Anaiya throws herself at an impossibly thin Air Elemental.

The target is quicker and more agile than expected. He steps gracefully to the left, evading her first attempt to grab and restrain him. Laughing, he starts throwing pidgin expletives at her.

As a normal, pure-aligned Fire Elemental, his antics would have no impact on her and she would transition easily into the next stage of pursuit. But there is nothing pure about Anaiya, anymore. She is a mongrel like the pup she left behind in her apartment, filled with a strange kind of rage that ripples along her nerves. Irrational and convoluted; mixed up in the mess of emotions wreaking havoc in her core.

Her focus zones in on random details – the smirk on his lips, the fraying of his jeans, the ugly skin ink that twists around his calves. It all works to notch the rage higher. Until Anaiya is just a flame seeking out oxygen in its desperate attempts to grow and explode.

The Air pushes up on his toes, preparing for another evasion. Her Fire identity judges his posture and energy levels, anticipating a move to the right. But her Air identity sees his movements as an intricate dance and, in that moment, she knows the positioning to the right is just a feint – a trap to get her off-balance.

Game on.

She positions her body to lunge right, relying on the Air affinity for identifying spatial patterns to create her own deception. Her target smirks and Anaiya's rage flickers hotter. But she holds it in place and gives away nothing. She has this.

The Elemental steps off his right foot, pitching backwards and into a pirouette. But Anaiya is already moving into her own unconventional positioning, springing forward with more force and speed that she would otherwise. The fall in the Air's face shifts her rage into something much more satisfying. Her hand clenches comfortably around his upper arm, twisting it until she has it, and him, in submission.

With her free hand, she reaches seamlessly for the syringe at her belt and, with no hesitation, pushes the needle into the vein bulging in his neck.

As he slides to the ground, her sense of victory evaporates. A spiky sensation she knows all too well rushes to fill the void.

Guilt.

She whips her head around, suddenly aware that Kaide may still be watching her, tiny pinpricks of dread alighting on her skin.

The street behind her is empty and relief washes over her. The emotion confuses as much as it comforts.

What do I care what Kaide thinks? He knows nothing about what I'm going through. The emotion is strong, but the words feel hollow. She swats the distraction away and turns to Jenna.

Ahead, the street lies empty save for three bodies lying motionless on the street and Jenna grappling with a larger Earth.

Anaiya advances towards them, the Earth whipping her head up as she comes into vision. The Earth's demeanour changes, her frown of concentration replaced by a smile strangely reminiscent of the Air Elemental's smirk. With a rough push of surprising force, she shoves Jenna to the ground and runs back towards the laneway.

Catching up, Anaiya reaches down to offer Jenna her hand. The Peacekeeper brushes it away with a scowl and leaps to her feet unaided.

"Moronic Earths," she spits. "Why start an altercation and then run from it?"

Anaiya shrugs and bends to help Jenna record the incident onto the wristplates of unconscious Elementals. "Why do Elementals do anything?"

The words draw up from her subconscious, echoing conversations held a lifetime ago. Jenna frowns at her.

"I mean," Anaiya continues, trying to pull attention away

from her genuine musing, "why do Airs dance? Why are Waters so annoying? It's all conditioning, right?"

Jenna shakes her head and resumes her tagging. "Whatever you say, Premie."

EIGHT

Time drags long nails along Anaiya's frustration. She has never been good at waiting, and keeping watch over unconscious Earth and Air Elementals wears down her patience to rough, scratchy fibres.

Jenna is also frustrated, her feet pacing tight circles around the unconscious forms lying prostrate on the street. Both of them want to be chasing after the insolent Earth that melded into the shadows of the laneway, but abandoning restrained Elementals is only permitted in extreme circumstances. And boredom does not qualify, no matter how extreme it is.

Anaiya drags the toe of her boot in the deep layers of sand, watching as grains skittle over one another to form deep grooves and swirly patterns. Her fingers constantly seek the paper hidden in her pocket, the skin of her fingertips tingling as they run over the crinkly edges.

"I thought you had limped out on me," Jenna says.

Anaiya snatches her hand out of the pocket and looks up, heat colouring her cheeks, grateful for the dying light that hides them.

"What do you mean?" She is stalling; she knows exactly what Jenna means.

"Well, you didn't exactly leap into the action." Jenna's arms are crossed, but she still shifts her balance from foot to foot.

"They were Earth Elementals," Anaiya replies, working hard to lace her words with as much scorn as she can muster. "I didn't think you needed any help."

Jenna laughs. The tension stiffening along Anaiya's shoulder blades wavers and then relaxes.

"When did they get so feisty?" Jenna asks, gesturing at the restrained Elementals. "I thought they were all just dumb brutes."

Something inside Anaiya cringes – at the rough assessment, at the raw truth. They are just dumb brutes; all brawn and simplicity and easy pleasures.

Are they?

She looks down at the unconscious bodies, seeing something beyond restrained Unorthodoxy. Does the characterisation match the reality or merely reflect the bias of her Fire conditioning? She shakes her head to clear the confusion.

"Heterodoxy has everyone acting strange." It is a weak response to cover for her reaction.

Jenna tilts her head and looks at her closely; a Peacekeeper profiling. And there it is again, too much scrutiny threatening to uncover her secrets. Secrets that could kill her.

Stillness, like liquid silicon, drapes over Anaiya's body and sets it in place. Jenna frowns; a quick flash of ... what? Suspicion? Irritation?

The moment is over just as soon as it begins; Jenna turns her attention back to the Earth Elemental, reaching down to shake the shoulder of the immobile body, testing for consciousness.

Noise echoes from the street behind them and Anaiya turns to see two Forensics appear in view.

"Finally," Jenna says, stepping forward to meet them.

Anaiya hangs back, letting Jenna brief them on the incident. The evening shadows are longer now and the streetscape has taken on a menacing tone. The restrained bodies seem too lifeless; their stillness holds an accusation. She turns away.

Jenna has finished talking and the two Forensics are striding towards her, their red neoprene aprons darker in the oncoming night. Like old blood.

"What are you waiting for, Premie? Let's go."

The moniker irritates old wounds, but she ignores it. Turning from the bodies and the sand-blasted street, she jogs up to Jenna and joins her in the free-run.

The rest of the shift passes in a strange state of familiarity and discomfort. Anaiya's body dredges up the free-run forms from its muscle memory as her mind repeats visions of lifeless, injured and dead Elementals. Hours slip by in the passing of moments, hidden from view by the constant demands of the harsh environment and the ever-present threat of violence.

Otpor is not the city she remembers. Hot-spots of Unorthdox and Heterodox activity seem to overrun the northern precincts; tight mazes of narrow streets and laneways are punctuated with swathes of rough graffiti and the empty shops and office spaces seem to leave a trail of debris to announce invisible borders.

The lack of Orthodoxy in the environment seems to permeate the stale air, saturating the minds and colouring the eyes of the Elementals that turn vicious and antagonistic. There is a wild abandon in the challenges they throw at the two Peacekeepers, a complete untethering from the discipline instilled by their conditioning.

It makes them unpredictable. And dangerous.

Anaiya trails a finger across the gash near her right ear. It comes away wet and sticky; the skin-mending serum not strong enough to completely knit the cells across the deep cut. The wound was the work of a younger Earth Elemental, her eyes bright with the promise of violence. Anaiya had easily evaded her clumsy attempts at grabbing, but the erratic whirling of broken glass at the end of a piece of nylon rope had eventually found a mark.

The sting had connected Anaiya to a deeper, hotter rage and the encounter had ended with the Elemental lying broken on the bitumen, a cut to match Anaiya's perfectly carved into her young face.

She flushes at the memory, with residual adrenalin. And shame.

"Patrol's over, Premie. Let's drink." Jenna looks as calm and assured as she did at the beginning of the shift. Yet, despite her demeanour, a long row of three red scratches trails down the side of her neck, courtesy of a spritely eighth lustrum Air Elemental.

Anaiya smiles at their presence, grateful for the buffer that prevents Jenna from remarking on her own injury. Only an assault by a forty-three-year-old Air could compensate the embarrassment of injury at the hands of a Trainee Earth.

Their free-run to the izkaya is an easy one – a warm down, a chance to stretch and soothe tired muscles before they become laced with drug-enhanced synthetic alcohol. She tunes out the stimulation of the broken and run-down spaces around her, letting the drumming of her feet against the road and the feel of rough texture underneath her fingers drown out any distractions.

The arrival in Precinct 2 is heralded with bright lights and a welcomed semblance of order. The new landscape gives Anaiya's mind room to finally breathe and her body responds in turn – her legs stretching longer, her forms more fluid.

Not for the first time tonight, she feels like a Peacekeeper.

When Jenna turns down a small laneway, her adrenalin levels briefly spike, but the neon sign announcing *Le Pas Sage* izakaya eases the tension. The only traps to be found here will be born from too much alcohol or a wandering eye.

The izakaya itself is a little unusual, set in a narrow arcade rather than fronting the street. A lack of lighting and the stone facade set it apart from the typical Fire drinking spaces and, at the far end, a nondescript door is noticeable only for the steady stream of Peacekeepers, Compliance Inspectors and Infrastructure Protectors that pass through it.

Inside, the izakaya opens up to her. At first, it appears smaller than she expects, but deeper inspection reveals an L-shaped layout that extends well beyond the bar and into an unknown space. It is disorienting, but Jenna seems to know the space intimately and Anaiya finds herself following the Peacekeeper.

Just like a good Premie.

She shoves her hands in her pockets to hide her frustration, her fingertips grazing the crumpled sheet that had almost become forgotten as the night's events had distracted her. Fire Elementals press in against her, lining up to get their synth fix from the bar. She pushes back against them, seeking her exit.

"Where are you going, Premie?" Jenna calls out to her, two tall glasses of blue effervescence cradled in her hands.

Looking around, Anaiya searches for an alibi, an excuse to disappear. Beyond the crowd, at a table unoccupied by anyone else, she spies a sixth lustrum Peacekeeper. Broad shoulders and angular features attract her attention, but it is the way he runs his fingers through the errant strands of his hair that reminds her of Seth.

Jenna follows her gaze, her laugh reaching Anaiya's ears over the increasing volume of noise in the izakaya.

"Don't go in thirsty," she calls out, extending one of the glasses towards Anaiya.

Anaiya takes the dodeca and begins pushing her way through the crowd. A quick glance over her shoulder confirms that Jenna has already forgotten her, caught up in her own distractions. Free from scrutiny, Anaiya can escape.

The Peacekeeper at the table looks up at her. Perfect features in ideal symmetry – a more successful genetic manipulation from the Nursery than she has seen in a while. He smiles at her – not the genuine display of pleasure that she had become used to as an Air Elemental, but the quiet seduction of a Fire who has never known rejection.

It would be so easy to accept that unspoken invitation, to let the dodeca work its magic on her and submit to the pure carnal urges of her core. But her curiosity – a state she had never experienced before her realignment – sings to her.

Lifting the glass to her lips, she lets the concoction run across her tongue and fill her insides with fire. Her fingers curl over the delicate folds of paper in her pocket, and she leaves the izakaya without a backwards glance.

NINE

The air outside is cooler than it should be, the heat from the sun already leached from the concrete and steel of the city. Anaiya's boots pad silently against the tiles of the arcade, her gaze firmly centred on the laneway ahead.

Despite the temptation, she leaves the paper hidden until the next darkened alley presents itself. Concealing herself in the shadows, lit only by the echoes of neon signs and muted streetlights, she pulls the unfamiliar material from her pocket and unfolds it. In a world of technological communication, the simple action feels Heterodox.

The words are scrawled in awkward lettering, the crude ink running and bleeding across the page. *Need to talk. Back entry to Veritas at 2100.*

Meeting as curfew starts is smart. Peacekeepers will be on shift change, presenting the opportunity to rendezvous unobserved. Still, Kaide must be crazy if he thinks she will turn up.

She remembers the words he said to her as he pushed the note into her hand. *You can make things right again, Anaiya.*

What had he meant by that? *What exactly did he think was wrong?*

It doesn't matter. She is not going. It would be foolish, and unhelpful, and …

It's not going to happen.

Still, the threads of curiosity loop around her conviction. Her fingers fidget at the edges of the paper, betraying the uncertainty blooming in her core. Even with all that has come since, she still wants to believe there is a way to correct the wrongs of her past.

Her fingers clench with the frustration of it all; the vulnerable material of Kaide's note crumpling and separating at the edges. Pulling at the top corner, the sheet peels apart into two distinct layers, revealing rows of hidden text.

Heart racing, she glances up, checking to confirm that she is still alone. The space around her feels tight, as if the brick walls are leaning in to peer at the Heterodox lacing her fingers.

She shuffles further back into the recesses of the alley, hiding from the growing stretch of activity out on the street beyond. Crouching in the corner, letting the dark envelop her, she turns her back on the street and activates the diode on her wristplate. At its lowest setting, the light is little more than a hum of photons – just enough to illuminate the paper, not enough to attract attention.

Perfectly formed letters, too rigid and straight to be handwritten, fill the page.

The mind of the citizen is weak – a vulnerable and transient ether. A variable that must be both nurtured and controlled. Freedom does the citizen no favours, provides it no benefit. Success of the Cooperative depends on the governing body assuming the role that parents once performed. Love and security must be met with discipline and submission. Divide and conquer, weaken and dominate, love and enslave; this is the path to progress and achievement.

The words are not Kaide's. And they are not Seth's or Kane 148's – they are the words of the Cooperative. Of the Principals who first gifted the city Orthodoxy and its conditioning.

Anaiya's fingers tremble and the paper falls from her grip. She bends quickly to pick the pages up, recoiling as if a hidden disease lurks in the fibres, as if they are Heterodox.

Which is absurd, because there could be nothing more Orthodox than the writings of Otpor's founders.

Then why does my heart feel like it is about to explode from my chest?

Still reeling, it takes her a while to see that the second sheet also hides forbidden words; not the perfectly stylised and angular text of the first, but long, looping forms that appear misshapen and hesitant.

They say I am Heterodox. That my mind is so damaged it is no longer capable of knowing or keeping the Orthodoxy. They will kill me for this. My convictions should shield me from fear, but I find myself scared of this great unknown. It is why I hide from them now. Why I hide from the inevitable. Not because I fear death. Death comes to us all. But because I fear my death will be in vain. That I will pass into the darkness and nothing will change. No one will change. Their narrative will continue and my voice will be lost.

She reads the page again. And again. Even with the fear of someone discovering her with it, she cannot put it away. Cannot tear her gaze from Kane's beautiful, tragic words.

Is she really holding the same sheet of paper that he committed his confession to?

His voice is so clear in the choice of words, the rhythm of the sentences, that she can almost hear it again. The deep cadence, the hint of roughness at the edges …

Unable to withstand the painful hammering of her heart any longer, she pushes the pages into her pockets, shoving them deep while taking care not to destroy them.

Wiping her hands against the rough texture of her jeans, she makes her way back into the light of the street. Elementals move about her, oblivious to the inner turmoil sending tremors along her nerves. Forcing her unsteady legs to keep moving, she pushes deeper into the city.

How had Kaide got his hands on these documents? Was the first as real as the second, or just a clever forgery lent credibility by Kane's words? What dangerous game has he invited her into?

He is more calculating than Seth – he has always seen more; has always been more suspicious, more attentive. Where Seth is unadulterated emotion and inspiration, shaped by a purity of ideology and charisma, Kaide is more strategic. More grounded.

If the message to meet had come from Seth, she would have assumed retribution. But knowing it had come from Kaide, remembering his entreaty and the lack of emotion colouring his eyes, suggested a more Machiavellian motivation.

She had seen it during her deployment – the way he would subtly shift a conversation or direct attention to where he thought the focus should be. Pulling hidden strings from behind shadowed curtains.

Knowing how dangerous he is – knowing that all of this could be a trap or a manipulation – doesn't diminish the need to confirm whether the words are real. And whether there are more.

With curfew approaching, the streets become quieter. The silence and shadows work their way into Anaiya's mind, stealing her earlier conviction. Doubt ripples along the edges, growing with each block she passes on her way to Veritas.

The first thing Anaiya notices when the familiar izakaya comes into view is that Kaide is not alone. Seth stands next to him, arms folded and muscles tense. Like Kaide, he is mostly still, except for the symphony of short, sharp micro-movements that hint at a barely restrained agitation.

He looks different to her now.

Once, she had dismissed the violence Earth and Air lovers inflicted on one another as just more evidence to the fantasy of their mind-warped 'love'. Once, the thought of two Elementals professing to connect on the deepest level one second, only to lunge at each other with blades the next, had convinced her of the futility of emotion.

Now, she understands it.

She had connected with Seth. But that connection was double-edged. And now the blade had flipped.

Hostility and suspicion radiates from him and the urge to step up to him, treat him like just another Unorthodox Elemental whose insubordination needs restraining, tickles in her Peacekeeper mind.

Control the fire.

The words have lost their original meaning, but they still have the desired effect. She slows her advance and calms her breathing. This fight, as much as she wants it, is not what she is here for.

She turns her attention to Kaide. He is harder to read than

Seth – standing with arms hanging loosely at his side, his gaze never wavers from hers.

The paper in her pocket crumples again in her grip. She transfers all of her unexpressed rage and emotion into it before lifting it out and presenting it to its deliverer.

"What is this?" she demands, ignoring Seth.

"An incentive."

In those two words, Anaiya sees his angle – it is not an original one; she has seen it many times before with Niamh. Anaiya is the uncomfortable asset; a necessary evil, a means to be justified by its end.

They are just metres away from each other, close enough to see the details flickering across the other's face, distant enough to bolster the animosity that tinges the air.

"Are they real?"

"Yes."

"Not the pages, Kaide. The words. Are they his? Are they Kane's?" Her throat constricts with the effort of saying his name aloud.

He doesn't hesitate. "Yes."

"Where did you steal them from?"

"Not stolen." It is Seth who speaks, stepping in from Anaiya's peripheral vision. "Found."

"Back off, Seth." Kaide's tone surprises her, as does the flash of anger Seth directs back at him.

Kaide turns to her. "Kane's Heterodoxy wasn't as impulsive as you have been led to believe. He knew things. We know things."

He reaches for the pages, fingers closing over them before her reflexes can recover from the strange admission.

"This is just a sample. Two pages of many. Hundreds. An entire book-full."

Book. Pages. Kane. All words and images and abstract concepts that should not be spoken aloud, should not be remembered. Should not exist.

"You shouldn't have them."

Because they are not Orthodox. They are not meant for you.

"We will gladly give them to you," Seth speaks again, his eyes hard, his voice thick with challenge.

Kaide frowns at him but turns back to Anaiya. "For a price."

Always for a price. She knew it would come, this negotiation, this tit-for-tat. And as much as she wants Kane 148's notes – the chance to learn about his Heterodoxy, and hers – she still bristles at the implied challenge of Kaide's words.

He is close. Closer than Seth. Closer than he should be.

Anaiya's instinct is to step back, to give herself space to position for the most effective attack. But her Air identity takes ascendancy and she steps forward into his challenge; all bravado, no sense.

The corners of his mouth quirk unexpectedly, the smile gone before it flourishes.

Not to be outdone, he also steps forward. Too close. The air shimmers with tension between them.

"Nice Peacekeeper uniform." His eyes trail down the kevlar threads.

The spoken observation takes her by surprise.

"What are you playing at, Kaide?"

"Why the promotion?" Something in his tone echoes the same questions she wants to ask Niamh. The same suspicion and caution. It irritates her that this rebellious Air Elemental is so perceptive.

"Old habits die hard," she replies. "Still keeping tabs on me?"

He shrugs. "You're a liability. Or an asset. Pays to keep track of both."

"What do you want?"

"What do *you* want?"

Frustration boils from within. She steps back, ready to turn and walk away from this endless circle of conversation.

His hand reaches out and grabs her. She swivels back, the rage that had threatened Seth now focussed on a new target. He holds his hands up in submission.

"Careful, Kaide. She bites."

Flicking her head to the right, she bristles at the sight of Seth scowling. How had she ever drowned in those eyes of his?

"Ignore him," Kaide says.

Harder to ignore a sandstorm. Still, she pushes his presence to the back of her mind.

"Senior Peacekeepers are planning a major offensive in the next couple of months," Kaide continues. "We need to know where and when."

She stares at him incredulously.

"This isn't you, Anaiya." He says it calmly. Matter-of-factly. Like he knows who she really is.

"You don't know the first thing about me." *I don't know the first thing about me.*

"I heard your music."

There is a pause. The two of them stand facing one another, forcing the other to remember things they would rather not.

"How do you know about the offensive?" she finally asks.

"We have our contacts."

Again, she looks over to Seth. He frowns at her. At Kaide.

"Then get your contacts to give you the intel," she says, looking back to Kaide.

"They're not that sort of contact."

Water, maybe? Kaide definitely has contacts there. And a full offensive would need Water support – profiling, comms, surveillance tech.

"And I am?"

"No," he replies, folding his arms across his chest. "But you are a contact who wants something we can give."

"Forget it, Kaide." Seth steps forward, breaking the intensity. "She's not going to do it."

His voice is sharp with loathing, but his eyes shine with that same tortured sadness she had witnessed at Rehhd's Execution.

"We can't trust her. She is not one of us. She is one of them. The worst of them, of what they really are."

Frustration and anger build to a peak within her. "And what is that?"

"Replaceable," Seth replies.

"Irredeemable," Kaide says simultaneously.

Her heart hardens. This was a mistake.

She steps up to Kaide. Flicking her arm out, she takes back the offending pages, taking petty satisfaction as he flinches. "Seth's right – I'm not interested. I protected you once, but I won't do it again."

Seth frowns, but Kaide is unreadable. Sirens punctuate the night sky, heralding the start of curfew.

"Keep the Orthodoxy or keep out of my way. I'm done with you."

TEN

The next few days pass by in a blur of patrols, violence and tiredness. Anaiya's muscles scream in protest and the tension between her shoulder blades pulls tighter with each new confrontation.

"Keep up, Anaiya!"

Jenna is frustrated with her. A week of shadowing has seen the Peacekeeper drop the insulting 'Premie', but Anaiya is still not living up to expectations – her speeds are slow, her timing is off and her forms are erratic.

It would be easy to explain it away as the result of her failed realignment, but she knows that's not the entire truth. Her body is underperforming because her mind is distracted.

She had been unable to destroy the pages she snatched back from Kaide, instead hiding them away in the air vent beside her bed. Each night, she would remove them and re-read the words, as if they would reveal their hidden meaning if she would just cast her eyes over them again.

The concepts themselves were not so disturbing – merely a re-telling of the same Orthodoxy she had been conditioned with in the Nursery. But the words leave a sickly sweet residue in her thoughts – like a veniamph with too much cordial and not enough alcohol. *Control. Submission. Conquer. Enslave. Damaged. Death.*

She shakes the clinging thoughts away, pushing her legs to lengthen their stride, feeling the muscles burn as she makes ground and catches up to Jenna.

"You need more training," Jenna says, speaking easily despite the physical exertion of the run. "Take tomorrow off and go to the gym. You need to build up your speed and endurance. I'll get Niamh to send over a Biomechanic Conditioner."

It's not a suggestion or a request.

Jenna slows and Anaiya breathes a sigh of relief at the chance to pause. The Peacekeeper reaches for Anaiya's wristplate, pulling up the vitals with a familiar sequence of swipes and clicks. She frowns and shakes her head.

"Your body chemicals are all over the place. You are as slow as an Earth Elemental on kava, but your noradrenaline levels are too high. How are you feeling?"

Like a specimen in a Water lab. Like puking up the bile twisting in my stomach. Like going home and sleeping for a few days.

"A little unconditioned," she replies.

Jenna rolls her eyes and nods. "Understatement. Go home, Anaiya. Or better yet, go to the nearest izakaya for some dodecas and sex. You need to reset your body."

She drops Anaiya's arm and looks around the street. They are in a quieter precinct, on duty for minor Unorthodoxy instances; more a show of force than any real tactical response.

"I'll finish the patrol," Jenna continues. "Report to the gym on Rue Daljair tomorrow morning. No point pretending to be a Peacekeeper if you're not conditioned like one."

Anaiya pauses, wondering whether this is another test.

"What are you waiting for?" Jenna is frowning at her again. "Get out of here."

Anaiya reluctantly turns around and starts jogging back down the street. She glances over her shoulder, expecting Jenna to still be watching her, scrutinising her, but the Peacekeeper is already free-running in the opposite direction.

A day at the gym should be a relief – a welcome respite from the gruelling demands of Jenna and precinct patrol – but anxiety is fast rising in her core. Her results will be passed on to Niamh, her movements placed under more scrutiny. It is an additional burden she doesn't need, an additional opportunity for her to misstep and be caught out in her lie.

Without warning, an arm reaches from a narrow service-alley and grabs at her wrist. She reacts instinctively, dragging down the captured arm and bringing the other up for a palm strike. Her hand connects with its target and she feels the familiar jolt as the assailant's skull is thrown back.

There is a grunt and her hand comes away wet with the blood from a broken nose. Pivoting, she pulls her leg in, positioning herself for a roundhouse kick.

"Anaiya." The words are muffled, distorted through the broken nasal passage.

She lowers her leg slowly and turns around. Peering into the shadows, arms up and ready to unleash, she sees a figure hunched over against the side wall.

"It's me." The figure looks up at her, blood dripping through his fingers.

Kaide.

A shot of guilt slams into Anaiya at seeing him incapacitated. "What are you doing, Kaide?"

He stays on his haunches, head bent again, the blood splattering against the bitumen. Anaiya looks away, unable to stomach the weakness, the brokenness.

"Here," she says, reaching into her belt, pulling out the skin-mending serum and handing it to him.

He grasps at the bottle clumsily and sprays two short bursts into each nostril. The blood stops dribbling from his nose and he wipes away the residue on his sleeve.

"Thanks," he mutters, holding the bottle out to her.

"It's OK," she replies, frowning at the blood-streaked plastic, "keep it."

Kaide puts the serum in his pocket and straightens. "Well, you still have your Fire tendencies."

"What are you doing here?"

"I needed to talk to you," he replies, feeling gingerly at his nose and grimacing.

"I'm done talking with you, remember?"

"Yeah, I remember."

He leans back against the wall and looks at her. She returns his gaze evenly but softens her stance when she sees no challenge in it.

"I know there is more to you than this Peacekeeper facade."

Anaiya shakes her head and begins to turn away.

"Wait," he mutters. "Just hear me out."

Something in the vulnerability of his voice makes her pause.

"There's a conflict in you, Anaiya. I see it. Even if no one else can. I know what it looks like. I know what it feels like."

Despite herself, she turns around. The words aren't shallow platitudes to disarm her. Unlike Anaiya, Kaide has suffered real hypoxia; he knows what it is like to live with a fractured identity, to be caught between what you were and what you are left with.

He is still there leaning against the wall, but his arm is outstretched, offering her the pages gripped in his hand. "He was conflicted, too, you know?"

She stares at the pages, wanting to reach out and take them, knowing that their hidden strings will bind her to Kaide, and Seth, again.

She shakes her head.

Kaide sighs and places the pages on the ground.

"I'll be at Lei Zhardan de Ruiso at 2000 hours for the next three nights. If you change your mind, come and find me. If the third night comes and I don't see you, you won't hear from any of us again."

"You can take your pages with you."

He steps away from them, the sheets ruffling in the soft echoes of the Wasteland breeze.

"I think you need them more," he says softly as he brushes past her and out into the street.

She stands there, eyes trained on the erratic twitching of the paper. Like her, they are caught in a moment of indecision – succumbing to, and fighting against, the gravity that presses them to the ground.

When a gust of wind barrels into the alley, she leaps forward, snatching the incriminating evidence before the wind can carry it out of her grasp and into the street.

There is nothing for it – she folds the pages tightly into a compact square and presses them deep into her pocket. Just because she has them, doesn't mean she wants them. Doesn't mean she'll keep them.

Doesn't mean I'll meet him.

Nonetheless, her run home is anxious and plagued with visions of the Ruiso Gardens and Resistance.

ELEVEN

Long shadows sneak into Anaiya's apartment, falling across her meagre belongings. Three days have come and gone, but the sunset on the third leaves a new sense of disquiet.

The pages, still unfolded, tumble across her fingers as she lies on her bed and stares at the paint cracking and flaking on the ceiling. Every night she has done the same, holding but not opening them – caught between her curiosity and fear. Even now, she picks at their edges, still unable to open up the creases and read what lies within.

Delacroix whimpers beside her bed, the dog picking up on her strange mood. She reaches down to scratch the patchy fur behind his ears. "OK, OK. I'll read them."

Slowly she sits up. Reaching above her head, she switches on the overhead light and pulls apart the folds of paper. Like the original pages that Kaide had given her, these new sheets are filled with both angular typesetting and looping hand script.

The text itself is clearly an early manifesto of the Fire Element – a relic of the days after the Singularity and Emancipation, when Otpor had risen from the ashes and a new order had been established. It reveals nothing she doesn't already know about the Orthodoxy – the role of the Fire Element, the essential balance it brings to the other Elements, the contribution of its various corps, the righteousness of their calling.

Instead, it is the handwritten commentary, formed in what she now recognises as Kane 148's characteristic style, that captures her attention. It fills the margins, languid in some places, harsh and erratic in others. Unfamiliar words and jargon are underlined with force, leading arrows connecting them with more handwritten commentary.

Brainwashing. Not conditioning!!

The Collective Lie – We perpetuate it ourselves! We deny the truth of our existence every day. We refuse our history.

There is NO controlling the Fire. We have become the Fire. We are the Fire.

Kane's words cause Anaiya's mind to tremble, not only because of their blatant Heterodoxy, but because of the anti-Fire sentiment that echoes too closely with that of the Resistance. And because of the culpability he lies at the feet of all Fire Elementals.

His is not a rebellion against the Fire Elementals who lose their discipline, who become too violent or ambitious or cruel. It is an indictment of the entire Element, an accusation that all Fire Elementals have lost their way. It is the verdict that Seth and Kaide levelled at her when they first negotiated the trade. The Fire cannot be controlled. The Element is irredeemable.

And yet, despite the damning conclusion, Kane's notes end with a way out, a solution of sorts.

The future is in the hands of the Premies. They must be reconditioned. They must learn the Truth.

Taken in its entirety, the page would be underwhelming if not for the mention of reconditioning – too close to the realignment that was supposed to be impossible – and for one last word found almost hidden, small and smudged at the page's bottom corner. *Anaiyasha.*

She can still hear it – the singsong teasing, the infuriating nom de doceur; the infantilism of it and the hidden insult behind it. In the beginning, he had used it to shame her, to motivate her to do better. Be better.

In the end, right up to the day of his Execution, he had murmured it with melancholy and something else. Something she had failed to place until now.

Hope.

Had Kane 148 seen her as the Premie who held the key to his imagined future? Had he tried to recondition her away from the Fire Element, to convince her of his alternative truth? Was that why her realignment to the Air Element had succeeded while her realignment back to the Fire Element had failed?

Re-reading the pages, her eyes scan for more clues, more meaning. But the words escape interpretation. His notes are otherwise indecipherable. Nothing but the chaotic ramblings of a damaged mind.

She struggles to remember the conversations they had in the weeks before his detention. *Had he hinted at this madness?*

It is useless. Neither the pages nor her memory will yield to her interrogation. So many hours of psychotherapy and conditioning in the aftermath of Kane's Execution have stripped her mind not only of any 'nascent Heterodox tendencies', but also of the ability to remember things as they truly were.

Glancing at her wristplate, she notes the time. More than an hour has passed. Stuffing the papers into the vent with the other Heterodoxy, she rushes to exit her apartment. With less than fifteen minutes till 2000 hours, she will need to race to make it to Kaide's rendezvous point in time.

Delacroix yelps and follows her out the apartment. She will easily outrun the pup, but the sense of a companion is comforting. Leaving the door ajar for him to return, she vaults over the staircase, letting her body segue into the lache form as she swings and repels to the bottom in seconds.

The pup is barking as he bounds down the stairs, upset at being left behind. But she has no time to spare, Delacroix forgotten as she sprints towards Lei Zhardan de Ruiso.

The gardens feel different this time around. Descending to the concrete courtyard feels as though she is entering a new world. A new beginning.

She shakes away the dark feelings of premonition and glances around for Kaide.

"You came," his deep voice echoes in the shadows. She turns towards it, finding him standing a few metres away, the darkness softening his form into something amorphous. Like an apparition that could disappear on the slightest breeze. "I didn't think you would turn up."

She holds up the sheets of paper. "Are they really his?"

Kaide nods. The simple confirmation sending her belly fluttering like so many synthflies on a rotting carcass. "How? How did they survive his Execution?"

He saunters towards her, calm while she is on edge. The disconnect makes her defensive, and she steps back as he sits down on the edge of the ablutions pool.

"There are more pages," he says, ignoring her questions.

"Where did you find them?"

"Not me. Seth."

The name has the same effect on her as it had on Kaide not so long ago. Her body stills, caught in an invisible amber.

"Are they what inspired his Resistance?" she murmurs, her voice shaking with the hesitance of speaking her thoughts aloud. "Did Seth really build this rebellion on the back of Kane's Heterodoxy?"

"Finding those pages changed a lot," Kaide says, his gaze never wandering from hers. "They gave us a manifesto, a call to resistance. But we were already primed to take up that call. We'd been suffering for years at the hands of a corrupt Fire Element. We were already searching for a way to fight back."

The papers feel like dead weights in her hand. Sighing, she steps forward and sits down next to Kaide.

"Do you understand his vision? Do you see what he saw?"

Kaide sighs softly. He is reluctant to talk about these things. "Kane was a visionary, not a prophet. His view of the world, his vision for the future, was enlightened, but it was still coloured through his subjective experience. His words hold guidance and inspiration, but they are not an infallible plan of action."

"What does that mean?" Irritation coats the words; she came here for answers, not more riddles with hidden solutions.

"Kane's words were his own. They hold an undeniable truth,

but that truth still needs to be interpreted."

"Is that why the Resistance has turned from passive protest to violent aggression?" She throws the question out in anger and frustration, and he returns with the same.

"Don't speak to me of violent aggression, Anaiya. Or have you forgotten the piles of unconscious bodies that littered the Ravignan Strip?" He pauses, the tight silence hinting at an attempt to control his anger and diffuse the situation. "We all interpret Kane's message a little differently. If you want to derive your own interpretation, look at the rest of his notes."

And so their mutual bitterness has led them to the bargaining of it. Kane's notes for Peacekeeper intel.

She looks down at her hands. "What do you want?"

"You know what we want."

"I can't betray my Element." Her voice wavers, signalling her inner conflict.

"You already have."

It is cruel, and unnecessary. But not untrue. Just by being here, by indulging this Heterodox conversation, she has turned her back on her original Element and conditioning. *Not for the first time.*

"Give us the intel on the intended raid," he says, calling an end to the tension that risks spiralling to a place of no negotiation, "and we'll deliver Kane's message."

She turns to face him. "We?"

"I. I'll give you the rest of the pages."

It is a noticeable shift. A hint of instability amongst the Resistance core. How much, exactly, does Seth know about this secret negotiation?

"And you're sure there is a raid?"

"They are planning something big."

The 'they' instead of 'you' is strangely comforting, but she swipes it away before it can cloud her judgement. She needs to stay focussed. Rational. Cold.

"What is the exchange?"

"Time and place of the raid," he says, his posture tensing with the same hard practicality she feels, "and I'll give you the rest of his notes."

It takes her less time than it should to come to her decision. "Deal."

TWELVE

The empty streets and broken buildings are less confronting than they used to be. Scarred by recent battles, they broadcast the damage that is hidden amongst the conflict's victims. And yet, after weeks of Peacekeeper duty, Anaiya no longer sees the level of destruction, only more props for her free-run.

She wonders if her Fire identity has recovered, is reasserting itself. The thought isn't as comforting as it used to be.

And it is not only her mind that has shifted in this new environment; her body is also growing and changing, realigning itself back to her past competency. Her technique and her speed continue to improve, not enough to rival Jenna, but enough to limit her glares and grunts of frustration.

Anaiya watches her now, assessing her patrol Shadow as she repels off the wall ahead, turning a perfect somersault and landing with precision to segue into a flawless kash vault. Rolling her eyes, Anaiya takes a simpler option; pop vaulting and letting her arms use the balcony as leverage for a monkey swing to the ground. It doesn't look as pretty, but it does the job.

Landing, she notices movement in the recess of a nearby door. *How does Jenna not see him?*

For weeks, Kaide has followed her, emerging without warning at some random location and then disappearing when Anaiya flashes the agreed hand signal for 'no news to report'. She knows he is getting frustrated with the lack of intel; his face contorts again as her fingers twitch in rapid succession.

What can she do? It's not like Niamh trusts her enough to share Element secrets. He doesn't even trust her to run without supervision.

She moves into the next transition and accelerates after Jenna. Glancing over her shoulder, she sees that Kaide still hasn't moved and her heart rate spikes at the thought of him continuing his own shadowing.

She searches ahead for Jenna. Her Shadow seems oblivious, completely focussed on the free-run; her training conditioning her to observe real threats and ignore distractions. Anaiya knows it won't hold indefinitely, knows that at any minute Jenna will turn around to see just how far her Trainee has fallen behind.

Her hands gesture furiously, repeating the same code over and over. No news to report. No news to report.

Jenna turns around. Her eyes flick from Anaiya to the street beyond. Heart in her throat, Anaiya also turns around. The street is empty save for sand drifts and debris.

"What are you slowing for, Anaiya? Keep up."

Adrenalin from the near miss runs like electricity along her veins and she uses the chemical surge to push her legs to pump harder.

She can't afford close calls like that, things are precarious enough as it is. She needs to reassure Kaide that their agreement still holds, that he doesn't need to keep her under constant surveillance.

"Do you think it will ever stop?" she asks, catching up to Jenna with some effort.

The Peacekeeper raises an eyebrow – at the question? Or at the fact she has caught up? – but doesn't respond.

"Even with the curfew and heat-map patrols," Anaiya continues, keeping her focus on the road ahead, forcing her voice to something casual, "it seems like the clashes are becoming more frequent and violent. Is Niamh planning to escalate his efforts?"

"It's not for us to question, is it?" Jenna finally replies.

"No. I mean, it's not *my* place to question. I just thought he would have had you leading his next stage of attack … instead of this babysitting duty."

It is a risky ploy to raise Jenna's ire, but with limited means of getting Kaide's intel she needs to work with what she has. No Peacekeeper enjoyed Premie shadowing – looking after pre-forms was for Water Conditioners in the Nursery. Being tied to a Premie – a *baby* – was like an insult, a punishment. And sometimes it was exactly that.

Jenna lands a flawless lache and comes to a stop. Worst-case scenario, she will shut down all communications and Anaiya will have lost one of the few available avenues of intel. Best-case scenario, she will respond to the slight and give some indication of what she knows or has exposure to.

"If this was just babysitting duty," Jenna finally says, voice cold and flat, "I wouldn't be doing it."

"Then what is it? And why are you doing it?"

"Enough with the questions, Anaiya," Jenna says, exasperation spilling into her tone. "You forget yourself. We're not partners, I don't owe you any answers. You're a Trainee. I'm your Shadow."

It is the way she says it, like it is a condemnation. Like Anaiya will never be anything more than a substandard Peacekeeper, like her pretence can only ever amount to Trainee standards.

She is used to Niamh holding his superiority over her, she is not willing to give Jenna the same opportunity.

"I'm not less than you, Jenna," she says, feeling the heat build in her core and taint her voice. "We have the same amount of career years, I easily have more Task Force hours than you and, though you're probably still pissed about it, there hasn't been a symbiotic Peacekeeper in generations. So, while you may have that little circle around your flame insignia, you can stop acting superior."

Jenna laughs, a sharp bark of derision. "You are *damaged*. I am not acting superior. I *am* superior."

Just like in Niamh's office, thoughts of launching at Jenna and physically erasing the natural display of ego are hard to fight. And then the memory of Kane's forbidden words pull her up. *There is no controlling the Fire. We have become the Fire.*

The reprimand stings, but she still needs an avenue to expend the frustrated rage. Turning from Jenna, she tucks tight in on herself, letting all of the emotion compress, before springing into a somersault across the broken road. Absorbed in the emotion and numbed by the adrenalin, she barely feels the tiny rocks and shards of glass that stab uselessly through her kevlar uniform.

Leaping to her feet, she accelerates into a sprint, launching at the nearest wall and grabbing at the windowsills. Her arms burn with the effort, but she ignores the pain and pushes her muscles to propel her higher. Kash vaulting to the nearest balcony, she forces her body into precise alignment and runs along the narrow railing, leaping to the next and to the next.

Not bothering to look down to see whether Jenna follows, she turns an aerial vault off the end of a railing. There is a moment in the free-fall, as gravity takes over and the descent accelerates, that she gives into it. No fighting the inevitable, no fighting for dominance.

At the last moment, her arms snap out to grab a balcony floor, to command control again. The free-fall becomes a choreography, her arms swinging her downward in a series of reverse sauts du bras.

With the ground only one floor away, and exultation coursing through her blood, she turns a reverse pike somersault, her feet thudding against the ground at the end of its perfect execution.

Jenna stands just metres away, arms folded, a frown marring her fine features.

Anaiya opens her mouth to say something, to shout the words that had torn along her brain with every form she had created. But there is no need to speak them. Jenna's rigid body language tells her that she has heard them loud and clear.

You are not superior. You will never *be superior.*

"Finished your little display?" Her voice drips with casual scorn, but there is a tension, a readiness, to her posture.

Anaiya, satisfied, remains silent and still.

"Then let's drop this babysitting facade and do some actual patrolling."

Hours later, the sun tinges the sky a darker brown as it nears the horizon. Anaiya allows herself a small breath of relief, the arrival of dusk heralding the end of shift. Beside her, Jenna slows the pace to a brisk walk.

The Peacekeeper had been unforgiving in her patrolling; streaking away at every opportunity and seeking out the most difficult routes to free-run. A torment that only slowed when minor instances of Unorthodoxy required restraint or wristplate recording.

Surprisingly, Anaiya had done well to keep up, but now her body shivers with the prophesying of future pain to come.

Stretching her tired calf muscles, she looks around the immediate surrounds. The central line of Precinct 8, where the Northern and Western Cardinal Areas collide, is less-densely populated than other parts. With no other distraction, her gaze is immediately drawn to the figure at the crossroads a few blocks ahead.

On instinct, her heart catches in her throat, her mind immediately turning to Kaide and his incessant following. But the figure ahead is slighter across the shoulders, moves lighter on his feet, with a casual confidence. Undoubtedly an Air Elemental, but not the one that has been following her these past weeks.

Beside her, Jenna adjusts her stride – slowing her pace and softening her footfalls. "There you are," she murmurs.

They are now close enough to see the Elemental more clearly, but not so close as to attract attention themselves. From the new perspective, Anaiya is able to put a name to the figure.

Seth.

Panic's barbed tentacles start to sneak around her core. It is like there is an invisible magnet that keeps drawing her back to him, even when she is trying to avoid him. What is he doing here? Where is Kaide? Is this a trap? And, if yes, who set it?

"Does he look familiar?" Jenna asks softly, still looking ahead.

The question ratchets her panic higher. "Should he?"

Jenna shakes her head in obvious frustration, her face flashing between annoyance and exasperation. "It's a simple question, Anaiya."

Anaiya's attempt at future-searching is a mess. Her thoughts race with a hundred possibilities, a thousand variables. What does Jenna know? Why does she recognise him?

In the early weeks of her deployment, when Anaiya had only just begun to get familiar with Seth, she had run into Jenna restraining Eamon. Anaiya had intervened to stop her from doing the same to Seth. But it had been quick and dark and Peacekeepers remembered crimes not faces.

Surely Jenna doesn't remember him.

"No," she murmurs, the lie threatening to steal away the last of her bravado. "Why? Who is he?"

Jenna is moving slowly now, keeping to the walls of the silent manufacturing plants.

"Remember the briefing on Rehhd associates? Just before the riverside incident?"

With everything that has happened since, the briefing should barely be a blip in Anaiya's memory, but the recollection comes back fast and clear: A briefing room in Peacekeeper Headquarters, not two kilometres from where she now stands; a bright room, with ceiling-to-floor windows and an imposing Niamh; dangerous questions about her alliance and loyalty.

"Are you getting too involved with your targets?"

She had been.

I still am.

"You identified Eamon 801 and Kaide 177," Anaiya says, remembering their faces flashing up on a wallscreen that also listed their past crimes; Affray, Stealing Manufactured Goods, Destroying or Damaging Property …

"We've been tracking both of them since her Execution," Jenna murmurs, her eyes never wavering from Seth's retreating form.

Anaiya startles at the realisation that Eamon, Rehhd's co-conspirator, has served his punishment and has been released from detention. The surprise only overshadowed by the fact that Kaide has also been under surveillance.

A new fear races in to replace the relief at Jenna not remembering her original run-in with Seth. Has she seen Anaiya with Kaide? Seen him following? Witnessed the exchange of Heterodox material?

Despite the cooling air, sweat rises at her jugular, the precise point where a restraint needle would pinch the skin.

"I always suspected a third accomplice," Jenna continues, unaware of Anaiya's anxiety.

Anaiya remembers. After the brief on Eamon and Kaide, a white space had flickered on the wall next to their profiles; the spot where Jenna's hypothetical third associate was to be analysed.

It had been Seth. There was no other Elemental who fit the profile generated by Peacekeeper intel and Water psychoanalysis. And yet, despite all of Anaiya's misgivings, despite what she knew and should have known, she had stayed silent. Pretended ignorance.

Just as she is doing now.

"I've narrowed down the list of candidates," Jenna says, still slinking along the brick walls. "Cressida 161, Yve 416, Seth 137, Tomas 257, Issau 091."

The last two are unfamiliar – not that she was paying much attention; her thoughts had grinded to a halt after the third name was uttered.

"And that," Jenna murmurs, gaze squarely focussed on the figure now only one block ahead, "is Seth 137."

Underneath the deep sense of dread that has anchored Anaiya's stomach, a bright point of irritation flashes. The familiar prick of jealousy; a keen sense of being slighted. In the seconds that it takes her to recognise the source, she flushes with the shame and embarrassment of it. That Jenna should know Seth's suffix, before she did.

"Does Niamh know you are tracking them?"

It is not the question she wants to ask. *How do you know about him?*

"Of course he does. Why else would he reinstate you as a Peacekeeper? Why else would I be paired as your Shadow?"

Because I'm good at what I do. Because I'm more than a tool to be used for whatever plans Niamh has for his next promotion. The frustration feels hollow, overwhelmed by the implications of Niamh getting closer to the truth of the Resistance.

"Why are you still tracking Rehhd's associates after her

Execution?"

They had always been so careful to avoid detection. Just how reckless had they become for Seth to land on Niamh's radar?

"Because the Heterodoxy continues," Jenna says. The reply leaves Anaiya confused, until she connects it with the original question.

"You think one of them still leads it?" Her heart seizes just to say it.

"Don't be ridiculous, Anaiya," Jenna whispers, exasperation flashing again on her features. "Obviously the source of the disease has been terminated. But for some reason the Heterodoxy is lingering longer than it should. I want to … expedite … its eradication. And I think one of these associates may be the key to getting what I want."

The streets and laneways pull and distract Anaiya as she follows Jenna on her shadowing of Seth. Every hundred metres or so, she looks around for Kaide, desperately wishing to see his face, even complete with its typical frown of disapproval. But the streets are empty, save for Anaiya, Jenna and their target.

Each new laneway, arcade and crossroad deepens her unease, the open spaces fraught with opportunities for Seth to see them or for another Elemental to emerge and be implicated. The temptation to create a distraction – a well-timed stumble, a louder than necessary footfall – itches along her frayed nerves. But warning Seth will only lead to added scrutiny or conflict.

"What do we know about him?" she asks, the 'we' sounding more forced in her head than it does aloud.

"Literature competency, historical co-locations with Rehhd, Kaide and Eamon. Current co-locations with other persons of interest." Jenna rattles off the list of statistics like all good Peacekeepers, except the last point trips up Anaiya's interest.

"Current co-locations with old persons of interest or new?"

"Not co-locations exactly," Jenna whispers, eyes still trained on Seth, "but I've seen him with peripheral players, connected to one or more of the core three."

"And that's important?" It is hard to keep her voice steady.

"Maybe not important. But definitely interesting."

"You really think an acquaintance of an Elemental randomly connected to a Rehhd associate is your third accomplice?"

The fake disbelief is convincing; there really is no reason for Jenna to have Seth under surveillance as a potential accomplice. Either she is desperate or she knows something.

"I think—"

A shrill beeping interrupts their hushed conversation and stealth surveillance. Jenna flattens herself against the warehouse wall, pulling Anaiya with her, but their advantage is lost. Anaiya stops herself from showing any visible signs of emotion – relief at the avoided disaster, disappointment at the lost opportunity for intel – as Jenna swipes at her wristplate to cease the beeping and check the communication.

"Unconfirmed Alert," she says, exasperation thick on her tongue.

About time. The Peacekeeper protocol of checking on field officers who hadn't returned from shift or applied for an extension has put an end to Jenna's covert surveillance.

Anaiya peers out of the building's shadows, in time to see Seth throw a quick glance over his shoulder towards where she and Jenna are hidden. He doesn't visibly react; shows no indication of surprise or satisfaction. Nothing to hint that he knew or didn't know of their shadowing.

Leave it, Anaiya. He is dead to you. But the words lack the same vehemence they had back when she first thought them.

"What now?" she asks, turning back to Jenna.

The Peacekeeper throws a longing glance towards her disappearing target. Her muscles tense, and Anaiya sees in her posture the desire, the want of the chase.

But, Fire Elementals are disciplined. And Jenna is perhaps the most disciplined she has come across.

"We go drink."

THIRTEEN

It was easier to leave the izakaya this time. Jenna's bruised ego had sought the only medicated solutions available – alcohol, drugs and random sex. Leaving her to a younger Border Watcher Trainee, Anaiya had withdrawn without notice.

Her first instinct had been to return home. To the simple and predictable. To Delacroix and peeling lino and pretending that nothing mattered. Except that returning home wouldn't take her back to how things were months ago. Before she was pulled back into this mess of Fires versus Airs.

So here she is, sometimes walking, sometimes free-running, towards Veritas and the rendezvous point Kaide had nominated.

The space in front of the izakaya is crowded – typical for the hours before curfew. But, even amidst the crowd of eclectic Air Elementals, her gaze is drawn to him. And to Seth.

Finding them together unnerves her enough that it takes a moment for her to recognise Eamon beside them. He looks thinner than he had six months ago; detention has ravaged his skin, the restraint serum and lack of sunlight leaving his face gaunt and pale. While he still holds the same arrogance and defiance, he seems less dominant. Less self-assured.

Curses and insults from nearby Elementals draw his gaze to Anaiya. The flash of recognition and open scorn on his face makes her hesitate, but she runs her hands down the kevlar of her

Peacekeeper threads and steps forward.

A nudge from Eamon attracts Kaide's attention and Anaiya flashes the hand signal for 'intel to report'. Kaide's eyes widen and he flicks a cautious glance towards Seth.

And that's when Anaiya notices her.

A tall, supple Elemental. Dressed in soft folds of rayon, she appears the exact opposite of Anaiya. She is laughing; a pure, almost unfair, joy magnifying her genetically manipulated features. Anaiya would be captivated by this unnatural expression if not for the pull of Seth's arm resting casually, intimately, on her hip.

He glances at Anaiya, their eyes meeting for the briefest of moments just like they had only an hour ago, before he pulls this unknown Elemental into a passionate embrace.

Anaiya averts her gaze, drifting past Kaide, who frowns and shakes his head at the pair. She stands still, her arms resting casually at her side, waiting for Kaide to fulfil his terms of the arrangement and meet her.

"Sorry," he says, throwing another glance over his shoulder. "You weren't supposed to have seen that."

Because it was unnecessarily hurtful or because it might change my mind about our agreement?

She shrugs it off. "I have intel."

"About the offensive?"

"I want more of Kane's notes."

"Intel first." His arms are folded. He thinks he has the leverage.

"No." Her voice is the cutting of a single grain of sand in a storm. "Pages first."

He looks over his shoulder again, drawing Anaiya's gaze to Eamon's scowl and Seth's indiscretion. Her eyes travel to errant fingers drawing invisible lines around curves.

Turning back, she finds Kaide matching her gaze, entering an unspoken challenge. He shakes his head, opening his mouth to voice a new negotiation. But she is having none of it. She is not beholden to them anymore.

Her feet pivot in a flawless Peacekeeper turn. She can live without him and the shadow of Kane's legacy.

"Feu mort."

Eamon's slur turns her back around. Other Elementals are looking at her – laughing at her, scowling at her. She turns her attention to Seth, waiting for his reaction, but he merely stands there; arm still draped around the blonde, posture still casual, eyes still dead.

The female Elemental murmurs something. Eamon laughs, a caustic ringing of bells, but Seth remains impassive. His eyes regarding Anaiya much like they did all those nights ago at Rehhd's Execution.

She turns to Kaide. Dead inside. "Pages first."

He looks at her. And, for a moment, she sees him really looking. Seeing her for the first time.

"Fine," he says, unfolding his arms and letting them hang loose. "Two pages only. You'll get the rest if and when the intel is good."

He reaches for her arm. She pulls away and is surprised to see the brief beginnings of a smile appearing on his lips.

"It's OK, Anaiya," he says, tapping his nose. "I know you can damage me."

Reluctantly, she lets him take her arm, frowning as he pulls out a thin stylus from the pocket of his hoodie.

"Meet me here," he says, pulling up the sleeve of her uniform and inking coordinates on her skin. "Three hours."

She pulls the sleeve down hurriedly and looks around. No other Peacekeepers.

Careful, Anaiya.

The danger of the situation sends apprehension skittering along her nerves like so many beats of synthfly wings.

Kaide ducks his head, forcing her to meet his eyes. "Yes?"

She looks over his shoulder to where the other three still stand; each of them casually observing her engagement with Kaide, each broadcasting their own unique mix of emotions – anger, incredulity, torment. Emotions she was unable to process, or understand, before her realignment.

"Yes?" Kaide's voice is louder now, more insistent.

She turns back to him, breaking the intoxication the others

hold over her. It would be so easy to walk away. But Kane 148's words echo in her memory, hinting at an enlightenment just out of reach. She needs to know his message. Needs to know more about his Heterodoxy. And her own.

"Yes."

She arrives early. The Edges, as always, are empty.

As a Peacekeeper, she had patrolled here – back when detecting secret rendezvous and Unorthodox activities were still a priority. But now, with all the real-world violence and Heterodoxy, the Edges are an afterthought.

Out of habit, she throws a quick glance up to the Border Wall, trying to find a Watcher on patrol. But, as always, they are well-hidden.

The coordinates that Kaide had given her put her uncomfortably close to the place where she had found the first Resistance mural. Walking past it, she had tentatively run her hand across the rough surface of the recycler. The forbidden paint had long since disappeared, but she could still feel the faint echo of slick chemicals under her fingertips, smell the harsh, sweet scent of synthetic colour.

A faint buzzing echoes in the silence, the electricity of the substation calling to the charged particles of the night air. She stares at the structure in the post-curfew hours, almost tempted to reach out and touch it. Just to feel its power. Just to feel something real and unambiguous.

"You made quite an entrance." Kaide's voice bounces off the terraces around her. He emerges seconds later, camouflaged in black jeans and hoodie.

A hundred retorts leap to mind.

"He's changed," she says instead.

Kaide laughs. Soft and genuine. "That surprises you?"

No. Yes. Everything about Seth was both familiar and unexpected.

She glances down at Kaide's hands, his left gripping folded pages.

"How did you find them?" she asks, reaching for them.

He doesn't pull them back, letting her grasp them, but not letting go either.

For a second they are caught in this moment; a tug-of-war, a detente.

She wonders why she hadn't paid attention to this side of him earlier; this intense, enigmatic confidence that makes it seem like he has all the answers and is just waiting for everyone else to catch up.

Had she really been that distracted by Seth? Or had he just blended into the background like he has on so many of her recent patrols?

He lets go of the pages, his fingers appearing to slip almost carelessly.

"Do you remember much of him?"

With the pages secure in her hands, she allows herself to be honest. "A little."

He steps forward, shortening the gap between them. There is a genuine interest and curiosity burning behind those eyes. And, for a moment, she is caught in them.

It has been so long since someone, anyone, has looked at her with something other than anger, frustration, disappointment, suspicion.

Her body reacts involuntarily, stepping forward to meet him. Mid-step, she hesitates; her muscles tensing, her mind warning her of unknown consequences.

Kaide's eyes narrow and his face hardens.

She forces her body to relax and carefully folds the paper into precise sections, tucking the pages away.

"What intel do you have?" Kaide asks, folding his arms across his chest.

"They've been following you."

He laughs, the noise unnerving in the relative silence of the Edges. "That's not intel."

"And Cress, and Yve. And Seth."

She expects her voice to catch on the last name, but there is nothing but a medicated numbness, like the dull edge that comes after so many dodecas.

Kaide is not as immune. He sobers at the mention of Seth's name. "Is that who they're targeting for the offensive?"

"I don't know. Maybe. He's definitely an Elemental of interest. It's hard to get access to the right information."

"We need that intel, Anaiya."

"I'm doing what I can. I'm not exactly the most trusted or respected Peacekeeper around. Hypoxia tends to limit credibility."

She stops herself too late. The scorn in her voice had been thick and Kaide's reaction tells her it has hit too close. She doesn't know much of the details of his hypoxia – Kaide was also one to keep intel to himself – but she knew it still weighed heavy on him.

"It won't be the same ... It won't be better and it won't be worse. You will heal, but it will be different. You will be different." He had uttered those words to her a lifetime ago, when they had first met. It is disconcerting that they still hold true.

"I'm sorr—"

He waves away the apology. "We still need the intel."

"I can't do it."

"Get the intel and you can have the rest of the pages. And trust me, you'll want them."

Sighing, she throws up her hands in frustration. "Kaide, I'm not lying to you. It can't be done. Niamh doesn't trust me. I'm not the same Peacekeeper I was. I'm damaged. And, anyway, it's not in his nature to give something away for free. He'll want something in return. Something he can manipulate for leverage."

Kaide is unmoved. "So give him something."

She groans, her feet twitching with an irritability that threatens to explode.

"He is a senior Fire Elemental." She pushes the words through clenched teeth. "I can't just give him anything. He needs something genuine."

"I'm not going to hand over intel on our movements."

"Then you make something up. Create a diversion – something that gives Niamh a taste of what he wants. Just make it believable."

This is madness. She feels the wrongness of it in every cell of her body, sees Kaide struggling with the same insane proposition in the way he knuckles his chin. They stare at each other, weighing up the trustworthiness of the other against the fatal consequences of a miscalculation.

"D'accord," he finally mutters. "The Fourth day. Next week. 0700 hours at the cemetery. I'll make something happen."

Her mind screams its opposition, her body tingling with the threat of promised danger. "It will have to be big enough to buy me legitimacy."

"OK, OK." The tension in his voice emphasises his furrowed brow and clenched fists. "Just make sure you live up to your end."

FOURTEEN

My Element is a lie. I serve to protect the Orthodoxy, but only enslave other Elementals to violence and submission. All my life, I have been conditioned to be separate. Apart. But I am no different from them, and them no different to me. Is our blood not the same colour? Are we not all citizens of Otpor?

When I was a boy, I did as boys do. Now I am a man, and I can pretend no longer.

I can no longer crave the protective arm of a parent, when I desire to carve my own mark in this world. I can no longer believe that order is the most important, when I know that order strips away my freedom.

And there can be no freedom while my Element remains.

The light from Anaiya's wristplate diode spills over the pages and onto the concrete below. It would have felt strange to sit atop the recycler alone, if not for the words that hold her completely captive.

She doesn't glance at her wristplate for the time, doesn't wonder about Delacroix back at her apartment, doesn't worry about her insane agreement with Kaide.

Kane 148's now-familiar scrawl steals all of her focus. She stares at the angular lines and looping curves, seeing in this archaic script a mirror to the Heterodoxy of his words.

Those words. They run with blades through her thoughts, not

because they are Heterodox.

Kane's conviction of Heterodoxy had been more than a verdict of guilty action, it had been a diagnosis of an infected and damaged mind. The ramblings of the original Resistor were nothing more than a manifestation of his incurable disease.

But unlike the incoherent exhortations of the previous pages, the words that cling to the page in her lap are clear and coherent. Terrible for how right-minded they are. For how similar they are to the vision of Resistance now tearing Otpor apart.

Was the elimination of the Fire Element the only way to restore peace to Otpor? Was that the radical conclusion Kane had come to all those years ago? The conclusion that had led to his Execution?

Had Rehhd been right all along?

Anaiya falters at the last question. Turning off her wristplate light, she lies back against the cool surface of the recycler and begs for the dark to file away the edges of her thoughts. Except her mind keeps returning to the past.

Rehhd, as angry as she was, had also been clear-minded in her rebellion. What had she said that afternoon her words had turned witness against her?

Resistance leads to growth. Resistance is about restoring the proper order of things.

Both Kane and Rehhd had tried to show her the corruption of the Fire Element but she had remained blind to it. Occasionally she had caught glimpses of it – the scars, the unrestrained aggression, the pure efficiency of the chase and the restraint – but it had never been enough to erode her conditioning. To make her question it.

The uncertainty overwhelms her and she chokes on the bile that rises up from her core.

Is this what you felt, Kane? Is this why you were so distracted?

There had been times in that last six months of his life where patrols weren't just patrols anymore. Like something more important hinged on them, that pervasive feeling that the pauses in between the free-run were not just recovery sessions but a lesson in something bigger.

Every patrol punctuated with an ever-present question: *Why?*

In his final months it had become an obsession. *Why did you kash vault instead of kong dash? Why did you leap when you could have climbed? Why did you restrain this perpetrator and not that one? Why did you sound a warning now, but remained quiet then?*

It had been the start of her demise – the question burrowing itself in her mind and shifting easily from a superficial question to a deep sense of self-doubt. Was she doing it wrong? Was she disappointing him? Was she not seeing something she was supposed to? Was she not living up to her potential?

And with the incessant questioning had come doubt and second-guessing. Her times had slipped, her ranking corrupted, her position as the best undone. Her star had fallen, and Niamh's had risen.

It had been so easy for the why to turn into a what. To shift from questioning motivations to something deeper, more personal. *What am I missing? What does he want from me? What is wrong with me?*

But, maybe, the question really had been 'why' all along.

She had been unable to see it as a Peacekeeper Trainee; 'why' was not a question asked by Fire Elementals – it needed a more malleable mind to take root, a predilection for imagination.

Now it assaults her. Even knowing it had led to Kane's demise doesn't stop it from taking root in her shattered mind, from taking over.

Why is the Fire Element so corrupted? Why does it need to be eliminated?

FIFTEEN

"Why are you still standing? Sit down already." Niamh sits behind his desk, tapping his fingers impatiently while Anaiya takes her time to comply with the demand. "Jenna tells me your free-running is improving. She began with the impression your mission had compromised your body as well as your mind."

The assessment brings to mind their last patrol and the covert surveillance of Seth. "What else has Jenna been telling you?"

"That's not why we are here, Anaiya. You said you had some intel."

Her fingers tremble with the urge to fidget. She clenches her hands into fists, pausing until every inch of her body is calm and collected. Just like a good Peacekeeper. An Orthodox, honest, trustworthy Peacekeeper.

"I think Rehhd's old associates are planning something for the Fourth day next week."

Finally, Niamh deigns to raise his head.

"What did you find?"

"Nothing definitive. I overheard a conversation on the worm about something Heterodox taking place at the cemetery."

"You were on the worm?"

He has every right to be suspicious – Peacekeepers have always shunned the city's only form of public transport in favour of the free-run.

"How else was I supposed to get intel?"

89

She pushes up her sleeves, revealing the skin ink that was supposed to be temporary. "And the worm is the only place where this will give me access to Air spaces."

"Who were the offenders?"

"I didn't get a visual," she replies, retelling the backstory she had meticulously crafted the night before. "It was peak hour and visibility was no more than twenty per cent."

Every word she uses, every inflection, has been practised for hours. She may not be a genuine Peacekeeper anymore, but the evolution of her Air identity has uncovered an uncanny skill for pretending.

"What exactly did you hear?"

"A female voice, pitch and language structure would indicate fourth lustrum. I didn't pick up on what she was saying until I heard her say 'Rehhd'. From that point she said: 'It's happening at the cemetery on the Fourth day.' Her companion, also female and fourth lustrum, replied: 'You can't be thinking of going. There are plagues of Peacekeepers everywhere. You've already been detained twice this year, why risk it?' And the first female said: 'Because it's taking place at 0700 hours. Their patrols are light in the early morning. They think we are lazy and unorganised. They'll never suspect it and won't be prepared for it.'"

She watches in satisfaction as Niamh's eyes flare with a cold rage. The casual insult to Peacekeepers, the obvious reference to a significant Unorthodoxy record, and the attribution to irreverent fourth lustrum Trainees – it was all designed to appeal to his superiority, leverage his ambition.

But it was the final insult – the hubris of a Trainee Air Elemental thinking a Senior Peacekeeper, thinking *Niamh*, could be bested – that Anaiya has built her charade on.

"Won't be prepared for it." His voice is cold. Hard. Her ploy has worked. "Let them see how prepared we are."

The morning is dark and cold. A blanket of thick grey clouds covers the sky, blotting out the weak Otpor sun and casting shadows over everything.

Stepping out onto the Courcelles Boulevarde, Anaiya shivers and looks around her. A contingent of Peacekeepers fans out beside her. Too many. She counts at least thirty of them, ranging from first-year Peacekeepers to Senior Enforcers. No Trainees; all hardened professionals with that familiar glint of expectation in their eyes.

Heart racing, she scans the uniform-clad clones around her, searching for someone, anyone, that will reassure her. The rippling of heightened energy reveals a new viewpoint and she spies two Peacekeepers standing apart from the others. Niamh looks as calm as ever; a recycler wall invulnerable to the pitiful beating of a synthfly's wings. Jenna looks focussed; a perfectly weighted syringe ready to be deployed.

Staring at them, Anaiya finds it difficult to imagine she ever appeared that way – assured, rigid, intimidating. She looks away before they can see her, shaking off the anger and confusion that always comes when the purity of her past identity confronts its corruption.

The Peacekeepers set a slow and measured pace to begin with, letting the steady jolt of feet against the road warm up muscles tense with anticipation and excitement. Once they reach the Northern Area, they will split into four groups – each heading to the same destination via a different maze of streets and alleys, maintaining stealth and speed to optimise the surprise attack.

With curfew only just over, it is still too early for Water and Earth Elementals to be in the streets – the former not due in their laboratories and offices until the sun has risen, the latter still recovering from whatever debauchery they indulged in last night.

Only a few clusters of Air Elementals interrupt the otherwise silent landscape. They stumble from too much alcohol, but their eyes are guarded and their faces pinched at the sight of so many Peacekeepers.

Anaiya waits for it – the inevitable catcall, the foolhardy challenge, the degrading insult.

It doesn't come.

She stares at the nearest cluster, a smaller group of five older Elementals. In their eighth lustrum, the synth toxin that will kill them in the next decade is already evident in their pockmarked skin and haggard features. They don't shrink under Anaiya's scrutiny, but they don't rise to any perceived challenge.

The male of the group turns to the female at his left, grabbing her hand and gripping it tightly. She tilts her face up to whisper something to him and the tension in his face disappears as a smile breaks across it.

Anaiya wonders how long they have been connected. At forty-three, they could have had more than twenty connections in their lifetime. Or they could have had just one – each other.

Connection. It had been an alien concept when she had first been realigned. Fire Elementals do not 'connect' with other Elementals. Intimacy is just a poorly constructed euphemism for strings-free sex. Air Elementals, soft and cerebral as they are, see Elemental intimacy as something deeper. More personal. More symbiotic. A joining of bodies and minds. Of souls.

Connection. Souls. Words that were foreign to her as a Peacekeeper. Worthy of ridicule.

And, yet, she had felt them. Experienced them.

Had I?

It is hard to tell in the cold light of her new reality. A reality she still can't fully trust – not while it tips and sways between a Fire and Air identity. Not while she still can't discern which identity is right. Which is hers.

The thought unsettles her and her stride falls out of sync with the others. Quickly reorienting herself, she looks around to see if the other Peacekeepers have noticed. But they merely stare ahead, fully consumed in their surveillance of the area and the mission at hand.

She looks back towards the couple, but the moment has passed and the silent city has swallowed them up.

The pace of the Peacekeeper advance has picked up, freeing Anaiya's mind of frivolous thoughts and forcing her to focus instead on the escalating free-run.

Ahead, the street comes to a large intersection, the metal rails of the worm's Uropa station visible as they stretch off to the north-west. So early in the morning, most of the worms are still retired;

they sit idle at the end of the tracks, banked up nose to tail to appear as one giant mass of sleeping metal.

The landmark acts as a trigger. Beside her, Peacekeepers peel off into their separate groups, not needing any further instruction. As if pulled by a different polarity, they do not slow down, just merely adjust their trajectory. Seconds later, the dispersion is complete.

Now it is just Anaiya and seven other Fire Elementals, the other three groups completely hidden by the dense infrastructure of the Northern Area.

A quick glance over her shoulder confirms Niamh is following, but Jenna is nowhere to be seen. Niamh catches her gaze and flicks a confident smile before his attention is taken by a Senior Enforcer who is advising him on something she will never be privy to.

They are close to the Montmartre necropolis. Wide streets give way to laneways lined with white concrete walls, the bold carvings of geometric patterns giving away the Air Elemental residents within.

Once, their corners would have been dotted with garishly clad Sex Workers and the flotsam of Airs that always gravitated to such spaces and their carnival atmospheres. Now, in the early hours after curfew, the laneways are silent and still. The walls, once contrasted with a kaleidoscope of innuendo and erotica, now appear too white. As if the curfew has leached all the colour from them, has sucked away their secrets and left them empty shells of a past life.

Keep it together, Anaiya.

The tension within her is bubbling up and hijacking her thoughts. Her Air identity immediately latches onto its natural environment, giving everything a dramatic narrative, even as her Fire identity free-runs towards inevitable conflict.

Ahead the stone walls of the cemetery flash into view.

"Game time," Niamh says beside her.

His whole body radiates an entirely different tension than the one Anaiya struggles with. He doesn't slow at the sight of the walls – what self-respecting Peacekeeper would? – simply launches at them, his hands and feet finding purchase on the uneven stones and propelling his body up as the other Fire Elementals follow suit.

For a moment, Anaiya hesitates, memories of another conflict in the shadow of the cemetery's walls distracting her. It had been here that she had stopped Jenna's needle from finding its place in Seth's neck.

That moment had been the turning point on which everything had hung. It had cemented her place amongst the core Resistance members. And kick-started the real deception.

I pretended then, I can pretend now.

The assurance rings hollow; overwhelmed by a growing sense of unease. Regardless, she pushes the memory back to the depths of her mind and sprints towards the necropolis wall.

She grabs clumsily at its facade, the sharp edges of the stones cutting into her palms, the skin still soft from her time away from Peacekeeping. She curses under her breath and side vaults over the top of the wall.

Landing roughly on the hard-packed dirt, she recovers and brushes the infertile grains from her jeans. Her belly heaves with heightened adrenalin that has nothing to do with her stumble.

There is no more time for hesitation. The rest of her group are already fifteen, maybe twenty, metres ahead of her. She shakes off the remnants of her indecision and accelerates to catch up to them.

Passing the first row of headstones, she enters into the maze of tombs and mausoleums. Her heart thunders as she runs through their shadows, the chill radiating from their cancer-ridden shells reaching out to caress the bare skin at her neck.

Finally, she catches up and settles into her stride at the end of the single file of Peacekeepers. The echoes of their footfalls mimic the frenetic heartbeat of the cemetery.

For a few brief minutes, it is the only sound she hears.

And then the screaming begins.

The level of violence that floods Anaiya's vision when she arrives at the small courtyard leaves her breathless. Bodies clad in black kevlar clash with those clad in black mourning clothes. The former restrain with abandon, the latter weep and wail but do not fight back.

Anaiya struggles to locate the Unorthodoxy that has triggered such an extreme response, her gaze drawn to the broken bodies falling at the hands of overzealous Peacekeepers.

With each new blow, the Air Elementals reach for one another, grasping fervently at each other's hands. In some places the links hold, in others the circle of solidarity is severed by the unconscious.

Slowly the chaos in front of her falls into a recognisable image. The Airs – a disparate group made common only by their Element and black threads – are attempting to form a barrier. Even as the Peacekeepers attack them, they rush to fill the gaps in the circle, holding desperately to each other to make their circle complete.

She glances over to the gap provided by the lifeless Airs that have been detained.

At the centre of the melee, still untouched by the Fire Elemental advance, is an oddly shaped sarcophagus. The white concrete reminds her of the walls outside the cemetery, marked with the same deep gouges as though an Elemental has tried to carve into the unforgiving material.

"Anaiya!"

Niamh's voice breaks her away from her thoughts. A male Air Trainee, his eighteen years evident in his lithe body and soft skin, stalks towards her.

"Not happy to just hold hands?" she asks, regretting the taunt as soon as it leaves her lips.

He glances over at the carnage behind him, the Fire Elementals outnumbered three to one, but still dominating the conflict. She follows his gaze, her own distracted by the tomb, all angular except at the top, where its form becomes more organic …

"Run at me, Peacekeeper."

His eyes glitter and his stance, although clumsy, is clear with intent. Only a lustrum younger than her, the five-year gulf is made more immense by the fact that he is only two years out of the Nursery.

She steps towards him and, to his credit, he doesn't flinch.

"Back down, Trainee."

"Run at me," he screams.

It all happens at once. The anxiety swelling in her belly, the chaos and violence stretching around her, the pure and untainted aggression in this boy's voice.

She responds to his challenge and launches at him. Her fingers reach and sink into soft pressure points, claw back flailing arms into unnatural positions. An errant kick is easily diffused with a simple sweep of her leg as the syringe in her hand finds its target in the boy's neck.

Boy. The familiarity of the Unorthodox word pricks at her subconscious. As the body beneath her hands drops to the ground, she recalls the word in its original context – remembers it in the angular lines and looping swirls of Kane's script.

When I was a boy, I did as boys do. Now I am a man, and I can pretend no longer.

She looks down. The anguished face on the broken boy below her steals all oxygen from the air around her. An urgent need to retch pulls at the bile in her stomach and floods her mouth with acid.

Metres away an Air Elemental twists out of a Peacekeeper's grasp. His roar, a tortured wail, ricochets off the death markers surrounding the courtyard. He barrels towards Anaiya, rage and abandon twisting his face into something desperate and ugly.

Rooted to the spot, Anaiya can do nothing but watch as he rushes at her. Peacekeepers' heads swivel towards the sound, a Senior Enforcer breaking away from the central struggle and running towards the new target.

The Air falters in his advance, but it is too late. The Enforcer takes him down with a perfectly timed interception. The body lifeless before it hits the ground.

The conflict is over; the last remnants of resistance silenced by Peacekeeper blows and syringes full of restrain serum.

More of Kane's words float to her in the quiet. *My Element is a lie. I serve to protect the Orthodoxy, but only enslave other Elementals to violence and submission.*

With the action ceased, Anaiya is finally presented with an uninterrupted view of the memorial that had distracted her earlier. There, in concrete relief, as if resurrected under the hands of an Air Designer, is the reclining form of Rehhd.

In perfect detail her curves are carved in a passionate embrace with another. With every neuron in her brain screaming at her to look away, Anaiya lets her gaze be pulled to the second concrete figure.

She moves towards the sculpture unconsciously, unaware of the mess around her, not caring whether she is being observed or not. Not caring about anything.

In her mind's eye, she sees herself reaching out to touch the figure. It is all so lifelike – as if a single caress would crack the surface and life would return to them both. Would flood Rehhd's cheeks with colour.

Would awaken Kane 148 from his slumber.

SIXTEEN

Anaiya's heart seizes and her knees buckle in protest against the onslaught of emotion. She feels it – the very real, almost tangible, lifting of the deception she has clung to for so long. And, in the bright light of this new perspective, she sees it – the answers to the questions that have plagued her for weeks.

Maybe years …

Kane 148's despondency had been built on the same blood that now turns her stomach. His Heterodoxy, and Rehhd's, and Seth's and Kaide's, was a call away from this madness and back to the true Orthodoxy.

Heart still exploding in her chest, she glances back to the memorial, the surprise at seeing Kane's likeness no less than it was the first time. His name and image have been forbidden for so long, she had thought Otpor had erased all trace of him from the collective memory. And yet here he is, his sharp angles and deep shadows perfectly captured in the hard concrete.

Seeing him again with her thoughts still wrapped up in his words, brings all of the inner turmoil and conflict to the surface. For so long she admired him, wanted only to follow in his footsteps. And then for so long she had resented him, desperate to shake off the weight of his legacy.

In the months since her failed realignment, the clear dichotomy had faltered, the emotions all mixed up inside her.

Loving and loathing him at the same time. Proud and angry, sympathetic and immovable, inspired and offended.

And now, in the aftermath of the Peacekeeper violence, they all converge on her at once and she realises that her love for her mentor had come from her experience, whereas her loathing had been conditioned.

The tearing away of her old conditioning is painful, but it pales in comparison to the grief that wells up from a much deeper place. A grief borne of the realisation that she had denied her mentor for so long after his Execution. That she had failed him.

She wonders if this was Kaide's true motivation behind this manipulated spectacle. A way to remind Anaiya of her mentor, a way to re-establish a connection that his Heterodoxy and death had severed.

"Anaiya!" Niamh's voice explodes in the silence. He is livid; arms rigid by his side, his face a thundercloud of rage.

The cemetery is emptier now, mostly cleared of Air and Fire Elementals and cordoned off from unauthorised access until the Forensics arrive.

Niamh strides towards her, stopping just centimetres away. His features are pinched but he lowers his voice, soft enough to be heard by Anaiya and no one else. "What the *fuck* was that?"

Every word makes her skin crawl, makes her want to recoil from his scrutiny. But the memory of the unrestrained violence, of seeing Kane's censure of the Fire Element validated in front of her, makes her angry.

"You tell me," she spits back, careful to keep her own voice low. "I give you intel on a planned event related to Rehhd and you organise a mass-scale takedown that would make any sane Elemental think she is still alive. What did you expect to find here? What exactly is going on?"

"No, Anaiya – you gave me intel on Rehhd's associates planning a public act of Heterodoxy. So, where were they? Where were these associates? We've searched the entire vicinity – no Eamon, no Kaide. No Issau or Seth or Cressida. None, Anaiya. *None.*"

So, Jenna was telling the truth. You're just as interested in Rehhd's cadre as she is. What are you up to?

"You got your Heterodoxy, Niamh – you got your code 545, your 'idolisation of Heterodox persons', not to mention scores of detained Elementals who can provide you with new leads. Why are you still pissed?"

"I am still *pissed*," he says, the Air colloquialism sounding rough and uncultured and full of sarcasm, "because I need more than just another Heterodoxy offence, Ani. I need more than a fucked-up Air celebration of two dead dissenters. I need—"

"What? What do you need?" It is an effort to keep from shouting, to match Niamh's cold, controlled anger.

He shakes his head. "This was a mistake. You're not a Peacekeeper."

"I was a Peacekeeper today." She keeps her voice steady, but something inside her wavers. For all her recent patrolling, it feels like the morning's events have picked at the edges of her identity and peeled away the layers like so many Heterodoxy pages.

"Today was a fucking debacle," Niamh seethes.

"Get over it, Niamh. Tell me what's going on?"

He pauses. The tension in his body has relaxed but the aggression has not dissipated. He looks past her, over to the concrete forms of Rehhd and Kane.

"What happened to you?"

Dread turns her mouth dry. There is no explaining her distraction, her new fixation on anything connected with her old mentor, especially when Niamh has seen her avoid it all for years. She tries to offer an excuse, but he waves her attempt away. "You just stood there. You restrained, what? One Air? A Trainee. You let another rush you. And you just stood there. Staring at that monstrosity."

"I wasn't st—"

"You were staring at it, Ani." His voice is cold, deadly. "You were just standing there. Standing there like an Earth moron, like you thought the dead had been resurrected."

The world is shrinking in on her. Thoughts of an Executioner's needle turn the heat too oppressive, the sun too bright.

Niamh turns back to her, all casual dominance and

intimidation. "I thought you could be useful – provide access to old Resistance networks. Or at least boost Peacekeeper numbers. It was a mistake to reinstate you."

"You can't do this to me, Niamh." The words are razors against her lips. "You can't just discard me again."

He is unmoved. Desperation is like a vice around her core – without access to Niamh's plans she has no leverage over Kaide. No way of getting Kane 148's notes and figuring out why he had abandoned his Fire Element and why her realignment back to that Element failed.

No way of knowing what she needs to do to carry out the vision he was never able to achieve.

"Dammit, Niamh." Her voice is so hoarse, she feels it cracking against the weight of all that hangs between them. "You did this to me. You made me this abomination. You sent me away and then you brought me back. *You* did this."

He just looks at her; weighing up his options, calculating the risk to him against any advantages he can still wrench from this mess.

Belatedly, she realises she is playing this all wrong, trying to appeal to emotions that aren't there. Guilt and mercy don't factor into Niamh's world.

"I can get you what you want," she blurts out. "I'll get you an associate. Just tell me what you need."

He can hear the desperation in her voice, she sees it in the way he tilts his head and appraises her from a different angle. No doubt he thinks it is her desperation to remain a Peacekeeper. Let him think that. Let him think that she still clings to her old Element; that she is no longer a threat to be managed, but a tool to be employed.

Finally, he nods. "Fine. Get me the associate that is stopping this madness from ending and you'll get to stay a Peacekeeper."

SEVENTEEN

Fluorescent light fills the Evidence Hall, bleaching everything it touches and making Anaiya's eyes sting.

Long rows of polymer-inlaid desks are arranged in perfect symmetry down the centre of the room, the strict organisation marking the space as the domain of Water Elementals. At capacity the room would seat thirty Elementals; today just two.

Beside her, an attractive Archivist scrolls through image after image, his quintessential Water neatness not detracting from a face that would make Air Trainees swoon. Maybe it would have distracted her once, but the thoughts that consume her are too heavy for a pretty male to break.

Niamh had given her three weeks to find the Air Elemental who was stopping the Heterodoxy from dying out like it should have after Rehhd's Execution. Jenna's shortlist of likely candidates was still in play, but Niamh was adamant he wouldn't be blindsided again.

"You've been exposed to the networks," he had said. "You can find the relevant secondary links."

"Why do you need secondary links? Why not just target Eamon?"

Throwing his name around when she knows who the real agitator is has a dark deja vu about it, but she is desperate to keep Kaide and Seth out of it, especially while they still have Kane 148's notes and may be her best chance of fulfilling his vision to bring down the Fire Element.

"I don't want the obvious choice," Niamh had replied to her suggestion of targeting Eamon. "We Executed the obvious choice months ago and Heterodoxy continues. I need this disease eliminated. I need to eliminate all the key players."

And, so, here she is. Locked away in a windowless space, three levels below the ground floor of Last Defence, reviewing every piece of evidence from the fatal mission that had begun seventeen floors up with her realignment procedure and ended with Rehhd Executed and herself corrupted.

Here she is, tasked with finding a new target but set on removing existing targets from scrutiny.

Just until I find something else of interest for Niamh. Just until I can find something that will unlock more of Kane's notes.

Her stomach still roils at the betrayal. Even with the ascendancy of her Air identity and the revelation of Kane's words, there is still something that feels … wrong … about completely abandoning the Fire.

Will I ever be free of this conflict?

It doesn't help that her Peacekeeper conditioning still rails against being stationary for so long. It has already been four days and she has only managed to work through ten per cent of the images on file. With each swipe across the desk screen, her breath stalls painfully, expecting to see a familiar face. Or worse, expecting to see her own.

It never happens – the images filled only with random Elementals and Heterodox murals. It is a small comfort.

She stares at the wall opposite, its white facade interrupted with tall columns of in-built cabinets and shelves, each filled with rows upon rows of hard drives. The dark grey boxes are hidden from the oppressive light, the zettabytes of evidence they contain safe in the shadows.

"There was only minimal audio recorded," the Archivist says, suddenly too close and too loud.

He reaches over and plugs a hard drive into the desk terminal. Tapping on the screen brings up a list of files, each with their unfamiliar, impersonal name consisting entirely of numbers.

"Minimal?" There are at least a hundred files. Anaiya does the quick calculation in her head. Over fifteen hours of listening. Of sitting in a windowless room with nothing but the drone of bad audio recordings to focus on.

The click of the door behind her spins her around, her pulse betraying the rush of relief she feels at the intrusion.

Niamh steps into the room and the relief evaporates. Spiky emotions have always assailed her in his presence, but once they had been only linked to ego and competition. Now they fracture in more complex patterns, tied to more difficult emotions and caught up in the thrill and guilt of her new plans.

"How is it coming along?" Like the Archivist, he speaks too loud for the small room – completely oblivious to its acoustic capacity.

Anaiya opens her mouth to respond, but the Archivist beats her to it. "She is slower than I expected. And I didn't expect much."

Tact; another thing that was glaringly absent in both Water and Fire Elementals.

"Have you discovered anything yet?" Niamh directs the question to Anaiya.

"The images didn't show anything of note. But there's still a lot to review."

"What about the audio?"

"Niamh, there are a hundred files to go through. Surely you don't expect me to go through them one by one." *I need to get out of here. I need to find Kaide.*

In the immediate aftermath of the cemetery incursion, she had tried to find Kaide. To warn him of their failed plan, to confess her shifting loyalties. But he had been absent from the Ravignan Strip the times she had visited and, with Niamh's focus firmly on Rehhd associates, she is unwilling to show too much interest in either his studio or Seth's apartment.

"It is torture."

Rolling his eyes at her exaggeration, Niamh nods to the Archivist. The Water stands up from the table and walks over to one of the cabinets.

"Yes, I expect you to go through each of them. In detail."

"But why? What can possibly be hidden in them that would be of use? What do you think I'll find?"

The Archivist returns with a carbonite box, five handspans across and deep. With a coordinated series of taps on the top surface, the lid springs open to reveal an assortment of items within.

Ignoring the Archivist, Niamh steps forward and plucks a small black cube from the box. A very sharp sense of foreboding, like fingernails clawing at a pressure point, comes over Anaiya.

Niamh holds up the soundmatcher, twisting it only centimetres from his face.

"The Developers were never able to properly replicate it. Did you know that?" He speaks softly, caught in a memory of a distant time. "They worked for weeks before the Execution, building and testing and tweaking. They got close – close enough to confirm the technology was legitimate – but never close enough to duplicate the sound match functionality."

After a moment's pause, he blinks and places the replica on the table. It is hard to look at it.

She had been so jubilant when she had first used it to match Rehhd's voice to the one inciting Heterodoxy. But that was before she had discovered the truth. Before she had discovered it was Seth, and not Rehhd, who was leading the Resistance. Before she had started to think that maybe the Resistance was necessary. And righteous.

"Audio brought them down once," Niamh says. "It will do it again. Somewhere in those audio files is something that will condemn one of Rehhd's associates. Find it. And report directly back to me."

The directive is menacing enough, but the last order makes her uncomfortable for other reasons. It reminds her too much of Niamh's casual disregard for rules he sees as irrelevant or constricting; of clandestine missions that bolstered his ego while they tore down everything else.

"Anaiya, is there a problem?"

Startling, she looks up at Niamh – a frown furrowing his brow, his eyes narrowed. She has been silent for too long.

She shakes her head. "No problem. Report directly to you."

The frown doesn't disappear immediately. He is assessing her again – looking for faults that need to be repaired. Or eradicated.

"Don't mess this up, Ani. You know the consequences."

It is hard to concentrate after Niamh leaves. Anaiya plugs in her earphones and starts working her way through the audio files, but it all takes much longer than it should. Thoughts of Heterodoxy and trials and Executions distract her from the sounds and conversations filtering in from the terminal. Only when an unexpected sound or word pulls her attention back does she realise she has glazed over entire sections of recordings and forces herself to replay the file from the beginning.

Shaking her head, she forces herself to focus on more immediate things – the hard edges of the desk, the smooth feel of the laminate, the contrast of light and shadow in the wall recesses. Her gaze tracks along the opposite wall, grounding her in the present environment, taking in the tiniest of details – the occasional spaces in hard drives, the rows of grey interspersed with a white highlight, the cracks in the stucco …

The too-straight line pulls at Anaiya's gaze. It is faint, a hairline fracture. She follows it up the wall, sitting up straighter when she sees it cut in at a right angle.

Not a crack. *A panel.*

What is behind there? It unnerves her that Water Elementals are so damn secretive. As if they alone should have the knowledge. As if no one else deserves it.

She scowls at the Archivist, watching as he methodically works through evidence collections, organising them into data groups with indecipherable filenames that only an Archivist would understand.

Like these audio files. If only she had some indication of what was on them, some way of navigating to what she wants to hear instead of wading through terabytes of useless interrogations.

She needs to find out what Niamh holds on the real core members of the Resistance. And she needs to find something of low-level impact to give to him if she is ever going to learn about his intentions for the attack Kaide is so certain is being planned.

Sighing, she taps on the next file, ready for the same monotonous voice to announce another interview. But this one doesn't start like the others. There is no formal introduction, no tirade of standard questions.

This one starts with an Elemental screaming for blood.

"Where is the bitch?"

It is not the words that send adrenalin spiking in her blood, but the voice. It comes to her with all the memories of a hot-headed Elemental with grey eyes and bronze hair.

"You have that look, Anaiya," Eamon had said all those nights ago, when he was just another confident Air and she was just an interesting arrival in the Northern Area precincts, *"of rage. Hunger."*

She had brushed it off as bravado, a crude Air Elemental form of flirting.

"That rebellion that makes us the same. We're the same, Anaiya."

The truth of it had made her shiver then. And is no less chilling now.

"Interrogation 280." Below Eamon's screaming she can hear the Truthseeker introduce the session. "Aquario 18, 0421 hours. Present, Truthseeker 111624 and Truthseeker 111504. Subject, Eamon 801." It is the first of Eamon's interrogations. The one after the curfew lockdown party, when the world had tilted on its axis.

"Where is she?" he shrieks.

She can hear the hoarseness of his voice; how it strains against his throat, cuts through clenched teeth.

"When did you first make contact with the Peacekeeper?" the Truthseeker asks in her monotone voice.

Anaiya's heart slams into her ribcage, panic blooming at the Truthseeker so casually referencing her. Her realignment and deployment had been a Sec Level 5 mission – no one beyond the Task Force was supposed to know of it.

If knowledge of her realignment to the Air Element had grown beyond Niamh and his trusted network, then knowledge of her failed realignment back to Fire could also be too wide. Knowledge of the Heterodoxy she had tried to hide for so long, that could lead to her Execution …

"When did you take him?" the Truthseeker continues, louder, more aggressive. And Anaiya realises the 'Peacekeeper' reference is not to her, but the Trainee Eamon and Rehhd had blinded and gagged in the basement of the Veritas izakaya.

Sweet relief evaporates the adrenalin that flooded her veins seconds earlier.

"She will burn for this," Eamon wails, derision clear and bright in his tone.

"Who will burn for this?"

But Eamon doesn't answer, his rage and panic sending him manic. The Interrogation is concluded and Eamon sedated. They will interview him again to get their answers.

It doesn't matter. While the Truthseeker had not been referring to Anaiya, Eamon clearly had been.

Why have they released him so early?

Six months' detention seems too lenient for someone so closely associated with Rehhd. Even if Rehhd had confessed to it all, which explained Niamh's inability to detain other known associates, surely there was enough on Eamon to warrant a longer sentence … unless Niamh had another use for him.

Had Eamon really escaped a longer detention or was Niamh manipulating him? And testing her?

She shakes away the thoughts before they take hold. As dramatic as they are, as easy for her Air brain to believe them, she knows the truth is much simpler. Eamon escaped a longer detention because the upgraded, violent version of the Resistance started while he was still detained.

Niamh's reluctance to target Eamon as the key Element of interest wasn't prudence, but a case of Eamon already being eliminated as an option.

And while Niamh may be manipulating Eamon to uncover more of Rehhd's old network, it's unlikely he's testing Anaiya. Unlikely that Niamh expects her to be anything but willingly and gratefully obedient.

Just like a good little Peacekeeper.

Still, he must have something on the others to be so singularly focussed on them. And must still need something to put the right one on the Execution Pillar. Something he thinks either Eamon can lead him to or Anaiya can find in the Archives.

She slams the headphones down on the desk, earning a frown from the Archivist. It is useless.

Even if the answer lies somewhere in the files, it will take too long for her to find them. Attacks and counterattacks were due any day; Otpor will burn before she can find them.

Despite days of reviewing images and hours of reviewing audio, Eamon's interrogation has been the only relevant sound bite, and all it has gifted is a tight ball of anxiety to her core.

"Is there something you need help with?" the Archivist asks in his clipped tone.

"Yes," she says through gritted teeth. "I need more useful file names."

"How could they possibly be any more useful?" he asks. "Time, date, Truthseeker number, target's lifeline serial number."

Anaiya blinks and looks back at the name of Eamon's file. The jumble of numbers had been indecipherable minutes ago. Now she sees the hidden code clearly.

Finding Eamon's lifeline number at the end of the long string of numbers, she begins entering it into the search function. And then she pauses.

There are more important targets she needs to run searches on.

"Rough day?"

The Infrastructure Protector posted outside the Hall offers her a sympathetic smile. *Or sardonic?*

She pushes away the vague confusion, in no mood for the usual distraction of her identity conflict. Things were so much easier when her Fire identity only knew and responded to a limited set of emotions.

"Peacekeepers were not meant to stay still," she replies,

inwardly cringing. Her life has become a poor sketch of pretence and cliche.

"Story of my life," he replies, grinning.

She laughs. How many times had she laughed with Niamh at the expense of Infrastructure Protectors wishing they were Peacekeepers?

"You heading back to your apartment?" he asks.

That was the other thing about Fire Elementals, no subtlety when it came to their desire for sex.

The Protector is not unattractive. He lacks the arresting symmetry of the Archivist, but there is a nice broadness to his shoulders. For a moment she contemplates the silent, yet obvious, entreaty.

"Not tonight," she replies. "Think I need some open space."

His face betrays no emotion. Which is not unexpected from a Fire. No doubt he will put it aside as a minor inconvenience and try again the next shift.

"Flame speed, then," he says.

Pushing aside errant thoughts, Anaiya heads up the stairs and through the lobby of Last Defence. The morning would be pleasant if not for her unconditioned limbs and the echo of Eamon's rage still bouncing around her skull.

Slowly, her pace becomes more consistent, the heat burning in her calves settling her into the free-run. Entering the Ravignan Strip, she accelerates, leaping atop a wobbly awning and scrabbling up the wall until she reaches the roof of the three-storey building. From here she has an uninterrupted view of the street and the throng of Air Elementals making their way to various izakaya, galleries and studios.

There is no guarantee that Kaide or any of the other core Resistance members will make their way here today, but it still remains her best option for finding at least one of them without raising unwanted suspicion. Tapping on her wristplate to bring up the remote scanning app standard to all Peacekeeper configurations, Anaiya settles against the roof cladding and begins searching the streetscape below.

EIGHTEEN

The sun beats down relentlessly. By mid-afternoon, Anaiya can no longer withstand it and swings down to the unoccupied balcony below.

Peering in through the broken, grime-covered window, she spies a similar state of disrepair. Water stains, like a splotchy pox, cover the walls and threadbare carpet is littered with rubbish. Nowhere is there a sign of colour or movement or habitation.

Satisfied that this apartment is just another of the thousands of unoccupied residential spaces strewn across the city, she sits down on the floor of the balcony and resumes her surveillance.

Hours slink by, filled only with the strange music she makes by beating out a rhythm against the broken columns of the guardrail. When her vigil is finally rewarded, it is not in the way she expects.

A familiar female, loose hair tumbling to her shoulders, moves in a way that is completely free of worry or distraction or frustration – something that should not be possible in this era of Heterodoxy. It is the Elemental that was at Seth's side the last time she saw him.

Seeing her makes Anaiya's heart clench and she shifts in her position, peering ahead to look for Seth. What would her shifting loyalties mean for their relationship? Would helping his Resistance get her any closer to the redemption she has been trying to earn? *Would it all be too little too late?*

Unable to see him, Anaiya turns her attention back to the nameless Air.

Who is she?

The curiosity about Seth's new interest pricks along her nerve endings – the itch building until it is intolerable. If she was being honest with herself, she would acknowledge that it is not the curiosity that is unsettling her, but the jealousy and hurt and regret.

Useless emotions.

But rejecting them intellectually is not the same as banishing them.

With the Air almost out of her sight, Anaiya grips the guardrail and swings down to the next level. She hits the ground with a satisfying jolt, attracting the heated glances and challenging stares of the Airs nearby.

Unconcerned, she weaves confidently in and around them – keeping her target in sight while maintaining a good distance behind.

Belatedly, she realises the female is not alone. Two other Elementals – a shorter female with close-cropped hair and a lean male, maybe two lustrums older – keep pace beside her. Using her wristplate, she remotely scans their lifeline numbers. A list of half a dozen numbers flashes up, the app picking up other lifelines in the vicinity. As she continues to follow them, the list reduces to just three.

No alerts are listed against any of them, but while that may be the purpose of the app, it's not the reason Anaiya is using it. She saves the list and continues following.

With evening well established, the crowds grow and swell around her. The trio occasionally slow to inspect the window displays of galleries or talk to other Elementals, but never deviate from their original direction. Heading north, they lead Anaiya away from the Strip and into the residential districts of Precinct 18.

As the taller buildings give way to the rambling terraces of Girardon Street, Anaiya slows. Two blocks later, she stops, unwilling to follow them any further.

Ahead, the dark facade of Seth's apartment building sits innocuously on the street corner; nothing to set it apart from the other nondescript towers, nothing to indicate it as a landmark of importance. Her gaze tracks up to the sixth floor, finding the window that identifies Seth's unit.

Movement at the ground level tears her attention away from the window and back to the three Air Elementals who are now entering the building. Anaiya grimaces at the weight in her core. Letting go of her past is proving less like a release and more like the tearing of old skin.

It is dark now. A quick glance at her wristplate tells her that curfew is less than an hour away. She pauses, the beginning of an idea – a stupid, reckless, irrational idea – firming in her mind.

Another quick glance around the street confirms that she is alone, for now. Swallowing hard, she shakes out of her inertia and strides towards the corner. Every step jolts fear and misgiving through her body, ratcheting it higher and higher with each metre gained.

Yet, even as her mind and body beg her to stop this foolishness, the need to learn more about this new Seth and why he is on Niamh's radar keeps her feet from slowing.

She passes by Seth's apartment building and turns the corner. The lights in his bedroom are out but she can still make out the window. With no one around to witness, she ignores the hammering of her heart, turns away from the building and steps out her run-up.

There is a moment, just before she pivots, when she can stop the madness before it descends any further. But determination and curiosity are twin rats gnawing at her insides. So, she turns and launches herself at the wall.

Entering an apartment by stealth is not unfamiliar to Anaiya, and yet small tremors thrill along her hands as she slides open Seth's bedroom window.

The light from the street below casts strange shadows around the room. Entering it is like stepping through to the past. She trails her fingers along nearby shelves and makeshift tables, skin grazing over shiny trinkets and objet d'art.

A slender plastic tube digs its pointy end into the skin under her fingernail, leaving behind a sticky residue. Her first thought is a nutrient syringe or synth injector, but holding her hand up to the light shows a dark, inky smudge.

Once, her hand would have burned to hold such a Heterodox object. Now, intrigue and desire see her grab it possessively and pocket it away in her hoodie.

Wiping her hand on her jeans, she looks over to the bed, briefly, and then to the ceiling above it.

Liberty. Egality. Fraternity. Or Death.

Individual freedom. Equality among the Elements. Interdependence between the Elements. Or death.

Seeing the Cooperative's motto carved into the polymer pulls her into a fresh turmoil. When she had last seen it, she had been unable to fathom how someone connected to the Resistance could show such clear loyalty to the Orthodoxy. Now she sees the motto through Kane 148's eyes, sees how much it has been corrupted in recent months.

Maybe the call to resistance is a call back to the original Orthodoxy...

"We have waited too long, already." Eamon's voice, rising unexpectedly from the room beyond, clears all other thoughts from her mind. "Her silence tells us everything we need to know."

"It's not that simple, Eamon."

Anaiya inches closer to the wall that separates her from the gathering in the next room. Tapping again on her wristplate activates the scanning app, presenting her with a list of six serial numbers, four of them already familiar.

"It doesn't get any simpler, Kaide."

Holding her breath, she closes her eyes and imagines them facing each other in the small lounge room. Seth sitting on the ground, arms wrapped around his knees, regarding them silently as is his way. Eamon pacing the worn carpet, anger and frustration taking turns to flash across his face. The nameless Air and her two companions, maybe standing near Seth, maybe reclining on the lounge. And Kaide, arms folded across his chest, leaning against the same wall she is hidden by.

"The attack at the cemetery proves how bold they have become." It is the older female who speaks. Her voice is deeper than Anaiya expects. "How they will stop at nothing to sate their aggression towards us."

"Lilith is right," says an unfamiliar voice, "the time to move is now."

"We're not ready," says Kaide. "Let's wait until we get intel from Anaiya—"

"*Anaiya.*" The derision in Eamon's voice cuts through the barrier between them.

She takes a step forward, she should reveal herself now, before they discover her and think the worst. She'll tell them that she understands their cause, that she wants to help them ...

"How can you trust her?" Eamon demands.

She can hear the same rage that tainted his voice in his interrogation. Except this time, it has less heat and sharper edges. Anaiya is caught – wanting to step into the next room; anxious to leave; unable to move.

"She is one of them. The worst of them. She is deceitful and treacherous and dangerous and—"

"She is an asset." Kaide's interjection should be welcome, but instead it twists in her gut. She had been naive to think they would welcome her into their rebellion again. That they would forgive her for the fire she had unleashed on them.

"Regardless," Seth says, his voice silencing the others, "we can no longer wait. It is true – the latest Peacekeeper attack has forced our hand. We can no longer let their violence be met with our passivity."

Anaiya's stomach clenches with a fierce and sudden dread. *No. No, no, no.*

She waits for Kaide to speak up, to call an end to this madness. He knows that the Peacekeepers were only there because the two of them manipulated the situation to lead them there. That the aggression had not been spontaneous, but a planned response to a made-up threat Anaiya and Kaide had fed them.

"What do you plan to do?" he asks instead.

"It's not enough to intercept their plans anymore," Seth

replies.

"Exactly," the female, Lilith, says.

It is easy to imagine her crossing the room to stand next to him, but the thought is just a vague distraction. Anaiya's heart is beating so hard she irrationally fears it will cause her to be discovered.

She clenches her hands and tries to control her breathing, swallowing hard against the invisible rocks that have lodged in her throat.

What have we started? Her head is pounding and she feels her core sway out of alignment. It is not an option anymore, she has to leave.

The cooler air that rushes in when she opens the window is a blessed relief. She pauses briefly to savour it, the final words of Lilith reduced by distance to a soft murmur.

"It is our time to strike."

NINETEEN

Just like she did hours ago, Anaiya scales the remaining floors of the building and swings herself up onto the roof.

Finding Kaide after looking for him for so long has filled her with mixed emotions. She is no longer sure that she wants to share with him her changed perspective or discuss their new opportunity for intelligence gathering. The overheard conversations in Seth's apartment have made her cautious.

Even though Kaide had defended her of a sort, there was still something cold in the way he had called her an asset. It reminds her of Niamh.

The comparison threatens to dredge up bad memories, memories she doesn't have time for. It doesn't matter; even if Kaide had been more genuine or persistent in his defence, it wouldn't have helped her.

She had thought the growing rebellion in her heart would find a natural home with Seth's Resistance. After the cemetery, it seemed inevitable she would join his efforts to dismantle the Fire. *Who better to help me fulfil Kane's vision?*

But in this new era, with Kaide's influence eroded and Eamon and Lilith sharpening Seth's hardness, there was no room for Anaiya. Even if they could accept her new ideology, they would never accept her.

She should leave.

An hour turns into two. Curfew is well entrenched; the streets quiet and Peacekeeper patrols less frequent.

Just when she is ready to cut her losses and call an end to her ill-planned vigil, they emerge. Not all at once; first Eamon, then Lilith's two companions. Then Kaide. In the dark, they appear as indistinct silhouettes, but Kaide's broad shoulders and easy confidence give him away.

She waits a little longer, to see if Lilith emerges. There is a dull sense of weight when she doesn't. Not a weight as Peacekeepers know it – the threat of violence or unrest – but a heaviness of emotion. An unwelcome reminder of just how alone she is in this world.

Rappelling down to street level, she begins her tracking of Kaide. He doesn't hurry, but still moves fast enough to make good time. There is a way he seems to avert the eye, keeping an even pace and straight path, occasionally ducking into doorways and alleys to escape possible scrutiny or check for trackers.

Anaiya thinks she has escaped his detection, until he pivots without warning to confront her. There is the briefest pause before he flashes a handcode and strides into the nearest alley.

Once again, she ignores the familiar trepidation and follows him. Glancing around for any indication of unwanted surveillance, she steps off the main road and into the narrow space. Her thoughts race with what she will say to him.

"What the fuck happened, Anaiya?" Kaide whispers harshly as she joins him, anger and frustration rolling off him in waves. "Forty detained, multiple injuries, at least three permanently incapacitated, and half a dozen with suspected hypoxia?"

The statistics from the cemetery incursion set ice to her chest; until that moment she had not known the full extent of the damage. What had Niamh done?

What have we *done?* How had they let their fake incursion turned into a real one? How had their efforts in discovering the next big attack become its catalyst?

Like some sick self-fulfilling prophecy.

"Scores of Elementals brutalised and damaged," Kaide continues, his face pinching in the effort to keep his voice low.

"Because why? Because you just had to be a Peacekeeper again? Because these people don't matter? Because you'll do anything your beloved leader tells you?"

He thinks the incursion was her fault, her plan all along. He doesn't see the incident as a mess they have both created, he sees it as evidence of a Peacekeeper returning to her old ways and her corrupted Element.

The accusation punches through to her core. In the seconds it has taken for him to deliver it, he has erased the last shred of hope she had for finding a home in his Resistance.

"You don't know anything," she whispers fiercely.

"I know that I trusted you and that you let your Peacekeepers slaughter them."

Her habitual rejoinder flashes in the back of her mind – *Not my Peacekeepers* – but the new truth of it makes it stick in her throat. "I implemented a plan we *both* agreed on."

Kaide shakes his head, eyes still flashing with rage. "You took our plans and turned them to your advantage. Seth was right – I should never have trusted you. It should never have happened."

His cruel words should push her into silence, but all she feels is her own rage building within. *No. You do not get to absolve yourself of this.* "You thought this would be *easy*?" The words escape without thought or restraint. "That I could just march up to Niamh – who, by the way, is as repulsed by me as you and your Resistance friends and who trusts me less – just march up and say 'Hey Niamh, just out of curiosity, because I have absolutely no need to know and no vested interest, what are the details about some supposed attack you're planning on the Air Elementals?'"

Kaide opens his mouth to respond, but she gives no quarter. "We're dealing with two very unpredictable forces who are intent on destroying one another. Getting involved in their games, trying to *manipulate* them, was always going to be dangerous. If you hadn't considered just how dangerous, you clearly weren't paying attention to Rehhd's Execution."

She shakes her head, angry and frustrated. This is not the conversation she wanted to have with him.

"You are right," Kaide finally says, his voice stripped of all emotion. "I should have paid more attention to Rehhd's Execution. I should have remembered that Peacekeepers, no matter what their disguise, can't be trusted."

His words are like a slap. She has suffered worse. "Save it, Kaide. You can delude yourself that you are on the right side of this battle, but Seth's planned attack is no more righteous than Niamh's."

His eyes glitter dangerously. "You don't know what you're talking about."

"I know *exactly* what I am talking about."

In the silence that follows, she watches his body tense. He has no way of knowing that her intel on the Air attack has come straight from the conspirators only hours ago. His only conclusion must be that the Peacekeepers are somehow aware of the plan. And that she is working with them to bring down his rebellion.

Fear, bright and sharp, flashes across his face and she knows that she has gone too far.

Control the Fire, Anaiya.

She opens her mouth to apologise, to tell Kaide what she had wanted to tell him from the beginning – that she sees the truth in the Peacekeeper violence, that she knows the Fire Element has become corrupted, that—

"This deal is over," Kaide says. "This *arrangement* is over. You don't get your redemption, you don't get Kane's notes. You get nothing."

He strides out of the alley without a backwards glance.

And just like that, her earlier resolve, her sensibility and restraint, evaporates. The rage that was simmering in her core explodes back into life. She is sick of being told what she can and can't do, what she can and can't have. Of being controlled and manipulated and leashed – leashed by the fear of her Heterodoxy, leashed by Niamh and his fatal ultimatum, and by Kaide and his promise of hidden truths.

He was within his rights to say their deal was over – it was his deal to break. But Kane 148's notes and her redemption are not his to give or take away. She will get both of them, with or without him.

"How far back do these files date?" Anaiya asks, glancing up from her desk to the Archivist.

He sits at the far end of the table, speaking in hushed tones with another Archivist who studies the soundmatcher. Both of them were there when Anaiya arrived and have largely ignored her since.

"Your assigned files date from the detention of Rehhd 020 to the commencement of her trial," the Archivist says without looking over to her.

"No, I meant how far do all these files date back to?"

After her covert surveillance in Seth's apartment and her run-in with Kaide, she had spent the night lying awake and figuring out her next plan of attack. In the early hours of dawn, with her brain numb and her body cold, she had come to the conclusion that fulfilling Kane 148's vision required three things: the complete picture of Kane's philosophy from the rest of his notes, the ability to stay off Niamh's radar and avoid the Execution needle, and a way to interrupt Seth's plans.

It had quickly become clear that while Kane 148 and Seth's rebellions had the same end goal, Seth's plans would only embolden the Fire Element rather than destroy it. With every Air attack and violent retaliation, the Resistance not only moved further from Kane's vision but lent legitimacy to the Fire Element.

With 'irrational' Elementals sending Otpor into disarray – leaving broken buildings, interrupted services, and uncertain market environments in their wake – who else will the Cooperative rely on to restore order and prosperity?

Seth's new Resistance will not erase the Fire Element, but legitimise it and its corrupted ways, cementing it in the Orthodoxy.

But that is a much bigger problem that needs solving. In the meantime, coming back to the Evidence Hall helps her avoid Niamh's suspicion and gives her the opportunity to learn more about the Resistance members from their interrogations and any seized lifeline data.

"Closed cases get relocated to the Historical Archives after twelve months," the other Archivist replies, her face betraying both the frustration at being interrupted and the delight at the chance to wax intellectual on a subject no one else could care about. "Derelict cases – cases that have not been closed but are older than ten years – get sent to the Holding Archives. Only current cases, closed cases less than twelve months old, and unsolved cases less than ten years old remain in the Evidence Archives."

The timeframes are generous – there should be enough scope to find more on Kaide, Seth and even Lilith to get a sense of who they really are and what they could be planning.

Maybe. They had remained undetected so far for a reason. Still, if she was stuck in the Evidence Hall to appease Niamh, she may as well use it to some other advantage.

"If I wanted to search through Code 150 offences in the last twelve months, how can I do that?" Cases involving theft from manufacturing plants would have been the first criminal foray of Resistance members as a collective, the appropriation of synthetic paints necessary for their Heterodox murals. If she can trace engagement from that point on, she may learn something important.

"An Archivist would have to run an index search, pull up relevant files and file names."

"Is that difficult to do?"

"No."

Anaiya sighs, biting down on her frustration and relaxing her throat enough to keep her voice calm. "Well, can you please run that search for me?"

"No," the other Archivist speaks up. "Your access parameters are strictly defined – only evidence directly related to the investigation of the Code 60 offence on Aquario 17. With the exception of specific requests regarding either the Peacekeeper Trainee that was abducted, or persons of interest you would like to evaluate further."

Anaiya grimaces. The Archivist speaks as if only relaying pertinent facts, but in between the words, Anaiya can see Niamh's obvious trap. If she requests files related specifically to Seth or Kaide or Lilith, Niamh will have a stronger lead for investigating them.

Her old patrol partner may not be testing her, but he certainly is manipulating her.

Bad luck, Niamh. I don't need names when I have numbers.

"If you want to broaden your search scope," the Archivist continues, his gaze suddenly too keen for Anaiya's liking, "you'll need approval from your sponsor." *Niamh.*

"No need," she replies. "It was just a hypothetical."

She shouldn't have bothered; the Archivists have already returned their attention back to the replica soundmatcher. Sighing, she pulls up the search function on her existing list of files and types in one of the lifeline numbers she had scanned the night before.

It takes a few attempts to find a number that has a match. Of the six serial numbers, three have been eliminated and one she already knows is Eamon's. Fingers hovering over the file name on the desk screen, she takes a deep breath and taps to begin the audio.

TWENTY

"Interrogation 314. Present, Truthseeker 111620 and Truthseeker 111499. Subject, Kaide 177."

"Please state the nature of your relationship with Rehhd 021."

"We've been friends for a few years. We met at an audiovisual event. Both of us were exhibiting pieces."

There is a pause, but this time it is the Truthseekers who are left speechless. Anaiya is also surprised by his unexpected candidacy. But that was Kaide – always doing the unexpected. Like hacking her lifeline data with the soundmatcher. Or following her lead at Veritas and betraying Rehhd. Or confronting her at Last Defence after her own detention.

"And Eamon 801?"

"Eamon and I aren't close. Rehhd introduced us a few years ago. They were working on a project together."

"Have they worked together lately?"

"On a project?" He sounds so relaxed, even more so than Lilith. As if this were just a random conversation rather than an interrogation. "Not that I know of. I've seen them together a few times out and about, usually with a large group. Rehhd hasn't mentioned anything – but then again, she's not one to talk about work."

"With you?" the second Truthseeker interjects. "Or with anyone?"

"Rehhd's got a lot of friends; who knows what she tells them."

"Friends closer than you?"

"Sure."

"Like Issau 091?"

"I don't know who that is." He says it with the same calm assuredness of someone with nothing to hide. But Anaiya knows it is a lie. A well-rehearsed collective lie. The Resistance members had been prepared for the possibility of interrogation all along.

"What about Seth 137?"

Anaiya's heart races at hearing his name. But Kaide seems unfazed. "I introduced Seth to Rehhd years ago. They never really hit it off – Graphics and Literature are not as compatible as other competencies."

"Seth was with you last night at Veritas izakaya?"

Kaide is finally silent and she worries that his pause will betray him. Everything up until this point has been carefully crafted, but there had been no way to anticipate what would eventuate the night of Rehhd's detention. No way to mask that chaos in a logical, well-rehearsed story …

"I saw him there."

"What did you speak about?"

"We didn't speak."

"Why is that?"

A longer pause. Even though Anaiya knows the outcome of these interrogations, knows that both Kaide and Seth escaped detection and punishment, the silence causes her throat to dry.

It is the primary Truthseeker who finally breaks it. "Your lifeline data suggests significant co-locations going back as far as five years ago and yet, that all seems to disappear three months ago." *When the murals started appearing …* "Why is that?"

The focus on Seth makes her unsettled. Both she and Kaide had risked so much to protect him from Peacekeeper scrutiny, to keep him hidden. That their betrayals could have been for nothing …

"Seth and I were close for a long time." Kaide's voice is deeper, a little huskier. The new focus has affected him as well. "A female he was connecting with brought us together." He laughs; the sound short and sharp and completely unexpected. "And then a female he connected with broke us apart."

Anaiya's blood fills with ice. There is no pretence now; every word he speaks is true.

"Which females are you referring to?"

"The first was Terani 105. She was a Music competency."

"What do you mean by was?"

"She died after taking some bad dex. Bought it from a shady Earth dealer. She was always the desperate type." He sounds melancholy, caught in the shadows of a past life.

"And the other female?"

Anaiya's heart is pounding in her chest. Flicking out her hand, she pauses the audio. Relief floods the same neural pathways that only seconds ago were firing with adrenalin. She closes her eyes and focuses on regulating her breathing.

Calm down. Even if Kaide had implicated her, it never went anywhere. Her interrogation had begun much earlier and never ended at the Execution Pillar.

Because Kaide held back the truth? Or because Niamh made it go away?

It is impossible to know who and when someone is an enemy or ally. Did Kaide save her, or did Niamh? *And why?*

Heart pounding and adrenalin spiking, she taps on the desk screen again, inviting Kaide's voice back to haunt her.

TWENTY-ONE

Her name was Anaiya.

The words crowd her mind, but they are not the words that Kaide speaks. "She came on the scene about two, three months ago."

Anaiya frowns. The timeline is wrong; her deployment to the Northern Area as an Air Elemental was only a month before Rehhd's Execution.

"She was pretty and intriguing; Seth fell for her almost immediately. He became distracted by her and she pulled him away from his friends. But that's Seth, impulsive when he needs to be cautious, patient when he needs to be decisive."

It is how he manages to sound so convincing – drawing on part-truths to deceive, lying only when he needs to. Being honest enough to sound authentic, but not so much as to give the important truths away.

"He ended a five-year friendship because he was distracted?"

"No, I ended a five-year friendship because he had her and I wanted her."

It is the boldest of his lies so far, but the easiest for the Truthseekers to believe. A jealous Air fits the stereotype better than a calculating one.

"Did he remain in contact with your other friends?" the Truthseeker asks.

"Like who?"

"Like Eamon?"

"Eamon and I aren't friends."

"Did you see Eamon and Rehhd at the izakaya?"

"I didn't stay long."

"Why is that?"

"I saw Seth, it kind of killed the night for me."

"You left before curfew?"

They are tying him up in knots, she can feel it as if she is watching it unfold in real time. The questions are coming too fast, he can't know what is a trap and what is general scanning for information. She can imagine him wracking his brain for details of the night – did he use his lifeline after curfew? To pay for a drink or download a song?

"No."

"You broke curfew?"

Unable to keep up with the Truthseekers' barrage of questions, Kaide has been pushed into a dead-end with no exit. While the interrogation hasn't been able to locate him with Rehhd and Eamon the night of the Trainee kidnapping, it has stung him with a curfew violation.

The inevitable charge is better than the death sentence its alternative would bring, but still leaves Kaide at the mercy of subsequent interrogations and justified monitoring.

"Truthseeker 111620 terminating this interrogation. Kaide 177 to be charged with a Code 548 offence and detained for forty-eight hours."

Anaiya ends the audio and quickly searches for the next involving Kaide's lifeline number. The forty-eight-hour period is long enough for Intel Analysts to do some more digging and for Data Forensics to scan his lifeline. The next interrogation will be more intense.

She runs the search again, checking that she hasn't messed up the long string of numbers. But no result is returned. A vague sense of uneasiness settles in her core – there is no good reason for the interrogations to have ceased.

And then she realises – Kaide's interrogation, like the others', would have ceased the moment they had enough on Rehhd to convict her. As soon as they had ruled out the other possibilities.

Hesitantly, she types in Seth's lifeline number into the search function. Like Kaide, there is only one result. Taking a deep breath, she taps on the listing to start the audio.

The familiar introduction does nothing to dampen the building sense of dread and anticipation. And then she hears his voice, and everything else fades.

"I met Rehhd a few years ago." Seth's voice is soft and bitter. Anaiya hears in it the lingering confusion triggered by Rehhd and Eamon's stupid ploy. And the sting of betrayal brought by her and Kaide's unfathomable betrayal.

He is sticking to the script, but just barely.

"How did you meet?"

"A common friend introduced us."

"Kaide 177?"

Seth's pause isn't as conflicted as Kaide's. It is one of restraint, of holding in rage and abandon.

"Yes."

"You two used to be close?"

"Yes."

"But not any longer?"

"No."

"Why is that?"

Anaiya holds her breath, waiting for him to repeat the same lie she had just listened to Kaide spin.

"Because I made a mistake."

Anaiya's heart clenches. Not because his story is deviating from Kaide's, but because she hears the truth in his words.

"A mistake? What kind of mistake?"

"I fell for someone. The wrong kind of someone."

"What makes someone 'the wrong kind of someone'?"

"When that someone betrays you."

"Why does that affect your relationship with Kaide 177?"

"Because he betrayed me, too."

Seth's interrogation finishes not long after. There isn't the same kind of scrutiny as there was for Kaide – the Truthseekers seemingly losing interest when he confirmed that his separation from Kaide was triggered by 'a bad relationship' and not some ideological difference. Belatedly she realises that the shift of focus from Rehhd in previous interrogations was never to Seth, but to Kaide.

In the aftermath that has all come before, she doesn't know how to feel about the unexpected realisation.

Kaide hadn't betrayed her, even though he easily could have. And he had absorbed enough of the Resistance heat to shift attention away from Seth and towards himself.

It was easy to cast him as a master manipulator, but there is another side that is becoming visible. A selflessness – or, at least, a tendency to self-sacrifice.

With questions plaguing her mind and conflicting emotions pulling at her core, she finds it hard to sit still. The interrogations have yielded nothing useful, nothing to indicate what the Air Resistance is planning.

Frustration threatens to boil over. Shifting in her seat, she forces herself to focus on anything but the list of file names in front of her. She glances around the room, at the rows of cabinets and the oblivious Archivists, who are still wrangling with the replica soundmatcher. Their frustration is as plain as her own; sharp frowns deepening as they inspect the object in turns.

How have they not figured it out yet? It was Water technology, after all. Could it really be that unfamiliar to them?

Her eyes fix on the cube, her mind racing with the threads of a half-formed plan.

"You're holding it wrong."

The female Archivist flips it around and looks over to her. "Like this?"

She shakes her head. "The other way."

"You used the original?" she asks, still frowning at the cube.

Anaiya nods.

"Show me."

Anaiya bristles at her tone, but bites back a retort. The soundmatcher slides easily along the table and into her hand. She picks it up and makes a show of examining it closely.

"There's a piece missing."

"What piece?"

"There should be a metal strip that runs along one of the faces."

It is a lie, of course. The cube is exactly the same as the one she had used to condemn Rehhd.

"You're certain?" the male Archivist speaks up, frustration spilling into his voice, turning it tight and short.

"Yes."

The Archivist sighs and stands. "Then I've just wasted fourteen hours studying a useless piece of carbonite."

His colleague stands and follows him as they exit the room, no doubt to brief their superiors on the situation.

Anaiya pockets the cube and makes her own exit a few minutes later.

TWENTY-TWO

The wait for curfew is an easier one this time around. As is the climb to Seth's bedroom.

Anaiya's heart races as it did previously, but this time with an anticipation and determination. She enters the room without fear; having seen Seth depart the building an hour ago, she knows it will be empty from now until dawn.

It is unchanged from her last visit; the same market trinkets by the window, the same sculptures cluttered with clothes and hard drives and assorted art pieces.

Focus, Anaiya. Remember what you are here for.

The black cube weighs down her cargo pocket, its hard edges biting into her thigh. She had originally intended to use the soundmatcher on Niamh – plant it in his office, use it to get the intel he would never share with her.

It was a stupid idea. She had entertained it for less than a minute – even if she could get it near Niamh, even if she could find a place where he and his tech sweepers wouldn't find it, there was no guarantee she would get access to it again.

And even if she did, she was smart enough to know that Niamh held all his important conversation in the dark and silence. Off the grid. Away from official spaces.

Seth as a surveillance target was an appealing alternative – she could get insight into his plans, track them against Niamh's movements, figure out impending clashes, run interference … Stop him from ruining Kane 148's vision just to satisfy his need for revenge.

She shakes her head, as if the motion will shake the distractions from her brain, and looks around. The room is small, and most of its contents are out in the open and on display. Perfect places for hiding the soundmatcher.

And, yet, she is tempted by a different opportunity. She knows Seth, knows he hides his secrets close. And what bigger secret than Kane 148's notes?

The soundmatcher temporarily forgotten, she centres her search and discovery on the hidden things; the places in shadow, the small nooks obscured by larger, more dominant objects. She trails her hand under shelves and behind furniture, looking for the rest of Kane's notes but finding only an assortment of random objects – tarnished and faded, some scuffed, others chipped.

Maybe once they had been prized possessions, had captured Seth's interest or appealed to him in some bright yet fleeting moment, but clearly no longer. Do they remain because they are hidden from view and forgotten? Or because Seth is unable to throw them away?

Stop getting distracted.

Even now, her mind betrays her and wanders towards the unimportant things. She sighs and sinks down onto the bed.

This room holds Kane 148's forbidden teachings. She just needs to find them.

She scans the room again. *Where would I hide my secrets?*

Thoughts of her own Heterodox pages stashed away in air vents set her heart racing and she quickly searches for the familiar grates in Seth's bedroom. With none in plain sight, she looks for furniture that could be hiding them. They are all so laden with objects, her Peacekeeper mind immediately dismisses them as illogical choices.

She tries to shift the bed, but there is nothing hidden but layers of dust.

Tch, tch, Seth. Cleanliness is next to righteousness.

There is only one other piece of furniture that is a logical candidate. She walks over to the wardrobe jammed into the far corner and runs her hands over its polyenamaline shell. The slick material resists purchase, pulling from her grasp with each attempted pull.

There has to be an easier way.

Opening the doors, she pulls out the clothes and throws them on the floor. When the wardrobe is empty, she sidesteps the pile of clothes and tries again. This time, the wardrobe shifts as she pulls it, providing enough of a gap at the other end for her to squeeze her hands in and push it along the wall.

Immediately, her gaze alights on the small vent near the floor. Bending down, her fingers scrape at the screws, twisting and tugging at them until they clatter to the floor. The grate comes away easily and she reaches into the void, hand searching for something she doesn't yet know exists, but that will change everything.

She pushes her hand in further, the hard edges of the vent opening scratching along her skin. She rechecks the walls, her fingers dragging along the cold metal, desperate to find something.

Finally, she gives up. Slamming her hands against the wall, she sits back on her haunches.

Forget it, Anaiya. You still have the soundmatcher.

Standing up, she shoves the wardrobe back into place. It thuds into the wall and she winces at the sound. After confirming there is no noticeable damage, she picks up the first armful of clothes and opens the doors.

And then she sees it. A panel, in the bottom left-hand corner. Before, its lines had been invisible, but now they are deep – the panel dislodged by the force of the wardrobe's collision.

Heart racing, she drops the clothes and pulls the panel aside.

Books fill the space, crammed into the small void to appear as a second wall.

Anaiya's breath catches in her chest, her hands reaching for the fragile volumes before her rational brain can catch up. She pulls out one after the other, rifling through pages, searching for the familiar scrawl of Kane 148.

She soon realises that the book she wants to find will not be found here.

Most are filled with printed text and strange, archaic language; ancient stories, relics of pre-Singularity times. But a small collection of orange-bound volumes opens up to an organic script. Not the erratic forms of Kane, but hypnotic loops and swirls that run across the page and trail off the edges.

She pauses her frantic rummaging and sits back on the floor. Piling the strange books beside her, she picks up the first and opens it to the first page.

The sky over the Edges is different tonight. Sharper. Brighter. As if the stars have finally reached their breaking point and are no longer content to let the city lights steal their glory. As if they, too, are starting their own rebellion.

The words, as beautiful and damning as they are, can only be Seth's.

She imagines him sitting atop a recycler, staring up at the night, letting the darkness draw the thoughts from his subconscious ... As it does from hers.

The pages skip under her fingers, her eyes drinking in his words, her heart lurching when a familiar name or turn of phrase leaps from the paper. It all reminds her of the old Seth she once knew – the one who saw beauty in the world and in her.

Reaching the last page, she reluctantly puts the book aside and picks up the next. Unlike the gentle, poetic ramblings of its predecessor, this one opens with a manic energy. Unlike its predecessor, which was all quiet reflection, this one reads like a confession, a manifesto of ideological conflicts and an urgent need.

Tonight it begins. The rebellious fruit of a broken Otpor, overripe and left too long on the vine, bursts from its fragile skin. Hidden away in the Edges, this simple act will be seen by no one. The anonymous birth of a new world order.

She realises that she is reading the volumes out of order – that somewhere in the rest of the pile of journals is an explanation of how and why Seth changed from a romantic to a renegade.

Closing the volume in her lap, she reaches for the next on the pile and then pauses.

Tentatively she re-opens the one in her possession and flicks to a page near the centre. Gone are the languid loops and swirls, replaced by heavy, tight script. Also gone are the familiar names, the page littered with initials, abbreviations and diminutives.

R's frustration is growing. The art is not sating her need for change, it's feeding her need for revenge. She's becoming erratic, suspicious, abrasive. And the barbs of her accusations are no longer content to pierce at the Fire and the ignorant masses.

She accuses me of being blind to need and opportunity. Of being distracted. Of prematurely enjoying the new order before it has been established.

She is jealous of the butterfly, incensed that someone could have my attention at a time when all of it should be consumed by the art.

Anaiya's chest tightens, the air suddenly too thin. Closing her eyes, she forces herself to breathe.

Inhale. Hold. Exhale. Pause.

The technique that had worked for her during her realignment is less effective this time, and it takes a few minutes of shaky breathing before she feels the panic subside.

Butterfly. It was what he had called her. An intoxicating nom de doceur that still causes her to shiver. She was the butterfly and R was Rehhd.

She closes the book, hiding away the words that have sent her into fresh turmoil. This journal covers her time with Seth. Will finally tell her the truth of what he felt.

And yet, now that she has found her answers, she finds herself unwilling to read them.

What good can come of this?

The ominous thought continues to circle even as she stashes the journal away in her hoodie, replaces the others and closes the panel.

TWENTY-THREE

It had been dark when Anaiya had finally left Seth's apartment.

The soundmatcher had been hidden amongst other assorted knick-knacks in the lounge room. She will have two, maybe three days, before the Archivist discovers it is missing and works up the courage to report it to his supervisor.

Anaiya can only hope that whatever conversations the Resistance core are having now, they will continue back at the apartment.

In the meantime, she has more than enough to preoccupy herself.

Seth's journal lays unopened in her lap. Delacroix sniffs around her feet, occasionally lifting his head to stare at Anaiya, but never attempting to jump up on the bed beside her. She scratches behind his ear absently, her other hand running over the book's soft cover.

"What do you think, Delacroix? Do I want to read this?"

The dog raises his head at her voice, but quickly resumes his stalking at her feet.

"Excellent advice as usual, pup."

Her Fire brain admonishes her hesitation. *They're just words; what harm can they do?*

But her Air brain reminds her how her chest had ached at hearing Seth's words. And she knows that words are not the soft, innocuous things she once knew.

Knowing they can hurt, knowing Seth can hurt, she hesitates.

And yet, it wasn't always that way. Once his words had enchanted her. Seduced her.

Heart in her throat, she opens the journal.

I knew as soon as I saw her that she was different. There was something about her – a strange mix of confidence and vulnerability.

K told me she was one of R's strays, but she was too headstrong. She reminds me a bit of him – their hypoxia makes them both unpredictable and erratic.

It's strange that she hasn't experienced the Subjugation before. She seems surprised by it, almost confused. And yet, she responds like someone who has suffered years of the same abuse that we have. Watching her rush that Peacekeeper, I knew she was one of us.

And yet, for all that bravado, she seems so vulnerable. She scaled the recycler like a Fire Elemental but cowered in its recess like a Premie.

She's nursing an injury. And she holds it so close to her chest. Like she is caught between the wanting to engage and win, and the utter fear of what will happen if she lets go and fails.

This is what the Resistance does. What the Resistance is.

It is a mirror held up to every Elemental. Forcing them to confront the lies of the Cooperative.

Forcing them to confront themselves.

It takes her hours to read through the journal; her body suffering the uncomfortable mattress and the room that grows stuffy with the lingering heat of the afternoon, her mind captivated by Seth's words.

Finishing it leaves her conflicted. The majority of the journal is a myriad of poetic thoughts and random observations – the encroachment of the Wasteland sands, the agitation of Elementals, the deep contours on the face of a ninth lustrum Earth Elemental.

While the pretty words have captured her imagination, they offer little else. Mentions of the Resistance members, and Anaiya herself, are few. Mentions of strategies, plans or missions, non-existent.

Back in Seth's room, she had been so sure that this journal would be his rebellious manifesto. She had let the opening take her in; seeing what she wanted to find, rather than what was there. Allowed her Air emotion to cloud what her Fire judgement should have been shouting at her. What she has known all along.

Seth isn't a strategist. His rebellion is poetry, not logistics.

For as long as she has known him, Seth has always been depth of emotion and pursuit of higher concepts – truth, beauty, purity, righteousness. He would never think of his rebellion as a set of strategies and plans; his journals, with their deeper contemplation of Elemental interactions, connections and the beauty to be found in overlooked details, confirm as much.

It is a conclusion she should have come to much sooner. If she hadn't been so conflicted and distracted.

While Seth may lead the Resistance, he definitely isn't running it.

I don't think he ever has.

She thinks of Kaide, the rational and strategic counterpoint to Seth's impulsiveness and fervency. One able to see the grey in the world, the other blinded by his own ideology and able to only see in black and white.

It makes sense that Kaide was the engine behind Seth's Resistance; the mechanism that kept things ticking over. Anaiya had witnessed it during her deployment, in the way Kaide was the voice of caution, the advisor, the one mobilising the troops while Seth was inspiring them.

But the dynamic has changed. There is a tension between the old friends, a shifting in the rankings – she hears it in the way Kaide has to fight for Seth's support where Lilith easily commands it. Kaide's position as Seth's second in command has been taken by another.

That Lilith's name is also notably absent from Seth's journal means little when all identities are coded. From the overheard conversation in Seth's apartment, Anaiya is convinced she is at the epicentre of this new rebellion. And that makes everything else unknown and uncertain.

Her Fire identity doesn't like it. It renders her future-searching impossible and makes the space at her jugular tingle with an expected but unknown threat.

The shadows in her room have lengthened, but it is still three hours until curfew. She glances from her wristplate to her door and back again. Her fingers pick at the corners of a nearby linoleum tile. The poor attempt at distraction is useless. All she can think about is the wardrobe of journals, a hidden soundmatcher, and an easy climb to a sixth-floor apartment.

TWENTY-FOUR

Despite her intentions, it is three days before she gets the opportunity to return to Seth's apartment. Night after night she waits for him to leave, but he stays put and other Elementals come to him.

Kaide isn't as regular a visitor as she expects, turning up only once and leaving minutes after arriving. Unlike Eamon and Lilith, who appear consistently – sometimes together, but always with a crew of random hangers-on.

Tonight, Seth exits the building with an unfamiliar Elemental. The two walk unhurriedly, heads bent in animated conversation. And then Seth laughs. The sound rings clear in the otherwise empty street and Anaiya's heart lurches.

It seems a lifetime since she has laughed.

The heat from the afternoon leaves a trail of sweat between her shoulder blades and breasts. She aches to scratch the itch it leaves behind, but she remains still, not daring to move until Seth and the other Elemental have turned down the intersecting street and retreated from view.

It is dangerous to risk entering his apartment during the day – there are too many potential eyes to catch sight of her, it is too easy for Niamh to keep tabs on her, and there's no guarantee that Seth and his friends won't return earlier.

But she can't wait any longer. She has waited too long as it is.

The climb to his window is easier this time around, spurred by a different kind of adrenalin and anticipation. When she steps down into his room, she ignores the things that distracted her last time and walks straight to the wardrobe. The space in front of the panel is cleared. She presses against it to release the catch, her heart racing again at the sight of the journals.

She grabs at random volumes, scanning the words and phrases – looking for something that explains the shift in the Resistance. Pages ripple under agitated fingers – she needs to be quick; every minute spent inside Seth's room before curfew is too much of a risk.

Three books later, she finds it.

K thinks the butterfly is a synthfly. Pretty wings hiding a poisoned barb. He is less vocal about it than R but I feel a fracturing between us.

The temptation to keep reading, to seek out reference to Lilith, is overruled by the fine hairs raising along the nape of her neck that remind her she needs to leave before Seth gets back. Pocketing the journal in her jacket, she stacks the other books back inside the hidden compartment.

Time to go, Anaiya.

Pressing the panel back into its place, she closes the wardrobe door and stands. The bedroom window is still open, but she turns from it and strides into the lounge room.

She finds the soundmatcher where she left it. For a moment she contemplates leaving it where it is – it can gather no more data if she takes it back now – but it has been a week and this time her curiosity wins the battle. Before she can change her mind, she pushes the cube into her cargo pocket and heads back into the bedroom.

The breeze through the open window stirs the trinkets hanging from the frame. She lets her hand trail over the coloured glass, looking down over the street below for any inconvenient witnesses. The street is empty, long shadows starting to creep up walls and casting elongated shapes on the dusty bitumen.

Grateful for the easy escape, she clambers through the window and scales down the wall in a series of simple forms. As she lands, her hand instinctively goes to her hoodie pocket, where the journal is tucked away.

"Find something to your liking?"

The voice is a vice grip around her chest. Heart hammering, she slowly turns around.

Seth stands only metres away, visible now amongst the shadows.

"Do I need to report an unauthorised entry, Peacekeeper?"

Once upon a time, the question would have been playful. Flirtatious. Now, there is only threat and malice.

It stings, but not as much as it used to.

"I wouldn't advise that, dear Resistance leader."

His frown deepens, but otherwise he betrays no emotion. "What are you doing here, Anaiya?"

She pauses. There is nothing keeping her here – she could walk away and there would be nothing he could do. But, even now, walking away from Seth is not an option.

"I wanted the rest of Kane's notes."

"I don't have them."

"Kaide said it was you that found them."

"I did. But the idea to feed them back to you was all his idea. I thought he was wasting his time."

The street is so quiet. It feels like they have been standing outside for hours, even though she knows only minutes have passed. With no other distractions, she is forced to confront him. Just him.

Green eyes still glitter and hands rake through short hair in that familiar tell, giving away his uncertainty … or anxiety. If he would just smile, if she could just see those features soften …

"Why?" It is so soft, almost whispered. A question she doesn't really want answered. "Why did you think he was wasting his time?"

"Because whatever Kane 148 saw in you as a Trainee had well and truly died by the time you sent Rehhd to her Execution."

He will never forgive you, Anaiya.

The truth of it is a sucker punch. She is unprepared for just how much it hurts, for how unwilling she is to let go of her need for redemption.

Stupid, stupid, foolish. "I did it to save you."

He laughs and the sound shatters against her ribcage. "No, you didn't. That Execution was in your plan the moment you came to the Northern Area."

Anger flickers in her belly. "That Execution was going to happen the moment you started painting Heterodoxy on air recyclers."

"It shouldn't have been Rehhd."

"It was her or you."

"It wasn't your choice to make."

Memories of that night in the izakaya, as always, come easily. Her stomach still drops remembering the moment when all the pieces had fallen into place and she had realised it was Seth and not Rehhd leading the anarchy; still shudders at the fear of seeing the bound and blindfolded Peacekeeper Trainee.

"It was the only choice I had."

And there it is. For all the guilt she bears from Rehhd's Execution, there would have been no recovering from Seth's Execution.

He regards her silently, the two of them trapped at an impasse. When he finally speaks, it is not what she expects to hear. "Can I have it back?"

He holds out his hand and Anaiya just stares at it.

"Have wh—"

"Whatever it is you stole." He looks pointedly at the bulky hoodie pocket and her heart sinks.

Reluctantly, she pulls the journal from her pocket, taking care not to displace the soundmatcher. He looks surprised to see it.

"I found it under your wardrobe," she says, looking for any indication he has seen through the lie. "It has my name in it."

Palms tingling, she hands it over, giving up her last chance to really understand him, understand the evolution of his rebellion. There is a moment when her fingers graze his. She expects an unseen current to pass between them, to feel the same heady racing of electricity she had six months ago. But there is nothing.

He flicks through the pages, orienting himself to its contents, before stashing it away in his own pocket. Its Unorthodoxy will attract attention. Its Heterodoxy will have him Executed.

"Did you read it?"

She shakes her head. "Why am I in it?"

"I thought you were one of us," he says, no longer meeting her gaze, "but I was wrong."

She should leave it there; just walk away … There was no fixing things with Seth, no reset button to erase all that sits heavy between them.

"It was real for me." The words spill out before she can second-guess herself.

"What was real for you?"

"Our connection."

She expects him to laugh. She prepares herself for how it will feel – the scorn tearing at her vulnerability. She braces against it.

"It was real for me, too."

"It was?" She is genuinely surprised.

He looks back at her with sad eyes. And then she realises, for Seth, admitting the connection is easy. The more important truth is in the past tense.

"It was doomed from the beginning, wasn't it?" she asks, more as a reflection than a need for confirmation.

"Yes."

"Because I deceived you?"

He laughs, and she feels every bit of judgement and irony crammed into it. "Airs deceive each other all the time. Everything is intrigue and secrets and half-truths. It was doomed because you are a Peacekeeper. Because violent suppression is all you know."

Unexpectedly, she thinks of Kaide. Strange that he sees the conflict in her, where Seth can only see the damage.

"I guess that makes us the same, then."

He shakes his head. "No, Anaiya. Violent resistance and violent suppression are two very different beasts."

TWENTY-FIVE

Anaiya's apartment is empty when she returns. Disappointment anchors her belly; she doesn't want to be alone tonight.

Sighing, she props the door open with a stale soylent brick for when Delacroix comes back from his hunt, wishing for the small comfort of his scrawny frame pressed against her; asking no questions, offering no judgement.

Heart heavy, she crawls into the space between the bed and the wall. The harsh angles of the replica soundmatcher bite into her thigh and her fingers scrabble at her cargo pocket to pull it free.

Resting her back against the wall and stretching out her legs, she turns the cube over in her hand. It is lighter than the original and the technology is not as slick, but it works in the ways that count.

She finds the playback function and starts the audio.

Silence and static fill the recording for the first couple of hours. She skips through it, waiting for the line on the soundmatcher to spike. It comes six hours into the recording, the bright green line peaking.

She rewinds it to the point where the flatline meets the incline and taps the carbonite face.

Click. The door shutting.

"What is it?" Seth. He sounds frustrated or amused. The words come out lazily, like they're weighed down under too much lys.

"You have to scale it back, Seth." Kaide's voice is clear and urgent.

"Not again. How many times are you going to beat this dead argument?"

"Is this really the rebellion you wanted to lead?"

"You've been spending too much time with your traitor friend."

Anaiya waits for the familiar sting, but the moment passes and it never comes.

"She knows."

"She knows nothing."

"Seth, she knows."

"Why do you still trust her?" Seth's voice explodes and Anaiya's heart rate echoes in response. *"She killed Rehhd. She restrained Yve. She disabled Jiah at the cemetery and her Peacekeepers laid waste to a peaceful mourning ceremony. What does she need to do for you to see what she is?"*

"She's not the monster you think she is." Soft. Reluctant. Anaiya's heart twinges.

"She is exactly the monster I think she is."

The soundmatcher's line falters in the silence that follows.

Anaiya's imagination expands into the void; she sees Seth pacing and Kaide standing resolutely, arms folded, body still. They stand facing off. They stand next to each other. They disagree. They empathise.

"Either way," Kaide says, *"she knows. They know. Know what you've been planning, what you intend to do."*

"Since when did 'we' become 'you'?"

"Seth ..." He is pleading, placating. *"Inciting violence will only create more violence."*

"They started it." It is such a weak argument. Juvenile. Reeking of the same delusional self-righteousness she heard in his differentiation between violent resistance and violent suppression.

"Did they?"

"Yes." It is a hand slamming on a wall. *"And I will finish it."*

Anaiya can hear her heat thumping in the pause that follows.

There is so much anger, so many secrets between these two.

And then Kaide speaks. *"When did the 'we' become 'I'?"*

The silence after Kaide leaves doesn't last as long as she thinks it will. Two hours later, the soundmatcher's audio line spikes again. Anaiya plays the recording, expecting to hear the resumption of Seth and Kaide's earlier argument.

"What happened?" Not Kaide. Lilith.

"Nothing. You shouldn't be out after curfew."

"I don't care about curfew. Why did you leave the izakaya without telling anyone?"

Concern and angst and intimacy mingle in the soundwaves coming from the cube. Anaiya shifts on the hard floor and places the soundmatcher next to her.

"Kaide wanted to talk."

"We can't keep waiting for her intel. We shouldn't have waited as long as we have."

"We're not waiting." Cold. Hard.

"Good. We can't be changing things up with ten days to go. Is Kaide going to be a problem?"

There is a hesitation before Seth answers. *"No."*

"No? Because we have other options."

"Lilith ..."

"I'm just saying. If we can't completely trust Kaide or if his heart isn't in it anymore, there are other places we can source the pituarmagn."

The strange word rings familiar to Anaiya. It tickles uneasily at the edges of her memory ...

"It's not just the pituarmagn. We need the right aural stimulation and without a symbiotic, Kaide is our best option."

"Se—"

"He can do it," Seth interrupts. And then, softer, *"We can trust him."*

There is no concession from Lilith, no backwards step. Anaiya can picture her frowning, watching Seth with scrutiny. Or sighing, not agreeing with him but not wanting to anger him.

The silence stretches on. Anaiya glances at the soundmatcher on the floor beside her; the line trembles, picking up sounds her ears can't. And then a murmur, that builds to a moan.

Belatedly, she recognises the sounds for what they are – the overtures of sex.

She flushes – with embarrassment or anger – and taps to halt the audio. Forwarding through the recording, her hand hovers above the cube, second-guessing whether the soft peaks are noises she does not want to hear, or whispered intel she needs to hear.

Sex talk is commonplace for clear-minded Fire Elementals, but she is not as confident that Air Elementals can be as rationally minded.

Glancing at the soundcube, she notes the timestamp. Fifteen minutes in. Twenty. For Fire Elementals, the act would be well over by now. The audio line continues to rise in small and intermittent peaks.

Sighing, she holds down the face and doesn't let up until the recording hits 1000 hours the next morning.

"So," Lilith says, "we tell Issau, Cress and Eamon the plan to move things forward. As far as Kaide knows, everything is still on schedule for the following Seventh day."

"Lilith ..."

There is a strange power dynamic between them. As if she pushes him to the boundaries of what he can accept and pulls back just as he is about to push back.

"Just tell me you'll stick to the plan." Her words are soft and come muffled. Is she embracing him? Kissing him?

"I'll see you tonight."

"Where are we at with the shipment?" The voice is male and vaguely familiar. From her previous surveillance or the recorded interrogations?

"Not your concern," Seth says, shutting down the train of conversation.

"And the sound manipulation?"

"Not your concern." Seth sounds terse.

"We're here to discuss the recording," Lilith says, interrupting whatever tension lies behind the short exchange. *"And the broadcast."*

"How many wristplates will be recording, then?" the unaccounted male voice asks, exasperation lacing his words.

"Why, Tomas? Worried that your grand performance will go unnoticed?" Unlike everyone else in the room, Eamon manages to sound both bored and sarcastic.

"Shut up, Eamon."

"Go fuck yourself, Seth."

Anaiya cringes. Even here, in the isolation of her apartment, she feels the tension building to explosive levels.

It surprises her, but then she remembers the conflict that had attached itself to Seth like a shadow during her time with him. The same conflict that had tipped the balance and ended with a bound and gagged Peacekeeper Trainee, a night in a detention cell, and an Executed Rehhd limp on the Pillar.

"We have a team of around thirty trusted sympathisers and active agitators to record the event," Lilith says, raising her voice. *"That's not our issue."*

In the background, the barbed exchange between Eamon and Tomas quietens.

"Our issue," Lilith continues, softer, more pointed, *"is hijacking all four high-vis distribution networks."*

"I'm working on it," Tomas says. *"With all the Kane 148 propaganda across all channels, we just need to splice in whatever footage we decide on."*

"Just need to splice some footage, that's all." Eamon's voice drips with scorn. *"No need to consider the vetting process by Communication Auditors or the fact that Water Controllers will shut down transmission as soon as they see the unauthorised vision."*

"Do you have anything useful to add, Eamon?" Seth's voice is tight. Anaiya imagines him with folded arms, clenched teeth and a barely suppressed anger.

"I'm sorry," Eamon says brightly, *"I thought that was useful. I mean, isn't that what you want, Dear Leader – restraint and control and no rash decisions."*

"Shut up, Eamon."

"Fuck off, Seth."

"You do not get to lecture me on rash decisions!" Anaiya flinches at the rawness of Seth's voice. *"Your idiocy with that Trainee killed Rehhd!"*

"No," Eamon says, cold and soft, *"your idiocy with your Peacekeeper killed Rehhd."*

Anaiya's breath is caught somewhere between her chest and throat, anticipating the roar of Seth's censure or the crash of a fight erupting. The silence builds the pressure at her temples, her body tight with expectation and apprehension.

But it is not Seth's voice of hot rage that comes next, but Eamon's cold analysis.

"And Kaide's idiocy with her will kill us all."

"We need to be smarter about this."

The others have left, leaving Seth and Lilith alone again.

"Don't lecture me, Lilith."

Footsteps recede and silence sends the soundmatcher flatlining.

"Why are you so fucking cold these days?" Lilith murmurs.

Anaiya frowns. Of all the things she knows Seth to be, 'cold' is not one of them.

"What is Eamon's fucking problem?" Seth has returned to the room.

"He's spent five months in a metal box, three metres by one. Cut him some slack."

The image turns Anaiya's chest to ice. Five hours in a similar detention cell had brought her close to breaking point. What had it done to an Air Elemental already on the edge?

"I've been cutting Eamon slack for four years. It's time for him to step up or back off."

"Hey, hey, hey." Lilith's soft murmur is a stark contrast to Seth's white rage. *"Hey."* More insistent. Seductive.

"Hey," Seth says softly. Reluctantly? The fire reduced to molten metal.

Anaiya fast forwards. She doesn't need to hear the sounds of their growing intimacy.

"Why am I here, Seth?" Eamon sounds tired.

It is the final night of the recording and Anaiya is still waiting for more details about this strange, secret plan of theirs. Lilith had spent most of the day at the apartment; but the conversation, when there was any, never strayed into heavy topics. Eamon turning up an hour after she had left and close to curfew is unexpected.

"What happened between us?"

She expects Eamon to laugh or reply with scorn and sarcasm, but instead the audio goes silent. Even from her limited time with these two very different Airs, she knows their history is long and complex. This is either going to get shut down real fast or get very, very interesting.

"You shut us out. Or forgot about us."

"I didn't forget about you, Eamon."

"Then why didn't you let us in? It was bad enough that you held your secret plans back from us – the Elementals who would have followed you into the Wasteland ..." Anger is creeping into his voice. *"But to tell that, that—"*

"There were no secret plans." Seth's voice is calm and firm. Whatever emotional spike Eamon is riding, Seth is staying distant from it. *"And I never told Anaiya anything about anything."*

"Bullshit."

"Why bullshit?"

The heat between the pair is starting to grow; Seth's calm fraying at the edges, Eamon's simmering rage beginning to boil.

"You took her everywhere. She was at your apartment, the Edges, Soylent, the spoken word at the Rabid Dog—"

"I didn't take her to the Rabid Dog," Seth interrupts, *"that was your little rendezvous, remember?"*

Silence. And then Eamon laughs. *"I knew she was different."*

Seth barks his own laugh and Eamon laughs again.

"Yeah, yeah. OK. We both knew she was different." His tone is light-hearted, almost friendly. And then it turns serious. *"Sitting*

with her that night, I saw that same hunger, that same aggression with no real target ..."

"I saw it, too."

Hearing Seth talk about her without acid in his tone, in a voice that is soft and weighed down by memories, threatens to file down the hard edges of her own emotions.

"But was that the real her, or just an act? How can Peacekeepers even act? All Fire Elementals are emotionally barren with no imagination."

She waits for Seth to answer; to shut her down, to defend her, to re-establish those hard edges.

"I don't know." He says it so softly, she almost misses it. *"Let's not talk about her. She's not important anymore."*

Anaiya's fingers twitch over the soundmatcher, fighting the urge to pause the recording. She swallows against the rising emotion and continues listening.

"So, what do you want to talk about?" Eamon's voice is calmer now.

"Where do you think Kaide's head is at?" Seth says it quickly, like he doesn't want the words in his head anymore, or needs to get them out before he changes his mind.

"Messed up with the Elemental you don't want to talk about."

"No, it's not like that. Kaide interacts, he doesn't connect. She's just an asset."

"Maybe." Eamon doesn't sound convinced. *"Either way, he's too invested in her."*

"No," Seth persists, *"there's something else. There's a reason why he's reluctant to move forward on this."*

"Why are you asking me? You know Kaide and I don't get along."

Anaiya imagines him running his knuckle along his jaw, remembering the punch that Kaide had landed on it at the lockdown party.

"Because I'm worried that I'm too close, that I'm making excuses for him. You don't like him, but you don't like me either. You're not going to sweeten the truth of what you see."

"What are you asking me to do, Seth?"

"Keep your eyes open and tell me what you see."

"With Kaide?"
"With everything."

For a long time, Anaiya just stares at the soundmatcher. With each new revelation, the pins in her brain had lengthened. The new timeframe for their plan of attack; the obvious influence of Lilith; the sudden shift in Seth's approach to Eamon; and the growing separation from Kaide.

Even without the clarity of her future-searching, she knows that all of it is building towards disaster. For her. For them.

The plan for a biochemical manipulation is a good one. After a while, Anaiya had remembered why 'pituarmagn' was familiar to her: Seth had introduced her to it during her deployment. A chemical composition designed to amplify dopamine triggers, it was mildly effective on its own as just another synth cocktail; but used with specific and complex sound patterns, it was powerful enough to provoke specific emotions.

And if those sound patterns were to be generated by a symbiotic, by an Elemental with complete affinity with their competence, the strength of that manipulation would be ten times greater. *Enough to what? Generate more complex emotions? Provoke a crowd? Manipulate their actions?*

Reluctantly, she downloads the soundmatcher's content to a data drive and deletes the original recordings. Hiding the drive in the vent with Kane's pages, she shoves the soundmatcher deep into the pocket of her hoodie. Its absence from the Archives Hall will soon be noticed, if it hasn't been already. Even if she gets the opportunity to steal it away again, it is unlikely that it will be in time to stop whatever Seth is planning.

She sighs and stands, groaning as stiff muscles and joints complain at the change in position.

No journals. No soundmatcher. No time.

Kane 148's words have finally triggered the rebellion he hoped to see in her when she was a Premie, but have come too late to stop whatever mutual destruction Seth and Niamh have planned.

Maybe Kane's Execution had eliminated his Heterodoxy.

Maybe his vision was supposed to have died with him.

TWENTY-SIX

The Evidence Hall is empty when Anaiya walks in. Immediately, her eyes roam the wall of shelves opposite, searching for the box that normally houses the soundmatcher. She locates it easily enough, sitting isolated on a shelf in the far corner. Next to the wall – the one with the panel.

The panel.

The subtle grooves in the wall pull at her memory.

Risking a quick glance at the door, she rests a hand against the panel's mid-section, testing its mechanism. It doesn't yield like the one in Seth's wardrobe. She pushes against it harder, with no success.

In frustration, she slams her fist against it. The sound reverberates in the empty room, raising the spectre of another memory.

Tentatively, she taps out a simple rhythm against the panel – a rhythm that her Fire brain would have quickly forgotten, but that her Air brain has retained. The same rhythm Niamh had once tapped to open a hidden staircase that had led all the way to the Water Commissioner and her realignment testing.

Three quick knocks. Two slow and deliberate knocks.

Click.

The lock mechanism swings the panel open and Anaiya breathes a sigh of gratitude to Water lack of imagination.

Another glance at the door; she weighs up the risks of the Air Archivist or, worse, Niamh, walking in.

Heart in her throat, she pulls at the panel. The space beyond is smaller than she expects – the size of her apartment's ensuite, it houses a single cabinet of shelves sparsely filled with the usual black hard drives ... and something more familiar. More Heterodox.

Her breath seizes at the sight of the journals and her thoughts immediately turn to Seth. Fingers shaking with too much adrenalin, she grabs the nearest one, opening it to a random page.

Order in times of chaos is imperative. Order can only come from loyalty and loyalty must be cultivated to the state. And for loyalty to be cultivated to the state, it must be eradicated from other distractions. Divide to conquer. Divide to unite.

The words bring their typical twinge, but it is the script at the margin that gets her heart racing. Long, looping, heartbreakingly earnest script trailing along the pages.

Kane.

Suddenly she sees the hard drives and the time-worn pages from a different perspective. This secret compartment isn't housing new Heterodoxy; it's safekeeping old Heterodoxy.

"What do you think you are doing?"

Whirling around, Anaiya sees a familiar Archivist enter the room.

"You can't be in there," she says, frowning at the journal in Anaiya's hand and raising her wristplate.

Panic spurs Anaiya forward. If the Archivist patches a call to report her unauthorised access ...

The Water's eyes widen at the sight of Anaiya advancing so quickly. Her lips part to raise a cry, but Anaiya's left hand smothers it while her right finds that soft spot of tissue that will shut off consciousness.

Anaiya glances at the door. If the Protector outside suspects anything, Anaiya will be shackled to the Execution Pillar before the First day comes back around.

The Archivist slumps against her. Shifting against the dead weight, Anaiya positions the unconscious body at one of the tables facing away from the door.

Work quick, Anaiya. Work smart.

She strides back to the compartment. Hands shaking, she opens the camera function on her wristplate and takes as many photos of the journal pages as she can. The Archivist will regain consciousness in ten minutes, maybe less. And when she does, there must be no sign of disturbance and no sign of Anaiya.

Her eyes keep returning to the hard drives.

Smart. Smart. Play it smart.

The adrenalin brings everything into hyperfocus – the light, the angles, the stale air, the unconscious Archivist, the insane urgency of her heartbeat.

Desperate to end it all and terrified of being caught in the act, her hand reaches for two of the hard drives. Stuffing them into her hoodie, she replaces them with two identical drives from the nearest wall of shelves.

Get out. Get out.

Her hands leave a sweaty trail on the plaster as she clicks the panel back into place. She hastily rubs it away with her sleeve, her eyes flicking to the Archivist still slumped over the far table. Every second ratchets the already suffocating terror of being discovered.

Her body screams to run from the room, her mind strains with the effort of maintaining a facade of calm.

The exit door exhales a sharp hiss as she approaches, springing open to reveal the lobby beyond.

"Leaving so soon?"

The Protector leans nonchantly against the wall, his arms folded to emphasise toned biceps. Anaiya falters, unprepared for the softly spoken challenge. The Protector smiles.

Belatedly, she realises it is not the smirk of an aggressor. But the seductive grin of a paramour.

"I'll be back later," she says, attempting a sexy smile of her own, inwardly relieved that her voice doesn't tremble. "Just following a lead."

"Guess I'll be seeing you later, then."

TWENTY-SEVEN

Anaiya's legs burn with the sudden and extreme exertion.

The hard drives slam against her ribs with each jolt of foot on bitumen. Their thrashing will leave bruises; the thought a trivial distraction.

Racing up the stairs to her apartment three at a time, she ignores the chunks of soylent scattered on the floor and the muffled echoes of arguments from neighbouring units.

Her fingers still twitch with adrenalin; they slip and scrape at the screws that hold the vent guard in place.

Come on, come on!

Pain flares and blood pools where a fingernail has been wrenched out of position. She ignores it all, clawing away the grate and grasping at the sheets of paper inside, cursing as the ink stylus she stole from Seth's apartment clatters loudly to the floor. Calling out for Delacroix and getting no answer, she can wait no longer. Stuffing the papers and stylus beside the hard drives in her hoodie, she leaps through the stairwell to the ground floor and doesn't stop running until she reaches the Edges.

Finding her usual recycler is like returning home.

Home.

It is still a strange concept – one that she has only recently come to truly understand.

She wastes no time in scaling the structure, her eyes immediately darting to the crevasse where she had last deposited the glass screen. The barest glimpse of a corner peeking above the crack fills her with relief that it is still there.

Glancing at her wristplate, the emotion evaporates and panic rushes back. Too much time has passed since she left the Archives Hall. She needs to be quick.

The rough concrete grazes her palms as she grabs for the screen, tearing skin and sending flashes of pain along nerve endings, even as she falls heavily to her knees. She ignores it all, racing to start the device, frantically plugging in her lifeline.

Nausea laps at her belly, the flickering of the screen taking too long to stabilise. She taps at it, fingers begging it to hurry.

Finally, the start screen crystallises and she begins the download of the recorded images. They flicker in static as they transfer from her wristplate to the screen, deleted from one, reborn in the other.

Only when the last image is erased from her wristplate does she eject her lifeline and sit back on the recycler roof. Her heart still thunders in its cage, but slower now, more deliberate. She pulls the hard drives from her jacket and curses – without a connection cable they are useless.

Her wristplate beeps – a rapid succession of three shrill tones. The sound stills everything.

Slowly, she puts the hard drives back in her hoodie. With trembling fingers, she taps on the wristplate – the notification flashing almost instantaneous in large, bold letters.

CODE 547B VIOLATION. WARRANT ISSUED. REPORT TO NEAREST PEACEKEEPER IMMEDIATELY.

The offence is ambiguous – designed to capture a range of crimes that don't fit neatly into one of the usual classifications.

How would you classify a Peacekeeper subduing an Archivist with no violence? Or accessing classified material that should have been destroyed a decade ago?

That a warrant has been issued so quickly hints at Niamh's hand. He is tugging on her leash. She is a liability – one that he will not hesitate to eliminate if it poses too much of a risk and not enough benefit.

She taps the wristplate in an effort to clear it, but it is useless. The warrant notice has effectively quarantined the device, cutting her off from data, calls and functions, and preserving it all as evidence for her impending trial.

The thought of a trial sucks the breath from her. A new kind of fear wells within her and nests deep in her mind.

All of her life, she had known Orthodoxy as righteous and Peacekeepers as infallible. But she's seen too much now – the scars, the violence, the Executions, the unregulated hubris.

And that is an Orthodoxy she will not die for.

TWENTY-EIGHT

Music from lockdown parties filters into the empty apartment. Anaiya stands to shut the window, accepting the stuffy heat as payment for the small buffer the glass provides. The muted sound of the Ravignan Strip still stirs up mixed emotions in her, but it is a small sacrifice to endure it. The abandoned space offers her a place to hide – somewhere she will not be noticed, where no one will be looking for her.

It looks different from how it had appeared all those afternoons ago, back when she had been looking for the lifeline serial numbers of Resistance members and all that she had to hide from was the stifling heat of the afternoon sun.

Sitting back down on the threadbare carpet, she balances the screen in her lap and tries to centre her thoughts. But her focus is distracted. She glances from her wristplate to the door and back again – expecting another notification, wishing for the sight of Delacroix bounding towards her.

Thoughts of Delacroix hit like a sneaky assault – striking where she is vulnerable and when she is least expecting it.

I'm sorry, pup.

She hadn't meant to abandon him. But she can't return to her apartment, or any of her old haunts. Not now, not ever.

Sighing, she pushes down the synthflies in her belly and taps on the screen.

There is, and always has been, an incurable chasm between humanity's two greatest desires: freedom and safety.

There is a vulnerability in us – a weakness that sees us yearn to always be children, to cling to our parents, to surrender the hard decisions and shattering consequences to a nurturing other.

We seek this security even while we rebel against the rules our protectors impose. The inner rebellion in us is a pure fire, but one with no direction. With no authenticity – because we don't really want it.

We want to act like we want it – to flex a poorly articulated muscle – but if we were forced to actually use it ... we would run crying back to the same protectors we rail against.

Once, our world was beholden to the golden principle of democracy. For a while it was celebrated as our greatest achievement. And then the heart of the people hardened against it. They said it was flawed, they declared it was dead. And it was dead – but not because it was flawed, but because it was too good for them. You cannot blame a tree for dying if you do not water it.

There had been a purity to the Fire once. Maybe there still is. Maybe it is just harder to find.

I see it in Anaiyasha. She has the Fire ambition, but not the singularity of vision. She is easily distracted – drawn to the creative over the functional, choosing the interesting free-run over the most efficient. But her conditioning is too strong – she refuses to see the corruption of her identity, the faults in her Element.

Still, she gives me hope. The inherent defects of the Element will not remain hidden forever. A new world order will be established.

This world is blind to the truth. But not because its vision is impaired, but rather that its vision is saturated with the unimportant and inconsequential. The alcohol, the enhancers, the high-vis stories, the false utopia. There is no awareness of the rot, no desire to change.

My words bring no enlightenment, my action no consequence. I fear they will make an example of me – take away my voice and my rebellion before its ripples are felt. Before the Element can be destroyed and reshaped.

It was the last entry. His last words.

Only when the pangs of hunger emerge as a distraction does Anaiya shake out of her daze. Days have passed since she first started reading the digital pages, hours since she read the last one.

Kane's words were elegant and poignant, but that was not the reason the Cooperative had secreted them away in the Evidence Hall. Heterodoxy filled every paragraph – forbidden words, romanticised notions of the past, deadly ideologies.

His words had achieved in death, what they could not in life – a gravitas. A sense of urgency.

And yet, the words were not for everyone. Too poetic for Water, too vague for Fire, too esoteric for Earth.

She understands now why Seth and Kaide were so drawn to his Heterodoxy. Why she can now understand it, when she had been deaf to it as a Trainee. Why it now finds an echo in her fractured identity and calls her to action.

Kane's ideology was always destined to be handed down to Air Elementals … *as if it were written for them.* And yet, the truth of that revelation sits uneasily. There is something odd about it …

Her fingers tremble again, the hunger insistent. With her wristplate disabled, she has no access to her account funds and no way of purchasing her regular quick dose of essential nutrients. The thought of stale soylent bricks back at her apartment is as nauseating as it is tempting.

She puts aside the glass screen and stands, the sudden rush of pain sending her stumbling. She steadies herself and waits for the pins in her brain to subside.

The need for nutrition threatens to undo her, but with her arrest warrant disabling her lifeline, there is only one place where she can safely satisfy it. And it is not her apartment.

TWENTY-NINE

Seeing Seth's apartment again affects Anaiya in an unexpected way. The usual rush of adrenalin is lost under the weight of her nutrient deficiency, but the trepidation at seeing Seth is also gone; even if she was right, and their connection had been real, she sees it now for what it is – well and truly severed.

No connection can survive an Execution.

She exhales, the effort sending sharp pins to the hunger headache that is already blooming in her skull. Squinting against the midday light, she curses the harsh brightness and hectic streetscape that do nothing to soothe frayed nerves.

The movement around her makes her shoulder blades itch. She scans the windows of Seth's apartment, looking for signs of occupancy, but her eyes flicker constantly back down to the activity on the street. The lovers walking hand in hand. The loners lost in their own thoughts. The laughter. The chatter. The innocence and ignorance and apathy.

She hates it as much as she yearns for it.

"You fucking bitch!" Eamon's wail pierces her daydreaming and sets a new edge to the pain crushing her skull. She swivels in its direction, immediately confronted with the sight of him in full flight headed straight towards her.

Behind him, Seth and Lilith have come to a standstill, staring at the unfolding situation in shock or interest or confusion.

Blink. The pain in her head is crushing.

Eamon is closer now, the threat of conflict inevitable. Kaide stands next to Seth, indecision clouding his face, even as his posture radiates confidence. And Cress. The effervescent pixie from her deployment days stands resolute next to Kaide, her usual smile a ghost on her face.

Blink.

Eamon is still advancing. Ten metres. Nine metres.

A movement to her left brings the dark kevlar of a Peacekeeper uniform into focus.

Fuck. This won't end well.

A generation older than Anaiya, the Peacekeeper doesn't have the rash enthusiasm of a Trainee, but still enough energy and confidence to inject himself into an interesting situation. He saunters towards them, the impending altercation enough to grab his attention, but not yet violent enough to put speed to his feet.

Anaiya's collision with Eamon hits like a sucker punch. She lets the pain sting before pulling him into a clumsy arm lock, sending them both stumbling away from the Peacekeeper and closer to Kaide. She feels Eamon reach up with his free arm and twists to avoid it, but she is too slow, her mind addled and her body flagging.

His fist hits her shoulder with enough force to loosen her grip, but not enough to send her stumbling. She retaliates with a hastily formed short punch of her own. Her knuckles sing with heat as they crack across his cheek. He stumbles, giving her time to survey the changing landscape around them.

Cress looks stricken, Lilith enraged. Seth is an immovable statue – so much like the unemotional Fire Elementals of her past than the passionate Air she once knew and desired. Kaide stands rigid, his face drawn in quiet panic and tortured indecision.

Blink.

Eamon has recovered and the Peacekeeper has broken into a jog.

There is no more time.

Desperately, she stumbles closer to Kaide, twisting her body in preparation for Eamon's next assault. He flinches at the forced proximity but doesn't step back. She stares at him, forcing him to meet her gaze, begging him to hear her silent communication.

Her hand flashes at her side, fingers stinging as the nerve endings resist the rough forms she shapes them into.

Meet at Edges. Danger. Danger. Need to Talk. Meet at Edges. Danger. Danger. Danger.

His eyes flit from her pointed gaze to her hands and back again, but he does not respond. Eamon is almost upon her, the Peacekeeper only steps behind.

Meet at Edges. Danger. Help. Danger. Da—

The force of Eamon's attack sends her sprawling to the ground, the rough bitumen tearing up her hands and ceasing all communication. He hasn't slowed, advancing on her quickly. He pulls his right leg back, positioning for an unforgiving kick to her exposed ribs.

She doesn't wait for it to connect, scrambling back and rolling out of its way.

Fresh pain alights on her hands and through her core. She grits her teeth and forces herself up to a crouch.

Eamon reacts quickly, shifting his trajectory and snarling as he launches himself at her. In his rage, it will be easy for him to see Anaiya's bent posture as a sign of weakness and submission. He comes at her too quickly, his body clearly communicating the violence he plans to unleash.

At the last possible second, she springs up, her knees screaming at the sudden exertion, the nutrient deficiency filling her joints with lactic acid. Her throat runs dry as it gives voice to the pain, her arm thrusting up, her palm finding its target in the underside of Eamon's chin.

His head ricochets back, presenting Anaiya with a perfectly sighted jugular. A well-weighted punch could silence his rage forever.

Instead, she throws out her leg, hooking it around his and sending him to the mercy of gravity.

His head bounces heavily off the stones and her breath catches. Nightmare visions of blood rivers between dirty cobblestones flash in her memory.

Blink.

Lilith is shouting, the sight of Eamon immobile on the street enough to push her into action. She rushes forward, her focus entirely on Anaiya. Seth reaches out to grab her, his hand glancing off her shoulder and sending her stumbling.

Blink.

The Peacekeeper crashes into Lilith. He is better prepared for the impact, rolling into a somersault to avoid more serious damage, even as Lilith crumples to the ground.

Around them, the street erupts. The lovers, the loners, the mismatch of onlookers now turned invested participants. They rush the Peacekeeper, swarm to Eamon and Lilith's aid.

Anaiya can't wait any longer. She pushes her shaking limbs to move. Frantically casting her gaze around, she finds the gap she needs and stumbles towards it. Breaking beyond the crowd's periphery, she looks over her shoulder to the scene unfolding.

All attention is directed to the centre of the melee, to the two incapacitated Air Elementals and the besieged Peacekeeper. From here, she can see Kaide pulling Seth to the safety of the shadows, even as he pulls violently from his friend's grasp. Cress is nowhere to be found; most likely at Lilith's side tending wounds or corralling other Elementals into disabling the Peacekeeper.

The crowd swells and shifts, obscuring her view for a second. And then it clears.

Kaide looks over at her, their eyes locking together. She feels it, the clicking into place, the slowing down of time, the palpable sense that something big hinges on this moment.

The moment stretches, pulling everything else out of focus, shortening the distance between them.

Blink.

Reality comes rushing back; the noise, the chaos, the crowd. She looks back to Kaide, but he is gone, swallowed up by the insanity, hidden in the darkness.

The tingling along her nerves is worse now. The heightened activity will only attract more Peacekeepers.

She needs to move.

THIRTY

The cold of the recycler's concrete does nothing to silence the spasms that race along Anaiya's body. She had initially tried to scale the industrial behemoth but had only made it to the two-metre mark before her damaged hands had given way.

For hours she drifts in and out of consciousness, the pure black of oblivion merging with the murky darkness of the coming evening.

Strange dreams float past to haunt her – visions of Delacroix bringing her soylent crumbs, his patchy fur scratching at her cheek; of stars falling from the sky in trails of fire; of the Border Wall shattering like glass and the fragments showering her like petals from extinct flowers; of strong arms lifting her up, cradling her, comforting her.

"Anaiya! Anaiya!"

Her name sounds distant and distorted. She wants to giggle. She imagines the laughter bubbling up her throat and tickling her lips. But no sound emerges; she lost the ability to move days ago. *Or hours?* Time has no meaning in her warped, dreamlike, deathlike state.

A pinch at her elbow radiates a strange warmth through her arm.

"Come on, Anaiya."

The words are clearer this time. And the cold against her back feels sharper.

Synthfly stingers prick at her feet and fingers. She shifts against the pain, moaning as fresh torture erupts in her core.

"Easy, Anaiya." Strong arms press her back against the recycler, stopping her from thrashing. "How long has it been since your last nutrient intake?"

Her eyes flutter open. Kaide kneels in front of her.

"You came." Her voice rasps like gravel underfoot.

"Yeah," he says, releasing his grip on her shoulder and sitting back on his haunches, "I came."

The pain is subsiding now. She shifts into a more stable position and hugs her knees to her chest.

"Why the fasting, Anaiya?"

Anxiety blooms in her heart. She knew this moment was coming the second her hands flashed their shared code back in Precinct 18. For such a long time she had never had to rely on anyone. And the scars of recent betrayals are still fresh enough to remind her that trusting others is a dangerous move.

She stares back at Kaide. Once, she had seen him as a stone in her boot – an obstacle to overcome, a distraction to avoid. Now, he is her only chance at survival.

"Not fasting. Hiding." She holds out her arm, wristplate up. His grip is warm, and softer. It lingers on her skin as he looks from the warrant alert, to her pathetic form, and back again.

"What happened?" He lets go of her arm and settles down against the gravel. She rubs her wrist, trying to recreate the warmth of his fingers.

She stalls. Still not ready to break down the final barrier and become completely vulnerable. "How did you know I was nutrient deficient?"

He stares at her, the subtle clench of his jaw betraying his frustration. Or indecision. Finally, he sighs and shifts to sit beside her against the recycler. Warmth radiates from him and she struggles to stop from leaning into it.

"I knew as soon as I saw you; you were disoriented and clumsy, but not wild-eyed or frantic."

"Yes, but *how* did you know?"

He sighs but doesn't answer; letting the silence stretch and hold. She doesn't begrudge him it – they have been enemies for too long to trust each other with their secrets.

Closing her eyes, she rests her head on her knees. Tiredness rolls through her, like a numb kind of exhaustion that leaves her body restored but her mind dark.

"It wasn't the first time I'd seen it." Kaide's voice comes softly, betraying his reluctance to speak. "Or the second time, or the third."

Anaiya lifts her head to look at him. He stares right back, gritting his teeth against the words that come next. "An old girlfriend … she had a penchant for bad dex. I'd find her passed out on her apartment floor with her eyes rolled back and faded at the edges. Like the colour was literally draining from them …

"She died a few years ago." His voice cracks. He is so still. Her fingers twitch to reach out and touch him, but she buries them in the sand and gravel that litters the space between them.

He sighs again, a long exhale that carries an age of emotions. "I think about her every day. And I still carry a nutrient booster."

He turns his head to look at her, dark eyes glittering in the muted light of nearby substations. "Old habits die hard."

Anaiya forces herself to maintain his gaze.

"What was her name?"

He shakes his head. "Why the warrant?"

"What was her name?" She is shivering now, the cold of the concrete like a stain in her flesh, but she doesn't look away.

"It doesn't matter," he says, breaking the eye contact.

"It does. It matters." Her voice fights against her dry throat, the words like glass shards along tortured skin.

He turns back to her, his vulnerability replaced with anger. "I will never understand what Seth saw in you."

"Neither will I."

"You are too stubborn and self-righteous to be an Air."

"I am too stubborn and self-righteous not to be."

They stare at each other, the reality of this strange, uncomfortable alliance sinking in.

"Terani." He says her name like he is whispering a prayer. "Her name was Terani."

Terani. The name acts like a key. Again, she feels it – the clicking into place, the shifting of fate. Kaide's interrogation file echoes in her memory …

Seth and I were close for a long time. A female he was connecting with brought us together. Terani. And then a female he connected with broke us apart.

His shared truth is enough for her to risk confiding in him.

"I restrained a Water Elemental," she says.

He frowns. "And? That's not a shocking revelation, An—"

"Because she found me accessing classified materials on Kane. Not classified, hidden. I found hidden information on Kane."

The words trip over each other, stumbling as her recovering body struggles to keep up with her mind. She tells him of the secret room, the panel accessed by a sound recognition not unlike the one that guards his own studio, and the pages of Heterodox text.

"He saw the corruption of the Fire Element. He knew it had to be destroyed." Her head thunders with the pressure of saying the words aloud.

Kaide regards her silently, shoulders hunched forward. "That is what we have always said," he murmurs. "That is the truth the Resistance is trying to set free. We've always known that the true Heterodoxy is the abuse of power by Peacekeepers."

"No!" she says, the vehemence rocking in her skull. "Not the abuse of power. The *creation* of that power. The Fire Element does not break the Orthodoxy – their structures and conditioning, it is all wrong. All set up for them to be placed in conflict with the other Elements. We don't need to bring Peacekeepers into Orthodoxy. We have to remove them from the Orthodoxy."

"Why are you telling me this?"

"Because your Resistance won't change that."

He frowns and shakes his head.

"It's true," she persists. "I—"

"No," he says, waving her away, "not that. That … That is another conversation. I need to know why you are telling *me*."

"Because you know what it's like to betray and be betrayed. Because I can't fulfil Kane's vision on my own."

As soon as the words are released, she feels her heart pause.

She waits for his incredulous stare, the scorn in his laugh, his final and ultimate rejection.

Her chest is so tight. Too tight. She needs to breathe, but her desperation is like a dead weight against her ribcage.

"I can't do that, Anaiya." He says it so quietly, and yet she still hears the sharp edges.

"Please," she begs, biting against the pathetic syllable, blood tainting her tongue.

"I can't. I won't betray him again."

The rage that flares in her belly is as welcome as it is unexpected. "Then why did you come? Why are you here?"

"I don't know."

"Bullshit. You see the senseless violence, the aimless aggression. You know that Seth's plan will not succeed. Yes, we need a rebellion. But you're wrong if you think antagonising Peacekeepers is the way to achieve that."

He flinches at the anger in her tone, but she knows none of it is getting through to him. None of it will shake his damned stubborn resolve.

"And you're wrong if you think you can protect Seth, or save him, or whatever it is you think you're doing. He's not a victim. And he's not the shining white hope of a better future. This rebellion needs to be emotionally charged and logically designed. But Seth is all emotion. You think you can stop the madness, the thrill of the aggression, before it infects him. But you're too late. He's already there and he's left you behind."

"You don't know—"

"I know everything!" The fury escapes before she can stop it, her voice echoing too loudly. Taking a shaking breath, she checks her emotions and modulates her voice. "I know whatever vision Seth once had of peaceful resistance is dead. And his new plan doesn't include you. How long has it been since you were part of the discussion? Since Seth trusted you with whatever it is that is going on inside his head? He doesn't need you for the pituarmagn and he doesn't need you for the sound manipulation. Everything is moving ahead without you."

Finally, she gets a reaction from him. He frowns at her, brown eyes unblinking. And when he talks, his words are slow and clear and deliberate. "How do you know about that?"

"Did Seth tell you I broke into his apartment?"

"He said you stole one of his journals."

"I did. But I also took the soundmatcher that had been recording everything for the previous three days."

Kaide leans in, his face centimetres away from hers, his gaze boring into hers. Testing her. Searching for the lie.

She doesn't shy away from his scrutiny. Even when the silence becomes uncomfortable.

Eventually, he breaks the eye contact and leans back against the recycler. "How can I trust you?"

"How can you trust them? Seth has Eamon following you. Lilith is agitating to keep you on the outer." It is too harsh a truth, she can't afford to alienate him now. Sighing, she softens her tone. "You don't have to trust me, Kaide. You have all the leverage at this point – you know there's a warrant out on me. You could leave me and I would die out here. You could turn me in, and they would kill me."

"So, what do you want, Anaiya?"

She doesn't know anymore. Before, when her mind was wrapped up in the haze of nutrient deficiency, she thought Kaide would understand. That they could stop the madness together. Fulfil Kane's legacy without creating their own of more violence and destruction.

"A trade. I just want to trade. Your soundmatcher for mine."

"Why do you need a soundmatcher when you've already got your own?"

"Why do you care? I'll give you my soundmatcher with all of Seth's plotting. You give me yours, wiped of data and no loss of functionality."

The temperature around them has dropped, the cold of the recycler no longer comforting. Still, he remains silent. Not looking at her, not looking away.

Finally, he stands. Gravel crunches underfoot and the cold rushes in to fill the void he leaves behind. She lets her head fall back to her knees, wrapping her arms tight around it. She won't survive this rejection. At best she has a couple of days before the hunger kills her or forces her to face the Executioner.

Her arms block out the sounds and the cold, so when Kaide says something it comes muffled as if through water. Reluctantly, she looks up at him.

He looks at her, head tilted to the side, arms crossed defensively across his chest.

"OK."

Relief washes over her. She stands quickly before he can change his mind, her legs wobbling and setting her off-balance. Her stumble puts her too close to him, but he doesn't back away.

Taking a deep breath, she forces herself to meet his gaze. His frown still draws creases across his forehead, but his eyes are softer than she expected. He looks angry and frustrated and sad. And lost. Like a man who is being worn down by the good fight.

She reaches into her hoodie pocket with one hand and for Kaide's wrist with the other. His frown deepens, but he doesn't shake her off.

Slowly, she prises his fist open and turns his hand so that the palm faces up. Her fingers tremble almost imperceptibly – from the cold, the chemicals still coursing in her veins, and the unexpected feeling of intimacy.

Without breaking contact, she pulls her other hand from her pocket. The stylus that she stole from Seth's apartment feels cool in comparison. She trails it across Kaide's palm, her eyes flicking from his face to the crude script the ink marks on his skin. The lines are clumsy and angular, but the name of the izakaya that sits across the road from her apartment hideaway is clear.

"There's a laneway," she says. "The izakaya supply door backs onto it. Meet me there tomorrow night an hour after curfew. I'll give you your soundmatcher, you give me mine."

He nods slowly and breaks eye contact. She exhales slowly, a vice lifted from her heart.

"And then we are done," he says softly.

Anaiya doesn't respond. His words aren't for her benefit.

He looks up at her one last time, eyes searching for some sort of promise or reassurance. Neither of which she can offer. He sighs and turns away from her, leaving her alone in the Edges.

Again.

THIRTY-ONE

Anaiya's palm tingles; she is clutching the soundmatcher too tightly. But, instead of relieving the tension, she digs the hard edges in further.

Her heart threatens to skittle her resolve and it is only the pain at her hand that stops her mind from entertaining the worst-case scenario – where Kaide doesn't show up and all of her chances for escaping the Executioner evaporate under the hot Otpor sun.

The lane next to the izakaya is narrow and smells of stale alcohol and dust. Pressed up against the brick wall, she can feel the dense beats of the music playing on the other side. If not for the rush of tension disabling her thoughts, she would be reminiscing about times she had spent on that other side; indulging in a hedonistic ignorance flush with alcohol and enhancers.

But, as it is, she finds herself in the dark and cold, staring at a service door that she is now convinced will not open.

Despite curfew, the street beyond is alive with the sounds of nearby izakaya and house parties. The noise will attract Peacekeeper patrols and the Air-dominant precinct will attract the more aggressive of them.

She pulls the hood of her jacket tighter around her face. The dark kevlar provides some camouflage, but foreboding itches between her shoulder blades, begging her to turn around and look for inevitable threats.

When the service door creaks open, Anaiya freezes; caught between fear and relief. Only when Kaide, and Kaide only, emerges does she relax.

"What?" he whispers, looking around her and out to the street.

"Nothing," she whispers back, shaking her head. He has already seen her too vulnerable. "It's nothing. Do you have it?"

He produces his own soundmatcher. "Where's yours?"

Anaiya slowly relaxes her grasp on the cube, its recordings restored from the data drive, and pulls it from her pocket. Kaide reaches to take it from her, but she closes her fingers over it before he can. His hand grazes hers and stops.

"Yours first," she whispers.

His hand hasn't moved from hers. "No way," he murmurs, his gaze shooting from her to the street and back again. She isn't the only one taking a risk by meeting him here after curfew. "How do I know yours has what you say it has."

She sighs in frustration. He is right, but handing over her soundmatcher first is problematic. He can take it and leave without making the trade, leaving her with no leverage and no option for survival. Or he can stand in this shadowed laneway listening to its contents, which will only increase the chances of them being discovered.

"Fine," she whispers, opening her hand and releasing the cube. "But hurry up about it."

Anaiya paces on the spot as he plugs his lifeline into the soundmatcher. With her eyes grown accustomed to the dark, she is able to see how his features shift with each passing second. Though the sound doesn't carry, she can still hear Seth's words ... hear him turn his back on his old friend.

When Kaide finally pulls away his earphones, his frown is replaced by something sadder. For a moment she forgets about the threat of nearby Peacekeepers.

"Are you OK?"

He looks up at her and offers a lopsided smile, one that never reaches his eyes.

"That's the thing about betrayal," he murmurs, handing over

the other soundmatcher, "it is never at the hands of your enemies."

THIRTY-TWO

There is a morbid sense of satisfaction that Anaiya revels in as she strides towards the Eastern Area Peacekeeper Headquarters. Most of the nearby Peacekeepers ignore her, oblivious to her status as a wanted Elemental, but one finds her amongst the crowd and immediately reacts.

She slows and holds her hands up in submission, but Jenna doesn't slow her advance. The unexpected activity attracts new attention, but no one interferes. This takedown will be Jenna's alone.

Anaiya raises her hands higher. "I'm here to surrender," she yells.

It makes no difference; the impact of Jenna's tackle sends her crashing to the ground. She lands awkwardly, pain ricocheting through her body and denying her any satisfaction from the grunt that comes as her knee connects with Jenna's hip.

She looks up, expecting to see rage in Jenna's face. But the Peacekeeper looks down at her with apathy. At just another offender with a warrant restrained. No mercy. No recognition of the time they have spent patrolling and drinking at izakaya.

The needle pricks at Anaiya's neck and, just before the world turns black, Jenna whispers to her, "Niamh wants to see you."

"What happened?"

Niamh sits rigid behind his desk. The tension in his shoulders belies the calm, clipped tone of his voice.

The sound ricochets in her skull, her brain ringing in pain. It has been thirty minutes since the restraint serum wore off and her body is still suffering.

"Jenna smashed my head against the pavement stones."

Niamh's eyes narrow at her tone. "What happened at the Evidence Hall?"

Anaiya frowns, feigning ignorance. It is a poor option, but her only one. "I don't know what you mean."

"What *happened* at the Evidence Hall?" He is in no mood to entertain her ignorance, feigned or real.

"Nothing happened at the Evidence Hall. That's kind of its thing."

His hand slaps down hard and fast on the desk. Her heart leaps to her throat.

"Stop with the bullshit, Ani. What. Happened. At. The. Evidence Hall."

Her stomach clenches and she wonders if she has the ability to follow this foolish plan through to the end.

"I. Don't. Know. What. You're. Talking. About."

Her attempt at sarcasm falls flat; Niamh's eyes glitter with the very real threat of violence. *Nothing comes between Niamh and his ambition.* She tenses her posture, shifting her feet and balance to anticipate any sudden movements. Even when Niamh's shoulders relax, her body remains taut.

"The Archivist alleges you restrained her." His voice is like liquid silicon; the raw emotion that erupted only moments ago, completely faded.

She laughs, letting it ring out long and clear, before sobering. "You can't be serious. With what? You took away my uniform and syringes weeks ago."

"With your hands."

"You really believe that?"

"Tell me what happened the last time you were at the Hall."

Anaiya sighs, attempting exasperation while giving herself time to calm her nerves and collect the backstory she has so carefully constructed.

"I arrived around 1100 hours. One of the female Archivists was there. I didn't pay her much attention. I went over to the shelves, looking for the hard drive that I had been reviewing the last time. It wasn't there. I asked the Archivist if she knew where it was, but she ignored me. Head bent over the desk screen."

Niamh hasn't reacted. He sits still, his face inscrutable. Anaiya's voice threatens to waver but she holds it in check and continues the fake narrative.

"I figured another Technician had checked it out for some reason or another, so I left."

"You left?"

"You would have stayed?"

Again, he ignores her attempt to dissemble. "That was days ago. Why didn't you respond to the warrant notice?"

"I saw the bullshit charge and figured it was your way of getting me to the Execution Pillar."

He pauses at that. It isn't true, of course – she had stayed away because she was guilty. But his silence makes her wonder whether she has inadvertently stumbled on the truth. Had her latest indiscretion spent what little mercy Niamh had left?

"Why would she lie, Anaiya?" His voice is so soft, but it is not the change in tone that unnerves her. Niamh only calls her by her full name when he wants to put distance between them. Or when he sees her as his weapon to manipulate.

"Why would I restrain her?"

He grimaces and shakes his head. Either he knows and can't say, or he doesn't know and is pissed about it. She suspects the latter – nothing frustrates her old patrol partner more than being kept from things he thinks he is entitled to.

"So why now?" The frustration has crept back into his voice. "Why turn up now? Why here?"

When she had been rehearsing her backstory, this had been the hardest answer to craft. There is no good reason to have waited this long. So, she tells the truth ... of a kind. Just like Kaide had done in his own interrogation.

"I needed something to bargain with." She reveals the

soundmatcher. "So I brought you this."

Niamh's eyes flick greedily to the black cube on her palm. She places it on his desk, close enough to the edge that he has to reach over to get it. She smiles inwardly; small victories are better than none.

"How did you get it?" He is no longer looking at her; completely captivated by the soundmatcher.

She ignores the question. Niamh turns the cube over in his fingers, inspecting it from all angles.

"How did you get it?" he repeats.

"I'm not going to tell you that."

His head whips up and he frowns. "Anaiya, how did you get it?"

She shakes her head. "No. I'm not going to tell you that."

Briefly, his frown deepens. One second his face is a portrait of contained rage, the next devoid of all emotion. Cold, hard, unresponsive.

"Why are you not going to tell me that?"

"Why would I?" she asks softly. "I tell you, I become disposable."

Her heart is quickening. Faustian bargains have always ended catastrophically for her. Everything rests on how well she has read Niamh; how accurately she has judged his ambition.

"There are other ways to become disposable, Ani."

She doesn't take his threat lightly; she is no longer blind to the disregard Peacekeepers have for life or limb. But she will not show any weakness to him. Surviving this negotiation depends on convincing Niamh she is just as strong as he is.

"I'll need to check it out," Niamh says.

Anaiya shrugs and leans back in her chair. A Water Technician is called into the office. Niamh hands over the soundmatcher. "I need this validated."

The Technician merely nods and exits the room. Not for the first time, she wonders about the strange partnerships between Water and other Elementals; with Niamh, with Kaide.

"I didn't realise your arrangement with Water was a permanent one."

"There's a lot you don't realise, Anaiya."

It is meant to shut her down, but she sees an unexpected opportunity. "Like your ambush plans for Airs in the Northern Area?"

His smirk tells her she is way off base. She tries a different tack.

"Or have your surveillance efforts finally produced a result?"

The smirk turns from sarcastic to smug.

Getting warmer, Anaiya.

Her interrogation is cut short by the return of the Technician. He ignores Anaiya as he strides over to Niamh and deposits the soundmatcher on the desk.

"It's legitimate."

Niamh nods and dismisses the Technician with a flick of his wrist. Imperious to the end. Only after the door closes does he return his attention to Anaiya.

"It seems you have found your reprieve, Anaiya."

THIRTY-THREE

Anaiya rubs at her wristplate in nervous irritation.

In the end, Niamh had let her go. What else could he do? But in letting her go, he had not made her free.

"You'll never be a Peacekeeper again." Niamh's words are not unexpected, but they still sting. "But you won't end up on the Execution Pillar. Not for this."

The Water Technician fiddles with her wristplate, the metal cuff twisting on her wrist and sending jolts of pain up her arm as the fine needles that channel below her skin are pulled with it.

She doesn't make a sound or pull away; just stares at Niamh, silently wishing all kinds of evil things to befall him.

Another tug at her wrist, another jolt of pain, and she turns her glare to the Technician. He keeps his head down, unravelling the lifeline from his own wristplate and plugging it into hers.

The glass panel lights up with an unfamiliar diagnostic screen. The Technician swipes and taps away, flicking between screens. Most of them contain lines of indecipherable code, but the final screen is a list of four coordinates. She squints to see them around the flashing of the Technician's hands, but the screen disappears only to be replaced by new lines of code.

The Technician finally ejects his lifeline. The pain in Anaiya's wrist subsides, but still she rubs at it – hating the violation of her wristplate being accessed more than the remaining twinges.

But the real insult is yet to come.

When the Technician's hands reach for her lifeline, her instincts kick in and she immediately moves into the standard disabling move. Rotating her arm, she turns her hand towards herself, brings it up and the Technician's with it.

It all happens in the space of a few seconds. She sees his eyes widen, his lips part. The fear and surprise is clear on his face, but strangely she takes no satisfaction from it.

That realisation gives her pause. She drops his hand and takes a step back.

"Anaiya." Niamh's voice grates along her already frayed nerves. "Submit or be Restrained."

She can't help herself; she turns her glare, full of hatred and promised retribution, on Niamh. It matters nought to him – he blinks it away like any career Peacekeeper would a Trainee's bravado.

Gritting her teeth, she steps back towards the Technician and holds her wrist out. She closes her eyes as he unravels the lifeline, hating every scrape of metal links against her wristplate. Only when the line pulls tight does she open her eyes.

The Technician stands in front of her. Her lifeline taut between her wrist and his ear. Rage and humiliation surge through her core and she fights with every instinct to not rip it back and run.

Her stomach churns, bile rising. She bites down on her tongue, and looks away, even as every fibre of her body screams to do something to escape this nightmare. Anything.

Finally, he ejects her lifeline. She yanks it from his grasp and wipes at it furiously with the sleeve of her shirt, taking no comfort as the metal links shimmer as the line coils back around her wristcuff.

So overwrought, she almost doesn't hear the final exchange between Niamh and the Technician.

"… functioning as expected." The Technician's lack of emotion elevates Niamh's subtle smile to a grin.

"Keep me updated."

The Technician nods and takes his leave.

Anaiya's rage radiates from her like a corporeal demon and fills the space between them, threatening to ignite with the slightest provocation.

And in that moment, she doesn't wonder whether the emotion is the Fire's flame of untempered aggression, or the Air's explosion of irrational passion.

In that moment, it is just her.

Her very personal, all-consuming, mind-shattering rage.

And its target.

"You're dismissed, Anaiya."

Thoughts of launching at Niamh flash in a red static, pulsing with the blood in her ears and hitching like the breath in her chest. But she will not give him the satisfaction. Will not waste her newly found reprieve for a shallow and short-lived victory.

She turns her back on him, happy to be rid of him even as the thought of him sets off another wave of torment. She will get her vengeance, but not today and not by cracking Niamh's head against his glass-topped desk.

The soft slap of her boots against the tiled floor is broken only as she reaches the exit. Niamh speaks up, almost as an afterthought. "Don't do anything stupid, Anaiya. I'll be watching you."

She swipes and taps again at her wristplate, trying in vain to bring up the same diagnostic screen the Technician had accessed. Each time she gets the same error message. *Unauthorised Access. You do not have the necessary clearance to activate this function.*

For two weeks she has waited for a message ordering her back to Peacekeepers HQ. For Niamh to call her back to collect whatever information he is tracking via her wristplate.

It makes her paranoid.

She hasn't been anywhere but her apartment and the warehouses she's been sent to protect; avoiding the Edges and the Ravignan Strip, lest Niamh uncover her secrets.

"Stop taking up valuable space." Spittle flies from the Warehouse Manager's lips, his rotund Earth frame wobbling with rage. "Your shift is over, or is your oxygen-deprived mind too damaged to understand that?"

He sounds ridiculous using words like 'oxygen-deprived'; like a poor imitation of a Water Elemental.

Pushing down the temptation to retaliate, she steps aside for him.

"And don't be late next time. Or your supervisor will hear of it."

She doesn't react, not because she is showing restraint or is numb to the insult, but because she is surviving. Like she did last week. And the week before that. And in the weeks after her realignment. And the weeks after Rehhd's Execution. And everything in between.

Stepping out into the street, she pauses; the thought of returning to an empty apartment sets a hard, sharp edge to her emotions. On her first return she had hoped to find Delacroix, imagined the pup racing to greet her, licking away her melancholy. But the apartment had been empty of the mutt when she had arrived, crumbs of soylent bricks scattered near the entrance, and had remained empty ever since.

No doubt the pup has grown tired of waiting for her. In the end, she had disappointed him like she had every other Elemental she'd grown close to.

Avoiding her usual route, she wanders closer to the Edges than she should, eyes scanning random streets for the familiar loping of the furball she misses more than she wants to admit. Her feet track haphazard lines in the sand drifts; a reminder of how life in Otpor has been disrupted by the Resistance. Or, maybe, of how the hard lines of a manipulated space will always be worn down by the organic.

The quiet of the streetscape should soothe her spiky thoughts, but all it does is give them more room to grow and swell. For so long she had been obedient and disciplined – the model of Orthodoxy. And now, when she is finally ready to fight, the fight is taken away from her – too late to fight for Kane's vision, too vulnerable to fight Niamh's manipulations, too hated to fight with Seth's Resistance.

And yet, the rebellion in her core hasn't lessened. With every failed attempt it has only notched higher, flooding her veins with the same feeling she had as a Peacekeeper chasing a target or competing with Niamh to be the best.

It's the same feeling that makes her look for the fight. Makes her see it in unexpected places. The same feeling she had tried to avoid for so long; when engagement meant detection, and detection meant death.

But avoiding detection is no longer an option. And all she wants to do is engage. So, when she hears the sound of a scuffle echoing from a nearby laneway, she doesn't hesitate.

Turning into the laneway, the sounds of the conflict are immediately amplified. They bounce off the walls and fracture into a thousand echoes. But Anaiya is used to being assaulted by a rush of voices.

Ahead, the laneway ends in a t-intersection. Her head whips to the left and then the right.

A Border Watcher, easily identified by the grey and brown camouflage, is toying with a young Air Prostitute. She pulls at his hair, even as he cowers and tries to curl in on himself.

"This is not the fantasy I had in mind," she says through gritted teeth, her hand poised above the neck pinch point.

Border Watchers, precise in observation but clumsy in technique, do not have the finesse of a Peacekeeper. The grip, if executed, will cause some dizziness and blurred vision; enough to put the victim off-balance and disorient him, but not render him unconscious.

Once upon a time, Anaiya had wanted to be a Border Watcher. Now, she just wants to tear one down. "Did your fantasy include something with a bit more of a fight?"

The Border Watcher spins around, her eyes flaring with the same abandon and aggression flaring in Anaiya.

"You want to rumble, IP?" the Border Watcher sneers. The Prostitute falls to the ground, dazed and confused.

Anaiya smiles and lets the adrenalin take over.

THIRTY-FOUR

The first punch cracks across Anaiya's cheek, not perfect enough to do damage, but hard enough to send a jolt of adrenalin along her veins. She will feel the pain later, but for now, the adrenalin is all the motivation she needs to throw herself into the fight.

Evading the next punch, she pivots and slashes her foot across the Border Watcher's jaw. Her opponent moves faster than she expects, is more agile. The rude awakening is softened only by the Watcher's frown and narrowed eyes. She was expecting an easier target as well.

Is she faster, or am I slower?

Neither option brings her comfort, so she banishes the question from her thoughts and focuses on landing a more punishing blow.

It is a scrappy fight, written with scratches and the promises of bruises. There is no snap of bone, no gut-wrenching scream as joints are damaged and body parts dislocated.

In the end it is finished with a sloppy punch that lands too soft to the Watcher's kidney. She stumbles, tripped up by a mix of debris and uncollected rubbish. There is a moment when it looks as if she will regain her balance.

And then the Prostitute, wild-eyed and still bleeding from a shallow gash on his cheek, throws his leg out. It is an act of desperation and vengeance; the last bite of a rat before it is crushed in the dog's maw.

But it is enough. The Border Watcher falls, already off-balance, and lands heavily into the wall behind.

It happens in a moment, but it comes to Anaiya in slow motion. In vivid detail she sees the skull ricochet off the concrete, sees the face contort with the impact, the eyes roll back to show the whites.

There is no satisfaction in it. Just relief.

Her shoulder aches and a fierce throbbing in her side is making her queasy. But she doesn't have time to feel sorry for herself; the volatility in the Border Watcher's vitals will have already alerted Water Security officials and a response team will soon be dispatched, if one hasn't been already.

"Get up." Her voice is hoarse, but still audible. The Prostitute stares up at her with blank eyes, cradling an arm that hangs awkwardly against his chest. "Get up!"

He flinches against the sharp point of her voice but shifts to stand up.

"Step away from him, Peacekeeper."

Anaiya whirls away from the Prostitute and towards the laneway entrance and the new voice.

Seeing Kaide, hearing the cold animosity in his voice, scrambles her thoughts. But only briefly.

He opens his mouth to say something else, but her mind is pulling together various threads of conversations and thoughts and is quickly arriving at a terrifying conclusion.

"Stop." The single syllable stops him in his advance. Briefly.

He takes another step forward. She shakes her head, urgency and fear radiating from her.

He looks from her to the Prostitute. And then he sees the Border Watcher.

In the seconds it takes to absorb the sight of an incapacitated Fire to looking back to Anaiya, his entire face has changed. In it, she sees her own fear reflected.

Anaiya takes a step towards him. Slowly. Hands held up in submission.

His gaze flits from her, to the Prostitute, to the Watcher.

"Wait," she mouths the word. Too cautious to say it aloud.

She points to her wristplate, tapping it to bring up the authentication error. Kaide is too distracted to understand.

The sand drifts stir around her feet. Slowly, she bends down, her hand burying into the fine grains to steady herself.

She glances up. Kaide still looks conflicted, but he hasn't moved. Trusting this new detente, she shifts her focus from the tense Air Elemental to the temporary parchment under her fingertips.

Dragging her index finger through the grains, she carves a simple word he will understand.

Hijacked.

Finally, he steps forward, crouching down beside her. He looks at her, the frown on his face softening into understanding and resignation. Shaking his head, he drags his hand across the word, erasing the i and the j.

Hacked.

His hand closes in over her wristplate and he leans in closer. His breath tickles her earlobe, "You're not the first. It's been happening for years."

She goes to pull away, but he grasps her wrist tighter.

"Looks like you've got an enhanced version. Do you think they're capturing audio or visual?"

She twists to stare at him, his hand still firmly clasped across her wristplate. He doesn't flinch from her scrutiny.

A sobbing interrupts them. The Prostitute is curled up in on himself, rocking back and forth, clutching at his damaged arm.

"Get him out of here," she whispers to Kaide.

He sighs, but nods. "We need to speak."

Quickly, she scrawls the name of the warehouse she will be Protecting later that night. There is a risk in meeting there, but it is the only place that won't attract Niamh's suspicion. A flash of her palm and the word is erased.

"When?" Kaide mouths.

"Eleven."

THIRTY-FIVE

The smell of grease hangs heavy in the workshop, caught up in the gears and conveyor belts and everything else that hums and grinds and murmurs.

But it's not just the smell that is skittering along Anaiya's nerves. The sounds – the incessant clicking and shuddering – it mirrors too closely the uneasy rhythm of her thoughts.

She glances again at the time on her wristplate. 2327.

Where are you, Kaide?

Images, like a strange mix of paranoia and premonition, flash in her subconscious – a contingent of Peacekeepers storming the warehouse; Niamh demanding to know about Kaide; Kaide struggling in a detention cell somewhere on a subterranean level of Peacekeeper HQ.

She swipes at the wristplate, accessing the entertainment function and bringing up columns of stacked cards. Once, it would have been enough to distract her, to speed up long hours of waiting. But now, the simple Fire game of instinct and order only heightens her frustration.

Minutes pass slowly, magnifying the noise and smells, dragging hooks along her patience.

When a knock finally sounds from the nearby service door, Anaiya all but runs to wrench it open. Kaide stands composed on the other side, his dark hair hidden under a thick beanie, his dark eyes clear and serious. But he is not alone.

A Water Elemental, tall and lean, stands beside him with arms folded. He frowns at her. They have met before. Both of them recognise the other simultaneously, their eyes widening at the revelation.

The Technician from my realignment.

She shakes her head. It's a set-up. Niamh has got to them.

Her fight or flight instinct kicks in and she lunges for the Technician, her shoulder colliding with Kaide and sending them both stumbling. The Technician scrambles back, evading her clutch.

Kaide has regained his balance; he strides towards them, arms reaching to detain the Technician. But detaining the Technician is only part of the problem.

What are we going to do with him? How much does Niamh know? Whe—

Strong arms wrap around her, cutting off the rest of her frantic thoughts.

"Sshhhh." Kaide's lips brush against her ear.

She struggles against him, desperate to warn him of the danger they are both in. He grips her tighter.

"Stop struggling," Kaide whispers, "He's a friend."

Anaiya stares at the Technician. He hasn't moved. The mere fact he hasn't attempted to escape, or patch a call to Niamh, slows her heart rate a little. But echoes of anxiety remain.

The Technician doesn't look at her; he stares unblinking at Kaide, his eyes narrowed. He isn't happy about this either.

"You have to calm down, Anaiya. Your heart rate and adrenalin levels will alert someone soon."

She startles. He is right. If their suspicions are correct, and Niamh has updated her wristplate with some of the same functionality as a Border Watcher's, any significant deviation from normal readings will be flagged.

Exhaling slowly, she closes her eyes and tries to normalise her heart rate. Kaide's grip on her loosens and she feels the jittering in her belly start to subside.

When she does open her eyes, Kaide stands with the Technician, engaged in a tense discussion. After a brief stand-off, Kaide disengages and walks over to Anaiya. He grabs her wrist, covering the plate and pulling her close. She lets him but doesn't take her eyes of the Technician.

"Come with me," he says, escorting her to the back of the workshop, where the sounds of the machines are loudest. The Technician follows them, eyes flitting from Kaide to Anaiya and constantly over his shoulder towards the exit. Maybe, like her, he has visions of a Peacekeeper intervention.

"So, you two know each other." Here, engulfed by the noise, Kaide can speak freely.

"He realigned me," she says, struggling to keep her emotions in check and her vital signs within normal ranges. "He knows Niamh."

The Technician ignores her. "You're playing a dangerous game, Kaide. This will not end well. She is damaged goods and will bring down anyone connected to her. You. Me. Niamh. Everyone."

"I hope Niamh does get brought down," Kaide says. "And I can take care of myself. As for you, you have to decide which side poses more of a risk to you."

The challenge does not go unnoticed by the Technician.

"I thought he was a friend," Anaiya mutters.

"He is," Kaide says, still looking at the Technician. "Just a conflicted one."

"Aren't we all," the Technician says, shaking his head and stepping forward.

"What do you know of it?" Kaide asks, looking down at Anaiya's wristplate.

The Technicians shrugs, still frowning. "I'd need to see it."

Kaide turns to her. Anaiya shakes her head.

"Anaiya, what is there to lose? If he is with Niamh, he already knows about it. And if he is with us, he can tell us just what we are up against. Anaiya – look at me."

She turns from the Technician and looks at Kaide. She knows her stare is as withering as a Wasteland breeze, but he doesn't baulk.

Unflinching, she holds her arm out to the Technician, only bristling when his hand clasps her wrist. She tries to control her breathing, but it is hard to banish the memory of another Water Technician violating her wristplate.

He drops her hand suddenly. "We have to leave. Now."

"What have you found?"

"It's more sophisticated than we anticipated. It's a live communication. They've got the Border Watcher vitals monitoring. And they're capturing audio, but not visual. Not as a standard, anyway. Maybe if something else flags."

Kaide gestures to the machines. "So, what's the problem?"

"They've enhanced the location function. They're calculating from three different points."

With anyone else, the words would mean nothing. But Anaiya and Kaide are not anyone; their minds don't obey the rigid definitions of their Elements. And Anaiya immediately grasps the importance of what the Technician is saying.

Maybe it's spatial. Or intuitive.

"They're triangulating our location?"

The Technician stares at Anaiya, surprised she has grasped the concept.

"Are they?" Kaide sounds surprised. And anxious.

"We have to leave." The Technician turns and strides towards the exit.

Kaide hesitates. Frowning as the Technician disappears, before turning back to Anaiya.

"Do you trust him?" Anaiya asks.

Kaide shakes his head. "No. But I hold enough leverage to keep him quiet for now."

"Why are you here, Kaide? Why did you find me? Wait. *How* did you find me?"

"No time to explain."

She shakes her head, unsatisfied with the answer. He scowls, gaze darting from Anaiya to the door. Sighing, he steps forward and lays a gentle hand on her arm, just above the wristplate.

"But I will. Later."

And then he leaves. And she is alone.

THIRTY-SIX

It is three days before Kaide returns. He appears unannounced at another curfew shift, sneaking through a first-storey window with a broken latch.

All manner of expletives threaten to leap from Anaiya's tongue, but she is silenced by her wristplate and the threat of discovery. Forcing herself to regulate her breathing, she glares at Kaide.

Once her vitals return to the green zone, she switches her wristplate to the music function and selects full volume. Fast and heavy beats erupt in the room, the simple chord progressions of Peacekeeper music hammering against the heavy walls and obliterating all other noises.

Kaide smirks and she can't help but smile wryly herself. It has been a long time since she has listened to the standard Peacekeeper soundtrack.

"For someone who advises I keep my vitals normal, climbing through a window is not your best choice of an entrance."

"Noted. But if you haven't already noticed, you've got random surveillance detail on your shifts."

She had noticed, but part of her had been hoping that it was just standard curfew detail.

"For an Air Elemental, you are extremely good at remaining hidden."

He laughs. With her hearing limited by the music distraction, she sees more clearly how it lights up his face, softening the angles and making him less distant.

"We both have hidden talents, Anaiyasha." The nom de doceur given by Kane 148 sounds natural on his tongue. It would distract her, except her thoughts stray to the Orthodoxy and conditioning.

"Why do you think that is?"

He frowns. "What do you mean?"

"Why do you think we're so ... *incompatible* with our Elements?"

His frown deepens. "Well, I know why *you* are."

It's true, her deviation is more obvious. But Kaide's eccentricities can't be explained away by typical Air inconsistencies or maybe even his hypoxia.

"Yes, but why are *you*?"

"What are you asking, Anaiya?"

She stops. She shouldn't have said anything, should be more careful with sharing her ideas.

Everything is so tenuous now. Weeks ago, when he had found her starving in the Edges, she had been ready to divulge everything to gain an ally. But she had been desperate then. Now, she is cautious.

Yes, she needs to be able to trust him. But while he is like her, he is not allied with her. Yet.

And it's not as if she has a plan, not really.

"How did you find me the other day? In the laneway?"

He shrugs. "It's not only Peacekeepers who have you under surveillance."

"Why?"

"Because you were right." She finds the reluctance in his answer, not from his tone, which is obliterated by the music, but by his guarded eyes and defensive posture. "Seth has been corrupted. And this new vision of his is one of reckless violence, not rebellion."

"So, you will help me?" The small flame of hope that flickers in her core takes her by surprise. Needing someone else has never factored into Anaiya's mindset.

"No. We will help each other."

Over the next hour, they pull together the rough outlines of a plan. Their conversation is tense, made difficult by a complicated history and legacy of distrust. But at the end of it they arrive at a shared conclusion.

"So, we agree. We need to attack both sides of the problem." Anaiya is tired and on edge. The same dense, quick rhythms have been playing incessantly since Kaide's arrival. Her head is pounding and it is getting harder to regulate her vitals by simple breathing exercises.

"I'll try to redirect Seth," Kaide says, rubbing at his temples. "You distract Niamh."

She nods, bringing down the volume of her wristplate. With each drop in decibels, her brain relaxes. Slowly she steps closer to him, reverting to their original way of secret communication.

"We need a better way of doing this," she whispers, her lips centimetres from his ear.

This time it is his turn to smile wryly. "Leave it with me."

It is a weird feeling trusting someone again. It is not the blind obedience she felt to Niamh and her Peacekeeper superiors. And not the irrational deep falling for Seth's charm. It is guarded and born of necessity, but somehow – for all its reluctance – it feels more genuine.

Kaide doesn't hesitate as he reaches the window and begins his exit. Only when he swings his leg over the sill does he look back at her.

As always, the air between them shimmers with tension and becomes almost sticky with unresolved emotion. And in that moment, she sees the same hesitancy. The same guarded hope.

Her throat aches with the impulse to say something, to remind him, or reassure him. But her wristplate tingles at her skin, reminding her of the risk.

Desperate to communicate something, she throws her hand out.

He looks at her, stopped in his descent, frowning at the unexpected action.

The tension increases and her brain races to come up with a

signal that will translate her complex thoughts.

She holds her index finger up. It is her alone. And then her middle finger. Kaide alone.

Slowly, she locks them together. Gently. And then increases the pressure, the middle finger dragging more insistently against the index.

She feels the heat and friction, the resistance, and then the pain.

The message is as clear as she can convey without words: If one of them stays too rigid to their original cause, they will be doomed. If one pulls too strongly on the other, forcing it too far from its alignment, they will be doomed. Either way, they will break the other.

And then she releases the tension, relaxing the signal until the two fingers fall into an uneasy support of the other.

We can hate each other and fail. Or we can find a way to support each other. Your win is my win.

They are uneasy allies. And yet, for all of that, they understand each other.

His frown softens, but he does not smile. This is their way – thrown together by fate against their will.

The hand that grips the sill relaxes. If it were Seth, he would wink and throw her a killer smile. But it is Kaide. He stares unblinking at her; sizing her up, contemplating the risks. Grimacing, as if banishing the internal voices that tell him otherwise, he raises his hand and mimics her signal, a strange melancholy plaguing his features.

He knows what she is feeling; the comfort of having someone on his side shadowed only by the uneasiness of knowing its price is betrayal. His lips move, but no sound is made. *Or Death.*

After Kaide leaves, Anaiya's thoughts turn to their plan.

Kaide had been quick to pick up on the risk of the soundmatcher in Niamh's hands. Coupled with the audio recording hack on her wristplate, any audible interaction with him or other members of the Resistance will be a death sentence for them all.

No more Ravignan Strip. No more covert entries into Seth's apartment. No more clandestine meetings in the Edges. *For now, at least.*

Kaide and his strange Water connections will look into a counter-hack, something subtle and undetectable, but it will take time. Time they don't have.

She glowers at her wristplate. Her fingers pick at its edges, lifting the cuff millimetres before the pain becomes intolerable. Implanted in her third lustrum, it was a badge of her maturity – a symbol to the rest of Otpor that her Premie days were over, that she was ready to be a contributing member of society.

Now it is a syringe at her jugular and all she wants to do is claw it out.

If only they knew exactly when Seth planned to unleash the mass-scale chemical manipulation. The particulars of the attack – the stockpiling and transportation of such a large volume of pituarmagn, the broadcast interruption and hijacking, the need for a location that can accommodate a large crowd of Elementals and provide for high visibility – they all offer opportunity for detection and destabilisation. They are all links in the chain that can be targeted.

But, with an unknown timeframe and undirected urgency, the challenge is knowing which link to focus their efforts on.

In the end, they had decided to target the three factors they agreed were key – reigniting Seth's original motivation and vision for the Resistance, removing the influence of Eamon and Lilith, and disrupting the pituarmagn distribution.

In Kaide's mind, all of the heavy lifting had fallen to him.

"You just have to distract Niamh. Keep him occupied for long enough so I can actually do all of this."

But distracting Niamh means deceiving him, and that has never ended well.

THIRTY-SEVEN

Anaiya squints against the sunlight. The crowd in Place Dela Concord is in a festive mood – it is the Sixth day, the weather is atypically pleasant, and the plaza has for weeks been immune to the violence that has plagued the rest of the city. It is almost as if it is a safe zone, quarantined from the chaos of the Resistance and backlash of the Peacekeepers.

The obelisk serves as her orientation point and she trains her gaze north to the Unbroken Fountain. The crowd is just as thick there as it is around the fountain's southern counterpart, but Anaiya's gaze easily finds its target.

He is dressed all in red, just as Kaide said he would be. But under the conspicuous attire, the Elemental himself is nondescript in every way. Not tall, not short. Not unattractive, but nothing interesting to draw the eye. Not awkward, not confident.

If she hadn't been expecting him, her gaze would slide right past him.

His eyes track briefly over her shoulder to where the Peacekeeper surveillance is undoubtedly loitering, but the falter is quickly overshadowed by the broad grin he offers Anaiya.

He strides over to meet her, arms wrapping around her, lips pressed against her ear. "Just follow my lead."

Releasing her, he steps back and smiles. "You came," he says, just loud enough for her wristplate to register the words and the voice. "I thought you were going to break my heart a second time. Where have you been?"

"I didn't think you would want to see me again." It is the backstory Kaide had scripted and passed her the evening before, scrawled on a torn piece of paper and memorised in her cold, threadbare apartment.

The stranger before her frowns and tenderly brushes strands of hair from her cheek. The presumed intimacy makes her shiver, but she resists the urge to pull away.

"I told you I would wait for you," he says, his hands dropping to hers. "When I said that I loved you, I meant it. What you've done and who you are doesn't change that."

He has to be an Actor. He is good – avoiding the urge to look and see if the intended audience is watching, varying the tone and emphasis in his voice, speaking as much with his body and face as his words. It would all be so absurd – to pretend the emotion could be real, to entertain the concept that an Air Elemental would ever wait for a disgraced and treacherous Fire Elemental – if it hadn't once been real.

"It's too dangerous for us, now," she says, sticking to the script and shrugging out of his grasp. "It's Unorthodox, they will punish us for it."

"Don't leave me again, Anaiya. I just got you back."

She looks around, eyes superficially scanning the crowd, finding the patrol Peacekeepers easily. They stick to the fringes, not finding the Unorthodoxy that would require their intervention and unwilling to provide the trigger that would manufacture it. But this farce isn't for them.

"We can't be seen together." She pulls away from him, surprised when he pulls her back.

"Don't push me away. Please." He looks so genuinely heart-stricken. Even knowing it is a charade, she baulks – the face may be a stranger's, but the words are ones she has yearned to hear for so long.

"What do you want from me?" She winces at the unsteadiness in her voice, only hoping that it adds credibility to her act.

"Let me see you again. I will come to you at night – when no one can see us. Or judge us."

"It is reckless."

He leans in and kisses her, the faintest brush of lips against hers. She pulls away and stares at him. *Part of your script, Kaide?*

"It is worth it," he says, winking at her before retreating into the crowd and disappearing from view.

Four days later, she sees the Actor again. He arrives just before curfew, winking at Anaiya before sauntering into the gallery that she is Protecting.

It had been easy to find an Infrastructure Protector wanting to swap a shift in the Air-dominated precinct for one in a low-risk warehouse tucked away in a quiet eastern precinct. Yet even as he accepted her offer, the crease of his forehead had broadcast his suspicion.

There were numerous reasons a Fire Elemental would want to put themselves in combatant territory – the Infrastructure Protector no doubt thinks she is doing it for the thrill of the fight, and Niamh, if her plan is working, will think she is doing it to rekindle an Unorthodox romance with an inconsequential Air Elemental.

But, of course, neither of them are right.

The street is emptying quickly now. Catcalls and dark stares are thrown at the gathering contingent of Peacekeepers, but no one takes it any further. For now.

Anaiya steps inside the gallery and closes the door behind her, shutting herself away from unwanted surveillance.

Almost. Her wristplate weighs heavy, a constant reminder that unwanted surveillance is her new reality.

The Actor is already lounging on a turquoise chaise in the first room. He doesn't look up as she walks past – the need for his Acting skills is spent. He will leave as soon as the dawn light cracks the sky; until then, all he needs to do is sleep and stay out of her way.

She takes the stairs to the second floor of the gallery, allowing her heart to flutter in its cage.

Hope you're enjoying the show, Niamh.

The room to the immediate right of the landing is identical to one directly below it. Except the room below is full of antique pieces and this one is full of holograms. Except the one below accommodates an inconsequential Air Elemental. And this one accommodates Kaide.

"Hello again, Anaiya."

He smiles at her – the grin of a Peacekeeper who has caught their perpetrator.

Anaiya's heart is properly racing now. Not at his presence or his smile; but at his voice. It is smooth and lyrical and completely unlike the deep and measured tones she knows are his.

He smiles wider, not bothering to mask his pleasure at her confusion. "You look surprised to see me. Tsk, tsk. I told you I would come."

Every syllable, every inflection, is the perfect copy of a voice she has heard only once before – the voice of the Air Elemental sitting in the room below.

"I just never thought …" Her voice is a little unsteady. She swallows against it.

"What? That I would come back?"

She shakes her head. "That it would work," she mouths.

Kaide had given her the basics of the technology at their previous meeting. A device, not unlike the soundmatcher, that when placed in the hollow of a throat could pick up on the vibrations indicating various words and phrases. And then manipulate and modulate them, based on parameters set by the user, so that they exited the mouth as a different voice altogether.

"Oh, Anaiya," he says softly, the voice pitching higher than it would otherwise, "you can't get rid of me that easily."

The first half hour is taken up with transmitting the fictitious back story – reminiscing over times they spent as lovers. The script is elaborate and convincing – there is no way Kaide could have written it.

His voice matches the emotion demanded by the story, but his posture is tense. They sit close to one another, approximating the distance between reunited lovers, allowing every murmur and whisper to be picked up by her wristplate. Alone, in the darkened room lit only by the glow of shimmering holograms, the false words take on a real intimacy.

"Why didn't you reach out to me? I could have helped you." Kaide doesn't blink, but the clench of his jaw makes his face harder. The words fit the story they need for their deception, but they also hint at their real shared past.

"And say what?" He has captured her tone perfectly, the script full of habitual phrases and her vocal idiosyncrasies. It makes it hard to keep the lines between the make believe and the real from blurring. "What did you want me to say? 'I lied to you from the beginning, you never knew the real me, I was never intending on staying in your life. Still love me?'"

Pain blooms in her palms and she glances down at them, releasing her clenched fists to reveal the red indents of her fingernails. She knows her heart rate is erratic. The thought that Niamh is monitoring it makes it skip more chaotically.

Just the flutters of a guilty, lovesick fool, Niamh. The thought is humourless – dulled by the uneasiness creeping along the back of her neck.

"You could have trusted me."

She stares at him. How much of these words are really his? His face is inscrutable. Shifting her gaze to the paper on the floor, she reads the next line of her script. *I wanted to, but it was too dangerous.*

It's trivial and trite and she can't bring herself to say it. Caught up in the subtext of the conversation and the urgency of their situation, she searches for a response that will fit their false narrative but also give Kaide a real answer to his question.

He taps her on the leg. His frown is still there but softened by confusion. "What's wrong?" he mouths, glancing between her and the script. "Just say the words."

"I …" She pauses, the words dying on her tongue. Unable to meet Kaide's gaze, she drops her gaze to her lap.

Frustration and trepidation are cinches around her stomach, pulling tighter with each second that passes. And when she can no longer bear the tension, she opens her mouth and lets the words rush out. "I did. I did trust you. I trusted you when I revealed myself to you. I'm trusting you now by being here."

The silence that follows brings a kind of relief and a new unease. Her heart settles into a slower rhythm, not normal but not the breakneck pace of moments ago.

"Come to me, Anaiya." The soft, lyrical voice sends synthflies to her stomach. But when she looks up, the serious Kaide is still looking back at her. Not frowning, but still guarded.

He points to the script, a simple capitalised statement standing out from the other lines of text: *DECEPTION ONE.* He opens his mouth to say something and stops. Eyes, dark and troubled, stare into her own. He shakes his head and grimaces, clenching his eyes shut.

When he finally opens them, they are softer but still tortured. He sighs. "Trust me."

THIRTY-EIGHT

The skin at her forearm tingles as Kaide places the strange rubber sphere over their clasped hands. Just before it clips into place, he activates the playlist on his wristplate. In the silence of the room, the sounds – muffled and muted by the rubber – take a while to register.

Anaiya's eyes widen when they finally do. She looks at Kaide, who shrugs and throws his hands up in defence. The belaboured and overly dramatic sounds of sex can only come from high-vis pornography.

Laughter bubbles up in her throat. She glances back at Kaide, who is also biting back a grin.

He shakes his head, attempting to glare at her – the lopsided smile undoing any approximation of sternness. The laughter bubbles higher. A particularly loud moan makes its way past the sound barrier and Anaiya's control shatters.

The giggle that emerges triggers the same from Kaide. The sound seems to erupt in the room around them. Their eyes widen momentarily before the threat of laughter sends them biting their lips and averting their gazes.

When Anaiya finally collects herself and looks back at Kaide, she finds him looking back at her. There is a sparkle in his eyes – echoes of laughter illuminated by the holographic light around them – but there is something else. A quiet consideration. The look of someone seeing something for the first time.

Her heart rate, only recently calmed, skitters and all thoughts of laughter evaporate.

Kaide looks away and the moment passes. He fumbles in his jacket and when he looks back at her, she expects to see the old Kaide – the closed, unreadable, sceptical Kaide. But while the curve of his lips is gone, his eyes still hold their softness.

"Take this." He opens his palm to reveal a chemical atomiser.

She takes the miniature canister and sprays two short bursts of a bitter liquid under her tongue. Her fingers itch to peel back the rubber sphere and peak at her vitals flashing on the wristplate.

The effect is almost instantaneous. Her eyes widen, sucking in the available light and drinking in every detail. Her fingers and palms tingle, hypersensitive to the graze of his fingers as they reach for the atomiser in her hand.

And the lightness – it engulfs her and sets every fibre of her body tingling with an unprovoked frisson.

A compelling and familiar warmth floods her veins. And, in that moment, the fiction of the contrived emotion is at war with the very real sensations manipulating her brain and body.

Seconds later, the sensation passes. She still feels her accelerated heartbeat, and intuitively she knows that her vitals will match the expectation of whoever is listening to the sex noises transmitted through her wristplate, but the pretence no longer entangles her mind.

Still, it is more difficult making eye contact with Kaide than it was just moments ago.

"We can talk freely," he murmurs. "The sound blocker and the playlist should mask anything we say."

"Playlist," Anaiya rejoinders, "is that what this is?"

Kaide grins and shrugs, the movement tugging at Anaiya's bound wrist. "I needed something obscure and vague. No chance of voice matching."

Another moan hums in the silence.

"Well you certainly managed that."

"Good thing Fire Elementals aren't prudish."

Now it is Anaiya's turn to grin. "Good thing your backstory didn't have me falling in love with a Water Elemental."

"Speaking of the technical Element, I think I have a way to distract your Peacekeeper friends …"

The sex noises are reaching their climax. The ridiculous sounds would send Anaiya into a new fit of laughter if it weren't for the knowledge of what is to come next.

Kaide looks calmer, but she notices his fingers tremble slightly as he fixes the voice modulator back against his throat and pulls a second atomiser from his pocket. The bitter scent of a different chemical composition fills the tight space between them as she fires two short bursts under her tongue.

The effect is less immediate and more subtle than the previous inhalation. She frowns at Kaide, concerned that the concoction is flawed. They are sitting closer together, now, their knees touching and heads still bent towards each other.

There is something comforting about the two of them pressed together in a small space when the rest of the gallery room expands around them. Her eyes seek out his and when she sees the softness in them she isn't surprised. It is more familiar to her now. Expected, welcomed. Wanted.

She startles. Confused as to how much of this is the chemical manipulation and how much is a genuine and growing affection.

"Ready?" The higher-pitched voice of the stranger in the room below brings the reality of her situation rushing back into focus.

There is a strange Air Elemental lounging in the room below. Niamh is monitoring every word, movement and reaction she has. The Resistance and its opposition are growing more violent. And she and Kaide are about to attempt a crazy, desperate deception that could shift everything.

Unwilling to trust her own voice, Anaiya nods. Kaide peels back the rubber sphere, revealing their hands still interlocked.

Keeping his eyes firmly on hers, he pulls her closer. Everything from here on in will be murmurs and whispers. And Niamh needs to hear it all.

THIRTY-NINE

"Things are starting to get out of control, Ani. I'm worried about you."

The sweet nothings have finally run their course and the true deception begins.

"I'm not a Peacekeeper anymore, there is nothing to worry about."

"Why do they continue to persecute us?"

They sit side by side. Occasionally, she risks a sideways glance at Kaide. He never looks back – focussed only on the script at their feet.

She ignores the strange fluttering in her stomach and reads the next line. "It's their duty to protect the Orthodoxy. Rehhd's Heterodoxy is more persistent than it should be …"

It is the greatest deception, because it is so close to the truth.

"Only because they didn't Execute the true source of Heterodoxy," Kaide says with his modulated voice.

"No?"

"Rumour says it was the Water Element who orchestrated this whole thing."

She laughs, low and soft, and then lets it trail off. "You're not serious?"

"It's just what I hear. And who better to manipulate the natural animosity between Fire and Air."

"But to what end?"

"Well, it's all a massive distraction, isn't it? Air is watching

Fire. Fire is watching Air. But who is watching Water?"

"You think they're up to something?"

"Don't ask me, Ani – I'm just a Choreographer. I'm just saying that Fire and Water have always been running this show, and maybe Water don't want to share anymore."

"But, Water were involved in … the mission, from the beginning."

"A good Director doesn't absent themselves from the performance, Anaiya."

It is such a clever story. For days afterwards, Anaiya's mind still turns it over and inside out, marvelling at the new layers of intricacy she uncovers each time.

The details will pique Niamh's curiosity. His ego will deny it at first, but the insinuation – that he has been played, when he was supposed to be the player – will keep itching in his mind. At first it will be an annoyance, a synthfly sting.

But he'll scratch at it. And scratch at it. And keep scratching at it – unable to banish it from his thoughts.

Scratch, scratch, scratch.

The level of detail was perfect. Any less and his ego would never have entertained the possibility of being crossed by the Water Element. Any more and his natural intelligence and instinct would become suspicious.

"… it's not enough." Kaide's true voice interrupts her thoughts. "We need to do more."

He's worried that Niamh hasn't taken the bait.

They sit in an empty warehouse, the rubber sphere around their wrists the only thing stopping their words from reaching Niamh and his surveillance team.

"Did you write it?"

"Write what?" He is chewing on his lip again, his frown making him look more serious again.

"The script. From the other day."

"Did I mess it up? I couldn't risk involving anyone else. It's risky enough as it is."

She shakes her head. "No. It was fine. It was good. I just … I just didn't think of you as a words person."

It is easy to see the spectre of Seth in the smile that fades before it fully reaches his eyes.

"I've picked up a few bad habits over the years … Lie down with dogs, wake up with fleas." It is a sombre attempt at humour.

"They're worse than you think."

"The words?"

She grins. "The fleas."

This time the smile does reach his eyes. "How is your mangy mutt?"

And now it is her smile that falters. *Stupid pup. Probably feasting on rats in the Edges with no care in the world.*

And yet, thoughts of the dog hit her harder than they should. In a world with no friends, having an ally – even of the matted-fur, four-legged kind – meant something. Means something.

Hidden away from sight, she feels Kaide's hand grip hers under the sphere.

He seems as surprised by the reaction as she is.

"I haven't seen him since the warrant." She doesn't owe him the clarification. And she knows he doesn't demand it. But it feels better to tell him.

"Loyalty is a fickle thing," he murmurs.

She squeezes his hand. This is a truth they both know all too well.

Shaking off the distracting emotions, she pulls the immediate problem back into focus. "We're good with part one of the plan; it will just take more time to see the outcome – Niamh won't act irrationally. What we need to do is move on with part two."

Kaide relaxes his grip. Anaiya hesitates before she does the same.

"Removing Lilith from the picture is … difficult." He is chewing on his lip again. And avoiding eye contact with her.

They had decided early on that separating Seth from Lilith would be their best chance at slowing down the Resistance plans. Targeting Eamon was too risky – since Rehhd's Execution, he had become more unpredictable; like the rage and the vengeance were all he lived for, and no consequence was too great for whatever would satisfy either of them.

"She's still our best option?" Anaiya asks.

"She's the only option."

"Well then, tell me what you know about her."

FORTY

Anaiya scratches at the skin that tickles along her neck. The day is hot, as most days are, but occasionally the air stirs, and when it does, she catches a new glimpse of the purple acrylic strands that blow around her face.

The wig was Kaide's idea. Fanciful and outrageous and completely in line with the Air style, it won't disguise her, but it will make her less conspicuous. Which is important, since she is trailing Lilith.

"If we are going to do this," she had said, *"we have to know where she goes, what she does, who she sees. If she has a routine, I need to know it."*

"I can't do it, Anaiya."

"Of course you can. I've seen you do it. You trailed me and Jenna for weeks without her noticing."

"That was different."

"Kaide!" The single syllable had come low and harsh through gritted teeth.

But he merely shook his head. *"No, Anaiya. This is your mission."*

In the end, she had relented. With Lilith monitored by Anaiya, Kaide had more opportunities for getting to Seth or uncovering the alternative pituarmagn supplier.

"So, how do I follow her? Niamh is tracking every step I take. If my path matches hers, she won't be detained for an Unorthodoxy charge, she'll

face an Execution trial."

Kaide was unconcerned. *"They won't match. You're generating continuous data, Lilith's location only pings if she engages her wristplate or lifeline. And she won't. Not often enough to force a match, anyway."*

"What do you mean? She engages her wristplate every time she swipes an entry panel or pays for a drink or patches a call."

"Except she rarely swipes to enter a building – she just follows someone else in. And she doesn't pay for drinks – Yve either supplies them for free or someone else gets the shout. And no one in the Resistance has patched a call in months – why do you think we're always meeting in person?"

The moment he had said the words, she had heard the truth in them. She had seen it herself – the holding open doors for others to enter, the endless shouting of drinks …

"The co-location numbers."

Kaide frowned. *"The* what *numbers?"*

There had always been something off about them. She'd just never known why.

"You were protecting Seth … Wait. Wait, wait, wait." And then it had clicked. *"It was you. You were protecting him – you were the set piece. It was supposed to be you, not Rehhd …"*

"That's not …" Kaide had frowned and looked away. *"That's not important. What's important is that there's practically zero chance of your lifeline data matching. We only need one entry swipe that fits the story; even if they do co-locate you, it will only lend credibility to your report."*

So here she was, tracking Lilith.

Kaide had set up the starting point, orchestrating a meeting with the strange Air Elemental, whose name she still didn't know, at a small square opposite the gallery Lilith was scheduled to visit. For over an hour, Anaiya had struggled to keep up the pretence of a secret and illicit rendezvous. Her counterpart, however, didn't appear to share her unease – revelling in the performance, playing up to the audience. Of one.

Seeing Lilith exit the gallery was almost a reprieve. Almost.

Leaving her fake paramour behind, she had settled into an easy pace at a safe distance. Twenty minutes into surveillance and nothing of interest had been uncovered. There was no pattern to her movements, no unusual stops along the way.

With the pituarmagn offensive due any day, Anaiya expects her to give something away – something that would hint at a location or supply networks. Either Lilith is being careful, or she knows she is being followed. Or, worse still, has no more preparations to make because everything is in hand.

"I don't understand," she had said to Kaide. *"How did she become so influential?"*

"Rehhd left a void. And a lot of people vied to fill it. I thought Eamon would step up, but I guess Seth needed another void filled as well. I underestimated how much you shattered his heart. Or ego."

Ahead, Lilith takes an unexpected turn down a side street and Anaiya's thoughts are cut short. The streets of the lower precincts in the Western Area are unfamiliar and the chaotic mix of warehouses, office buildings and cheap apartment towers makes it difficult for Anaiya to orient herself.

Once upon a time, she would have strode down the street without a second thought. But she has to play it smarter now. Even if Lilith's apparent detour is not a trap, the risk of Lilith spotting and identifying Anaiya is too much of a risk. She needs another option.

Tapping on her wristplate to access the location app, she finds her current position. The side street is a connector between two main boulevardes. A handful of small, dead-end alleyways branch off on either side, but otherwise, the only entry and exit points for Boileau Road are here and at the intersection of Boulevarde Exelmans to the south.

She pulls up the hood of her jacket to hide her fake purple hair, groaning at the amplified heat that threatens new rivulets of sweat. Pivoting, she sprints back along the way she has just come, leaping at the far wall of the intersection with Rue Michelange and continuing her sprint along the wall until gravity pulls her back down to the street.

Seconds later, she enters the busy intersection with Boulevarde Exelmans. She slows her feet, weaving her way into the dense crowds of Elementals until she is obscured by the masses. With a quick flick of her hand, she drops her hood and pulls the purple acrylic strands of hair around her face.

Confronted with limited options, she resorts to staking out the shuttered doorway of a performance space near the intersection. It will open again in an hour or so, transitioned from a formal rehearsal space to a makeshift space of dancing, drinking and debauchery. But, for now, it is quiet. Most Elementals who see her standing outside will simply assume she is an Infrastructure Protector who has arrived early for their shift. It's not a perfect deception, but it suits her purposes.

She waits for Lilith to exit, unconcerned that the slow sauntering Air Elemental could have outpaced her free-running detour. Each minute that passes presents different variations of two possibilities – either Lilith had picked up on the tail and used the side street to lose it, or she walked into that side street with a destination in mind.

Anaiya checks her wristplate. Fifteen minutes. Fifteen minutes of standing still and keeping quiet. She has to move. If Niamh isn't suspicious yet, he soon will be. There's no way of explaining it. At best she can justify it as a recovery moment after a spurt of free-running.

Reluctantly, she steps away from her post and continues walking down the boulevarde. Passing the intersection with Boileau, she risks a glance up the road. In the seconds it takes her to pass by, she notices the ancient cobblestones cut off by smooth bitumen, the strong and angular lines of seven-storey apartment blocks, and the complete lack of colour anywhere. But no Lilith.

The temptation to steal away into the street's shadows is insistent – an echo of her Fire competitiveness and Air impulsiveness – but she ignores it. She needs to be smarter.

Six months ago, her competitiveness and impulsiveness led to Rehhd's Execution and almost led to hers. Too much has happened in the meantime; she is not the same Elemental that infiltrated the Resistance.

Biting down on the inside of her cheek, she keeps walking.

The chagrin fades the further she gets from the side street and eventually other thoughts rise to the surface. When she had asked Kaide about Lilith, he had stuck to the basics – a Literature competent like Seth, originally from the Southern Area, lured to the Northern Area nine months ago by whispers of a Resistance.

"She was one of Rehhd's synthflies," he had said. *"Drawn by the promise of something radical and outrageous."*

"So, you were Seth's fall guy and she was his recruiter. He must be lost." The words were bitter, but her voice held no bite.

"Why do you think he resorted to sub-rate imposters like Eamon and Lilith?"

She smiles still thinking of the lopsided grin he had flashed. Seeing the cheekier side of Kaide, rare as it is, always resonates with her. It reminds her that joy can still be had in a world that tries at every turn to suck it from her.

Ahead, the marker to Precinct 7 introduces the shift to the Water-dominated section of the area. Bland office buildings compete with multi-storey laboratories and technology testing sites.

"I said, keep your mouth shut, wet-byte." The voice, and the aggression it carries, bounces off the walls around her. "I'm not here to debate with you, I'm here to detain you."

FORTY-ONE

Anaiya is calm as she stalks towards the source of the conflict.

The streets of the precinct, while not as busy as they were along Boulevarde Exelmans, still attract occasional Elementals moving between precincts. Technicians and Analysts hurry with heads down past the altercation, uninterested and unwilling to get involved.

Gritting her teeth, she moves around them, her eyes flicking to a grey administration building where a Peacekeeper is facing off with a higher-level Technician.

"You have no authority," the Technician shouts, her voice raspy. "There has been no Unorthodoxy."

The restraint syringe glints in the brown sunlight; the Peacekeeper unmoved by her distress.

There is no hesitation, the needle sinking into flesh, the Technician slumping to the ground.

"Something you need, Protector?"

Anaiya moves her gaze from the limp body to the Peacekeeper. His eyes are downcast, focussed on downloading the detention details to the victim's wristplate, but he has shifted his stance so that he is directly facing Anaiya.

"No," she starts, mind racing to find an advantage from this encounter, "I was just on my way to a shift; anything I need to know?"

Saying anything at all is a risk, knowing that someone else – maybe Niamh himself – is listening to it. But she is unwilling to just walk away without knowing whether this incident is random or an indication that the fake intel she and Kaide are using to cast shade on Water Elementals is working.

"What would you need to know?" The sarcasm is clear, but he still doesn't look up.

"Any break-ins?"

He laughs and shakes his head, finally glancing over to her. "Not exactly a Water offence, is it?"

"No, but most embezzlement and anti-trust offences don't attract such a public detention."

The Peacekeeper frowns at her and she swallows against the burst of anxiety that flares at her core.

"Nothing you need to be concerned with, Protector. Best be on your way before you're late to your shift."

She wants to challenge him, make him explain what is going on; her tongue tingles with the anticipation of it.

The Peacekeeper's frown deepens and his stance shifts again, subtle but meaningful.

Blood blooms in her cheek, her teeth clenching hard.

Shaking her head, she risks one last glance at the unconscious Elemental. And walks away.

"How long was she there for?"

Kaide taps his feet, the movement ricocheting up his leg and passing on the vibration where his knee meets hers. They sit side by side, legs bent and hands linked under the now-familiar black sphere.

"I told you. I don't know. She could have waited a few minutes and then exited the same way she went in."

"Unlikely – Lilith is savvy enough to keep tabs on nearby Peacekeepers; she wouldn't expect an incognito trail."

"You said she was intelligent, *astute*; that she knew how to interpret an environment and—"

"She is," he interrupts, "And she can. But you're too good a Peacekeeper to be made."

The compliment puts her off-balance. "I'm not a Peacekeeper."

"You are in the ways that count."

What is that supposed to mean?

In the silence that follows, she wonders if his words were meant as a compliment or insult.

"So, assuming she didn't pick up on your surveillance," he continues, "how long was she in there for?"

She sighs. "I waited for fifteen minutes. It would have taken me maybe three minutes to get to Exelmans and, given how slow she was moving and how long Rue Boileau is, it would have taken her six to get to the same intersection."

"So, fifteen minus six gives us a nine-minute minimum detour."

"If she didn't return the way she came in."

"What are the side streets on Boileau?"

"Jouvenay is the prominent one. Despero has more branches, but limited access."

"What did you see around Despero?"

"I didn't see anything; I didn't check it out." She waits for the frustration or disappointment to flash across his features, but it never comes. Just a slight cock of the head, and the continuation of his foot tapping.

He may be her partner in this, but he is not Niamh.

She pulls up their interlocked hands. "Thought it might attract the wrong kind of attention."

Kaide nods, chewing on his lip. "OK. I'll check it out first thing tomorrow. We still need something to pin on Lilith."

"It needs to be a low order offence that can be identified in real time. Nothing that requires witnesses or involves time delays. Just a straightforward detention that will take her out of action for a few days, nothing more."

"That doesn't leave us much, Anaiya."

They fall back into silence, the muffled soundtrack from Kaide's wristplate hovering in the air between them.

"You really need to get some new sex tracks."

He grins briefly. "I told you – it's not an easy task. Plus, it's not like I can purchase them; I've had to pirate them from random sources to guarantee total anonymity."

The thought of Kaide stealing pornography makes her laugh. As a Peacekeeper, she had detained scores of Air Elementals for Code 94 robbery offences, but never where the stolen object was porn.

"You find that funny?"

"I find that hilarious …" Something tickles at the back of her mind. *That's it.*

"What? What is it?"

"I know how we set Lilith up."

"Well, don't keep me in suspense."

FORTY-TWO

It takes Kaide three days to work his contacts and set Anaiya up with a Protector shift in the Northern Area.

The gallery is nestled amongst the stalls and display tables of Precinct 9's Lopera Markets. Like with any market shift, her area of responsibility will extend out into the market throng. But for now, her attention is on the trinket collective next door, and the Protector who patrols it.

Earlier in the morning, she had scanned the stalls as they had been assembled. Typical of Trinketeur offerings, most of the displayed pieces are cheap plastic decorations – gaudy knick-knacks designed to last only as long as they are fashionable. But amongst all the disposable items are a few pieces of superior craftsmanship and impeccable design. Expensive pieces – designed to catch the eye of high-earning Air Elementals who can appreciate their quality, or upper-level Earth Elementals who like to pretend they have more class than they do.

"Is this your normal gig?" she asks her counterpart, his heavyset frame leaning casually against a smaller table.

He looks over at her, boredom clear on his plain features. "Every Sixth day, without fail. Haven't seen you before. Are you new to the market or just the gallery?"

"First time at either. I usually Protect warehouses, mostly in the Eastern Area."

He pulls a face. "Protecting for Earth Elementals is a punishment. Although, Air Elementals are giving them some fierce competition these days."

"You get much trouble around here?"

"Sometimes there's a bit of catcalling at Peacekeepers, but it all gets shut down pretty quickly."

"What about stealing? Looks like you've got a few expensive pieces to protect."

The words have the desired effect – he follows her gaze to a nearby sculpture. Made entirely of glass, it twists like bodies intertwined. The colours dance in the sunlight, exposing the ripple of bubbles that mark the piece as hand-crafted and not machine-manufactured.

"I don't understand why anyone would pay a week's wage for anything that isn't digital."

The analogue piece is perfect – unique, expensive and hard to track.

The midday sun brings a fresh new torture. Trapped in her heavy uniform, the sweat pools between her shoulder blades and in the small of her back. The heat refracting off dark bitumen has thinned the morning crowds to clusters of small groups and individuals, making it easier to spot the few Peacekeepers loitering in the space.

No. Not loitering. *Stalking*. She sees it in the way they move – smooth, inconspicuous, deadly.

Air Elementals dominate the space – unsurprisingly; the precinct is Air-dominated and the market pieces more artistic and less functional. But a few Water Elementals can be found browsing high-tech visualisations and requisite Earth Elementals stand over smoking pits roasting cola pigeon or push carts from one stall to another.

Movement three stalls away pulls Anaiya's gaze away from the innocuous activity. Kaide's dark hair is mostly covered under the dark hood of his jacket, but the way he moves – comfortable, but not confident; quick, but unhurried – easily marks his presence.

She flashes her hands, communicating the description of the high-value piece with words they practised the night before.

Blue. Orange. Green. Tall. Twisted. Glass. Back. East.

He nods; clear to her, imperceptible to others.

His advance appears casual – he stops at the stalls in-between, strong hands running delicately over cheap, gaudy plastic. When he arrives at the stall next door, he becomes more assertive. Striding up to the shaded space, he towers over the fragile piece that has been his target all along.

Anaiya moves away. Close enough to still see, far enough to ensure her wristplate doesn't pick up on the voices.

"Are you sure this is the right price?"

She doesn't hear him say it, watching instead as his lips form the shapes that match their rehearsed script.

The Infrastructure Protector looks up. "Pay up or move on."

Kaide smirks. The action seems unnatural on him. Ugly.

But it works on the Protector; he scowls and takes a step forward. Kaide holds up his hands in mock submission – a more natural gesture – and steps away. Anaiya watches as he strolls past her area. At the last second, he glances up at her and winks.

Her heart jumps unexpectedly. She quickly looks away.

Shaking off the echo of synthflies in her belly, she turns her attention to the Infrastructure Protector next door. He smirks, a poor imitation of Kaide's earlier effort, and shakes his head. She smiles back, acknowledging his silent mocking of Kaide and Air Elementals in general.

Stage one complete. Protector attention drawn to target piece.

Three hours later, the heat is less oppressive but the day has taken its toll and the market vendors and Protectors are on edge. In the time since Kaide's appearance, there have been two bouts of violence and multiple arguments that have threatened the same.

When Lilith finally arrives, the tension in the market has well and truly ratcheted up. She approaches slowly, caught up in the conversation with her companions, oblivious to the activity around her.

Anaiya's heart rate picks up. She had argued this point with Kaide when they had first discussed his plan.

"What if she doesn't stop? Why would she stop?"

"Because she'll see you. And that will give her pause."
"But what if she doesn't? What if she doesn't see me."
"Trust me, Anaiya. She will see you."

He hadn't divulged any more details. As far as he was concerned, the less she knew the better – it would make her surprise more genuine and her denial of knowledge more plausible.

In the stall next to her, Kaide's other operatives go to work. One, a young and attractive Air Trainee with the moves of a Dancer but the body of a Sex Worker, saunters up to the Infrastructure Protector. His momentary distraction sets the next play in motion.

Another Air, clearly a Dancer by the sophistication and choreography of his movements, weaves almost imperceptibly through the stall's tables to where the target piece is displayed.

Anaiya looks back to where Lilith is continuing on her path through the market, still oblivious to Anaiya and showing no signs of stopping.

Her heart rate is frenetic, now. She glances back to the neighbouring stall – the Protector is still distracted by the Trainee, but the Dancer is gone and so is the art piece.

Desperate, she steps closer to the thoroughfare, conscious that she needs to attract Lilith's attention while not attracting the Protector's.

Time is against her; at any moment, the Protector will notice the missing piece and spring into action. And unless that piece is located in Lilith's bag and Lilith is reasonably in the proximity of the stall, all of the planning will be for nothing and Lilith will still be a problem that needs taking care of.

She hesitates and takes another step forward.

Still nothing. Lilith has passed the neighbouring stall and is only metres away from Anaiya.

Look up, look up.

"Anaiya!"

The voice is loud and clear and shatters the rhythm of the nearby space; random Elementals stop their browsing and turn to locate the source and Peacekeepers shift their stance in anticipation of another brawl or escalated argument. But more importantly, Lilith stops in her tracks and swivels her head, her eyes scanning the nearby area, her face hardening when her gaze alights on Anaiya.

Confusion briefly flits across her features. While she has every excuse to be looking at Anaiya, there is no reason for Anaiya to be looking at her.

Anaiya glances away, but not before she feels the emergence of a spiky emotion that is all too familiar and unwelcome. It has been a long time since she has felt guilt and she doesn't like it.

Next door, there is a shift in the weight. The changing mood of the crowd has pulled the Protector out of his distraction with the Air Trainee. He is scanning the surrounds, no doubt attempting a limited version of the Peacekeeper future-searching. It happens quickly – with each sweep of his gaze she can see him checking off potential threats. The direction of the shout, the nearby group of Elementals, the blind spot to the west.

And she knows what will come next.

His gaze tracks to where Lilith stands, pausing at her defiant stance and hardened features. Her emotion is not the mild curiosity or morbid fascination with likely violence that dominates other faces in the crowd. Her anger and confusion makes her different. It makes her memorable.

And then his gaze falls to the display table. Anaiya glances back at Lilith, wondering if she has any indication of what is about to happen. A slight movement behind her reveals the Dancer and as quick as he lifted the art piece from the stall, he deposits it in Lilith's bag.

The movement or the change in weight causes Lilith to glance down. Her hand instinctively pulls at the strange object, its multicoloured glass flashing above the lip of her black bag.

It is such a simple, natural, reaction. And it is her undoing.

The Protector calls out the code to the nearby Peacekeepers and they don't hesitate leaping to action.

Lilith spins around at the unexpected grip on her shoulder. Her companions try to intervene, but another Peacekeeper arrives and they back down. The Protector strides over to speak to the Peacekeepers. Lilith shakes her head violently, waving the 'stolen' artwork around in frustration. Eyes wild, she looks over to Anaiya, confusion clouding her features.

She knows she has been set up. And she knows that Anaiya could not have been the one to do it.

The first Peacekeeper strengthens her grip on Lilith's shoulder. Around her people are stepping away, leaving the Air alone in a circle of Fire Elementals.

Anaiya looks around – the Air Trainee has disappeared and there is no sign of the Dancer. Even Lilith's companions have left her; *to avoid guilt by association or relay the news back to Seth?*

A loud crash interrupts the raised voices, and then comes the tinkling of glass shattering against the street. Anaiya doesn't need to future-search to know what happens next.

She turns away – relief, anticipation and guilt a strange cocktail in her core – unwilling to watch as the inevitable restraint needle pierces Lilith's neck.

FORTY-THREE

The apartment is hot and stuffy when Anaiya returns. She calls out
for Delacroix, hoping the mutt will answer and come bounding
towards her. But there is nothing but the silence and heat to greet
her.

Stay alive, you stupid dog.

Striding to the utilities closet, she pulls her battered pedestal
fan into the small lounge room and plugs it in to the terminal under
the window. Flicking the heavy plastic switch, she waits for the
blades to bring some relief. But they do not spin.

Frustrated, she twists the fan's dial, to no effect. Yanking the
plug from the wall, she looks around the room for the other power
terminal. Wiring in the older apartments is a common problem; she
should have relocated sooner. If she is truly honest, she should have
relocated after the Execution. But the space had become familiar,
and with Delacroix it had become home.

Sighing, she gives up on the fan and pushes against the
window. Her effort brings no relief; the grains of sand accumulated
from westerly breezes jam the frame in place.

She pushes harder and then harder still. The windowpane
dislodges with force and falls five storeys to the street below,
exploding in a hailstorm of glass and stealing her breath.

Looking down, her anxiety morphs into panic at the sight of
an Elemental lying dazed and bloodied on the bitumen. Other
passers-by alternate between scanning the nearby buildings for the
source of the violence and tending to the barely conscious victim.

Can this day get any worse?

Biting down a curse, she grabs her hoodie from the bed, steps up into the naked window frame and rappels to the scene below.

The victim, a ninth lustrum Earth Elemental, is mumbling incoherently. Rivers of blood course from gashes on his forehead and shoulder.

With only ineffectual Airs and slow Earths nearby, Anaiya pushes through and kneels beside the bloodied male. The bottle of skin-mending serum tucked away in her pocket won't make much difference against the depth of his cuts, but she pulls it out and sprays them anyway.

The papery skin of the older Elemental struggles to respond to the healing properties of the serum, but the anaesthetic kicks in quickly. The Earth's face relaxes from its contorted frown and the mumbling and groaning subsides into whispers.

Anaiya taps on her wristplate to patch a call to the Paramedics. The white cross flashes on the screen.

Bloody Niamh messing around with my wristplate.

"Call the Paramedics," she calls to a nearby Air. "Tell them it's a Grade 4 multiple laceration to a ninth lustrum Earth."

The female scowls at the direction but taps on her wristplate. She frowns and taps again. "The comms function isn't working."

A nearby Earth Elemental brings up his wristplate. "Mine isn't working either."

The words cause a ripple in the small crowd. A failed comms function on one wristplate is uncommon, but not unheard of. But on three wristplates of three very different Elementals ...

Leaving the injured Elemental, Anaiya sprints over to the apartment building opposite. Rapping on the window brings a sleepy looking Air Elemental to the glass.

"Turn your lights on," Anaiya yells.

"What?" he yells back, not bothering to open the window.

"Lights. Turn your lights on."

"Why would I turn my lights on?"

Clenching her jaw, Anaiya banishes thoughts of punching through the glass and turning the lights on herself. "Turn the wallscreen on, then."

"It is on," he says, turning to the back wall. Anaiya squints against the glare of the sun's reflection and tilts her head to see around the Elemental. He walks away from her, revealing a dark, blank wall beyond. She sees him locate the controller and plug in his lifeline.

Nothing changes.

She doesn't wait for him to return and confirm what she already knows. No power in her apartment. No power here. No comms.

This isn't a normal curfew power-shutdown. Someone's hit a transmission hub.

Or maybe the network …

The thought sends adrenalin to her feet and she pivots to the west, where the nearest hub is located. Only to be confronted again with the sight of the injured Earth Elemental.

The anaesthetic qualities of the serum have clearly worn off and his agitated twisting has opened up the wounds again. Blood, thick and red, dribbles onto his already soaked shirt, attracting hungry synthflies.

Fuck, fuck, fuck.

The transmission hub to the west. The Infirmary to the south.

Groaning, she walks over to the Earth and kneels beside him. Placing her hands under his frame, she takes a deep breath and braces for the lift. "This is going to hurt. Don't struggle. Don't scream."

After eight blocks of silence, the sounds of wallscreens and music speakers finally swell in the stale air around her. Lowering the Earth from her shoulder and placing him against the nearest wall, Anaiya rubs some feeling back into her upper arms and patches a call to the Paramedics.

The Earth's eyes flutter as he drifts in and out of awareness, his blood-soaked shirt still wet and sticky.

"PK230 … Correction; IP879103. Grade 4 multiple laceration to a ninth lustrum Earth. Victim location is Ninth Precinct. Rue Poissonniere and … and …"

She looks around, scanning for the nearest street sign or coordinates plate. Finding a placard on the base of the building's corner, she kneels to wipe away the dust obscuring the location. "And Papillon."

Movement in her peripheral vision sends a shot of adrenalin through her body. She has been too distracted.

Not waiting for the Communication Operator's confirmation, she pulls the lifeline from her ear and disconnects the call. Straightening, she sets her feet and glances around for anything that will help or hinder her response to the emerging threat.

The tension and anxiety addle her brain and it takes her a few seconds before she can decipher the unfolding situation.

Jenna, her trademark platinum blonde hair and precise movement, sprints towards her. There is no hesitation and no flair, just straight lines and speed. Another two Peacekeepers flank her, moving in unison; their black uniforms melding together as one impenetrable wall.

Anaiya looks around, seeking the disturbance they are responding to. But there is nothing to draw her eyes or catch her ears. Whatever it is, it is blocks away.

Closer now, Jenna's gaze hits Anaiya's and she slows. The other two slow in response. Something itches between Anaiya's shoulder blades.

"Where have you been?" Jenna yells. She is pissed. "Niamh's been looking for you."

Slowly it dawns on her. There is no other disturbance. Jenna is here for her.

"Why is he looking for me?"

"Where have you been?"

The frustration in Jenna's voice does not come from her. Not really. It is an echo – an approximation of the frustration Niamh's voice would have held when he ordered her deployment.

But Niamh knows where I am ...

"I was at home. There was an incident." She glances over at the Earth Elemental; his trembling has worsened. If the Paramedics don't arrive soon, his chances of recovering will be destroyed.

Jenna briefly follows her gaze, but her frown doesn't shift.

"Then why are you here? And why didn't you answer your comms?"

"Comms were down …"

Anaiya looks back at the Earth, her brain racing to assemble the fragmented thoughts that are piling in on one another.

Niamh doesn't *know where I am.*

With the transmission hub down, the location triangulation had failed and Niamh's sound surveillance shut down. Anaiya had fallen off his radar. Until now.

She looks back at Jenna. "Why does he want to see me?"

"Not your place to question, IP." She uses the acronym like an insult, but Anaiya is immune to the barb. "He's waiting for you back at Headquarters. Let's go."

"What? Now?"

"Yes, now." Jenna's stance has become less combative, but there is still an edge to her voice.

"And what?" Anaiya throws her hand towards the Earth slumped against the wall. "Just leave him here?"

Jenna doesn't flinch at the accusatory tone. Doesn't take her eyes from Anaiya. "That's not my problem, IP. And it's not yours."

"So, what *is* your problem, Jenna?" She pours as much sarcasm and disdain as she can into the words, fully aware that Niamh is listening to the entire exchange.

One of the other Peacekeepers, a generation younger with a scar across his forehead, steps forwards. "Show some respect to your superior."

Anaiya laughs. "I'm not a Peacekeeper. She may be your superior, but she's not mine."

Jenna shakes her head at her shadow. Turning to Anaiya, she smirks. "You don't really believe that fiction, do you, Anaiya?"

"You mean the Orthodoxy?"

Now it is Jenna's turn to laugh. "Only a fool could be blind to the fact that Peacekeepers are the only thing keeping Otpor together."

"I'm pretty sure the Water Element feel the same way about their corps."

Jenna turns sombre. "Then they are not as smart as they think they are."

FORTY-FOUR

Anaiya adopts a slower pace on the way to Peacekeeper Headquarters. Partly because she is tired and partly because it is immensely satisfying to see the frustration radiate from her Peacekeeper guards.

A Paramedics Van, one of the few automobiles given reign on Otpor streets, had passed them two blocks ago. Unburdened from her guilt and worry over the damaged Earth Elemental, Anaiya had begun to formulate her approach to Niamh.

It has been weeks since she last saw him. Since he started tracking her.

Thinking of the violation still makes her skin crawl with invisible maggots, but she trains her face to remain neutral. She will need to play this smart if she is to blindside her old partner.

"You've been avoiding me, Anaiya."

Niamh nods at Jenna, dismissing her from his office. She doesn't betray any emotion – no scowl, no twitch of her lips – just nods in response and exits. The quintessential Peacekeeper – obedient to a fault.

"I thought we were avoiding each other," she replies as the door shuts behind Jenna. "We didn't exactly enjoy our last meeting."

"I don't know – I gained a soundmatcher, you gained your freedom. I would say that was a pretty good day."

"I thought it was to be our last day. Every time you say goodbye, you always find a reason to bring me back." She walks up to his desk, trailing a finger along the dulled edge of the glass. "You should be careful Deputy Commander or the Earth Cleaners will start gossiping about your improper dalliances with a lowly Protector."

Niamh doesn't smile. Humour is not valued among Fire Elementals. "That does sound scandalous ... Although not so scandalous as a tryst between two Elements."

Anaiya ducks her head and tries to imagine a naked Kaide. She pictures him as she has seen him all these weeks – coming to the galleries and warehouses she protects. Climbing in windows, the sleeves of his shirt riding up strong forearms. Chiselled jaw. Thick, dark hair to match serious, dark eyes.

She imagines those eyes tracking down her body as he removes her shirt and then removes hers.

Heat rises to her cheeks and flushes along her collarbone.

It is exactly the reaction she needs to make Niamh think he has hit a nerve with her. She looks up at him, shrinking away from his smug grin, even as she internally rejoices at seeing it.

"Why did you want to see me, Niamh? Or am I just here for you to torment?"

"I wanted to ask you about the Archivist."

This time her reaction is genuine. Of all the scenarios she had considered on the way to his office, this had not been one of them. "I've already told you everything. I didn't restrain her."

"Ease on, Anaiya. I believe you. That's not what I want to know."

She remains silent, too stunned by the turn of events to interject.

"What I want to know," he continues, "is what did you see her working on that week?"

There is no time to come up with a credible story; something that will shift suspicion from her or, better yet, increase paranoia about Water designs on power. So, she sticks to an approximation of the truth. "She had been working on the soundmatcher with the other Archivist. I hadn't paid much attention at first. But when I looked closely, I had seen that there was a part missing."

"What part?" Niamh leans forward, eyes intent and voice

tight.

"Like a panel or something. The cube was … I don't know … misshapen."

Anaiya waits for Niamh to say something else, but he merely leans back in his chair, so she continues. "I said something to them and she got angry. Well, as angry as Water Elementals get. But she was clearly pissed that I had said something. So, she snatched up the cube and left."

Niamh's entire posture has stiffened. Subtle, it would have been missed by her a year ago, but in her Air-enhanced state it is as if he is shouting the depth of his tension.

"The next time I saw her, I figured she was just ignoring me. For all their rationality, Waters tend to hold grudges."

Niamh sits still, his face inscrutable. "They do have long memories."

It is a cryptic answer, but there is nothing to be gained by questioning him on it. "Why are you asking me this, anyway? I thought you and the Waters had some sort of arrangement. With my alignment. With the soundmatcher."

He stares at her, as if weighing up what he knows of her against what his instincts are whispering to him. "It seems all partnerships eventually run their course."

"Is that why they're shutting down the Transmission Hubs?"

He frowns. There had been no time for Jenna to give him a full debrief on their way to Peacekeeper Headquarters.

"I mean, it makes sense," she continues, keeping her body language interested but not eager. "Shutting down power does hinder Resistance activities, but it also keeps the Peacekeepers out of the loop as well. What did the Fire Commissioner do to piss them off, Niamh?"

It is a nonsense question. She knows the paranoia clouding Niamh's features has nothing to do with the Commissioners and everything to do with the Unorthodox arrangements he has created to sate his ambition.

"We're investigating the power failures," he says, voice calm even though his jaw is tight. "We expect Air vandalism to be the cause. In any case, it will be easy to differentiate crude violence from sophisticated tech manipulation."

"What will you do if it is Water manipulations?"

"What I always do, Ani. I'll enforce the Orthodoxy."

FORTY-FIVE

"He's hiding something."

Anaiya and Kaide sit on the cool linoleum of her apartment floor. Curfew has brought with it a drop in temperature and the breeze that blows in through the open window carries the icy touch of a distant ocean. It plays with her hair and raises tiny bumps on her skin. With each gust, she shivers and grips Kaide's hand a little tighter under the sound-blocking sphere.

"Of course he's hiding something," Kaide replies, "He's a Peacekeeper."

She scowls at him and shakes her head. "He's hiding something big."

"Tell me more about the power outages. How many went down?"

"I'm not sure. Niamh definitely said 'power failures', plural, but he didn't say how many. I implied it was a Water ploy, but if the Forensics find vandalism, they'll conclude it's a Resistance attack."

Kaide shakes his head.

"They're not yours?"

"Maybe," he replies. "Indirectly. Seth mentioned something about tapping the water distribution lines for the pituarmagn distribution. They could have hit the power cables."

"You're still recording him?"

Kaide nods, his brow furrowed. "With Lilith detained, he may seek an old confidant. But, for now, it is the only way."

"The plan is still going ahead?"

"As far as I know; I'll check the soundmatcher again tomorrow. I checked out Boileau Road this morning."

"And?"

"It wasn't the alternative pituarmagn supply."

Anaiya groans. For every seeming victory, there arrives a multitude of obstacles in their path. "So, she did know I was tracking her. She saw me today at the market, she'll mention my name for sure."

"She didn't know you were following her. Her detour down Boileau wasn't evasive, she was there to see someone."

"Who?"

"I don't know. Not yet. But there's a gated community hidden behind the Danish Prince izakaya, I'm sure of it. One with lots of money, influence and anonymity."

Gated community. She had heard rumours of them when she was a Peacekeeper – hidden enclaves scattered around the city to accommodate the rich and high-ranking; to separate them from the common rabble of Elementals. Anaiya had dismissed it all as idle gossip of bored Elementals.

"What would Lilith be doing in a gated community?"

Kaide frowns. "Maybe we underestimated her. Maybe she is more influentially connected than we thought."

Frustration wells up inside Anaiya. "We need more information. Everything we have are hunches and innuendo and murky possibilities. We need something... tangible."

"More information means more time and less surveillance. Two luxuries we don't have."

Anaiya taps her foot against the nearby bed frame, impatient and anxious. More time. Less surveillance. More time. Less surveillance. *Less surveillance. Less surveillance ...*

"The Transmission Hubs."

"What about them? They won't distract Niamh for long."

"That's not where the opportunity lies. For the forty minutes and eight blocks of the power outage, I was offline."

Kaide's eyes light up as he grasps the implication of what she is saying. "Offline. No surveillance?"

Anaiya shakes her head.

"No audio surveillance? No triangulation?"

"Nothing."

"I wonder how many power stations need to be taken out for it to work ..." Kaide's whisper floats to Anaiya in the darkness.

She sits with her eyes closed and her back against the wall. The demands of the day are exacting their price, tightening already sore muscles and tempting her to sleep. She leans heavier against Kaide, squirming to find a more comfortable position. "One would be enough for the triangulation to lose accuracy."

Opening her eyes, she glances across at Kaide. He stares straight ahead at the window, chewing on his lip. "Maybe. Depending on which Transmission Hubs are affected and how close you are to one that is powered ... What's the minimum range for voice comms?"

"Three, maybe four kilometres. I always had voice comms in the Edges and there are no Hubs for at least a few blocks inside the city proper."

"How many Transmission Hubs to a power grid?"

Anaiya laughs. In her tiredness it comes out as a breathy giggle. Kaide laughs in return, his shoulder shaking hers. She nudges him and he nudges her back.

"What?" he asks, good-humoured sarcasm bright in his voice. "You don't know the city's infrastructure network? Can't calculate the power requirements of each Transmission Hub? I thought Peacekeepers knew everything."

She closes her eyes and smiles. "I keep reminding you, I'm not a Peacekeeper."

Kaide's hand unexpectedly squeezes hers under the sphere. "I think I'm starting to believe you."

"What makes you think there is an enclave behind Boileau Road, anyway?"

"There's too much wasted interior space on that block. No warehouses, no deep administration buildings, and no windows opening to the rear." He folds up his knees, the movement causing their linked hands to fall in the space between. "I tried to enter the izakaya, but it's more … exclusive … than the establishments I typically frequent."

She turns to Kaide. "You were turned away?"

A wry smile twitches on his lips. "The Protector was more than happy to follow that order …"

Anaiya's heart quickens, an echo of the chemical enhancer she had taken twenty minutes ago. "There's a power substation just off Exelmans Boulevarde, down near the river …"

Kaide shakes his head. "It powers the greater half of the Western Area. It will be too heavily guarded."

"We don't need to attack the substation. If you are right and it was Cress' handiwork that caused today's outage, we just need to damage the supply lines."

"What exactly are you planning, Anaiya?"

FORTY-SIX

The chill from the concrete facade of the Danish Prince izakaya bites through Anaiya's thin cottonex shirt. It is a welcome distraction from the building anxiety that comes from the quiet road and knowledge of what is yet to come.

Manipulating the izakaya's Protection roster had proven impossible for Kaide; much easier had been the distraction of its regular Protector by a high-quality and exorbitantly priced Sex Worker. After a few drinks and a sneak peek at the services on offer, he had been as eager to accept Anaiya's invitation to cover the shift as he had the entreaty of his new companion's body. A quick lifeline transaction and Anaiya's identification number was registered against the shift.

Nothing unusual, nothing to draw unwanted attention.

The hours of drinking at a nearby Fire izakaya had helped make the exchange appear more coincidental but has also made her less sharp. She digs her fingernails into her fingertips, pushing and prodding to elicit pain and clear her mind.

How is it that she finds herself in a strange izakaya looking for a treasure that exists, as yet, only in the mind of an Elemental that months ago was her enemy?

Enemy.

Even as she recognises the truth of the observation, she struggles to recall the emotion that was once associated with it. Kaide is no longer the Elemental she knew six months ago. And she doesn't know if it is him that has changed, or her.

A flicker of lights down the road brings the adrenalin rush she craves. Blood flushes her cheeks and her feet tingle with anticipation.

Flicker. Flicker. Falter. Out.

Darkness and silence explode on the street around her.

It doesn't take long for boredom or curiosity to tempt the izakaya's patrons out into the road. Anaiya checks her wristplate, testing the comms function. Nothing. It is the only invitation she needs.

Stepping into the izakaya is more disorienting than she expects. With so few patrons, the light from wristplates is not enough to navigate the unfamiliar space; even with the adrenalin rush, her mind is still dull from the residual alcohol and she has no idea where the hidden entry to the hidden community is located. Or if it exists.

"No, there is nothing for us to do out there." The nearby voice is slurred. Anaiya swivels instinctually, her eyes struggling against the dark to find its owner. "Let's just go back to le hameau. There are better things to do in the dark there, anyway."

The voice is fading. Anaiya stumbles around, attempting to follow it. A tinkling laugh to her left reorients her.

"The offer is tempting, Farasei, but we both know the lights will be on beyond the door."

Vague shapes start to materialise in Anaiya's limited vision. Snatches of other conversation drift to her; the quiet whispers of lovers enjoying the new darkness, the animated discussions of Elementals exploring heightened senses.

"Your loss, Amarelle. If you change your mind, you know where to find me."

Anaiya steps out of the path of the retreating Elemental, her eyes straining to follow the path of the rejected lover. A flash of light a few metres away reveals a swipe access panel.

Panicked, Anaiya brings up her wristplate. The comms function is still offline. Glancing around, she searches for other signs of light, for indications that the power network has been restored. But there is only darkness.

She turns back in time to see a sliver of dark grey appear,

interrupted only by the silhouette of her target. A different panic besets her. She needs to get through that doorway and she needs to do it undetected.

Her feet move quickly, as her brain races to consolidate the initial stirrings of a plan.

"Farasei!" Her voice is low and as seductive as she can make it. The figure at the doorway pauses and turns towards her. "I would be happy to take you up on that offer."

"And who might you be, my shadow seductress?" He sounds amused. And interested.

Anaiya twists at the last moment, careful to stay hidden in the darkness. Trailing one hand up his upper arm to cup the back of his neck, she places the other against the door to keep it ajar.

"I think I'm going to like you," he murmurs into her ear.

"Oh, I'm sure you will," she whispers, splaying her fingers till they find the sweet spot.

There is a moment, just before she presses, where her stomach flashes with guilt. But time and necessity overpower any softness and her fingers dig in, just enough to render the Elemental unconscious, but not damaged.

"Goodnight, Farasei," she whispers as his body slumps against the wall.

FORTY-SEVEN

The first thing Anaiya notices as she steps into the hidden world beyond the izakaya is the muted light. Not bright enough to attract the attention of the outside world, but sufficient to cast long shadows on the cobblestones.

The second thing she notices are the trees. Tall, impossible, beautiful structures whose tips never reach beyond the heights of the nearby buildings.

She walks slowly, keeping to the shadows, creeping closer and closer until she is only centimetres from the nearest one.

Her heartbeats furiously and her breath labours as if beset by a fresh terror. The last trees had disappeared from the Otpor landscape generations before Anaiya's conception.

Raising a trembling hand, she reaches out, fingertips grazing the finely textured trunk. Pressing her palm against it, her gaze travels up. Up to the slender branches and beyond to the canopy.

In the quiet, she can hear a slight rustling as the tree's uppermost leaves dance in what little of the south-easterly breeze that reaches them.

This is a dream. I'm in a dream.

Noise from the street ahead pulls her out of her reverie and returns the urgency of the mission. Ducking behind the cover of the tree, she peeks around its broad trunk.

Ahead, two shadowy Elementals emerge at an intersection. Deep in conversation, they remain unaware of Anaiya's presence.

"The Resistance has tampered with the power supply."

"They are becoming too bold."

"Yes, they are petulant children, but the balance will be reset. The Peacekeepers will not suffer the humiliation lightly."

"Peacekeepers! What are they, but overzealous bullies?"

The voices are fading, the Elementals continuing down the cross-street. Stepping out from her hiding spot, she stalks down the street towards them.

"… they are what they are conditioned to be. Everything in its place, everything in balance."

The cross-street emerges as a strange-angled intersection. She follows the Elementals as the street veers oddly to the left. Lights shine from unshuttered windows, illuminating the street and the Elementals.

They do not wear the fashion of the Air Element, or move with the same lightness.

"Perhaps. Then again, balance does not need to come from such volatility. If the pendulum continues to swing to such extremes, we may be its next victims."

"You worry too much. We are protected here. The outside world knows nothing of us. Even these enclaves are mere rumour and innuendo to them."

"Then why is Danai talking to random Air Elementals at the izakaya?"

They have arrived at an apartment building. The facade is a mosaic of brickwork, interrupted only by rows of large windows and a wide staircase that leads to the front entry.

"Danai sees it all as entertainment. He's reckless, but—"

The door shuts behind them, cutting Anaiya off from any further conversation.

She waits, hidden in the shadows, before continuing up the street. Rows of trees cast dappled shadows on the street and a faint music, unlike any she has heard before, drifts from an open window. With nothing else to orient her, she follows it.

Ahead, the enclave opens into a courtyard. The trees are thicker here, the light softer, the music louder.

Strange shadows reveal themselves as ornate benches; Anaiya finds one in the deepest part of the darkness and sits down.

The alcohol still lingers in her bloodstream, making her thoughts messy and disobedient. She has stumbled on something much bigger than Lilith's Resistance plans, but she can't piece together exactly what this strange new world means.

She recalls remnants of the overheard conversation and wonders if Lilith is one of the random Air Elementals that has visited the Danish Prince … maybe drawn by the same rumour that had piqued Kaide's interest? But if the enclave's residents were as reclusive as they seemed, it was unlikely Lilith had ever crossed the threshold.

Sighing, she stands. For all the questions she has, she knows the answers will not be found waiting in the shadows.

The streets are quiet on the way back to the izakaya. Anaiya pauses at the last tree, her fingers curling around the thick strips of its skin that peel away from the trunk. Her chest tightens and her fist clenches, distraught that she may never experience this ancient wonder again.

The papery material pulls away from its host. Anaiya knows she should leave it behind, but her legs carry her to the izakaya doorway with the piece tucked safely in her pocket, and three names on her mind.

"You really made it inside?"

"Yes."

Kaide's foot taps excitedly and he drags his hand through his hair. It is a move that reminds her of Seth.

"What were the names again?"

"Amarelle, Farasei and Danai."

"They're not Air names."

"Well, they aren't Fire, Water or Earth names."

"And Lilith was talking to Danai?"

"Maybe. It's a possibility. She may have just gone to the izakaya – it's exclusive enough that she could have had secret conversations. Secret negotiations."

"She could have made it inside."

Anaiya shakes her head. "No, you were right – the izakaya is exclusive. The enclave is … shut-down, classified. No outsiders allowed."

"What makes you think Lilith is an outsider?"

"Because. This place was different."

"You keep saying that, but it just sounds like a hideaway for the rich."

The remnant of the tree is still tucked in her hoodie jacket. She hasn't told Kaide about it. Her fingers curl around it, reminding her it wasn't a dream; wasn't some drug-induced hallucination or the workings of a mind under stress.

"In any case, you won't get answers there. Even if Lilith is an insider, you are definitely not." Kaide frowns but doesn't argue the point. "And whatever she was discussing, it wasn't low-level operations. She wasn't there to talk pituarmagn supply or sound development."

"So, what? She was looking for money?"

"Maybe. My guess would be sponsorship of some kind – either to lend finances or credibility. Having a high-profile supporter with connections …" She shrugs. "It could help get interest. Or supporters."

Kaide isn't looking at her. He stares straight ahead, eyes glazed over, foot still tapping.

"Don't do it, Kaide."

"Do what?" he murmurs, still wearing that far-away gaze.

"I see your mind working it over. I know what you're planning to do."

"Mmm?"

She sighs and shakes her head. "It won't work. You'll never get in."

Finally, his foot stops tapping. His face is all screwed up, a window to the conflict she knows rages inside him – the desire to solve the mystery, the frustration at knowing she speaks an unpalatable truth.

"You have to go back in," he says.

"No …"

He turns to her, face only centimetres from hers. Under that scrutiny, she becomes acutely aware of just how close they are;

where their legs touch, the press of his shoulder against hers, the grip of their hands.

"Anaiya, you have to."

"I don't have to do anything." She sounds more determined than she feels.

He cocks his head to the side, flashes her a smile. "Please."

During her realignment mission, she had never seen this side of him – playful, charming. It's disarming. "Are you trying to flirt with me?"

His smile widens. "I know you're too smart to fall for that, Anaiya."

She laughs. "Flattery?"

"The way to a Fire's heart is through her ego." His eyes twinkle with mischief, his foot nudging hers.

"And what is the way to an Air's heart?" It is meant as a sarcastic rejoinder, but her reply is too soft. Too hesitant. Holding her breath, she waits for him to laugh, or scoff, or respond with his own witty remark. Anything that will indicate he will not hold her to account for her words.

The silence stretches between them. Anaiya stares at a distant point, fixated on where their feet still touch.

Something has shifted in their dynamic. Weeks of secret rendezvous, whispered conversations and shared plotting has changed them. Changed how they interact. How they see the truth of the other.

He squeezes her hand, softly. She doesn't look up.

Theirs is a complex relationship. The brief moments of laughter and playfulness do not erase the troubled history or shared guilt. But they do dull them. Or change them somehow. Make them less fatal, more … *binding*.

He squeezes her hand, more insistent now. Still she avoids his gaze.

Sighing, he squeezes one last time. "The way to an Air heart, Anaiya, is through beauty and truth. Through what inspires, what is extraordinary. What intrigues them, or makes their heartbeat faster. Air hearts can be fickle, but genuine connections run deep."

Finally, she looks at him. Gone are the sparkling eyes and

cheeky grin.

The rush of emotion screams at her to pull from his gaze, to take breath. Heart racing, she forces herself to meet his eyes.

Everything is so raw with Kaide.

She looks away and immediately regrets it. His grip under the sphere relaxes and she knows that she has caused offence.

This connection will undo us both.

"Much easier to a Fire's heart, then," she says.

To her relief, he laughs. She looks up at him again, his eyes still sombre, but his face smiling.

"You have to go back in, Anaiya."

She sighs. He is more stubborn than other Airs she has known. "See what you can find out from Seth, first."

"His path is set, Anaiya. Even if he does come to trust me again, he has lost his way. His vision of the Resistance is too corrupted. Nothing I can say will resurrect his original vision."

The words trigger a memory of Kane 148 – his passion, his recklessness, and his unwavering conviction in a resistance uncovered by his Heterodoxy. His was the true, original vision. His resistance the one that had ultimately become corrupted …

"There is something you can do," she says slowly, still debating whether the potential gain in Seth's confidence is worth the risk of sharing more of her secrets with Kaide.

"What?"

She hesitates. Shaking her head, she squeezes her eyes shut. "There's an apartment out by the Ravignan Strip with loose floor panels and a large ventilation panel …"

FORTY-EIGHT

Each day that passes with no communication from Kaide is a steel coil around her chest. It is easy to think the worst – that he has turned on her, betrayed her to his Water Element contacts, or to Niamh in order to secure an amnesty for Seth. Harder to remember the things that bind them together.

The relentless heat strips her nerves, makes her restless. She waits for it all to come crashing down: for Niamh to order her detention, for the pituarmagn attack to commence, for the violence to start. Even when the sun goes down, the heat stays gathered within her apartment walls, holding tight to all of her dark thoughts.

Tonight, she sits on the floor next to the window, begging the night to admit a cooling Wasteland breeze. Sweat trickles along her neck and adheres loose hair to sticky skin. She strips off her singlet and flings it across the room at the pedestal fan that stands idle and useless in the corner.

The power is out again. Has been out for hours now.

She rests against the wall, the bare skin of her back seeking the relief of the cool plaster before the heat of her body can ruin it.

A bottle of tequila and cache of crystal enhancers sit beside her, her only refuge from the anxiety and sleeplessness. The synthetic cocktail is rough and bitter, but after a few minutes it starts to work its magic. The gears of her mind slow and her eyelids grow heavy. The floor and wall seem to lose their hard edges and unforgiving solidity, and her muscles no longer cry for the comfort of her bed.

Sleep does not come, but the quietness is still a blessing.

Except that it is not truly quiet. Without the typical wall of background noise from wallscreens and amplifiers, all the other sounds of life in Otpor filter through. The arguments, the sex, the buzzing of synthflies, the whimpering of hungry pups.

Her eyes fly open. The whimpering is louder, closer.

Pushing up from the floor, she rushes to open her apartment door. With the opening only centimetres wide, the door flings violently towards her and Delacroix bounds inside.

The pup barks excitedly and laps at her bare ankles. Anaiya snatches him up and hugs him tightly, her hand scratching through his patchy fur, eliciting more high-pitched barks. She laughs, the sound erupting from the darkest parts of her core and spilling out into her apartment.

"I missed you, pup! Where have you been?"

A shadow falls across their reunion, drawing Anaiya's gaze from the pup to the figure that stands at her threshold. Kaide leans against the door frame and pushes down the hood of his jacket.

His grin lights up his face and makes her heart quicken. She goes to open her mouth to say something – to ask what he is doing here, how he found Delacroix – but the itch of her wristplate keeps her quiet.

The pup barks louder, jumping from Anaiya's grasp to bounce around Kaide's feet. Kaide laughs and steps inside the apartment, shedding his hoodie and shutting the door behind him. "It's OK. The power's out – we are free."

The jacket drops from his fingers. With two quick steps he is just centimetres from her. Strong arms wrap around her bare waist and lift her high. He spins her around and the pure joy of it floods through her.

"Why are you so happy?" She is laughing, unable to take her eyes from his.

"It worked," he replies, slowing the spinning and finally setting her down. "Kane's notes, they changed him. I saw it – I saw Seth change as he read them. He trusts me again."

He is still smiling, but the news has spun Anaiya's emotions out of sync.

"Really?" Her voice is unsteady.

He still holds her tightly, stabilising her when her body still wants to sway. "Really."

"He'll reconsider his position?"

"Maybe. It's too early to know. But he's willing to indulge our relationship for a little while longer, which gives us more time."

"Our relationship? Is that what this is?"

Kaide's grip lightens and his smile loses some of its brightness, but not its warmth. He trails his hands up from her waist, across the sweat-drenched cottonex of her bra and along her arms.

Still she can't take her eyes from his; watching as they lose their sparkle and gain an intensity that sends her heart to her throat.

Fingers trail along her neck, cool against the sticky skin, hesitating only for a second before they bury into her messy hair and pull her in close.

There is a moment when it could all stop. When the madness could reveal itself as a minor glitch, a temporary insanity brought on by the uncertainty and the excitement and the unforgiving heat. And then his lips graze hers, the tingle running like electricity through her core to her toes.

As if drawn by an invisible magnet, she presses in against him, her own fingers roaming the expanse of his back, her lips crushing into his. The simple action ignites a firestorm and weeks of pretending shatter on impact.

Her brain whispers at her to be rational, to not be so reckless.

But the firestorm consumes her and she readily gives in to it.

FORTY-NINE

Anaiya wakes to Delacroix licking her bare feet. Entangled in threadbare sheets and Kaide's arms, she is reluctant to give into the pup's demands. But the dog is insistent, barking its discontent and causing Kaide to stir; stealing his arms from her side.

Sighing, she rolls onto her back and sits up. As if the motion were an invitation, Delacroix leaps up onto the bed and into her lap. Soft growls of satisfaction rumble in his throat as she scratches behind his ears.

Kaide murmurs against the sleep interruption but doesn't wake. Anaiya stares at him, her eyes roaming along his figure and fixating on bronzed skin peeking out from greyed sheets.

Her belly flutters with unfamiliar sensations as she recalls the night before and their unexpected intimacy. Sex with Fire Elementals was expedient, efficient – satisfying and high-energy – but all about the release and never about the connection. With Kaide, every caress, lick and kiss had been sweet torture. Never rushed, always urgent; never rough, but never soft.

Shaking off the tremors, she swings her legs over the edge of the bed and stands.

Delacroix pads after her, his paws racing across the linoleum floor to the apartment door.

"OK, pup, go get your feed." She opens the door wide enough for him to squeeze through. "Just make sure you come back."

She waits until the sound of him rushing down the stairs recedes to a dull beat before turning back to Kaide. They have been reckless; Kaide should have left hours ago, while the power was still off or curfew still in force. He is awake now, propped up on his elbow and gaze firmly settled on her naked body.

A moment of indecision attacks her. In the raw passion of the night before, there had been no time to second-guess their folly. But now that the shadows have dissipated and the morning light taints everything a soft shade of brown …

Kaide smiles at her. It is not the exuberant grin of the previous afternoon or the seductive smile that had followed. It is softer. He sees her hesitation, reads her conflicted thoughts, knows the strange mix of emotions coursing through her; she finds them reflected in the quiet intensity of his gaze.

He stretches out his arm, beckoning her to join him. Banishing her dark thoughts, she lets him pull her back into his arms. He hugs her tight.

The minutes steal precious time from them, and still they lie there. Not moving, not speaking. Just being.

She knows it can't last. Wriggling out from under his arm, she turns to face him. He reaches up to trail a finger along her cheek. She pulls his hand away, interlocking it with hers and nestling it between them.

"You have to go," she whispers.

He closes his eyes and brings their grasped hands up to his lips. Slowly, she extricates her hand from his.

The coolness that rushes in as he leaves the bed should be welcome, but she resents it. He dresses quickly, looking at her with serious eyes. Sighing, he shrugs into his hoodie.

Before he leaves, he pauses at her desk and scribbles something on a sheaf of paper he has rescued from his jacket. His fingers push and pull the note into a complex series of folds; an angular, fragile bird emerging from his efforts. He places it gingerly on the pillow beside her and leans down to kiss her temple.

"We're allowed to be happy, Anaiya," he whispers into her ear. And then, without a backwards glance, he leaves.

Left alone, she runs her fingertips over the edges of the folded bird in front of her. *Happiness.* It is a nice sentiment, an easy throw-away line. *Everyone is allowed to be happy. That doesn't stop misery crushing everyone who seeks it.*

She rolls onto her back and looks up at the ceiling.

I'll be happy *when we put an end to all of this madness.*

Sighing, she unravels the paper sculpture. The underside is printed in small, tight characters. She tries to make sense of it, her brain stumbling over the unfamiliar words and strange rhythm.

> *How if, when I am laid into the tomb,*
> *I wake before the time that Romeo*
> *Come to redeem me? there's a fearful point!*
> *Shall I not, then, be stifled in the vault,*
> *To whose foul mouth no healthsome air breathes in,*
> *And there die strangled ere my Romeo comes?*

The rest of the page continues in the same strange manner. She reads and re-reads it, finding no new clarity. Frustrated, she gives up and turns the sheet over. Kaide's haphazard scrawl contains a much simpler text. *You're not alone in this.*

FIFTY

The afternoon streets thrum with activity. Sounds and colours and scents call for Anaiya's attention, tempting her away from the warehouse that is expecting her.

She takes two steps to the left, following a yellow scarf fluttering in the breeze and chasing the smell of sweet glucose caramel. Glancing down at her wristplate, she calculates whether there is enough time for a detour. Her shift at the warehouse isn't due to start for another forty minutes. If she takes the subworm from San Lazar to Nation, she can cut twenty minutes from her journey ...

Her idea to orchestrate shifts at the warehouses likely producing pituarmagn, or at least its precursor chemicals, had been more difficult to implement than she or Kaide had anticipated. Security at chemical warehouses had always been tight, but with the escalation in violence and the persistent Resistance murals, getting their number and locations was impossible.

A week ago, Kaide had tracked down a few warehouses in Precinct 20 from his own contacts. They are unlikely to be the source of Seth's planned pituarmagn attack, but if nothing else they may offer hints of where the other warehouses are located.

She banishes thoughts of pituarmagn and warehouses and covert missions. The afternoon's heat is tempered by an insistent north-westerly wind and the streets of the Northern precincts, while busy, are not heavy with the weight of inevitable violence.

Almost pleasant.

The thought pulls her up short. Around her, Elementals move and weave between and around each other. She looks more closely at them. And doubt creeps along the edges of her mind.

Is the weight really as light as it seems? Or is she merely seeing her own joy reflected back at her?

Is that what this is?

She had thought she had known joy before. The thrill, the swelling of heart, the anticipation of what will come next – that was all familiar. But it had always been a loud emotion – exuberant. It had shouted through her body, whereas this new sensation skips and dances.

Belatedly, she realises her distracted stare has fallen on an eighth lustrum Earth Elemental who struggles to set up the remaining street-side stalls. There is no joy in her movements and no restraint in her return stare.

Anaiya looks away. The lightness she had felt just moments ago dissipates with the rising taint of guilt. While all Elementals are impacted by the Heterodoxy and its violence, for some the burden is heavier.

Confronted with this new realisation, the emotional filter falls from her eyes and a different streetscape is revealed.

She sees defeat and fear in the hunched postures of older Elementals. The drunken bravado in others falters, revealing itself as a thin disguise for the anxiety that spirals out of control below.

And so it goes; each block on the way to San Lazar teems with the scared, the tired, the angry, the resentful.

And with each block, the day seems darker, the heat wilder. And the weight heavier.

The same Peacekeepers her gaze had slid over at the start of her journey now call to her attention. She expects to see arrogance or indifference. Expects these black-clad sentinels to stand in stark contrast to the Elementals they oppress. And yet all she sees are the same troubling emotions lurking beneath their hard exteriors. Not as obviously as they are in the faces and stances of other Elementals. But there, nonetheless.

Why so surprised, Anaiya?

Her guilt ratchets higher. How had she come to so easily

demonise her former corps? To so easily reduce them to a simple stereotype – the same thing she accused them of doing to other Elements?

Not every Peacekeeper is Niamh.

It's an easy truth to accept. But it scratches at her mind, working away at deeper levels, raising more troublesome questions.

Not every Fire is corrupted?

She pushes down the errant thought. Just because there are decent Fire Elementals doesn't mean the Element itself isn't corrupt. *And just because there are corrupted Fire Elementals doesn't mean the Element itself needs eradication.*

She shakes her head and tunes out the streets and Peacekeepers.

Leave it be, Anaiya. Kaide is turning you soft. The sight of the station marker less than a block away lifts her from her dark thoughts but does not eradicate them entirely. As she descends the stairs and steps into an almost-empty carriage, she feels them twisting in her belly.

The sound of the worm speeding along the underground tracks grows louder as it enters the lower precincts. The infrastructure is older here, built on pre-Singularity foundations and cursed with all the erratic flaws of its past.

Fluorescent bars run like white ribbons cursed with static. Their light bounces around the metal walls of the carriage. Flicker. Flicker. Flicker. Flash.

She rests her head against the window; pressing her cheek to the cool glass, letting the vibrations of the worm echo through her body.

It is only when the rhythm slows and the darkness deepens that she opens her eyes.

Faced with pitch darkness, she blinks; trying to clear her vision and wipe away the shadows. Slowly, vague details emerge against the green glow of her wristplate and she stands to manoeuvre down the aisle towards the doors. Shining her wristplate against the frames, she runs her fingertips downwards until she feels a ridge in the metal.

The manual override panel pulls away under the pressure from her fingers and she holds the light of her wristplate up to illuminate the matrix of ports. Remembering the combination from her Peacekeeper days, she locates the one at position D6 and jams her lifeline in. A full twist to the right and half to the left disables the lock and the interim panel comes away, revealing the manual lever beneath.

Gripping it tight, she pulls down hard, expecting it to resist. It flicks down quickly, accompanied by the sound of the doors losing pressure and releasing from their grip to each other.

She prises them apart and peers down along the train and beyond. No lights anywhere.

Unwilling to trust the obvious conclusion that leaps to mind, she grimaces and clambers down to the tracks.

Have they really done it?

The subworm network, being the second-largest power-sucker after the air recyclers, is hooked up to its own power grid; quartermetre-thick cables buried below the more recent power structures built for the residential and commercial sectors. If Cress and her merry band of vandals have managed to hit it, they haven't done so by accident.

Her heart races with thoughts that the pituarmagn attack has started. She looks again to her wristplate, surprised to see the comms function still online.

But why shut down the subworm?

Why shut down any network at all? The whole attack rests on people recording it on their wristplates and uploading it for mass consumption.

Maybe it has nothing to do with the attack.

Maybe it's just a taunt. Something to wave at the Fire and Water Elementals who think they are superior, but who are so easily bested by the Air Elementals they look down on and despise.

Her ankle rolls on a loose piece of concrete, her wristplate diode sending light scattering as she stumbles. Cursing out loud, she stabilises and looks around. The tunnel stretches on and on in darkness.

If she hadn't zoned out, she would know where she is and how far she needs to walk until she reaches the next station.

There is a danger in being on the tracks for too long. Her nerves tingle in anticipation of the sound of an oncoming worm. With no escape route, all she has is the assumption that the power is out and that no other worms can come racing through the tunnel.

The darkness and disquiet follow her for the next eight hundred metres until her diode hits the sharp edges of a platform station. With tired legs she hoists herself up, the light catching the name of the station: Sully-Morland.

She knows the name. Knows this place. Three blocks away lies her old headquarters; the Eastern Peacekeeper HQ. And Niamh.

FIFTY-ONE

Her feet race up the stairs that lead from the station to the street and, before she hits the surface, she has crafted the backstory she'll need to explain why she will turn up late to her Protection shift.

Exiting into the light of late afternoon is disconcerting. While the power outage has pulled her off the digital surveillance grid, the lack of darkness still threatens her ability to remain undetected.

This is foolish, Anaiya.

The berating rings true but doesn't slow her feet. With her surveillance disabled, she has an opportunity to enter the HQ undetected. And once inside, she'll have access to the designated areas and the back-up data systems, the ones that run off their own quarantined power supply. She will have to restrain a Peacekeeper in order to use their lifeline, a task that will be infinitely harder than restraining the Archivist, but —

She stops suddenly, her body and thoughts shocked into stillness by what lies ahead. A block from the headquarters, a line of Peacekeepers stretch along the intersection.

Her hackles raise and a heady mix of suspicion and foreboding slow her feet.

This is not a threat response – they are too still. If there had been an attack or incident, bodies would be in motion and the streets would be echoing with aggressive voices issuing commands. This is a defensive manoeuvre; they are there to keep something out or create a distraction to disguise something else.

Whatever the motivation, she knows that Niamh is orchestrating it. *He must have moved quick to take advantage of the power outage.*

The thought draws her up. There is no way he could have set the defensive line in place unless he knew about the shortage in advance. Or planned it himself.

What are you up to, Niamh?

Backtracking around the block presents the same picture. Rows of Peacekeepers standing like sentinels.

She is losing time. If this is all a master plan, Niamh will be wasting no time in implementing it.

Her belly cramps with anxiety. It all has the same feel as her realignment mission. The feel of something that is outside the bounds of Orthodoxy, of a crazy plan borne of Niamh's ego and ambition.

Is this the start of his attack against the Air?

Her need to get inside HQ is suddenly overshadowed by her need to find Niamh. His hubris and paranoia won't let him delegate anything important to someone else; if something is happening, Niamh will be getting his hands dirty with it.

But where is he? Is it all unfolding here at HQ or is Niamh using the power shortage and defensive line to sneak out undetected?

Ducking into a side street and away from any line of sight, she pulls up the call function on her wristplate, cursing at the blank screen even as she expects it. Adrenalin courses through her body, sending her fingers trembling and her brain screaming at her to do anything but stand still.

Stepping out into the main thoroughfare, she walks towards the HQ entry.

"Halt, Protector," a senior Peacekeeper calls out. "This building is on lockdown."

Anaiya slows her advance but doesn't stop. "I have urgent intel for the Deputy Commissioner."

"Not going to happen tonight."

Still she advances, heart racing as the line of Peacekeepers shift in unison to a more active position.

"He'll have your badge if you don't let me tell him."

"And who are you to claim that?"

"The Peacekeeper who brought down Rehhd 020."

There is movement as the senior Peacekeeper steps out of line and up to Anaiya. Her wristplate diode lights up the space around them, blinding Anaiya and giving the Peacekeeper the visual confirmation she needs.

Vision from Rehhd's Execution is still on high rotation across the broadcast channels and Anaiya had been front and centre for most of it.

The Peacekeeper baulks at the recognition and pulls the analogue comms device from her belt. The rest of the precinct may be without power, but Peacekeepers still had ways to stay in contact.

"PK1351797. Request patch to PK6051951." She stares at Anaiya, still sizing her up in the light of her wristplate.

"Transferring now," an anonymous voice crackles through the device.

"Do you need a reminder, Peacekeeper?" Jenna's voice, despite the distortion, is easily recognisable. "HQ is on lockdown. No calls unless there's a level four threat. Is there a level four threat?"

"No, Peacekeeper."

"Do I need someone else to lead the southern line?"

"I have Anaiya 234 here. She claims she has critical intel for the Deputy Commissioner."

Anaiya's heart is beating too fast, too loud. Things are becoming too complicated, she hasn't thought this through.

"Put her on."

The Peacekeeper hands over the plastic intercom and stands back with arms folded.

"This is Anaiya." She prays Jenna won't hear the hesitancy in her voice.

"What do you want, Anaiya?"

"I need to speak to Niamh."

"It's not a good time, Anaiya."

"The world's on fire, Jenna. There's no such thing as a good time anymore."

"Then this is really not a good time."

Jenna is just as intractable and infuriating as ever. Anaiya chews her lip and punches tight fists into her thighs. "Where is he?"

"Unless you have something valuable to offer, Anaiya, I am terminating this call."

She needs to tell her something. Something that will keep her on the call, something that will command Niamh's attention.

"I saw the Archivist. The one that claimed I restrained her." The words rush from her mouth, the idea half-formed and rough around the edges. Jenna's silence at the other end of the line emboldens her.

"She passed me near Chatelet." She rattles off the name of the station immediately before Sully-Morland, hoping that it also suffers from power outages, reassured that in the worst case, there is no way for Jenna to check the veracity of her claim in real time. "She said something. Something about Kane 148. Something about Fire gone bad. Or turned bad …"

"What exactly did she say?"

"She said that Kane's sins would undo us all."

A faint clicking transmits through the call. Of Jenna's wristplate against a desk? Or her tongue against her teeth?

Either way, it is the sound of indecision, and angst, and frustration. It is music to Anaiya's ears.

"Stay on the call."

The line goes silent. Two seconds, five seconds, ten. Any more than fifteen and the chances of Niamh being away from the building increase.

Fifteen seconds. Twenty. Thirty.

Sixty seconds of silence later, the call becomes active again.

"Don't approach. Niamh will contact you tomorrow for more details."

The call is disconnected before Anaiya can reply. It doesn't matter. Niamh is not inside, leaving only Jenna as someone who might spy her sneaking around undetected and attempting to access the data systems. It is a risk, but one she is more than prepared to take if it gets her intel on what the Peacekeepers are planning.

The subworm platform is still empty when Anaiya arrives back at the station. She wastes no time jumping down to the tracks and pacing down the tunnel.

A few hundred metres in and her wristplate diode catches the start of the ventilation network. With the power out, the fans will be idle and every subterranean space on the network will evacuate without windows to relieve the heat. Including the basement levels of the Eastern Area's Peacekeeper Command.

She checks her wristplate. It's been twelve minutes since the power went out. The average duration of recent outages has been around forty-five minutes – leaving her enough time to reach the HQ before the fans switch back on. But this outage is different. And unpredictable.

Ignoring the lock on the grate, she turns her attention to the hinge. Like the lock, its metal shines with strength. But the weak point isn't the hinge itself, but the bolt that holds it in place.

She bends to inspect the underside, her fingernail testing the gap between the hinge and the bolt's head. It's enough.

Removing her belt, she jams the buckle in the space and picks up a chunk of loose concrete that litters the tunnel floor. The weld that holds the bolt head to the shaft is the most vulnerable component; so close to the floor of the tunnel, rising dampness should have weakened it further, which means just a few heavy strikes …

The disembodied head skitters on the tunnel floor. Pulling the rest of the bolt from the hinge, the grate pivots around the still-intact lock and swings outwards.

Securing her belt back in place, she clambers up into the pipe, and sends out a silent prayer that Niamh's plan doesn't conclude before she can get there. And that the power doesn't return before she can get back.

FIFTY-TWO

The network is simpler than Anaiya expects. She navigates it easily, her Peacekeeper affinity for spatial awareness overlaying a map of the above streetscape in her mind's eye.

Crawling on her belly, she shivers as the cold metal hits the skin where her shirt has ridden up. She shuffles through intersections and around silent blades, moving as quickly and quietly as possible. Only when she gets closer to her destination does she shut down her wristplate and plunge into darkness.

Adrenalin spikes along her veins as memories of her time in a detention cell flood her mind.

It's not a metal cage, it's just a tunnel. Keep moving.

Twenty metres later, her fingers hit ridges in the metal where the main ventilation system joins a local network. She pauses and listens. Blood thrums in her ears, but otherwise there is silence. She creeps forwards slowly until her fingertips graze the crosshatch of a vent opening.

Turning on her wristplate light brings the room beyond into focus. Like all the other interrogation rooms on the third sub-floor, it is sparse – a plastic table, four plastic chairs, restraint anchor points bolted to the floor and audio-visual recording equipment set into the wall.

Her heart sinks, the adrenalin condensing into disappointment.

It is a dead end. The room's door won't open from the inside without authorised wristplate activation, even in the event of a power blackout – a failsafe against unlikely, but not impossible, escapes.

She resists the urge to pound her fists against the metal panels. *Think, think, think.*

She shuffles forward and shines her diode upwards, finding the spot where the ventilation tunnel opens up into one of the shafts ascending to the upper levels. Standing in the narrow space does little to relieve her claustrophobia, but she ignores it and instead focuses on maintaining traction against the slick facade as she pulls her legs up and pushes her back against the wall to hold her suspended.

With her body stabilised, she uses her hands and feet to inch her body upwards. Her first attempt takes her halfway to the next level, before her traction slips and she falls with a thud to the tunnel below. Wincing more at the noise than the pain, she wipes her sweaty palms against her jeans and starts again.

The second and third attempts are no more successful.

I don't have time for this.

The threat of the power returning makes her rush her next attempt, her hands scrabble too quickly, her balance is never settled from the beginning. She gets higher than her other attempts, but the eventual crash to the tunnel below comes louder and harder.

Groaning, she rolls onto her side and massages the throbbing in her hip. Biting down on the pain, she braces to pull herself up for another attempt. And then the sound of a door slamming sets ice to her chest. She scrambles to shut down her wristplate, wincing as her elbow collects the wall and the dull thud echoes around her.

Holding her breath, she strains to hear any reaction above the sound of her racing heart.

"This is ridiculous, Deputy. Why are we here?" The female voice is familiar. It tickles at the edges of her memory.

"These rooms are completely soundproofed," Niamh's voice rings out, clear and confident. Anaiya's heart lurches; he was not supposed to be in the building. "All wristplate functionality is scrambled. And with the power off, nothing can be recorded."

"What game do you think you're playing, *Deputy*." She says the word like an insult. Like it is beneath her.

And that's when it clicks. Anaiya does know this voice – it is the voice of the Water Commissioner.

"It's not a new game, Commissioner. And it should be one that is familiar to you. After all, you've been playing it for some time."

"Don't let our arrangement embolden you. You have more culpability and much more to lose. Your ambition may have got you this far, but it may yet bring you undone."

"Don't lecture me."

"Then stop wasting my time. Why did you invite me here? What is so urgent, and secretive, that we must discuss it three storeys below surface during a power outage?"

The strength of familiarity between them is unsettling.

"You brought me in on your plan to uncover the Resistance all those months ago. Why?"

"I needed a Fire Elemental with desire and imagination. Two things your superiors clearly lacked."

"You needed someone you could manipulate."

"You sound ungrateful, Deputy. Yes, you gave me the tool and opportunity I needed to trial realignment procedures. But I gave you the pathway for your fast-tracked promotions. And let's not forget, when it comes to future Fire Commissioner nominees, I wield a veto power that will be of much benefit."

"You would like that, wouldn't you? A Fire Commissioner in your pocket giving you free reign over the Cooperative."

The Commissioner laughs, short and sharp. "Don't be naive, Deputy. That's not how the Cooperative works."

"Oh really?" Niamh sounds equally smug.

"I fear you have overstepped this time. I don't know what you hoped to achieve from this reminiscence, but our arrangement is concluded. I have no more use for your hubris or your insubordination."

"Shall we make the separation official?"

"What are you do—?"

The change in tone and sound of movement pushes Anaiya to inch forward, until she can peer through the nearest ventilation grid. The glow from the wristplates below illuminates an impossible scene.

Niamh stands over the Commissioner, his hands gripping the restraint points in her shoulders.

No. Not restraint points. There is no point in restraining her; all that can result is her recovery and Niamh's ultimate fall from grace.

While Anaiya can't see it, she knows his fingers are not digging into the soft tissue of the Commissioner's neck. They are splayed and pressing into the spot just below the chin, stimulating the carotid sinus.

There will be no violent struggling, no excessive violence. The Commissioner's heart will seize and …

Niamh lets go and the lifeless body falls from his hands.

"I'm tying up loose ends."

FIFTY-THREE

The power comes back on half an hour later. Anaiya hears the sound of the fans kick into gear as the lights of the subworm tunnel flicker on. She moves quickly, racing to get to the next station before a freshly powered worm comes hurtling through the tunnel and squashes her on its tracks.

Her wristplate will be pinging her location. Niamh will know she is close.

Jenna already knows you're close. It won't matter.

And yet her belly still flutters with unease.

She slows as she nears the next subworm station. With the power back on, there are more Elementals milling about. The last thing she needs is to attract unwanted attention. Or witnesses.

Casting about for some loose concrete, she finds a piece the size of her fist and launches it down the tracks. It has the desired effect – curious Elementals peer in the opposite direction, allowing Anaiya to leap up onto the platform unnoticed.

She paces towards the stairs, the subterranean space suddenly claustrophobic. Taking the steps two at a time, she stumbles near the exit; her ankle twists and falters under the pressure, sending pain ricocheting up her calf. Wincing, she hobbles up the final steps to the station concourse.

More Elementals roam on the mezzanine level. Grateful for the lack of black kevlar, she ducks her head and limps towards the exit. Swiping her wristplate over a barrier gate, she hurries as best she can through the rest of the concourse and up to street level.

Dusk has arrived in her absence. Long shadows run down Boulevarde Bastille and music floats across the still waters of the nearby Basin Delarrsenal.

She and Kaide have underestimated Niamh and his willingness to break the Orthodoxy if it serves his purposes. Distracting him is no longer an option – they had thought giving him the scent of blood would pique his curiosity, but what rat practises restraint when the blood leads it to a fresh carcass?

Thoughts of blood and rats and carcasses circle in her mind and distract her from the pain still buzzing in her foot.

What did he do with her body?

There was no way that Niamh could leave it in the interrogation room. And half an hour wasn't long enough to move her up three storeys and out of HQ without anyone else seeing.

How is he going to hide this?

He was obviously bold enough to set everything in motion. And while he is ambitious, he isn't reckless – he would have planned every detail and every detail would point in a direction that could never implicate him.

The pain has turned white-hot. She will not make it to Precinct 20 on foot.

Reluctantly, she turns and heads back to the Bastille subworm station.

"You lost, Protector?"

And with three words, the pain in her ankle is pushed aside.

"No, Jenna, not lost. Just … injured." She wants to bite down on the last word. As it is, it comes out strangled and defeated.

Jenna stands at the station entry, flanked by two other Peacekeepers. "What are you doing here, Anaiya? You were told to move on."

"I'm on my way to a job."

"You were on your way forty-five minutes ago."

"There was a power outage, if you hadn't noticed."

"You don't need power to free-run. Or walk." Jenna's smirk adds acid to injury.

"Can't walk on an injured ankle," Anaiya spits back, making no attempt to stay calm or school her tone. "I tried catching the subworm – they do need power to run."

"So, how did you injure your ankle?"

"I thought Niamh had you off heat-map duty. What did you do this time to piss him off?"

"This isn't heat-map duty, Anaiya."

Then what is it? Does she know about the Water Commissioner?

"Cleaning up Niamh's mess, Jenna?"

It's the way she narrows her eyes and the way her posture shifts from intimidating to defensive. *She knows. She knows everything.*

"How much Unorthodoxy do you need to see before you stop obeying orders?" She spits the words out, no longer caring that Niamh can hear them. Wanting him to hear them.

"Watch yourself, Protector."

Testing her ankle sends waves of pain through her body. She won't be able to outrun Jenna. And Jenna is too beholden to Niamh to do anything but turn her over. It doesn't matter that Jenna knows her superior is flaunting the Orthodoxy for his own ambition; if Niamh wants Anaiya detained, Jenna will not hesitate to follow his direction.

Just like a good Peacekeeper.

"He's using you, Jenna. He'll keep on using you and when he's wrung all the use he can from you, he'll discard your empty shell."

"I'm not you, Anaiya."

"You're *exactly* me, Jenna. You're me right up to the point Niamh threw me in a Sec Level 5 briefing with the Water Commissioner and left me alone while Technicians stripped away my identity and reconditioned my brain."

It's enough for Jenna to detain her. Speaking of a Sec Level 5 briefing in front of other Peacekeepers warrants an Unorthodoxy code, should lead to some sort of disciplinary action. But Jenna stays where she is.

Maybe Niamh has pushed her boundaries too far after all.

"Get to your shift, Protector," Jenna says, ignoring the quizzical looks from her colleagues. "I don't want to see you again."

FIFTY-FOUR

"You didn't find anything?" Kaide's lips send tiny tremors along her earlobe. The sensation is immediately reminiscent of the night before, but this time Anaiya's core is beset with worry, not desire.

He had been waiting for her at the warehouse when she arrived. She had stopped him before he could speak. Even with the voice manipulator and their well-established backstory, she was no longer keen to take unnecessary risks.

Like crawling through a ventilation tunnel to spy on Niamh?

She had been rash. Maybe it wasn't Niamh who had the ego problem.

"No," she whispers back to Kaide, her lips brushing against his cheek. "Niamh had the HQ on lockdown."

The lie coats her tongue, but she is not ready to share what she has seen. As far as he knows, all Anaiya had done that evening was find a back way into the Eastern Area HQ through a ventilation shaft. Part of her feels guilty about the omission, but she still doesn't trust the Water Technician he seems affiliated with.

The memory of her realignment warns her about the dangers of keeping secrets. Secrets have stolen her identity and killed innocent Elementals. But secrets have also kept her alive. And so, she is content to keep the matter of the Commissioner secret for now.

Kaide nods and pulls away. They sit side by side with their backs against a large mixing vat. The sound of the internal blades grips Anaiya's brain in a vice. She pushes her palms against her ears and pushes her head into her knees.

Seconds later, Kaide's hands tilt up her chin and gently tug her hands away. He pulls her up to standing and leads her to the far corner of the room, where other vats sit waiting for transportation.

Condensation trails large beads of sweat around the metal bodies. Kaide trails his fingertip across, sending rivulets of liquid down like tears. *Why are you worried?*

These secrets will kill them. She can't tell him the truth, so she turns the question back on him. *Why aren't you more worried?*

He shrugs and smiles. *Everything is working out the way we planned. Seth. Niamh. Lilith.*

That had been the reason he had showed up unexpectedly at the warehouse. He had come from Seth's apartment; Seth had finally confided in him and reached out for help. He was worried about the pituarmagn attack, uncertain whether they could pull it off without Lilith around.

Kaide had used the opportunity to cast more doubt; questioning whether it had ever been the right plan, whether it could ever be the catalyst for the change Seth wanted to bring about.

Too many unknowns, she writes. *Too many things out of our control.*

Kaide shakes his head. *No. Just one – the pituarmagn. Stop that, we stop the attack.*

Anaiya sighs. That was what it had always been about for Kaide – stopping the violence, saving his friend, respecting the original vision for the Resistance. But shifting his perspective is a problem that doesn't require an immediate solution.

Kaide ducks his head to meet her gaze. "Yes?" he mouths.

There is no point denying him. Shift end is still hours away; they may as well use the time to find out what they can about the pituarmagn distribution.

"Fine," she mouths back and then steps up beside him to whisper directly in his ear. "We'll check the transport manifests and schedules."

They are the only documentation she has access to as a Protector. Knowing who is arriving to deliver or collect stock, and whether their requests or protocols are in keeping with past behaviour, is all part of the standard risk assessment. There won't be a lot of detail, but maybe it will be enough.

She turns away from the vat and heads for the loading bay mezzanine, the pain in her ankle reduced to a dull thud. Kaide's hand darts out to grab hers. She startles, trying to find the danger he has seen before her. But he merely links his fingers in hers, his grip strong and reassuring.

The words he wrote to her on that strange piece of paper sound in her mind, as if she is hearing them direct from his lips. *You're not alone in this.*

She wants to believe it, but she's not so naive to believe it for the want of it. The last time she had let herself be distracted by her feelings for an Air Elemental, her entire world had been destroyed.

Kaide is not Seth.

The truism feels defensive and triggers an unsettling case of deja vu. Her earlier words to Jenna re-translate – *He's exactly Seth. He's Seth right up to the point you betrayed him and let an innocent Elemental be Executed.*

The void below the bay's mezzanine is empty, save for the harsh fluorescent light that paints everything white.

She stands apart from Kaide, putting more distance between them than is necessary. Not enough to call his attention, but enough to satisfy the dark thoughts plaguing her.

Her lifeline slots soundlessly into the transport management terminal, powering up the glass screen and initiating the verification protocols. Knowing that every tap and swipe from this point on will be monitored makes her nervous.

It is nothing she can't explain away. But the thought of needing to explain it away makes her hesitant.

She knows Kaide is watching her, waiting for her to start the search, but she avoids eye contact. Reluctantly she swipes to the past month's deliveries.

From what Kaide has gleaned from his Water contacts, there are two main precursor chemicals needed to produce pituarmagn. The first, proloxy, is a common ingredient in a range of synth products on the market. But the second, lutraden, is complex and difficult to produce. Highly unstable, it requires specialist conditions for production, storage and transportation. Anaiya reasons there can only be two or three warehouses producing it, if that. Which means that all pituarmagn producers are relying on the same small handful of suppliers.

Which means we just have to find an entry for lutraden deliveries and work our way back to the supplier. Find them, find the warehouses that are purchasing it to make pituarmagn.

She wants to explain all this to Kaide, to reassure him that she has a plan and is not just wildly scanning the system for something to pin their hopes to. Looking up from the terminal, she expects to see him frowning at the screen. Instead he peers at her, not frowning, not smiling.

"What?" she mouths.

He shakes his head, as if to clear it as much as assuage her suspicion. *Nothing.*

"What?" she persists.

Sighing, he closes the space between them and presses his lips to her ear. There is a pause before he whispers anything. "You've changed ..."

He pulls back to look at her. To check her reaction? His own face is loaded with too many complex emotions for her to decipher. "You're not thinking like a Fire anymore. Or an Air." He pauses, uncertainty flashing across his features. "It's like you've transcended the Orthodoxy ..."

She pulls away to look at him. His face is soft, but otherwise unreadable. But his eyes, there is something burning behind them – a revelation, a desire. It finds an echo in Anaiya's belly and she feels her senses heighten.

She wants to lean in ... but, instead, she clenches her eyes shut and hurriedly turns away. Her breath threatens to become shallow and fast, but she forces it into a normal rhythm. Counting to five, she opens her eyes and swipes at her wristplate to bring up her vitals. Elevated, but within the normal range.

Kaide pauses, hurt and rejection flashing briefly in his eyes. She flashes her wristplate at him and sees his face register recognition. There can be no conversations, no sounds of another presence and no sudden spikes in her vitals. Any anomaly will tip Niamh off.

"Sorry," he mouths, stepping back.

She snatches at his hand before he can get too far and squeezes it, forcing him to look at her. *Don't be.*

In the unforgiving light and wide expanse, the moment feels raw and naked. Part of her wants to let go, but she holds his gaze and her grip until the hesitation passes.

Only when he smiles at her – easy and uncomplicated – does she squeeze his hand and release it. He is right – they may not be in this mess equally, but they are in it together.

Turning back to the terminal, she resumes her search.

"Tell me something," Anaiya murmurs.

The two of them sit facing each other on the carpeted floor of the Manager's office. The now-familiar dome covers their hands, muting the sounds of Anaiya's playlist.

"What would you like to know?"

"The note you left me the other morning, the *'you're not alone in this'* message ..."

"I meant it." He says it matter-of-factly. Not earnest. Just genuine.

"Do you remember what was printed on the other side?"

He frowns.

"The strange language?" she prompts. "The *'when I am laid into the tomb'*?"

The unorthodox words feel familiar now. Reading and re-reading them have carved them into her memory.

"Romeo and Juliet?" Kaide asks, his face softening into one of recognition.

She recognises the first name and nods. "What is it? Where did it come from?"

Smiling, Kaide leans into her until their foreheads are touching. It feels as though a final piece has slotted into place, the two of them connected at the head, hands, knees and feet. A completed circuit.

"As far as I can tell," he murmurs, "it's an ancient story. I found only a handful of pages under an old storage cabinet out in Precinct 19. The building was empty – completely derelict. I think the Cooperative had condemned it years ago. The pages were stuffed under the cabinet to stabilise it."

"How many pages?"

"Fifteen, maybe twenty."

"What do they say? What is the story?"

"It's hard to be exact – the language is difficult to translate and I'm missing more than a hundred pages—"

"Then don't be exact."

He lifts his head, breaking contact to look her in the eye. She can imagine the questions he wants to ask her, the questions she would ask if the situation was reversed.

Why do you want to know? Why is this so important to you? Don't we have more pressing concerns to discuss?

He doesn't voice them, though.

"Romeo and Juliet come from two warring factions." His voice is soft. Anaiya closes her eyes and lets it wash over her. "These factions have hated each other for forever. But, somehow, the paths of Romeo and Juliet have crossed. And despite the Unorthodoxy of it all, despite the weight of everything else against it, these two have connected.

"Everyone thinks it's a bad idea. People are dying around them, because of them. The leaders of the two factions are enraged and do everything they can to separate them. But Romeo and Juliet don't care – they can't deny the strength of their connection because of an ancient conflict. Romeo is sent away, but Juliet devises a plan.

"She fakes her death, sending word to Romeo that he should come back and rescue her from her tomb. The two of them can escape unnoticed – As far as everyone else is concerned, he is banished and she is dead.

"It's a perfect plan. But she is worried."

"How if, when I am laid into the tomb," Anaiya murmurs, recalling the words of the story, "I wake before the time that Romeo come to redeem me? There's a fearful point!"

"She's worried her fake death will turn into a real one."

Anaiya opens her eyes and looks into Kaide's. "Does it?"

Kaide sighs and squeezes her hand under the dome. "I don't know; the page I gave you was the last."

FIFTY-FIVE

The next few days are spent hustling Protection shifts at the warehouses they have identified as potential pituarmagn distributors. At each, Anaiya checks the schedule for unusually large shipments or lots of smaller shipments to the one destination, but she finds nothing out of the ordinary.

Kaide's visits become less frequent as Seth leans more heavily on him in Lilith's absence. Without him around to distract or reassure her, she finds herself scanning gossip sites and social forums for word on the Water Commissioner's death.

Sighing, she swipes to close the browsing screen on her wristplate. It is a useless endeavour; the affairs of Water Elementals are not of interest to Airs, and Waters themselves would never deign to engage in frivolous speculation online.

The sound of a shrill bell echoes through the warehouse, announcing the arrival of a transporter.

Anaiya walks to the loading bay and checks the terminal for details.

DELIVERY – 18:10 – AQ78ZG – AMOXYLON 10kL – WAREHOUSE IEA23 (J8)

It is a large delivery, but of an innocuous chemical. She scans the plates on the delivery truck to check they match the registration number provided in the manifest and, satisfied, presses the button to permit entry.

Walking down to the bay, she greets the seventh-lustrum

Earth Elemental who steps down from the driver's cabin.

"How's your night been?" he replies, moving to the back of the truck to unload the consignment.

"Slow. Yours?"

"Same old, same old." His fingers flick across a control panel at the back of the truck, releasing the vat from its vice and initiating the conveyer belt. "I have instructions that it needs to be refrigerated immediately."

Anaiya frowns and steps closer to the truck, surprised to feel the waves of chilled air radiating from its body.

"I thought amoxylon was stable at room temperature?"

The Earth shakes his head. "Not my carcass, not my rats. Boss says it has to be refrigerated."

"OK. I'll check the notes and send it for storage."

The vat lands on the bay's conveyor with a thud.

"It should all be in there," the Deliverer says. "It's been the same instructions the last three times."

Anaiya pauses and stares at the vat. Stepping closer, she inspects the consignment sticker. It matches the details on the terminal.

"Three times?" She runs her hand over the sticker, looking for signs of tampering. "What? In the last year?"

He laughs and starts walking back to the driver's cabin. "In the last week."

That can't be right. There is no way this place has needed thirty thousand litres of amoxylon in the last week.

Anaiya walks around the truck, following the Earth. "All from the same warehouse?"

The door to the cabin slams shut and he leans out the window. "Yep, all from IEA23."

"Where is that again?" she yells over the sound of the engine starting up.

"Precinct 20. Boulevard Picpus. Just a f—" She loses the sound of his voice as the engine hits throttle and exits the warehouse. It doesn't matter, she knows what he would have said.

Just a few blocks from the Nation subworm station.

FIFTY-SIX

Anaiya's eyes grow heavy with waiting. She had left a message for Kaide – a blue stone thrown through his studio window – to tell him she had something urgent to share. But that was hours ago.

Her discovery changed everything; they finally had what they needed to head off what had seemed to be an inevitable clash between Niamh's Peacekeepers and Seth's Resistance. They needed to meet immediately – to plan their next course of action. To finally put an end to the madness.

Where are you?

The dark of the curfew hours stretches long and tight. All too soon, the coming grey of dawn filters into her apartment and brings with it a mixed torment – borne equally of sleep deprivation and Kaide's failure to arrive.

His absence brings with it a new kind of worry. It was naive to think she was the only one with secrets. The thought puts spikes to her mind, the tips dulled only by the heavy tiredness that weighs down her body and mind. *A problem for another day.*

Every blink of her eyes lasts a little longer than the previous, does a little more to file down the edges of her worry. Each time she lingers in the soft darkness a while more. Embracing it. Hiding in it. Until it obliterates all thoughts and torment and she crashes fully into sleep.

When she awakes, the apartment is transformed in mid-morning light. Long shadows and heat infiltrate the small space, and still Kaide is absent. Blinking against the light, she runs her fingers over her wristplate looking for something that will indicate Kaide's reasons or intentions.

There is nothing.

Rolling out of bed, she showers quickly and dresses in the clothes lying wrinkled on the floor. Brushing off the dog hair that clings to the fibres, she whistles for Delacroix, hoping to hear the pup's excited yelp and scurry of filthy paws.

The silence hurts more than it should.

Calm down. He's a dog – he's out hunting. And Kaide is just caught up in managing Seth. No one has betrayed you.

Biting down on the rising emotion, she races from the apartment, free-falling over the balustrade and letting the rush obliterate everything else.

The streets of the city move slowly in the day's growing heat. Anaiya, too, moves more slowly than she would otherwise, spending too much time looking for Kaide's face in the shadows.

A street hawker, with sun-damaged skin and raspy voice, calls out the flavours of her nutrient boosters. Cheaper than the convenience of pills or syringe shots, more palatable than soylent bricks, they satisfy key dietary requirements while offering a poor approximation of the flavours found in synth alcohol and cocktails.

"Mademoiselle, you look thirsty." She winks at Anaiya.

Anaiya smiles despite herself. Who knew Earth Elementals had a sense of humour? "It's a warm day."

"What?" the older woman replies, grinning as Anaiya steps closer. "I hadn't noticed."

In her tenth lustrum, she has done well to so far avoid the inevitable death from synth toxin build-up. "You must have lived through some hot summers."

The hawker laughs. "Are you calling me old? How impertinent."

Anaiya laughs in reply and cocks her head. "You don't speak like other Earth Elementals."

"Ha. When was the last time you spoke with an Earth?"

The accusation is a fair one. While Earth and Fire are not diametrically opposed, their shared preference for action over introspection is not enough to dull the disdain they have for one another.

"Besides," she continues, "when you get to my age, time has a way of erasing the mind's conditioning as much as it poisons the body. Now, enough talk – What flavour would you like?"

"I'm not sure …"

"What's your choice of poison at the izakaya?"

Anaiya pauses, genuinely caught between two favourites. "Some days I like a dodecahedrazine. Other days I like a lyseracid."

The older female frowns, looking at Anaiya closer. "And what day is it today?"

"Today is the day I don't like either."

"Ha. We all have days like that." She rummages through her collection and hands Anaiya a blue booster. "Here; it's never too late to try something different."

Anaiya tucks the lightweight box in her pocket and swipes her wristplate over the payment terminal. Looking up, she finds the hawker still staring at her.

"You don't act like a Fire Elemental," she says.

Anaiya smiles. "I guess that makes us the same."

The streets are quiet when Anaiya finishes her shift. With curfew still in place for another four hours and no residential or entertainment quarters nearby, there is no music or laughter. No sound of wallscreens blaring mindless entertainment and propaganda. No grunts or squeals of aggressive sex from open windows, no shouts or thuds of domestic violence.

Just darkness and stillness. And heat.

With no white noise taking up space in her mind, her thoughts seem excessively loud.

Minutes after the Deliverer had left the warehouse, the pieces all fell into place. Finally, she knew what was going on and why she had never found any unusual lutraden shipments in her searches. Checking the transport history had confirmed her theory.

They were disguising the shipments – passing them off as amoxylon or tetraskar or any other low-grade, low-risk chemical. More ingeniously, they were shipping the vats between warehouses, moving them around so that no one warehouse was recorded as moving the whole shipment alone.

In analysing the manifests deeper, patterns began to emerge. With some effort, she had been able to decode the shorthand descriptions, identifying the unique prefixes for production and storage warehouses and the strange alpha-numeric reference that located them on a ten by ten grid of the city.

After that, it had been easy to identify the storage warehouses that were receiving the shipments. At first, she had been disappointed that there hadn't been just one. And then she realised that if they were moving shipments between production warehouses, they were probably doing the same with the storage warehouses.

All she needs to do now is get access to those warehouses and see which one isn't passing the shipments on.

She moves quickly towards the centre of the city, wishing not for the first time that she could just call Kaide and speak openly to him.

It takes her just under forty minutes to get to his studio. She doesn't stop, running past as if she is lost in the free-run, glancing up to see if the lights are on. This area of Precinct 18 is mixed use, pushing apartment buildings up against commercial spaces and filling the gaps with izakaya and galleries. Lights and music and colour filter out from open windows, hinting at life beyond curfew, but Kaide's window is dark.

The empty booster container sits crumpled in her pocket and a tart aftertaste lingers on her tongue. With nowhere else to go and no desire to head back to her apartment, she has found her way to the storage warehouses of grid reference A8.

They sit in a cluster, their faded facades an echo of the recyclers that hum nearby in the Edges. Anaiya doesn't linger, still conscious of her wristplate surveillance. She turns north, keeping to the riverside.

With each step her surroundings become more familiar, taking her back to Boileau Road, where she had first tracked Lilith. Unlike other riverside districts, the left bank of Precinct 16's River Syn is quiet and degraded. The cobblestones are blistered and broken up, running together in long gashes that reveal the dark bitumen beneath. Windowless walls face outwards, saving the inhabitants from the stench of sludgy water and Anaiya from prying eyes.

The river walls are corroded, so she sticks to the uneven walkway. For three blocks she walks without seeing another Elemental. Only at the intersection with Boulevarde Exelmans do the familiar sounds and movement of the city start flooding back.

A small izakaya sits isolated on the corner, lost amongst the tall administration buildings that shadow it like bulwarks. Her gaze wants to slide right past it, drawn to the brighter lights and louder noises further down the boulevarde. And that's why she knows that something is off.

Despite the afternoon hour and the high volume of traffic, there is no movement around the izakaya. She steps closer, taking in the camouflaged door and tiny slits for windows.

What is this place?

It is too simple to be an Air izakaya, too small to be Fire, and too inconspicuous to be Earth. If not for the fact that Waters drank infrequently and always alone, she could almost imagine it as a Water izakaya.

There is no light that spills from the windows and no music that echoes from behind the nondescript facade. There is no way it could be abandoned, the real estate it occupies is too lucrative. And there is no reason for it to be closed with curfew still hours away.

Concocting a half-formed fiction for entering the property, something about suspecting a disturbance or seeing Elementals fleeing, she swipes her wristplate over the access terminal and waits for the door to click open. She swipes again, the terminal beeping to acknowledge the request, but the door refuses to open.

She pauses, stepping away from the door and looking around. Comfortable that no one suspects her of anything Unorthodox, she switches on her diode and shines it through one of the narrow windows. A few tables and lounge chairs are scattered around the small space, but beyond the furniture the space is empty.

Backtracking to the riverside pathway, she drags her foot

along the crease where the wall meets the pathway, sweeping away the pools of sand and debris. About three metres along, her boot hits a heavy, metal knuckle. Bending down, she trails her finger across the smooth facade, finding the subtle grooves that will reveal the service entry.

It is a small panel, no more than half a metre high or wide, just enough for deliveries to fit. And, if she is lucky, an Elemental.

She lines up her kick, aiming for a spot just below the top of the panel where the hinges will be. And then, on the follow-through, just centimetres from impact, she pulls back. Her boot skitters harmlessly across the wall.

She looks around, taking in her surroundings, focusing on the details her subconscious has already stumbled upon.

It is an old part of the city; the crumbling river wall, the cobblestone streets, and the lack of modern infrastructure dating the quarter like pockmarks and wrinkles on final lustrum Elementals. The river is deeper in this part of the city; the water darker, the current slower.

Normally, service entries burrow down into subterranean levels of Otpor; hinged from the top to allow access panels to lift up. But burrowing down is not an option here – the river is too close, the water too deep, the infrastructure too vulnerable.

She taps along both sides of the panel; her left hand eliciting dense, almost soundless thuds, in contrast to the tinny rattling from her right.

Repositioning herself, she brings her foot in hard and fast against the left side of the panel. The hinges explode and the panel shudders away from the wall. Grateful for the absence of watchful eyes, she crouches down and squeezes through the small opening.

The elation at gaining entry to the mystery izakaya is quickly replaced by confusion. Instead of opening up into a larger space, the access point continues as a narrow tunnel.

Anaiya's chest constricts and panic, thick and hot, screams at her to scramble backwards, to return to wide, open spaces, to escape the oppressive dark confines of this extended coffin.

Her brain, fuzzy with emotional feedback, struggles to form the rational demand that filters through vague and weak.

Keep moving.

It doesn't have the power it had five nights ago. With shaky fingers, she taps on her diode and lights the way ahead. The tunnel seems to continue indefinitely.

Heart in throat, her hands and knees scrabble to propel her back to the street. The light from her diode bounces around the walls, picking up the irregularities in the polyethelene cladding.

She pauses. The lines in the ceiling aren't random flaws – they are too straight, their depth too uniform.

Breathing heavily, she inches forward. Turning onto her back, she pulls her knees to her chest, flexing her feet against the ceiling panel.

Three. Two. One.

She flinches against the sound as her legs push up and through the barrier. The panel comes away easier than the first and her muscles pull tight at the over-extension.

For a while she just lies there, her legs resting against the edge of the opening. From her positioning, the light crests over the edge and into the room beyond. It should all appear unfamiliar, except her brain reconfigures it – rotating it, turning it upside down, flipping it – until it fits the same view she first saw peering through the narrow windows of the izakaya.

Her first instinct is to crawl through and explore the space beyond. It is her Fire instinct calling her, tempting her to investigate and confirm. It lasts a few, brief seconds, before another part of her mind takes dominance. A part that tells her the more interesting lead is the tunnel that runs from the river wall, underneath the izakaya and beyond. Under Boulevarde Exelmans. Towards the enclave.

The tunnel widens the further she progresses, shifting Anaiya from crawling on her belly, to all fours, to eventually standing.

Each vertical shift is a reprieve – her claustrophobia fading, anticipation building.

Calmer now, she can pace out her progress. Her eyes constantly scan upwards, searching for the next panel into another room in another building. The first one had opened up into the basement level of an administration tower next to the izakaya.

Her subconscious tickles with the potential consequences of her detour. The triangulation will pick up her location to the nearest five metres, maybe less. It's enough for the surveillance team to assume she is on the nearby streets. Her slow movement may attract attention, but hopefully they will put that down to the depression of not being a Peacekeeper anymore.

Ha!

Five minutes later, when she thinks she has reached six hundred metres in, she sees the tell-tale lines that mark an entryway. By her calculations, it is the Danish Prince.

Adrenalin courses through her body, her hands reaching up to run fingertips along the grooves. And, yet, she doesn't attempt to push through. Instead, she shines her wristplate diode ahead. Unlike before, when the light would dissipate as distance gained dominance, the light terminates ten metres ahead. It shines off the back wall, speckling it grey.

But it's not the back wall that interests her.

She slows her advance, shining the light up at the ceiling. Finding the panel, she stands directly under it, stilling her body and straining to hear for any sounds from above. Her fingers flex against the smooth metal. She pushes a little harder, testing the strength of the lock, only to find the panel shift against the contact.

Swiping off her diode, she pushes again, lifting the panel just enough to peer through the crack that results.

Late afternoon light filters down into the tunnel. It could be any street or dilapidated plaza in the city, except the rush of air is cooler and smells sweeter. No long shadows interrupt the view, no inane chatter fills the silence.

A piece of debris pushes its way through the crack and floats down. Anaiya lets the panel click down into place and turns her diode back on. Shining it down, the light picks up the layers of dirt and grime that have accumulated over the years.

And something lighter, more fragile.

Bending down, she picks it up. The dry, papery leaf splinters in her grasp. She lets it fall back to the ground and picks up another.

And another.

Her mind races to make sense of it all; tiredness and anxiety stopping the pieces from falling into place.

She will not get the answers she needs from fallen leaves in a dark tunnel. And with her wristplate surveillance, she can't sate her curiosity in any event.

Glancing over to the next panel, her mind turns to the world of the Danish Prince above and to Kaide, the echoes of frustration and confusion at his absence still keenly felt. He had done his best to convince her to go back to the izakaya. To get more answers.

Looks like you will get your wish after all.

FIFTY-SEVEN

Kaide is waiting for her when she returns to her apartment. He sits on her bed, back resting against the wall, legs crossed.

"Where have you been?" he asks, the voice modulator rendering his words in the higher-pitched tone of his alter ego. He is not angry or frustrated, but she still has to bite down the retort that burns on her tongue, that demands the same answers from him. It has been more than two days since she threw the stone through his window.

"Out."

He frowns at her, chewing his lip. There are things he wants to say, things he can't say while her wristplate is sending every sound in real-time back to Niamh. "I was surprised to see your message…"

"I had something important to tell you."

He cocks his head to the side, still chewing his lip. Part of her is a little satisfied at his obvious discomfort, the other part just relieved to see him again.

"Do you still have something important to tell me?" He looks over at the sphere laying on the bed next to him.

She laughs and lets go of the frustration she had been stubbornly holding on to. "Are you trying to seduce me?"

There is a pause, a moment where confusion deepens his frown and stills his incessant fidgeting. And then he laughs. "Would you like me to?"

"Ah, lover." She walks over and sits next to him on the bed. He wraps an arm around her. "You kept me waiting two days. That ship has sailed."

He laughs again, softer, and leans his head against hers. "I would have come sooner," he whispers into her ear. "But Lilith's detention is due to end any day now and I need to make sure Seth doesn't fall back into bad habits when she returns."

"Well that's not good news."

"Maybe. What about you? Did you find anything at the warehouses?"

"Actually, I did."

Kaide pulls back to look at her. "Really?"

"Mm-hmm. And I've got better news."

"Oh, yeah?" He picks up her hand and intertwines his fingers in hers. "What's that?"

"You owe me a date at the Danish Prince."

Anaiya tugs at the strange fabric. Tight at the bodice, flowing to her ankles, it is completely alien from anything she has ever worn. And yet, there is something liberating in wearing it. In being someone different.

There had been no time to organise a shift swap or a power failure. After divulging her intel, Kaide had insisted on going back to the Danish Prince that evening. Their only option was to turn up to the izakaya and try to gain legitimate access.

The rivets of her boots flash in the light, kicking out from under black skirts that shimmer silver in the street light. Boileau Road is empty, save for the Protector leaning against the wall of the izakaya and a shadowy figure half-illuminated in the intersection with Jouvenet Street.

She approaches slowly, her heart hammering away with each step. When she is around twenty metres away, Kaide steps out.

Gone is his familiar messy hair and mismatched clothing. Replaced by curls that frame his face in waves and dark threads that shadow curves and angles.

Her heart quickens. He looks good.

He is staring at her and something about the intensity makes her look down. She knows, in the rational part of her brain, that she hasn't slowed her advance, and yet everything seems to wind down. Crystallise.

She looks up. He hasn't looked away.

Ten metres. Eight. Five.

He is still. No chewing of the lip, no fidgeting of the hands.

Four metres. Three.

He lets out a low whistle. Soft. Seductive.

This close, the fire in his eyes burns hot. They aren't the kind of eyes you drown in. They're the kind that strip away everything inconsequential.

Two metres. One.

He offers his hand, but she steps past it. She collides with him, feeling his body rock back, tingling as his arms wrap around her and his core stabilises their faltering. Lips crash onto his and all rational thought is silenced.

Heat rushes through her body, followed by crazy, impossible thoughts, imagining things they could do, that she wants him to do.

The kiss turns deeper, slower. His hands shift lower, trailing the groove of her lower back. Hers entwine in the curls left unsubdued at the nape of his neck.

Finally, she breaks away.

"I missed you, too, Anaiyasha." His voice is soft and raspy. It sends new synthflies to her belly.

"You look good," she says, drawing her gaze up from his chest to his eyes.

"You look stunning," he murmurs. Even with the manipulator, she hears his true voice. "I was worried you weren't going to show. Thought you might have changed your mind."

"Was never an option."

She still hasn't told him about the tunnel that leads from the riverbank to the enclave. He still hasn't told her about what he and Seth have discussed.

She takes his hand. "Ready?"

"Ready."

Closer to the izakaya, she pauses, her stride faltering when she recognises the Protector at the entrance.

"What?" Kaide whispers, looking around.

She doesn't say anything, just squeezes his hand and looks straight ahead. Kaide follows her gaze, pausing when he sees what she does.

Leaning into her, he whispers in her ear, "I've got this. Follow my lead."

FIFTY-EIGHT

"Name." The Protector sounds bored.

Anaiya buries her head into Kaide's shoulder.

"Farasei invited us," Kaide says, speaking the name of the Elemental that had first granted Anaiya access to the enclave.

The seconds seems to stretch longer than they should. She feels Kaide's lips graze her cheek. Another subterfuge. And then the door clicks open, trance music escapes into the space outside, and they are moving.

Only when the cool breeze at her back ceases and the bassline synchronises with her heartbeat does she look up. Luxe carpet and copper inlaid walls serve as the backdrop to a collection of finely dressed Air Elementals. They lounge around on intricately carved armchairs. The moulded plastic has been worked to imitate the heavy timber of extinct trees.

Except they aren't extinct.

Anaiya looks closer. *Is it real timber?*

No one pays attention to her and Kaide as they move further inside the space. Perfect faces, stunning bodies, expensive threads. These are Otpor's most beautiful mixing with its most rich and powerful.

At any moment, she expects someone to really notice them, to notice how out of place they are. That they don't belong.

And then she looks over at Kaide.

In the golden light of the izakaya, his hard angles are softened and his skin glows like bronze. He looks strong and assured and beautiful.

Maybe it's just me that doesn't belong.

The thought pricks at her core and she bites down on the uncertainty. She is not here to belong, she is here for answers.

Closing her eyes, she pulls herself back through time, remembering the izakaya as she had experienced it during the power outage. The access panel had not been far from the entrance, maybe twelve strides ahead and slightly to the left.

She opens her eyes and lets her gaze recreate the pathway from her memory. Past the lounges, all the way to the back wall. She expects to see the light of the access panel, but all she sees is her reflection.

Somewhere behind that ceiling-to-floor mirror is the doorway to the enclave.

Kaide bends in towards her. "This is not what I expected."

"Welcome to the other side," she whispers back. "Let's get a drink."

The walk to the bar serves two purposes – it gets her closer to the mirror wall and it gives her time to think about her next move.

"What can I get you?" The voice pulls Anaiya out of her thoughts. It is too light, too musical, to be an Earth Server. But there is no Air Elemental who would work in such a mundane role. It throws her.

"What's popular?" Kaide asks.

The Server laughs. "Your first time, huh? Who is your sponsor?"

Kaide looks at Anaiya with a frown. They are woefully unprepared for this.

"Farasei?" Anaiya replies softly.

"That boy has good taste. Although, it's been a while since he's brought in outsiders." The Server starts pouring two drinks; a clear liquid set bubbling with a blue crystal enhancer. "I haven't seen him yet. Did he give you a set time?"

Anaiya shakes her head.

"Sounds about right. He has always been a little vague. I'll send him over your way once he arrives." She pushes the two tumblers across the bar and waves towards an empty corner of the izakaya. "His space is over there. Take a seat and enjoy."

Anaiya picks up her glass and looks for the payment terminal, but the bar is one long, uninterrupted piece of stone. Still confused, she looks to Kaide. He shrugs and starts walking towards the cluster of empty chairs. With no other option, she follows.

"Check your wristplate."

Kaide looks up from his drink. "What?"

"Check it." She holds out her own, the thick white cross dominating the screen.

No time stamp, no connectivity, no apps, nothing.

Kaide frowns and holds his own out to Anaiya. The same white cross flashes across his screen. She leans over and waits for him to meet her halfway.

"I need Kaide to be here," she mouths.

"I am here," he mouths back.

"No. I need *Kaide* to be here. I need to hear your real voice. I need Niamh to hear your real voice."

He pulls away from her, his frown deepening when he understands what she is asking him.

"Go to the bar," she mouths, "Follow my lead."

He hesitates. Every muscle seems to tense with the weight of the proposal. With the weight of how much they stand to gain versus how much he trusts her.

Her own palms tingle. What he does next will shape their time at the izakaya. And will speak to how he feels about her.

And for some reason, that matters.

Unspoken secrets and past betrayals stack up silently between them. How can they trust each other? How have they ever worked together?

Everything feels dark. Even with the golden light and decadent surroundings, it all feels shaded. As if what makes them beautiful is corrupted. Fatally flawed.

And then he stands up.

Anaiya's breath catches in her throat as she approaches the bar, still debating whether the risk is worth the potential reward. Kaide is already there, scanning the nearby Elementals, smiling at the Server, and generally looking like he was created to be in this exact space.

Please let this work. She isn't sure who she sends the silent plea to, but the fervency of it makes her nauseous.

She strides up to the bar, purposefully bumping into his shoulder.

"Hey, livewire, watch where you're going." His tone is light-hearted, but his face betrays the same anxiety that makes her feel like she has skipped a nutrient supplement.

Is it enough? Is a random encounter enough for Niamh to formally link her to a key target?

"My mistake," she says, louder than she needs to. "Let me buy you a drink."

"I'm not one to pass up a free drink from a beautiful woman."

The compliment, delivered with Kaide's trademark sincerity, isn't what sets her heart racing. It's his use of the word woman. An ancient, Heterodox word – one that gives identity to something other than Element.

If Niamh is listening, the stakes just got higher – he'll not hesitate to act and once they are detained, they will face the highest consequence for their rebellion. But, if he's not – if the izakaya is somehow off the communication grid – they have free reign within the izakaya's walls to talk to whoever they want about whatever they want.

Swallowing the anticipation rising in her throat, she orders two more drinks.

"Have you got eyes on Niamh?" she mouths. Kaide nods. It is as she expected. "And Jenna?"

He nods again. "And all four of his direct reports."

Smart. And useful. She glances down at her wristplate again, the white cross still prominent on the screen. "Find out if any are moving our way."

Sitting alone in Farasei's section of the izakaya draws more attention than Anaiya is comfortable with. Two glasses sit empty on the low-lying table in front of her and the temptation to down the third grows with every minute Kaide stays outside.

Thoughts of Kaide being detained play with increasing volume. But if he has, Anaiya going outside will only make things worse. Her only option is to wait until he comes back or until enough time has passed for her exit to be seen as unconnected.

With nothing else to distract her or pass the time, she scans the room – her gaze avoiding the more obvious stares and flitting between the bar and the mirrored wall.

Unlike other izakaya, the weight is different. Still light, but sharper.

There are no large groups or loud conversations. The music is eclectic and the lustrum range of Elementals narrow. None of it makes sense.

Fitting for an izakaya that serves as the doorway to an enclave.

The mirror seems to shimmer. A tall male steps into the space, as if he has crystallised from the invisible photons of light.

She looks closer, squinting until the optical illusion reveals itself. The mirror is not seamless – it diverges as it nears the adjacent wall, where the light is softer and the angles of the room present a distraction for the eye. Behind that illusion is the access point, and beyond that point the enclave.

Distracted by the mirror, she realises too late that the male is staring at her. He is attractive. Not that anyone in the izakaya is unattractive. But this Elemental … *What is it about him?*

She stares back at him, fighting against the uncomfortable knot in her belly that a silent confrontation with a beautiful stranger inevitably produces. He smiles – a slight quirk of the lips that transitions into a full grin within three steps.

And she realises what it is that makes him attractive. It's the confidence, the casual assuredness, and the look of amusement that hints at a recklessness motivated by pleasure and not self-destruction.

Like the weight of the world hasn't touched his shoulders.

That still doesn't explain why he is staring at you.

He stops at the bar. The Server inclines her head towards Anaiya. The stranger follows her gaze. Nodding, he picks up his drink and walks over to the table.

"Elatrice tells me I'm your sponsor," he says, his voice low and oddly familiar. "Which explains why you are in my section … and, yet, doesn't."

Anaiya's heart rate accelerates and her senses become distorted with the fight or flight response; the music sounds as if her ears are plugged with gauze and the once-muted light seems impossibly bright.

"Farasei," she whispers.

"Yes." He takes Kaide's empty seat. "I think we've established that you know my name. Time for you to tell me yours."

FIFTY-NINE

"Is my name really important?"

Farasei cocks his head and then laughs. "No, I guess it isn't. For now."

The laughter fades and he leans in closer to really look at her. "Why are you here? No, don't tell me, let me guess. It's more interesting that way."

Around them, life inside the izakaya continues uninterrupted. No one but Anaiya is aware of this strange interrogation.

"You're not like the others, are you?" He throws his hand around at the other Elementals but keeps his eyes on her. "I mean, you're obviously not like us, but you're not like them either. Why is that?"

Anaiya picks up one of Kaide's drinks, the reluctance she felt earlier outweighed by a rising panic. "I have no idea what you're talking about."

Farasei laughs again. "Ah, but I think you do. If you were one of them you wouldn't, and if you were one of us you would, but wouldn't care. But you do know. And you do care."

"What's going on here?" Anaiya's hand stumbles as she places the glass back down, the sweet liquid spilling over her fingers.

Farasei notices but doesn't say anything. Because he's right. Elementals like him don't care. Not about the trivialities of Otpor life.

"Are you really so protected – so removed – from life back there in your enclave?" The question comes from a genuine

304

curiosity, but her voice is sharp and clipped.

"Protected, yes. Removed – well, that's a matter of personal preference. Some like the outside world more than others. Me? I prefer le hameau."

He takes a sip from his own drink, still appraising her over the glass. "Which is why you being here – sitting in my exclusive section, throwing around my name, claiming I'm your sponsor – is all so intriguing."

The way he says the last word makes her think that he finds this situation much more than intriguing. She looks over at the entry.

Where are you, Kaide? It is a desperate thought. Deep down she knows that Kaide is not returning.

"What do you know about the pituarmagn stockpiling?" The question races out before her rational brain can vet it.

There is no laugh this time, yet even without the mirth, he still appears amused. "You really are a different species, aren't you? The pituarmagn initiative isn't my project. I'm an interested spectator, but violence and destruction aren't my thing."

"Whose thing is it?"

"That is my secret to keep and yours to find out."

"Are they here in the izakaya?"

He looks around, the break in eye contact allowing Anaiya a small reprieve to collect her thoughts. She has to be careful. If Niamh is listening, she'll be sent to the Execution Pillar for sure.

"As a matter of fact, they are."

"Are they a friend of yours?"

"No more questions." He leans back and sips his drink. "I've indulged you long enough. Tell me why you are here or leave."

She shrugs and stands up slowly. Her mind scrambles, trying to remember the name she had overheard during her time in the enclave.

Looking to the mirrored wall, she scans the reflection of the room.

"Danai!" She yells it, her voice jarring against the civilised murmurs and music. A lot of heads turn, but only one stays trained on her.

Anaiya turns from the mirror and finds the owner of the reflection. He stands and excuses himself from the larger group of four Elementals he was sitting with. Walking over, his gaze flits from Anaiya to Farasei.

"Are you not going to chastise your charge, Farasei?" He sounds pissed.

So, not friends.

"I am not her sponsor." Farasei sounds bored, but the way he leans forward betrays his interest.

"Then why is she here?"

"I asked her the same thing, but she seems to prefer asking questions than answering them."

"How did you meet Lilith?" Anaiya's heart races as she asks the question. She is treading a very fine precipice. Lilith is already a person of interest; the mere mention of her name in conjunction with her recent questioning about pituarmagn and Farasei's comments about violence and destruction is dangerous. Not conclusive enough yet for a clear conviction, but enough to motivate Niamh to employ his Unorthodox tactics.

Danai frowns. "Lilith said she would bring by two others, both male, both senior leaders. She said nothing about a third. Why are you here without her?"

She is running out of time. If Danai is here to meet with Lilith and other Resistance members, she needs to get her answers and get out quickly.

"Why are you stockpiling the pituarmagn for them?"

"Who do you think you are questioning me? You forget your place, *Elemental*." He says the word like it is an insult, like it is somehow lacking or inferior.

"If you let this madness go ahead, not even your enclave will protect you."

"See, Danai?" Farasei stands. "Even this Elemental can see the stupidity of your plans."

"Don't lecture me on stupidity. Either sponsor her and make her behave or remove her. I won't tolerate such insolence."

The izakaya has turned quiet and still, the unfolding spectacle drawing every eye in the room.

Farasei sighs and turns to Anaiya. "I think you have outstayed your welcome, wabi-sabi."

The last term is unfamiliar but sounds less insulting than Danai's strange inflection on Elemental. In any case, he is right – there is no point staying any longer; Kaide is surely gone by now, these strange enclave Elementals are unlikely to reveal anything of use, and she has already pushed the limits of acceptable risk.

"I'll see myself out."

And head back to the tunnel. She can access the enclave and wait for Danai to arrive; figure out where he lives and then come back with a soundmatcher …

Reaching the door, she hangs her head low; ready to avoid the gaze and recognition of the Protector. She slides the door open, resisting the urge to turn around and see what has come of the interaction between Farasei and Danai.

Distracted and looking down, she collides with an unseen body, the force of it sending her stumbling.

Arms grab her before she can hit the footpath.

"Woah. Easy there."

No, no, no.

She looks up in horror, finding the face she expects and fears. Seth.

SIXTY

"An—"

He is cut short from saying her full name; Kaide's arm pulling him back hard and fast.

"Move on, Protector – this is not your fight." Kaide stares at her, the intensity of his gaze broadcasting his desperation.

She shakes her head. Not at the suggestion, which she knows is just his way to stop Seth from saying anything more and revealing himself to Niamh, but at his self-sacrifice to protect his friend. And at her own stupidity; for letting her guard down, for being so desperate for connection, for believing that she could ever mean more to him than Seth.

She steps aside. Away from them both. Something has happened here, the balance of power shifted. But she is too amped, from the encounter and the one that preceded it, to see it clearly. Her only option is retreat.

"What the fuck is she doing here?" Eamon is livid. He strides towards her, emboldened by the environment or his companions.

She looks beyond him. Lilith has paused, taking in the scene but not engaging.

"It's his fault," Eamon shouts, flinging his arm in Kaide's direction.

Anaiya ignores it all, stepping around Eamon even as he tries to grab her.

"Your sponsor is waiting for you," she says to Lilith. Seeing her surprise files down some of the sharpness in Anaiya's mind. "For all of you."

She doesn't wait for a response, continuing her journey down Boileau Road towards Exelmans.

"Run, Anaiya," Eamon calls out after her, "when we unleash the chaos, you will be the first to suffer."

Her heart turns to ice. Not in response to his words, but to the knowledge that Niamh has heard them and that they have condemned them both to Execution. If her and Kaide's charade inside the izakaya hasn't motivated Niamh to action, this certainly will.

And so she runs.

The familiar lines of Boulevarde Exelmans appear sooner than she expects. Faced with the intersection, she is suddenly unsure of her destination.

It is only a matter of time until the warrant notification appears on her wristplate – there is nothing to gain from entering the tunnel; even if she finds something, her detention will prevent her from making use of it.

And, yet, there is also nothing to lose. If Niamh is coming to take her to the Pillar, nothing she does in the tunnel or the enclave will make things worse. In the end, it is curiosity that drives her east, back to the tunnel access point.

The tunnel seems shorter, the journey quicker, than it had when she had first explored it. She doesn't stop to investigate each access panel, she knows where she is going this time.

Only when she arrives at the tunnel's end does she pause. Listening for any sound of nearby Elementals, she slowly pushes the access panel up. It is riskier than before. Even with night approaching, it is still too light and the shadows aren't deep enough to hide her.

With her vision limited to what the opening affords, she sighs and flings the panel fully open. Better to risk a sudden movement attracting attention than a slow one guaranteeing it.

The panel opens up into a small space between two buildings. Ahead she can see the trees that line the main road leading from the izakaya, but here she is protected from casual glances.

A beeping sounds from her wristplate – three shrill tones that are now all-too familiar. Tapping on the screen brings up the notification.

CODE 547B VIOLATION. WARRANT ISSUED. REPORT TO NEAREST PEACEKEEPER IMMEDIATELY.

They will be coming for her. She needs to be quick.

Climbing out of the tunnel, she shuts the panel and looks around. There are no side doors to either of the buildings, but the one to her right has a few narrow windows running up its three storeys.

Without waiting, she starts climbing, finding footholds in the intricate stonework that decorates the facade. It is quick work and she reaches the first window in less than a minute.

Peering in, she sees only a bathroom.

This is a fool's mission.

The other three will only yield the same view. There will be nothing to find in these rooms, nothing that will help her understand the pituarmagn attack or the role of the enclave.

Still, she is curious. *Do they really live such different lives?*

Sliding the window open, she squeezes inside, landing quietly on the tiles. Padding towards the door, she presses her ear against the wood.

Wood. Real timber.

In the outside world, a piece this size would be exhibited in a gallery or seized as evidence of Heterodoxy. Here it is used for a door.

With no sound to alert her of activity beyond, she pushes it open. A long hallway extends before her, the walls hidden beneath heavy frames and sheets covered with textured paint. She runs her fingers along them as she walks by, her eyes flitting ever ahead to see what other exotic scenes and objects will be presented.

At the end of the hallway is a large room, its space filled with unfamiliar-looking furniture and contraptions. A large wooden table dominates the space to her left. Strange implements litter its top, scattered around what looks to be the remains of a misshapen soylent bar.

She picks it up, her fingers sinking into its soft and spongy texture, when they should shatter brittle and dry layers. Bringing it up to her nose, she smells it. It is so unlike anything else she has encountered and yet her body responds immediately to it. Saliva pools in her mouth and her stomach grumbles as it always has at the scent of cola pigeon. Biting into it releases its full flavour, sending all other thoughts fleeing from her mind.

Only after the last morsel is gone does she regain her focus. Her gaze falls on the wall opposite and the rows and rows of books it holds.

She strides towards them but stops before she reaches them. Pausing, she looks around again. This time she focuses her gaze, taking in all the details, trying to make sense of what she sees.

Everything here is a relic of the past. As if this place is protected from the power of time, as if it never suffered the Singularity. Never witnessed the Emancipation. Never was tethered to the Orthodoxy and all it entailed.

A high-pitched ringing echoes in the apartment. She instinctively looks to her wristplate, even though she knows the sound does not originate there. Beneath the incessant ringing is a lower-pitched rumble. A vibration.

Over on the table, a small device – like a miniature glass screen – flashes with blue light. She walks over to inspect it, surprised to see similar icons and functionality as on her wristplate.

She looks for a lifeline to plug into her ear, but the device is untethered. Regardless, she swipes right to answer the call.

Without a lifeline to transmit the sound directly to her ear, the communication is fuzzy; faded at the edges and lacking any distinct voice. But it is clear enough for her to hear the message.

Unauthorised Access. Intruder located in building 4A. Remain in place and await inspection.

She drops the device and hurries to the main window. A small group of Elementals, who move like Peacekeepers but who lack the uniform, are amassed below.

Hurrying to the bathroom, she glances down from the narrow window. The view to the tunnel access panel is clear.

Pain, hot and insistent, ricochets up through her body as the free-fall to the street below ends abruptly. Ignoring the burning in her feet, she launches into a roll towards the panel. With adrenalin bestowing extra strength, she flings open the access door and falls again to the tunnel below, reaching up at the last minute to pull the panel shut again.

She emerges a few minutes later, not at Boulevarde Exelmans, but in the basement of what appears to be an Administration building. Using her diode, the only thing that still works on her disabled wristplate, she makes her way to the stairwell and up to the ground level.

Artificial light streams through large windows, the hour still too early for curfew, but late enough for the floor to be empty.

Never losing pace, she races for the exit. Her abrupt exit attracts a few stares from wandering Elementals, but none of them are Peacekeepers.

Slowing her pace, she walks away from the tunnel line, heading north towards her apartment.

She barely makes it two blocks before she sees the advancing pair of Peacekeepers.

Jenna leads, but it is not the Senior Peacekeeper that calls out the restraint warning.

"Surrender, Protector. You are to be detained for a Code 547B violation." The Peacekeeper who speaks is young, only a lustrum out of her traineeship. There is no passion in her announcement, no anger or fire. Just a Peacekeeper doing her duty.

Anaiya holds her hands up in submission. There is nothing to be gained from flighting or fleeing. Jenna smiles and advances, the restraint needle flashing in her hand. And then her satisfaction falters, the smile turning to a grimace. Her hand reaches up to her throat even as she stumbles and falls to the ground.

The other Peacekeeper hesitates only briefly before she advances with her own syringe. She rushes it; her future-searching would have already predicted Anaiya taking advantage of the new situation and fleeing.

The needle glances off Anaiya's collarbone, tearing at the skin in her neck and jamming into the jugular. Pain sings along her nerves and her vision starts to distort. Shadows seem to emerge from hidden spaces as the inevitable blackness comes for her.

But it is not the loss of consciousness that she fears, it is the knowledge that another needle awaits her. A needle that will end her life.

SIXTY-ONE

The waking from a restraint sleep is always cursed with disorientation. There is a strange moment when the boundary between dreaming and reality is less a line and more a shadow.

Last time, Anaiya had awoken to the darkness of a detention cell. Now she awakens to a cold, hard floor below her and chains on her wrists. But the darkness is still there.

With no way to reach her wristplate and switch on the diode, she waits for her eyes to adjust and reveal new details. In the darkness, time becomes amorphous and she can't be sure whether seconds or minutes have passed.

Seconds, minutes – it doesn't matter – there is no change. Nothing but a dense darkness that stretches to infinity. The panic that had started itching between her shoulder blades on waking has now erupted into fear.

I am blind.

She brings her knees up and presses her face against them, begging her limited sight to register something in the close proximity. There is nothing.

Metal bites into her wrists as she thrashes about, pain burning up her arms as she tries to wrench them out of her restraints. Memories of the murdered Water Commissioner swell in the dark silence, growing and shifting until all Anaiya can see is Niamh's hands around her own neck.

She howls; a wild, desperate wailing that strips her already dry throat. The darkness pulls it from her, the sound bouncing off the walls of her prison, reverberating and layering until her mind breaks under its weight.

Even after her throat gives up the sound, it still rings in her ears.

Her body, once invincible, is betraying her. Her breath comes fast and shallow, and her heart skips to an unsustainable beat.

Still, she continues to work her wrists against the cuffs.

She doesn't want to die this way. Not with her hands chained behind her back. With no way to fight.

Sometimes she dozes, other times she screams.

Her wrists ache with the pain of unseen bruises and lacerations. Her eyes hurt with the effort of straining to see something, anything.

Nothing good has ever come at the end of the darkness and yet she is desperate to be free of it.

"Rise and shine." The voice comes to her in a dream.

And then the dream explodes in a fireball of fluorescent light. Spikes in her brain. Eyes clamped tight. Adrenalin like electricity.

Pain burns behind her eyelids and still she tries to open them, to suck the light in, to bathe in it.

"Open your eyes, Anaiya." The voice, though not Niamh's, is familiar. The realisation comes to her like an afterthought.

"Open them."

She stands slowly, the shackles pulling at tired and mangled wrists. Squinting against the brightness, she prises her eyelids apart. The needles in her eyes grow dull and bearable, enough to make out the figure standing in front of her.

Eamon.

His rugged handsomeness is marred by the dark circles and shadowed lines on his perfect face. It is a slight comfort to know that he has also been suffering.

She is surprised it is not Niamh who confronts her. And then realises the error in her earlier panic. Niamh would never kill her disabled. He loves the fight as much as she does.

"What are you doing, Eamon?"

"You don't get to ask the questions, Protector," he spits, face contorted.

"So, you ask the questions." Rage bubbles up her throat and tumbles over her tongue. With Niamh she would have been more careful, but this Air delinquent? *Bring on the fight.*

"All bravado, no action," Eamon shouts, eyes wild with a chemical-induced fervour.

"Easy to say when you have me in chains."

"Deja vu, no? I remember another bound Peacekeeper once upon time. But we all know how that ended."

Memories of an izakaya basement and a blindfolded Trainee dance at the edges of her mind.

"What are you doing, Eamon?"

"I'm changing the world."

A needle pricks at her neck. She waits for the darkness but a rush of energy comes to her instead.

A nutrient booster?

"Can't have you failing at your moment of glory," he says, grinning maniacally before striding through the exit and plunging her back into darkness.

SIXTY-TWO

You were stupid to think it was Niamh.

With the booster resetting her energy levels, Anaiya is thinking clearer. Niamh didn't need to secret her away to kill her. The truth of her Heterodoxy is enough for an uncontested Execution. If he wanted her dead, he just had to catch her. And it appeared he had, before Eamon had stolen his prize.

How *had* Eamon managed that? She struggles to remember the details of her restraint – there had been a younger Peacekeeper and Jenna. *Jenna* ... something had distracted her, she had fallen? Had that been Eamon? Is that how he had grabbed her from the Peacekeepers? Had kept her from Niamh's clutches?

The thought of Niamh seething at her disappearance is almost satisfying. But escaping the Executioner's needle only to die alone in a dark bunker is no cause for celebration.

Details of her prison had flashed bright when Eamon had switched the lights on – a large circular room with a dirt floor and high walls. The fact that Niamh hasn't stormed the place with Peacekeepers strengthens her conclusion that Eamon has hidden her in a retired air recycler – the isolation and dense concrete the perfect obstacle to any triangulation or communication efforts.

She pulls again at the chains that hold her arms behind her back and tether her to the wall. Fresh pain alights on old and she stops. Kicking her foot back against the wall in frustration, she winces as a piece of concrete dislodges and tears along her calf.

Her scream tears through her throat and manic energy sends

her limbs into spasms, her hands pulling at their shackles, her feet pounding into the wall.

She screams and flails until the pain is too much. Slowly she sinks back down to the floor, tolerating the sting of rocky fragments under tired legs. Her heartbeat synchronises with the slow ticking of time, everything grinding down to the lowest gear.

Flexing her wrists, the cuffs jangle against the bar that ties her to the wall. It is the reason she can stand. And also the reason she can't escape the shackles. With the cuffs threaded behind the bar, there is no need for a long chain. Her tether is kept short, allowing her no leverage, limiting her strength to her lower arms.

It was smart.

But Eamon is not smart. Impulsive, egotistical, dangerous. But not smart.

Which means this bar wasn't recently installed.

She'd been playing this wrong the whole time. Escaping the cuffs wasn't her key to freedom, escaping the wall was.

Ignoring the groan from her legs, she stands. Her fingers grip the bar and, setting her shoulders, she pulls.

Nothing.

She changes tack – pulling the bar left and right, begging for it to move.

Still nothing.

She stops, the chamber echoing with her accelerated heartbeat and the sound of rain. Except it is not the sound of water hitting the ground, but fine concrete particles.

She pulls again, attempting to shake the bar, her hands getting coated in a fine grit.

If only she could get more leverage. Stretch her arms a bit, extend the dimension between her and the bar.

With her legs untethered, they have enough range of movement to achieve what her arms can't. But attempting a flat scissor kick from a standing position won't give her the power she needs. Pulling her hands up the bar until they rest in the small of her back, she grips hard on the metal and uses her feet against the wall to push up.

Her arms tremble with the exertion and her legs don't have

the power they should to get her as high as she would like to be. Still, she gets high enough.

Knowing she doesn't have it in her for a second attempt, she draws on the last of her energy reserves and puts it all into one kick.

Her foot reverberates off the metal, bones and tendons shivering at the impact. She lands awkwardly and waits in hope for the clang of the bar on the ground, knowing it will never come. She had felt it when her foot had connected; despite the decaying concrete, the bar is tightly secured. Most likely it ran all the way up the height of the recycler. One kick was never going to dislodge a ten-metre bar.

Groaning, she sinks back down.

Rest. Recover. Try again in a couple of hours.

They are hollow thoughts. Already the pain in her right foot is eclipsing the raw heat in her wrists. A grade one fracture, maybe a grade two. There's no way she can attempt the kick again without exacerbating the fracture, and escaping the bar is only half her problem – she will still need to escape the recycler.

SIXTY-THREE

The pain and paranoia make sleeping difficult. In the pitch black, Anaiya treads a vague line between waking and dreaming – her reality too surreal to trust, her dreams too real to dismiss.

Sometimes it is Kaide who comes to rescue her, other times he enters with Eamon to check that the shackles still hold her tight. Rehhd's voice floats to her in the darkness, as does Kane 148's – both berate her for her stupidity, her misplaced loyalty and her litany of failures. And Farasei makes the occasional appearance, turning the lights on only to smile and then turn them off.

It is only when the pain is bright and sharp and clear that she knows she is really awake. It is the pain that lets her know when Eamon's visits are real.

His bitter voice crashes into her sleep and prises her eyes open. "Your little stunt at the Prince created some major headaches for us. There was even talk of calling off the attack." He laughs. "But I was never going to let that happen. Lilith is empire building, Seth has gone soft again, and Kaide – well, let's just say I still don't trust him, no matter what secrets he divulges about you. I'm the only one with an eye on the real prize."

Squinting against the light, she pins her gaze to Eamon. He looks smug.

"And what a prize you are. A Fire hero. A fallen Peacekeeper."

She looks away from him, only to be confronted with the dark kevlar of her old uniform, her Protector uniform nowhere to be seen.

The thought of Eamon touching her bare skin and seeing her naked makes her shiver.

To cover the weakness, she manipulates the feeling into an approximation of rage, urging her body into a dominant stance.

She flexes her legs against the ground and pushes up, but her cuffs catch on an unseen obstacle and she crashes back down. Pain slams into her coccyx and ricochets along her spine, pulling the cry from her lips before she can trap it.

Eamon laughs again. "No wonder they demoted you to Protector. I always thought the hypoxia story was a distraction, but maybe your old friends roughed you up the same way you roughed me up that night at Veritas."

She is only half listening. Her fingers skitter down the bar, searching for the flaw that stopped the shackles from letting her stand up. Down, down, down, until they reach the curve that marks the place where the bar connects to the wall.

Her earlier kick may not have compromised the bar, but the surrounding wall is damaged. A fissure, big enough to capture the links of her cuffs, has opened up.

"What did you say?" Somewhere on the periphery of her subconscious, something Eamon has said has shaken her out of her distraction.

"I said I'm sick of all our dances happening behind closed doors. It's time for the fight to come out into the streets."

"This isn't exactly out in the streets, Eamon."

"Never fear, Anaiya. This is just your holding cell. Today, you are hidden away. Tomorrow, your Execution will trigger the pituarmagn response and be viewed by everyone in Otpor."

She looks back down at her uniform. "So, you want to Execute a Peacekeeper and broadcast it to your drugged masses."

"Poetic, no? We were thinking about it all wrong. Showing Elementals the injustice and subjugation – boring – when what we really needed to show them was the thrill of fighting back. Show them how weak Peacekeepers really are. Show them how easy it is to overthrow their masters."

Her fingernails scratch and pull at the concrete, her heart races, and her eyes never leave Eamon's.

"If you wanted to publicly Execute a Peacekeeper for broadcast, why not take one of the Peacekeepers that restrained me?"

His smile falters and the real undercurrent of emotion surfaces. Eamon is enraged and desperate and determined. When he speaks, it is slow and measured and tainted with all that is cold and hard and immovable.

"Because there would be no justice for Rehhd in that. Because Executing you will deaden this cancerous feeling inside me every time I think of her or you – which is often. Because to everyone who matters, you are the ultimate Peacekeeper who destroyed the Resistance, and in destroying you I can restore it.

"And because I needed those other Peacekeepers to take back a story that would distract your Deputy Commissioner and his lackeys and stop them from interrupting the attack."

SIXTY-FOUR

After Eamon leaves, it is all Anaiya can do not to cut her fingers to the bone against the jagged concrete. Larger fragments fall and bounce off the floor. They sound like sonic booms in the empty chamber and she expects Eamon to come racing back in to investigate. Each time he doesn't is like a whip at her back, spurring her to go faster.

When her fingers are slick with blood and numb with pain, she stops digging and puts her tired muscles back to work. Gripping the bar as securely as she can, she wiggles it back and forth, throwing her body around, begging for the chaos to dislodge the metal.

She tires quickly, her protests against her fatigued muscles shouted down by hours of pain and exertion.

Lowering herself gently to the ground, she bites down hard, stifling the wail of frustration that is burning along every nerve, every tendon, every fibre.

Large chunks of rock make sitting uncomfortable. She shimmies until there are no more jagged pieces digging into tormented skin.

Details are emerging in the darkness. Her eyes are growing accustomed to their prison.

No. Dawn light is turning the sky grey and filtering down the throat of the recycler.

Eamon will Execute her tonight in a manipulated frenzy of chemically enhanced rage. Broadcast for all to see and revel in and cower from.

She is running out of time.

Clenching her fists against the onslaught of pain, she resumes her struggle against the metal shackles and concrete wall.

In the end, her escape comes not with the dramatic breaking of the bar but the subtle shifting of chain links within a groove.

With one hand, she pulls the bar away from the wall, with the other, dragging the chain of her cuffs into the space that opens up. Millimetre by millimetre, she forces the links into the tiniest of cracks, leveraging their girth to widen the next crack.

There is no clang of metal reverberating against the hard ground, just a release of tension.

Disbelief and fear of the unknown give her pause. But it is only brief, seconds not passing before she has pulled away from the bar and stood up. Grunting, she throws her arms in a series of practised manoeuvres; dislocating her shoulders and pulling her mangled arms above and over her head.

The popping sound as her shoulders click back into place echo louder than her racing heartbeat. Nausea rushes over her in a toxic wave, bringing pain and relief in equal measure.

Though still bound, she is freer now.

She rushes to the door, searching for a way to open it, but every prod, shove and poke yields nothing. It is not unexpected – doors like this can only be opened from the outside.

Spinning around, her gaze is drawn to a large piece of fallen concrete. She imagines crushing Eamon's skull with it. But that satisfaction will have to wait.

For now, she needs to get word to Niamh.

The Peacekeeper uniform had been meant as an insult, a source of shame. But Eamon has gifted her the only opportunity to bring undone the pituarmagn attack.

Using the compromised bar as a launching point, she leaps at the wall; cuffed hands gripping the smooth metal while her boots find the natural footholds in the wall's surface.

She climbs as high as the bar and her tired muscles allow her.

Hands and legs tremble with exertion.

"Niamh, I know you can hear me. I'm trapped in a decommissioned air recycler somewhere in the Edges. There's a chemical manipulation attack planned for tonight. I don't know where, but I do know that whatever the blindsided Peacekeepers told you is just a distraction. Follow my movements, it will lead you to where you really need to be."

Her hands, still slick with blood and sweat, falter. Off-balance and spent, she falls hard to the ground below.

There is no way to know if Niamh has got her message. Or whether he believes it.

She needs a back-up plan. Picking up the piece of concrete she found earlier, she positions herself by the door and waits for Eamon to return.

SIXTY-FIVE

She hadn't meant to fall asleep. The adrenalin should have made it impossible. And yet, the sound of footsteps echoing in the recycler wakes her before the evening chill can.

Scrabbling to her feet, Anaiya finds the concrete shard and grips it tight. The footsteps are closer. Positioning herself for the attack, the door swings in and she launches.

It is a bloodier, messier attack than she's used to; her makeshift weapon slamming repeatedly into Eamon's skull and tearing at his skin.

At the last second, she pulls back – she doesn't want to bludgeon him to death, she just needs to get past him. Still, the concrete comes away slick and Eamon plummets to the ground.

The shard drops from her bloodied hand as though it is electrified. And then her gaze slides past Eamon.

Seth's stricken face takes seconds to transform into something harder. He strides into the room, focus switching from her bound hands to her set feet, but never to her eyes. She lifts her foot to place the standard roundhouse kick – her best option given the tight space and her compromised physical ability.

The kick connects, but Seth moves quicker than she expects; the blow glancing off his chest and landing with a thud against his arm.

Crying out at the impact, Seth throws a clumsy punch in retaliation. His fist moves like a blur, a shadow in her peripheral vision. She should be able to easily avoid it, but with her arms immobilised and her balance still offset, it slams into her jaw.

She falls to the floor, the blood that pools from her mouth a torrent compared to the trickle that had come from Eamon's temple. His face looks peaceful. And then she blacks out.

Consciousness comes back to her with a flood of sensations. Vaguely, she is aware of the cold touch of the ground against her cheek, but more insistent is the pressure. It feels as though someone is standing on her face, stomping on it, grinding her head into the floor.

She tries to bite down against the pain, but that only makes it more excruciating. She can feel them, random pieces of bone moving around in her jaw.

Nausea hits her like a fallen wall, rolls through her belly like a violent storm.

Only when it passes does she hear their voices.

"Don't lose your nerve, now," Eamon is shouting.

"I'm not a monster," Seth shouts back, "I don't want to be a monster."

"We're not the monsters! They are! This is why we are doing this. What they've forced us to do." Eamon's voice slows and softens. "We kill one monster to stop the advance of the others."

"It's not that simple."

"It's always been that simple. They took Rehhd, we take Anaiya."

Anaiya opens her eyes, just in time to see Seth slam his hand against the wall. He looks agitated and indecisive. It makes him appear older. And weaker.

"So, we do what they do – Is that supposed to justify our actions or condemn them?"

"You're overthinking it. And you're starting to sound like Kaide."

"What's your issue with Kaide?"

"My issue isn't with Kaide, it's with her." Eamon flings his hand in Anaiya's direction, eyes widening at seeing her conscious. Seth follows his gaze and physically baulks at meeting her gaze.

She wants to speak, but the pain in her jaw teeters on the edge of pure agony. So, she puts all of her unsaid words into a glare that she sets on Seth.

Seth looks away, foot tapping rapidly on the floor, hand raking through short-cropped hair. "No surprises, Eamon. We do this according to the plan. Quick, painless, silent. You get to kill her, not torture her."

"You're no fun anymore, Seth."

"Enough!" He slams his hand against the wall again. "I mean it, Eamon. This is necessity, not retribution."

Eamon scowls, the movement made uglier by the gashes that still dribble blood at his temple, but he doesn't say anything. It's not a confirmation, but it seems sufficient for Seth. He nods and strides out of the room without a backwards glance.

Eventually, Eamon returns his gaze to Anaiya. "Seth can think what he likes. I think we both know, it's *all* about retribution."

SIXTY-SIX

The evening sky is just starting to shift when Eamon leads Anaiya out of the recycler. With only an hour until sunset, the streets are uncrowded, and yet there are still enough Elementals who stare with mouths agape at the sight of a shackled Peacekeeper being led through the precincts.

He plays it smart, sticking to quiet streets. Still, she expects to see some Fire presence; waits for a Peacekeeper patrol or off-duty Border Patroller to see her and intervene.

She glances down at her bound wrists, stretching her fingers to reach her wristplate, the cuffs digging in to already raw skin. The disabled screen still flashes her warrant notice.

Niamh, are you still listening?

Not that it matters. The pain in her jaw has been sending her in and out of consciousness for the last few hours. Even without the pain, there would be no way her mangled mouth could form the words she needs.

Her only hope is that her original cry for help, back in the recycler, made it to Niamh. And that he listened to it. But each block that passes without Peacekeeper presence anchors her core with fear.

The crowds are getting thicker. Air and Water Elementals line the streets, their excited chatter the sound of rats feasting on bones. And in every hand are the ubiquitous red plastic cups that no doubt hold the pituarmagn-spiked alcohol she and Kaide had worked so hard to find and destroy.

An older Air Elemental, face pockmarked with synth toxin, strides right up to her. Anaiya twists her head away from him, the gob of saliva hitting her swollen cheek. The crowd around them erupts into raucous laughter and catcalling.

She tries to raise her hands to wipe it off, but Eamon pulls her chain tight and continues pulling her through the street.

Other Elementals, emboldened by the display, step forward to do the same. Spit rains on her; dirty, phlegm-tainted stickiness catching on her hair, her skin, her clothes.

She draws down into herself, disassociating herself from body, cocooning her mind from the pain and subjugation. Still, she feels the tears gathering at the corners of her eyes, feels her clenched fists digging tighter and tighter.

Retreating further in mind, she narrows her field of vision. The world around her warps down to a single tunnel of sight; the crowd either side of her fades into a vague blur of colour until only Eamon remains in focus.

She holds the illusion tight, forcing everything else to turn soft and numb and transient.

The punch that lands on her belly bends her double. The illusion shatters and the chaotic scene comes rushing back into focus. Eamon yanks the chain hard to pull her up, instead sending her sprawling.

She lands awkwardly on her wrist, her face crashing into forearm.

The searing heat of pain flashes bright for just a second and then everything turns black.

When consciousness comes back, it does not come back gently. It tears her eyes open and wraps her in barbed wire. Pain, sharp and insistent, sends ice to her chest and fire to her brain. But her torment has only just begun.

Eamon tugs on the chain that connects them, forcing her to stand up or be dragged along the rough bitumen. The world is sent into a spiral of distorted images. She slams her feet into the ground, desperate to regain her balance.

Faces race along the periphery of her vision, until one pulls her out of her static feedback loop. Cress, her pixie features contorted into a frown, stands closer than the others. Anaiya follows her gaze a few metres behind to where Lilith and Seth stand.

Lilith is all calmness and control. Arms folded, her gaze flits from the crowd to Eamon to something hidden ahead. Never to Anaiya. Occasionally to Seth.

Seth. It hurts to look at him.

He stands with the full weight of culpability bearing down on him. She sees it in his tormented eyes and clenched jaw. She knows this betrayal, remembers the sharp prick of conscience that accompanies it. This guilt will last longer than his rage. Will eat away at his mind long after the anger and self-righteousness has subsided.

Good.

It would be easy to hate him, but hate is too simple an emotion for what she feels for Seth.

He doesn't flinch under her gaze. Doesn't turn away in disgust at her swollen jaw, misshapen face or cowed posture. He bears his accountability with a determination she hasn't seen since the early days of their first meeting.

So, this is how we balance our ledger.

But, being even with Seth offers no relief – it doesn't lessen the guilt of her past and it doesn't diminish the rage and desperation that now grips her core. A rage and desperation that is tainted with something heavier and more insidious.

Even with all the animosity that has grown between them since Rehhd's Execution, she still can't imagine passing a death sentence on him.

She had said that he was dead to her, but she hadn't known the depth of coldness that was required to genuinely mean it.

She wants to shout at him – to rail against this monster who sends her to Execution with the same breath he blames her for Rehhd's – but her mangled jaw and swollen cheek deny her.

A sharp tug at her chain breaks the moment and threatens to send her falling. Heart racing at the impending pain, she throws her arms out and braces for the impact. Her feet stumble beneath her, frantically trying to maintain her balance. Ankles twist to absorb the impact, her legs straining to stay upright.

She feels the momentum shift; feels gravity step in to support her rather than conspire against her. Relief, cool and strong, floods her body. And then another tug from Eamon sends her off-kilter.

This time it is an arm that stops her from falling. Cress, her lithe Dancer body, has stepped in to support her. Anaiya expects the crowd to erupt in outrage, but then she notices the way the Trainee has positioned her body – squaring away the footpath, posture rigid, arms soft.

Something light and cool tingles in Anaiya's grazed palms.

"You need to escape, Nisha."

SIXTY-SEVEN

Cress vanishes in the crowd, heading away from Seth and Lilith. Anaiya keeps her hands clenched, not daring to glance at the tiny key that is imprisoned within. Eamon can't see it. She can't drop it. This little piece of metal is all that stands between her and her Execution.

She scans the crowd, searching for Kaide. Is this his idea? Has he orchestrated her escape? She wants so desperately to find him; her heart seizes with the pure *need* of it.

But he is nowhere to be seen. If he is watching the spectacle unfold, he is well hidden.

Music starts to filter through the murmur of the crowd and Anaiya's eyes are drawn to the large, black speakers that are scattered along the street. The notes are soft and fuzzy, like static before a storm. The chatter of Elementals rises louder.

Another sharp tug at the chain pulls Anaiya sideways. She stumbles, clutches the key tighter, but regains her balance quickly. Eamon drags her through a bottleneck in the crowd, the view finally opening up.

The small square is cordoned off in a way, speakers and burly Earth Elementals holding back the crowd. A makeshift platform has been erected, unadorned save for a mural that has been painted on a large swathe of fabric and hung from the balcony of the nearest building.

The picture is familiar. It is the same one that had been painted on the warehouses Anaiya Protected in the aftermath of

Rehhd's Execution: a female Peacekeeper shackled to the Execution Pillar, her solar plexus a blackened flame crumbling to ash, her head crowned with one word – Resistance.

Movement on the balcony pulls her gaze from the mural. Standing with arms draped over the railing, a look of casual interest etched on perfect features, is Danai. Beside him, less casual and more interested, is Farasei.

Outside of the Danish Prince, they appear less impressive but just as arrogant. Danai leans in to say something, sending the small group of elite Elementals around them laughing. But not Farasei. He just stands silent, surveying the scene below.

The music is building, shifting from a soft buzz to a frenetic pulsating. It filters through her skin until she feels it hammering in her chest. The Elementals around her are growing restless; small fights break out in pockets of the crowd, the chatter transformed to angry chants and high-energy shouting.

Eamon pulls her to the square, hauling her up the stairs to the platform. With no Execution Pillar, Anaiya is gripped by two Earth Elementals. They hold her tight, but she doesn't struggle. That will come later, when her hands are free. For now, she stays still and compliant. They need to think she is not a threat; to see her as beaten down and defeated.

But she doesn't have much time.

"Citizens of Otpor," Eamon's voice rings out through the speakers, "for too long we have suffered under Peacekeeper oppression."

The rest of his words become lost, obliterated by the glint of metal that consumes every part of her mind. He brandishes it above his head, the blade three-fingers thick.

One slice to her jugular and she will bleed out like a bitch in labour.

He has advanced to the stage, standing beside her. His eyes never leave the crowd, hers never leave the blade.

The crowd is reaching fever pitch, their chanting matching the energy of the music; both building to a crescendo.

"We Execute one of them tonight," Eamon bellows over the rising noise.

She flexes her empty hand, fear setting her fingers trembling. Heart racing, she tries to regulate her breathing, begging her hands to be steady.

"Tonight, we become ascendant."

The Earth guards tighten their grip and Eamon turns away from the crowd. His eyes are crazed, bloodlust warps his face, manic energy pouring off him in invisible waves.

He steps up close to her, tracing a finger along her broken jaw.

"Time to die, Peacekeeper."

Blood thrumming in Anaiya's ears distorts the sounds around her. Desperate and out of time, she takes a deep breath.

With Eamon so close, her hands are blocked from his view. She pulls the key from her sweaty palm, twisting her wrists to drag the key along the surface of the cuffs.

The blade pivots in Eamon's hand. He takes a step back, giving him the space he needs to perform the killing blow.

Her fingers scrabble in search of the lock's opening, pressing the key into every groove and indention. Panicked, she breaks eye contact with Eamon and looks down.

He follows her gaze, shouting as the key locks into the tiny opening.

Time shudders down its gears, turning everything to liquid silicon. Even her heartbeat, which seemed to whir only moments ago, now warps into a dense, heavy thudding.

The key turns in her grip, pulling hidden mechanisms into alignment. The cuffs unlock their jaws and release her battered wrists, sending time spinning back to its normal tempo.

Eamon lunges at her, his face contorted in a wail of rage she doesn't hear.

Her hands are free, but she has no time to use them. Instead, she brings her knees up, leveraging the stability of the two sentinels either side of her. They catch Eamon in the chest as his blade grazes her neck.

She extends her legs, pushing at Eamon with all of her adrenalin-fuelled strength. The impact sends him crashing to the stage, the blade falling from his grip and skittering over the edge to the street below.

The crowd is in full frenzy. And everywhere are arms raised to capture it all on wristplates.

Another voice booms above the chaos. Lilith stands on a speaker not five metres from the stage.

"Your oppressors are here. Your time of rebellion is now." She points down the street. A small contingent of Peacekeepers rushes into the chaos, tic tacking off nearby buildings and vaulting from speakers.

And in that moment, Anaiya feels it.

The weight of the crowd has reached its peak. The pituarmagn attack has commenced.

SIXTY-EIGHT

The Earth to her right releases his grip on Anaiya's arm, the unexpected freedom shaking her out of her thoughts.

Confusion tinges the pain and adrenalin clouding her brain. And then she feels the Earth to her left strengthen his grip and pivot, reaching for the arm his friend has released.

With her hands freed, Anaiya snatches her arm away, bringing her leg up into a roundhouse kick directed at the Earth in front of her.

The move glances off his cheek, causing him to step back. But, more importantly, the momentum has pulled her from the other's grasp. In her weakened state, she cannot hope to fight them, not with any chance of success, so she runs.

Her moves are clumsy and her pace slow, putting her on equal footing with her two assailants. But, unlike them, she has the element of surprise. And the ability to climb.

She launches at the fabric mural that was to be the backdrop for her Execution. Clutching the folds in her fists, she pulls herself up. It is hard going, but not unlike scaling a rope. It takes her less than a minute to reach the balcony.

Across from her, three balconies along, Danai and Farasei stare at her. If she lives to survive this ordeal, she will learn more of their machinations. But for now, she just needs to escape.

Climbing up to perch on the railing, she leaps up to grab the balcony above. Up and up she goes, never stopping to look down, eyes focussed only on the next balcony above. Her body aches and sweat streams from her temples.

Blinking against the salty liquid, she launches herself at the final balcony. Her weakened wrists and slick palms betray her, her grip slipping from the metal.

Before she can fall the seven storeys to the street below, she swings her body inwards. Her lower back collides with the railing below, but she falls on the right side of it, crashing harmlessly to the tiled floor of the balcony.

The panic of the near miss burns hot and brief, readily replaced by exhaustion's heavy embrace.

With the last of her energy, she crawls backwards and collapses against the wall of the empty apartment.

Her body thrashes out instinctively as she comes to. Visions of being chained to the recycler wall, of Eamon's blade against her neck, disorient her.

Slowly the chill of the tiles and the sound of the melee below remind her where she is.

She shuffles closer to the edge of the balcony and peers down through the railing's bars. The conflict below is in full force. More Peacekeepers have arrived, but the strength of their presence does nothing to temper the chaos. If anything, it seems to drive the crowd to higher levels of aggression.

Punches are thrown and landed on both sides. The Peacekeepers are more accurate and effective, but the sheer imbalance of numbers means a few of them go down. More Peacekeepers arrive, more bodies go down.

The brawl extends for a four-block radius. The fighting is heaviest at the centre point, around the stage. Air and Earth Elementals have formed a wall of defence, protecting the makeshift structure.

No. Protecting the speakers.

Music still streams from them, fuelling the drug-enhanced attack. The Peacekeepers are ignoring them, seeing them only as props for their free-running.

Taking a deep breath, Anaiya brings her wristplate up to her face, the screen only millimetres from her lips. Keeping her jaw as still as possible, she rasps the same command over and over.

"Shut down the power."

Damn it, Niamh. Just shut down the power.

She scans the crowd, looking for familiar faces. Eamon is easily spotted, jumping wildly from the stage to the speakers, gesticulating to the crowd, whipping up the frenzy. Lilith is less conspicuous; Anaiya spies her weaving along the line of defence, whispering in ears, shouting orders. Kaide is still nowhere to be seen and both Seth and Cress have either departed or are lost in the chaos.

She moves her gaze to the advancing Peacekeepers. More of them are familiar, but she doesn't find the one she is looking for.

Where are you, Jenna?

The Peacekeeper's absence sets a new tension between Anaiya's shoulder blades. If Jenna is not down there among the fray, perhaps she is stalking another target.

Anaiya throws her head around, looking up and across the nearby balconies.

And then the power goes out. It strips away the background noise to the conflict, turning the battle symphony into a harsh collection of shouts and grunts. The effect on the crowd is rapid. Fights at the fringes taper off; Earth and Air Elementals retreat into nearby side streets, no longer urged on by manufactured chemical reactions.

The breakdown of aggression spirals inward towards the stage. Peacekeepers gain more and more ground, leaving the core resistance more and more vulnerable.

Speakers are turned over, their hardened plastic shattering upon impact with the street. The advancing Peacekeepers are only metres from the stage.

The sound of the balcony door opening behind her spins her around.

She expects to find Jenna, but instead comes face to face with a Trainee Peacekeeper. She looks much younger than her eighteen years and moves much faster.

Anaiya flings up her hands to protect herself from the syringe, but she is too slow. The needle pricks the skin at her neck, perfectly positioned for the restraint serum to hit her bloodstream.

There are only microseconds before the plunger is depressed and the chemicals rush her veins. She tries to turn around, to see whether the Peacekeepers have captured Eamon or Lilith, but the darkness comes quicker than her reflexes.

SIXTY-NINE

Regaining consciousness this time is like shrugging off a thick blanket. Anaiya takes her time trading the dense, warm blackness for the cool, sharp reality.

Blinking open her eyes reveals the white tiles of the Infirmary. Relief explodes in her chest.

She had thought there to be only two outcomes of her restraint – waking up at Peacekeeper Headquarters for an interrogation and trial or waking up in an abandoned recycler at the mercy of Eamon again. She had never considered Niamh would remove her warrant and let her free.

She brings up her wrist to check the screen, heart plummeting when her hand is yanked to a stop by the cuffs that bind her to the bed. Panicked, she attempts to sit up, but is held tight around her chest and thighs by restraints hidden under the cottonex sheets.

Before her brain can make sense of the situation, she is thrashing; limbs pulling taut against their shackles, heart racing with the effort of railing against her captivity.

Shrill beeping floods her ears and a red light flashes on the ceiling above her bed. Adrenalin ramps higher, her thrashing becomes more desperate.

A Nurse races in, flanked by three others.

Wild with desperation, Anaiya throws her head side to side, trying hopelessly to avoid the needle she sees glinting in the Nurse's grasp. It is all for nought. The syringe is plunged into the wall beside her, the liquid trickling through hidden tubes to the catheter she can now feel in her hand.

Warmth travels along her arm and seems to flood her body, stilling her limbs and silencing her wails. In the forced calm, her focus sharpens on the Elementals in front of her. The Nurse looks shaken, his eyes flashing from Anaiya to the Technician beside him.

The Technician ignores his stares, focussed instead on the glass screen she has plugged into the wall. She swipes and taps away, tilting the screen to share the display with the other Technician. Kaide's friend.

Her eyes widen in recognition of the same Technician who had met her at the Warehouse after Niamh had hacked her wristplate. He keeps his eyes on his colleague's glass screen, never shifting his gaze to Anaiya.

The fourth Elemental steps forward and Anaiya's surprise ratchets higher. An Infrastructure Protector. She steps forward to Anaiya's bed and lifts the sheets, pulling on the thick restraints to tighten them and test their integrity.

"Are we good here?" she asks, lowering the sheets and resuming her position by the door.

The female Technician waits for the Nurse to nod before answering. "Yes, she's sedated. The jaw surgery was successful and the internal injuries are healing. You'll be able to transport her in an hour."

Anaiya blinks, trying to dispel the growing fuzziness in her brain. But even blinking feels strangely awkward. Her eyelids struggle with an invisible weight, her vision darkening, her mind shutting down.

It is well past curfew when the detention vehicle arrives at Peacekeeper Headquarters.

The driver that unshackles her from the bench doesn't look at her. A low-level Fire Elemental, only slightly more elevated than an Infrastructure Protector, knows better than to interact with detainees.

Two Peacekeepers are waiting to escort her inside. Neither are familiar.

She doesn't struggle or ask questions. They won't answer them, even if they have the answers. She just keeps her head down and bides her time; waiting until she reaches the interrogation room and can confront Niamh directly.

Her escorts take an unfamiliar route through the building, winding around the outer corridors, away from prying eyes. It is only when they take the stairs leading down to the subterranean floors that she feels the synthflies in her belly.

There is nothing in the lower levels except dispatch areas and holding cells. And she knows they aren't headed for the dispatch areas.

"Where are we going?"

They ignore her. She starts to drag her feet, pulling against their advances. They pull tighter, hauling her forward.

An irrational part of her brain, driven only by fear and anxiety, seeks a fight. She throws out her legs, twisting her body and wrenching her arms from the grip of her escorts.

It is a useless effort; her brief freedom is soon met with the now-familiar sting of a restraint syringe.

The holding cell is cold and small. Anaiya sits in the corner, forsaking the pallet bed for the floor. She doesn't expect to be here long. If she isn't to be interrogated, she will soon be marched to an expedited trial.

Voices echo down the corridor – heated chatter, aggressive demands for release, self-righteous gloating. The noise reverberates off hard floors, walls and bars, making it difficult to estimate how many mouths it comes from.

From the tone and language, she knows the voices don't just belong to Air Elementals. A few Earth Elementals are also awaiting trial and sentencing, and not for the stereotypical violence and public damage, although she is sure they were also a factor.

How long has it been since she was detained? Since the pituarmagn attack? Have they all been detained from the attack? Is the attack still raging?

The sound of footsteps turns up the dial on the energy of the room. Anaiya stands and waits for the Peacekeeper to arrive at her cell. Part of her wants to walk to the bars and peer down the corridor. Part of her doesn't want to give whoever is walking down that corridor the satisfaction of seeing her anxious.

The footsteps grow louder but are still drowned out by the erupting cacophony.

If it were Jenna approaching, she would have said something already. Taunted them or told them to shut up. But Niamh, he would be impervious to the noise. As if he couldn't hear it. As if it were irrelevant or beneath him.

She takes a step back; she didn't expect that he would show up personally.

The footsteps stop abruptly. An unfamiliar voice calls out an unfamiliar name.

Not her name.

Not Niamh.

SEVENTY

Hours stretch on, the same pattern repeating. Footsteps, cacophony, unfamiliar voice, unfamiliar name.

The first three or four, she had put down to procedural limitations – her case had been expedited, but it was still in a queue. The next few, she had concluded were an insult – they knew she was there, they wanted her to know she wasn't important enough to be expedited. That had made her both grit her teeth and smile.

And still it continued. Her mind turned to thoughts of a test; some strange, devious examination of her strength? Will? Temperance?

So, she had stayed silent. Eventually she shifted from the floor to the bed and stopped standing at every sound of footsteps. Her hands had begun twitching, desperate to relieve the awful stillness, and so she had started a silent count.

Twelve, thirteen, fourteen visits. Fourteen names of Elementals she didn't know and couldn't see.

With each departure, the noise of the holding cells had diminished in energy and volume. And had increased the fear and dread pooling in her belly.

When the fifteenth set of footsteps arrives in the corridor and the fifteenth unfamiliar name is called out, Anaiya snaps.

"Who are you? Where is Niamh? Where is Jenna?" It is too high-pitched, it betrays her desperation.

The Peacekeeper doesn't answer. A few wired Elementals pick up on her wild emotions and mimic it back to her. "Where is

Niamh? Where is Jenna?"

The singsong chant only ceases when the footsteps subside. Only to pick back up when she calls out again with the sixteenth visit and the seventeenth.

If there are nine circles to hell, as Airs believe, then Anaiya is firmly entrenched in the first.

After the last Elemental's name is called out, there are no more visits to count. Anaiya resorts to repeating the name over and over in her mind.

Depeter 206. Offence 93X.

It means nothing to her and is only mildly effective as a distraction. But for all its limited worth, it stands up against the rising tide of panic within her. It is enough to dampen the irrational desire to knock herself unconscious against the cell's walls until her name is called.

"Anaiya 234. Offence 12."

There is a closure that comes with it. A feeling that the end has begun. No more limbo.

The Peacekeeper who opens her cell looks tired. He ties her hands together with a plastic restraining cord and stands aside for her to exit.

"I thought a Heterodoxy charge would have earned a personal visit from the Deputy, himself," Anaiya says. "Or at least, one of his favourites."

The Peacekeeper escorts her down the corridor, past the empty cells that had seemed to heave just hours before with the unrestrained rage of Elementals. "The Deputy doesn't have favourites."

"What of Jenna?" she asks. "I thought she would have relished the chance to see this all unfold."

"Jenna is dead. Deputies don't concern themselves with transport. And it's not a charge; it's a conviction."

Anaiya's initial surprise at the news of Jenna's death is quickly overshadowed by her confusion at his mention of a conviction. "What do you mean 'conviction'? I haven't been tried."

The Peacekeeper doesn't pause. Anaiya's panic notches higher. Planting her feet, she looks around for an escape.

"Keep moving, detainee." He too has stopped, positioning himself to block the exits and advance on Anaiya.

"There's been a mistake. I haven't been tried yet." She is shouting now. "I haven't been tried."

It makes no difference. The Peacekeeper doesn't flinch or respond, just shoots out his hand to grab her arm. She struggles against his grasp, planting her feet and pulling all her weight in the opposite direction.

"Enough, Peacekeeper," he yells, stopping abruptly and pulling her back. "Your trial concluded three days ago. You were convicted by unanimous decision."

There is repulsion in his voice, but Anaiya's mind is tripping over itself, unhinged by the news that her Execution isn't just a possibility anymore. He ushers her forward and, this time, she doesn't resist.

"Are you taking me to the Execution Pillar?" Her voice cracks, scorching along her dry, constricted throat.

"No, Peacekeeper. Your Execution is tomorrow; I'm taking you for final prep."

SEVENTY-ONE

With no dark of night to conceal her, Anaiya's transport to the Palai is paraded along the streets of Otpor. Through the small barred window of the detention van she sees the curious stares and pointed fingers. Her transfer has not been kept a secret.

The sound of something slamming into the side of the van and shattering on impact sends Anaiya cowering to the floor. She expects the vehicle to stop and the offender detained, but the van speeds up instead, sending her crashing into the back wall.

From her position she sees the afternoon's brown sky blazing over the city's rooftops and, minutes later, the pillars of the Trocadero. She knows that if she stands to peer out the window, she will see the Execution Pillar and the scaffolding that will support massive outdoor screens.

And so she buries her head into her arms and clenches her eyes tight.

Moments later, the motion stops. Fluorescent light falls in panels on the floor and then floods in when the doors to the van are swung open. The sedation needle brings a welcome flood of heat through her veins and dulls the edges in her mind.

Corridors and stairwells and passageways come to her as in a fever dream. Time falls out of its regular rhythm.

Vaguely she is aware of hands reaching for her, stripping her of her clothes and replacing them with something softer and lighter. Of a push that feels like a caress. Of falling, falling, falling down for an eternity. Of thin sheets on a large bed.

Visions of Rehhd weave their way into her fractured consciousness. She lays with Anaiya on the bed they share before their Executions. Close, but not touching. Staring into each other's eyes and never blinking.

In that moment, Rehhd's fears become her own. She sees the needle, feels its sting, senses the coming blackness, and knows the terrible uncertainty that only the spectre of death can bring.

Or, if I live, is it not very like the horrible conceit of death and night? Together with the terror of the place.

Her mind is clearing and the vision of Rehhd fades.

There has been so much death lately. Too much death. Rehhd's. The Water Commissioner's. Jenna's.

It is as if Niamh is eradicating anyone he sees as a threat. And maybe he is.

As far as Niamh is concerned, only two other Elementals knew about her failed realignment and his transgressions – the Water Commissioner and Jenna. With them both dead, only Anaiya stands to cause problems for him.

And here she was, locked in a prep room under the Trocadero awaiting her Execution.

So, Niamh wins again.

The silent acknowledgement hits like a sucker punch.

She is so tired of Niamh winning. So tired of letting him win.

Lashing out, she beats her fists against the wall behind her and clenches her teeth. Again and again, she slams her hands against the unforgiving stonework, biting down until she think she will shatter her jaw. Again.

Her hands still. Her thoughts tripping over something in her subconscious.

Your trial concluded three days ago. They had convicted her. Her Execution had already been scheduled. And yet they had sent her to the Infirmary. Her surgery couldn't have happened more than a day ago.

So why heal her only to kill her?

Because they need me whole. They don't want a broken Elemental on the Execution Pillar. They need to prove a point, they need the stereotype for their propaganda. They need me whole, so they can strip me down for the nation to see.

If they need her whole, she needs to break herself.

The noise of her throwing herself around the cell eventually draws two Protectors to her room. They shout at her to stop, but she can't hear them with the blood pooling in her eardrums.

The pain is excruciating; her right leg shattered in at least two places, her left mangled, both arms hanging uselessly by her side. Bruises and cuts lace her skin, blood soaking through the thin cottonex and staining it red.

Only when the sedation serum taints her bloodstream does the pain subside. But sleep doesn't hit hard and she is still conscious when they bring in a Senior Peacekeeper and Nurse.

"What happened here?" The Peacekeeper's words sound stretched and faded.

"It was all self-inflicted," the larger Protector says, her voice equally as muted. She steps in front of Anaiya, blocking her view. Anaiya tries to move her head, but her neck feels as though it is filled with concrete. "We called the Peacekeepers as soon as we found her."

The Nurse steps around the Protector and starts his inspection, gently lifting broken limbs.

"This is a fucking debacle," the Peacekeeper says. "Where's the surveillance footage?"

"There is no surveillance footage," the other Protector says, her arms crossed defensively across her chest. "This whole complex is on lockdown. Total darkness by Commissioner's orders."

"She'll have to return to the Infirmary," the Nurse interrupts. "There's too much damage."

The Peacekeeper lets loose with a string of colourful curse words before patching a call on her wristplate.

Relief washes over Anaiya, placating her body's trauma better than any sedative. But she knows her stay of Execution is only temporary. If she is to truly escape her fate, she needs the rest of her plan to fall into place.

The Peacekeeper steps forward, her restraint syringe

gleaming. Before she can reach Anaiya, the Nurse stops her.

"You can't use that," he says. "She's been sedated. You'll kill her before she can be Executed."

The news sets off another session of cursing. "Can she be sedated again?"

The Nurse nods and the closest Protector steps forward with the injection. The warmth should be welcome, but Anaiya needs to fight its call to sleep. She needs to be awake when she reaches the Infirmary.

Her only hope now rests with the Technician. And with Kaide.

SEVENTY-TWO

Sleep's entreaty grows stronger the closer the transportation van gets to the Infirmary. With her body practically immobilised, Anaiya's only defence against its advances comes from the flickering of the city's night lights through the window.

She traces their path across the wall, watching them burst with colour and then succumb to the shadows. Her ears latch onto the regular beat of the van's tyres against the road, her mind filling in the melody with each new flash of light.

It should be a light and gentle piece, carved by the silence of the streets and the shimmering of the lights. Instead, it sounds sharp and edgy. She pours everything inside her into the silent symphony – the rage, the uncertainty, the desperate hope.

When the van finally stops, the music ends abruptly.

Nurses lift her onto a gurney and rush her through the Infirmary doors.

"She's had two sedation courses in the last hour," one calls out.

A Technician bends over her and prods at her eyelids. Anaiya's heart sinks – not Kaide's Technician. "Take her to the ward," he says. "We'll need to reschedule the surgery."

The clang of handcuffs attaching her wrists to the gurney are soon followed by the feeling of heavy straps falling across her thighs.

"No more sedation," he calls out, his voice fading as the Nurses push her along the corridor. "All sedation by Technicians only."

The initial adrenalin spike of her arrival is dissipating and the early sedation reasserting itself. Her eyelids fall heavy under the white lights bearing down.

Just a little longer. A little longer.

With all the fuss of protocol changes and handcuffs and protection detail, any Technician on shift will hear of her return.

"Water," she rasps, more to test her voice than sate any underlying thirst.

A syringe full of water is placed against her lips. She bites down on it, blinking as the cool liquid rushes down her throat.

"Thank you." Her voice is clearer. Clear enough to pass on her coded message if the Technician shows up.

"Thank you, Nurse. I'll take it from here."

The familiar voice filters into Anaiya's dozing mind and sends her eyes fluttering open.

Kaide's Technician stands over her, glass screen in hand but gaze firmly focussed on Anaiya. He doesn't look happy to be there.

"You have some very serious injuries," he says, flat and monotone. "I can give you sedation, but it will delay surgery ..."

And your Execution.

"I'd like the sedation," she whispers.

He nods and prepares the syringe. "Because of your earlier doses, you may experience some adverse reactions at first; disorientation, confusion, random babbling, shivering."

Anaiya blinks. He is well prepared, offering her all the outs she needs. Did he alert Kaide about her situation after her first attendance to the Infirmary?

What does Kaide hold over you?

The question evaporates as the warmth of the sedation swells. She doesn't have much time; sleep will come quicker this time around.

"How if, when I am laid into the tomb, I wake before the time that Romeo come to redeem me?"

He frowns at the seemingly nonsensical words. She repeats

them again.

Clenching his jaw, he bends down to her, his posture stiff. "This is the last time you will see me," he whispers fiercely. "If you have a message for your lover, say it now."

He stands again and folds his arms.

The sedation is lulling her back into sleep's grasp.

"How if, when I am laid into the tomb ..." Her voice is faltering now. "I wake before the time that Romeo come to redeem me?"

He shakes his head and looks away from her. "A Nurse will check on you shortly. If your pain gets any worse, you can request additional sedation."

She tries to repeat the line one last time, to force him to recognise its importance, but her throat seizes.

Under the weight of sedation, panic pricks at her fading consciousness. *What if he thinks it is just nonsense? What if he doesn't pass it on to Kaide?*

Time loses all structure. With each waking comes the echoes of pain and repeated requests for sedation.

True to his word, the Technician doesn't reappear. The bursts of hope with each visitor to her room grow colder and colder until they cease completely.

He won't return. And there is no way to know if Kaide has received her message.

Or understood it. Or agrees to it.

The sedation is her only way of stalling her inevitable Execution.

"More sedation," she rasps at the Nurse who has just entered her room.

The Nurse ignores her, striding to the end of the bed and lifting the sheet.

"More sedation," Anaiya rasps louder.

"No more sedation," she replies distractedly, flicking her finger against Anaiya's feet and checking the display on the wall at the head of the gurney. "The trauma has subsided. No more sedation before surgery."

Anaiya's heart rate spikes, sending the wall display beeping.

"Breathe," the Nurse says, replacing the sheet and hurrying to the wall to adjust hidden settings. "There is no cause for worry. You won't feel a thing and you'll be discharged in a few days."

"How long—"

"Tomorrow," the Nurse says, flicking her finger across a glass screen and turning towards the exit.

"Since I've been here?"

But the Nurse has already left.

SEVENTY-THREE

They don't transfer her back to the holding room under the Trocadero after her surgery. Anaiya's new room is smaller, but still windowless and barren of everything except her and her restraints.

Peacekeepers come to get her, their black uniforms interrupted by thick heavy vests. They don't say anything as they haul her to her feet and into the corridor.

The injection she received twenty minutes earlier acts like a mild restraint – it softens her mind and limbs, makes her pliable and compliant. Her footsteps come slow, but steady; never faltering, never stumbling.

Afternoon light hits her full-force as they exit the unknown building, but she doesn't flinch. It is like all emotion has been siphoned from her. She knows this is the day of her Execution. Knows that the Pillar will greet her at the end of this stroll. But the knowing of it doesn't affect her.

Rows of Peacekeepers line the street, facing out to the crowd beyond.

Someone is speaking loudly. Saying her name.

Blink.

The Peacekeepers are walking her out to the Trocadero.

Blink.

The Execution Pillar is cold against her back. The new shackles tighter.

Below, in the terraces, the crowd seems to shiver with anticipation.

She should be looking for someone.

Kaide.

The name floats across her brain. Vaguely, she is aware that something is wrong, but her thoughts seem to fade before they can take hold.

A prick at her arm sends liquid ice through her veins. It rushes to her brain. And everything explodes into sound, movement and colour.

She screams against the onslaught and the crowd below screams back in frenzied excitement. Memories of the manipulated emotions in the pituarmagn attack flash bright.

Whipping her head around, she flails against the restraints. They will come for her with a restraint serum at any second and she needs to escape.

Except they don't. Her thrashing and desperate wailing brings no retribution.

She slows, looking from the Peacekeepers standing at the front of the platform, to the officials to her right. Niamh stands there with the Fire Commissioner and the new Water Commissioner. Impassive. Occasionally, he whispers orders to Peacekeepers who go racing off to relay them to the rest of the cordon. He has learnt from the lessons of the past – there will be no riot tonight.

Something else tugs at her attention, drawing it away from Niamh. Just behind him glints the hard edges of another granite plinth.

The loud voice is speaking again, an Air Pronouncer gesturing wildly to the crowd. With the cloudiness gone from her mind, she feels the panic explode around her heart.

"Tonight, we cure our city's Heterodoxy with the Execution of two detractors. Anaiya 234, our fallen hero, and her Air lover and Resistance leader …"

No, no, no. She pulls against the cuffs, eyes wild and breath short.

The Peacekeepers escort him to the Pillar, his head bent, a hood shadowing his face.

All is lost. They are both doomed.

She stops her frantic scrambling and forces herself to breathe slowly. Everything has slowed, her vision tunnelled on the Peacekeepers as they shackle their prisoner to the Pillar.

The Pronouncer's voice booms against the stone and concrete as one of the Peacekeeper's whips the hood down. But it is not Kaide who is revealed.

SEVENTY-FOUR

"Eamon 801."

Eamon slumps against the Pillar, his eyes rolling to the back of his head.

The lights of the Trocadero have been switched on, tainting everything a harsh white. Anaiya can't see any bruises or cuts on him, but that doesn't mean they weren't there earlier.

She scans the crowd, searching for familiar faces and finding none. *Have the others also been detained? Or has the fear of reprisal finally kept them away?*

"Anaiya 234 and Eamon 801," the Pronouncer continues, pitching her voice deeper and louder, "as mandated by the Otpor Constitution, you are sentenced to Execution."

Technicians appear on the stage.

No. It is happening too quickly – there should be more time. I need more time.

For what? You're going to die, Anaiya. No one is here to rescue you. No amount of time will change anything.

The realisation acts like a magnet, dredging up all her emotions and sucking them into the one place. The weight of them drags at her core and fills her chest. Everything; the fear, the rage, the regret, the infinitely deep sadness – it all swells and pulls and crashes against her mind.

The scream is pulled from her, clawing its way up her throat with the barbs of a hundred untamed emotions.

The Technicians pause in their advance and the Pronouncer

turns to her. She ignores them, turning her head against the cold stone and fixing her gaze on Niamh.

Time may not change her fate, but it can change Niamh's.

"You fucking feu mort!" She yells the slur and it feels good.

Niamh finally deigns to look at her, but his face is unchanged.

"You think this world is your plaything," she continues, her voice breaking with the desperation of it. "You killed the Water Commissioner and Jenna and now you get to kill me."

The new Water Commissioner raises an eyebrow and shifts his gaze to Niamh. Visual recording drones buzz around them, capturing everything. Niamh frowns and beckons to the Technicians. The Pronouncer shakes out of her daze and continues her spiel.

"For the ultimate crime of Heterodoxy," she says, unsteadiness creeping into her voice, "Eamon 801 will now be Executed."

Anaiya's gaze flicks to Eamon. He hasn't moved. Doesn't flinch away from the syringe.

"You want to eliminate Heterodoxy?!" Anaiya screams, her voice pitching higher as she sees the needle plunged into Eamon's skull. "Eliminate your Deputy Commissioner! He flaunts the Orthodoxy in your face. He thinks he is above it."

The Technicians are walking towards her.

"He realigned me! He realigned me! I wasn't a Fire Elemental when I brought down the Rehhd 020. I was an Air Elemental."

She flings the accusation at Niamh, shouting it as loud as her cracked voice will allow.

It should reign down chaos, should disrupt the proceedings and turn the scrutiny of the Commissioners and crowd to Niamh. It should make some impact.

But the words merely bounce off the wall of officials. Niamh is cold and silent, the Commissioners still beside him. The Technicians do not halt their advance, the Pronouncer has returned her attention to the crowd.

Anaiya's final words are useless; nothing but the desperate ramblings of a doomed Elemental.

"Anaiya 234, for the ultimate crime of Heterodoxy, will now

be Executed."

Hands pull her head back into position, forcing her view away from Niamh and back to the crowd. Straps bite into the skin of her forehead, forcing her still. It's an unnecessary precaution. All the fight is gone from her.

She closes her eyes as the tip of the needle makes contact with her temple. Her heart slows its frenetic beating and her breath comes steady as she exhales.

The pressure increases. She can still hear the crowd and the whir of the drones, but the sound is fading; replaced by the echoes of a voice from a lifetime ago.

"Remember, Anaiyasha. You are more than what they condition you to be. And there are more important things than the Orthodoxy worth protecting."

The memory of Kane 148 lifeless against the same Execution Pillar is the last thing she sees before she dies.

SEVENTY-FIVE

"Easy, Anaiya."

The familiar voice cuts through the darkness. Cold bites into the skin at her back.

Am I still on the Execution Pillar?

Arms are wrapping around her core. She feels gravity press down on her as someone lifts her up.

"Things are going to hurt," the voice continues, "but I need you to open your eyes, Anaiya. You need to wake up."

No, no. I don't want to wake up. I'm happy here – in the dark and warm. There is no pain here. No Executioner needles. No Orthodoxy or Heterodoxy or Conditioning or Cooperative.

"I need you to wake up, Anaiya. I need you to help me finish this thing we started."

The voice is insistent, the grasp around her secure.

"Come on, Anaiyasha." The nom de doceur stirs something within her. "Don't let Niamh win."

Eyes flutter open. Kaide, dressed in dark kevlar, stands before her. She stares into his eyes, both of them unblinking.

"He has already won," she whispers. "I'm dead."

Kaide laughs, low and soft. "Not yet, Juliet. But we have to move if we're going to keep it that way."

Reality washes away the rest of her dreamlike state, her skin tingling with the flush of adrenalin at finding herself alive and Kaide in front of her.

He came. It worked.

Her naked body shivers and she wraps her arms around herself, startling to find a thick, blood-stained bandage around her wrist. Her right hand flies to it, pressing fingers into the soft, dense fabric; ignoring the pain, searching for the hard ridges of her wristplate.

"Hey." Kaide's hand gently brushes her own away and grips it tightly. "It's OK."

"What happened? Where is it?" Her voice pitches high with the fear and panic that is racing along her veins.

"The Technicians removed it," he whispers, stepping closer and taking her other hand. "All wristplates are retired on death. Sent to the Archives, or in your case some research facility."

Her heart is pounding. The thought of being without her wristplate, her lifeline, is terrifying.

"No," she whispers, "I need it."

She tries to shake out of Kaide's grip, to pull back the bandage and see for herself, but he holds her tight.

"No, you don't. You don't need it." He ducks his head and forces her to meet his gaze. "You don't, Anaiya. You're free now."

Memories of Niamh's surveillance, of hidden conversations and interrupted location triangulation – they all come flooding back. Once she had wanted to claw the wristplate from her own skin. Now, she aches to have its familiar weight wrapped around her arm.

Slowly, Kaide releases his grip and helps her to stand. Resisting the urge to run her fingers over the bandage, Anaiya looks around, taking in the white tiles and metal tables. "Where are we?"

"The Descartes Water Research Institute; they're planning to study your and Eamon's brains – find out what made you Heterodox."

"Is Eamon—"

"No." Kaide steps away from her, walking to the room's exit and putting his ear to the door. "Eamon is dead."

Her legs wobble and she reaches for the metal table to steady herself. She glances around the windowless room. The sterile environment is neatly ordered; unfamiliar instruments and vials stacked in sharp geometric patterns. Everything in its place.

"What happened?" she asks. "What are we doing?"

"I'll explain everything later," he says. "Right now, we just need to be quiet. And patient."

Seconds later, a quiet knock sounds on the door. Anaiya's gaze flies from it to Kaide.

"It's OK," Kaide whispers. "It will all be OK. Trust me."

SEVENTY-SIX

The Technician barges quickly into the room, pushing a gurney covered in black plastic. He glances at Anaiya briefly, before throwing Kaide the blue uniform.

"This is my debt paid," he whispers to Kaide. "I'm done after this."

Kaide nods and strips quickly, pulling on the blue as he discards the black. Satisfied, the Technician starts removing the plastic from the gurney.

"Will it work?" Kaide asks, smoothing his hair back and slicking it down.

"If it's tagged as Anaiya 234, it is Anaiya 234."

The plastic falls to the floor, revealing a pallid grey corpse.

"Who is that?" Anaiya whispers.

Kaide manoeuvres around her, looking and moving like a Water Elemental.

"It's you," the Technician replies, picking up the shoulders while Kaide lifts the legs. "And I hope to never see either of you again."

They transfer the body to the table Anaiya was lying on just minutes earlier.

"This is where my involvement ends," the Technician says. "You have seven minutes before shift change, so be quick."

He leaves the room without a backwards glance, leaving Anaiya and Kaide with the anonymous body.

"OK, Anaiya," Kaide says, turning to her, "time to get out of here."

Tapping on the gurney, he bends to pick up the plastic. There's an urgency in his posture, in the tension left behind by the Technician. A hundred questions burn through her brain and pain starts to inch its way along her extremities towards her core.

Slowly she reaches out to Kaide. Gripping her arm, he uses his body to stabilise the gurney against the wall. With shaking limbs, she scrambles up, flinching at the bite of cold metal against her skin.

"See you on the other side," Kaide murmurs, and pulls the black plastic over her.

The sounds of the Institute eventually fade, replaced only by Kaide's footsteps and the whirring of the gurney's wheels. Eventually, they cease, too.

"Time to move," Kaide murmurs, whipping the plastic off and restoring Anaiya's vision.

They are in a storage room.

"Here," he says, flinging her a blue uniform to match his own. "We have to exit through a service door. We're about five kilometres from the Edges, but if we can make it a few blocks, we should have a clear run."

She dresses quickly. The fabric is coarse and scratchy, but she is grateful for its instant warmth. She tugs the sleeves down to cover her bandage and looks up at Kaide.

He is staring at her, head cocked to the side, a look of puzzlement dancing across his face.

"What?" She tugs again at the uniform, suddenly self-conscious.

"Nothing," he replies, shaking his head and looking away.

"What?" she persists, stepping into his view.

He frowns. "It's just surreal. Being here with you. You being alive."

The words come too quickly, too light. They aren't the words he had intended to say, but it is not the time to pursue the truth.

"Let's keep it that way, hey? Which way to the service exit?"

Their path to the service exit is quick and unobstructed. Outside on the street, they move silently. There are hours until curfew, but the precinct is quiet.

Kaide leads the way, sticking to obscure laneways. In the quiet, their footsteps sound too loud. Anaiya finds herself switching to Peacekeeper mode, constantly scanning the environment for hidden threats. But none come and they arrive at the Edges unseen.

From there it is a quick journey through the maze of concrete recyclers to a small apartment in Precinct 16. Only when Kaide ushers her inside and shuts the door does Anaiya let go of the tension she has been holding in her muscles.

The adrenalin drains out of her body, giving room for the pain to come rushing in. It buckles her knees and sends her crashing to the floor. Black spots swim in front of her eyes, but strong arms wrap around her and Kaide's voice keeps her from slipping from consciousness.

"Hey, hey, hey," he murmurs, lifting her up and settling her on a soft bed. "Stay with me, Anaiya."

He sits beside her, wrapping an arm around her shoulders.

The security of it, the reassurance and comfort, undoes her. Tears fall in warm ribbons down her cheeks and she collapses in gut-wrenching sobs that seem as if they will never cease.

Kaide holds her silently, never letting his grip weaken.

SEVENTY-SEVEN

"I didn't understand it at first," Kaide says.

They sit on the bed together, interlocking hands like they have so many times before, but this time without fear of surveillance. Delacroix sleeps in her lap, the pup's warmth and mass a kind comfort. For the last few hours, Kaide has told her everything – his discovery of her kidnapping, the failed pituarmagn attack, Eamon's detention, the public trial, the Executions.

"Vincent had mangled the message so badly; his first attempt at repeating it went something like 'something about a tomb and redemption'. But I kept pressing him and when he said 'Romeo', I knew what you were trying to tell me."

"Was it Vincent who organised the swap?"

"Vincent got the syringes swapped, but the chemical concoction was Yve's."

"Rehhd's Yve?"

Kaide nods.

"Did she know who it was for?"

"No. Not who it was for or what it was for."

They lapse into silence. It made sense that Yve was behind the sleeping nightshade. Her synth alcohol creations always dabbled in the organic and unusual.

"She trusts you?"

Kaide sighs. "The Resistance began fracturing a long time ago. No one took sides, but some relationships are stronger than others."

"Like you and Cress?"

He frowns.

"I saw her – at the pituarmagn attack," Anaiya says. "She gave me the key to my handcuffs. She saved my life."

"Cress and I are close," he begins hesitantly, "but she was always closer to Seth."

Seth. He had been at the attack, had watched as Eamon marched her towards the stage.

"Have you spoken to him?"

"No. No one has. Rumour is he went into hiding after the pituarmagn attack."

"And Lilith?" She had expected to see the dominating Elemental at the Execution.

Kaide chews on his lip. "Lilith … is complicated."

"Is she still around?"

With Eamon dead, the first half of the Resistance fire has been extinguished. But if Lilith – the brains and motivation of this reformed rebellion – is still agitating, the violence will never stop until Otpor has burnt to the ground.

"No one has seen her since Eamon's detention. No one that talks to me, at least." There is hesitation in his voice. He is holding something back.

"Where do you think she is?"

Kaide disentangles his hand from Anaiya and frowns. "I think she's in the enclave. I saw them – Farasei and Danai – at the pituarmagn attack; their role in this is bigger than we think."

"You were there?"

She had searched everywhere for him; as Eamon dragged her through the streets, as she was held hostage on the stage, even as she looked down on the melee. She had searched for him. And never found him.

He ignores her question. "They won't be happy Lilith's mission failed. If she is anywhere, she is with them."

Anaiya stares at him, her mind dredging up every memory she has of him: Their first meeting at the izakaya, their wild night at Veritas, the spoken word, the mural revelation, cola pigeon on the riverbank … nutrient injections in the Edges, kisses in her apartment, dead bodies in the research institute.

"Why did you save me?"

His face softens. "Anaiya …"

"No," she interrupts. This is a question she needs answering. "Why did you save me?"

He leans into her, pressing his forehead against hers, forcing her to confront his intense gaze.

"I didn't save you, Anaiya." Every syllable is clear and bright. "You saved yourself. And maybe you can save Otpor."

SEVENTY-EIGHT

Sleep descends on her like a lover's embrace. Kaide had given her a heady mix of sedatives to ease the pain and her continued anxiety about Peacekeepers discovering their ruse and coming to detain her again.

But it is not Kaide's face that swells in her vision before she drifts off to sleep. It is Kane 148's.

"Remember, Anaiyasha. You are more than what they condition you to be. And there are more important things than the Orthodoxy worth protecting." Kane sits at her bedside, the dark kevlar of his Peacekeeper uniform in stark contrast to the white, sterile environment of her Infirmary recovery room.

Somewhere in the depths of her sleep, she knows that this is a forgotten memory – a moment in time that was erased from her mind with the sedatives from her biomechanic surgery and hours of psychotherapy after Kane's Execution.

"Why do you say these things?" She is frustrated and angry with him. "They are wrong, they are Heterodox. You know they are."

"Anaiya, it is not Heterodox to use the eyes you were created with to see how wrong this Orthodoxy is. It is not Heterodox to use the brain you were created with to know that the divisions in this city and in your mind are artificial."

She closes her eyes, shutting out Kane and his terrible words. But a few breach her defences before she succumbs to the medicated sleep.

"You know this, Anaiyasha. Your identity is not something that is dictated by others. Your identity is something you find yourself."

Don't want to stop reading?
Sign up at kyrija.com/mikhaeyla-kopievsky and follow Mikhaeyla
on Bookbub at https://www.bookbub.com/profile/mikhaeyla-
kopievsky to be the first to find out when *Revolution (Divided
Elements Book 3)* is released.

ABOUT THE AUTHOR

MIKHAEYLA KOPIEVSKY is an independent speculative fiction author who loves writing about complex and flawed characters in stories that explore philosophy, sociology and politics. She holds degrees in International Relations, Journalism and Environmental Science. A former counter-terrorism advisor, she has travelled to and worked in Asia, the Middle East and Africa.

Mikhaeyla lives in the Hunter Valley, Australia, with her husband and son. *Divided Elements* is her debut offering.

For exclusive content and VIP access to new releases, reader events and advance copies, sign up at
www.kyrija.com

Loved *Divided Elements* | *Rebellion* ? Spread the word by leaving a review on Goodreads and Amazon.